One-Night Alibi

Kara Lennox

HARLEQUIN® SUPER ROMANCE®

Recycling programs
for this product may
not exist in your area.

ISBN-13: 978-0-373-71862-7

ONE-NIGHT ALIBI

Copyright © 2013 by Karen Leabo

HARLEQUIN®
www.Harlequin.com

Printed in U.S.A.

"You have to leave."

The urgency had returned to Liz's voice. "We can't be seen together."

"We've already been seen together," Hudson said. "Your security man downstairs knows I came to see you. The valet at the wedding saw us leave together. You think cops won't figure that out?"

Her face fell. She returned to the living room and more or less collapsed onto the sofa. Hudson sat in the chair opposite her.

"Maybe you better tell me everything," he said. "Why would you want to kill Franklin Mandalay?"

"Because he's my father. And we're estranged. He is manipulative and controlling and a liar. And I'm his sole heir." With that, her eyes filled with tears. "I have no idea why I keep crying. He was not a very nice man."

Mandalay was her father? Hudson's head spun. "I knew there was something off about that night," he murmured. Then, louder, he said, "Tell me everything. All of it, Liz. If I get even a whiff of deception from you I'm going straight to the police."

Dear Reader,

Any writer will tell you that coming up with the title of a book can be an excruciating process. For me, I usually begin writing with some lame title in place. Then, as I get to know my story and my characters, other titles will come to mind. By the time I send the manuscript to my editor, I'll probably have a title I'm happy with.

Oh, but it doesn't end there. Editors have their own ideas about titles, and every title undergoes a great deal of scrutiny. Does it fit the story? Is it the right tone? Does it sound like a Harlequin Superromance title? Will it fit on the cover nicely? Although the title usually is something all parties can agree to, often it is not the author's original title.

One-Night Alibi is one of those titles that come up once in a blue moon. I had it before I even started the book. I love it because it tells you exactly what the book is about. It's sexy and it's suspenseful-sounding. Happily, the editors agreed with me on this one! I hope it caught your attention, too!

All best,

Kara Lennox

ABOUT THE AUTHOR

Kara Lennox has earned her living at various times as an art director, typesetter, textbook editor and reporter. She's worked in a boutique, a health club and an ad agency. She's been an antiques dealer, an artist and even a blackjack dealer. But no work has ever made her happier than writing romance novels. To date, she has written more than sixty books. Kara is a recent transplant to Southern California. When not writing, she indulges in an ever-changing array of hobbies. Her latest passions are bird-watching, long-distance bicycling, vintage jewelry and, by necessity, do-it-yourself home renovation. She loves to hear from readers. You can find her at www.karalennox.com.

Books by Kara Lennox

HARLEQUIN SUPERROMANCE

HARLEQUIN AMERICAN ROMANCE

‡Project Justice
*Blond Justice
**Firehouse 59
***Second Sons

Other titles by this author available in ebook format.

For Sally Slocum

Everyone should have such a wonderful mother-in-law

PROLOGUE

HUDSON VALE LIKED to brag that he never got sick. All the vitamin C in the Mountain Dew he drank kept him healthy as a horse. But today, he'd been made a liar. After sneezing his head off yesterday, he'd cut his shift early and gone home. A handful of extra vitamin C hadn't done the trick; he'd awakened with the mother of all colds. His head hurt. His chest hurt. His throat hurt. He couldn't breathe. And he had nothing resembling cold medicine in the house.

Like it or not, he had to drag himself out to his car, drive to the nearest convenience store and buy some Alka-Seltzer Plus.

Although it was October, Hudson didn't bother with a jacket. He shoved his badge in the pocket of a pair of disreputable jeans because he never went anywhere without it. Breaking his usual pattern, he didn't arm himself. In his current state of debilitation, he'd be more danger to bystanders than to anything he aimed at.

It was a brilliant, clear day outside, one of those rare instances when the humidity was low, the air crisp and fresh. Football season was in full swing, and citizens of the greater Houston area were focused on fall barbecues and tailgate parties.

Hudson climbed into his Datsun 280Z and headed for the local convenience store.

At this hour of a Sunday morning, most people were still in bed, sleeping off a wild Saturday night, or in church repenting for the same. But in an hour or two, the store would be filled with fishermen stocking up on bait and beer and charcoal briquettes, intent on wringing every ounce of recreation from the outstanding weather.

Hudson wished he could get out on the water today. But after sneezing four times in a row on the way to the store, he couldn't think fondly of anything except his bed and a box of tissues.

As he got out of his car, he noticed a familiar-looking woman in a red miniskirt and white patent-leather boots talking on the pay phone outside. On seeing him, she turned to face the wall.

It wasn't until he was inside the store, paying for his purchases, that he recalled her name. Jazz was a prostitute he'd arrested last year. Conroe had quite a few working girls, but most of them plied their trade near the strip clubs, liquor stores and pawn shops downtown or near the railroad tracks. They didn't normally trawl the Lake Conroe Stop 'n' Shop parking lot on a Sunday morning.

He might have tried to chat her up, find out why she was so far from her usual stomping grounds, but he was off duty and sick, and for once he was just going to stifle his innate curiosity and go on about his business.

That plan worked fine, until after he'd paid for his purchase and was heading out the door.

The first things he noticed were raised voices. Jazz was no longer alone; she was arguing with a middle-aged man in a baseball cap and sunglasses, his jacket collar pulled up to hide as much of his face as possible.

Classic "john" disguise.

Even so, Hudson was inclined to let it slide. He wasn't in Vice anymore. It was just an argument in a parking lot, no crime.

Still, he couldn't help wandering closer.

"You better do what you're told," the man growled. He was shoving something into Jazz's hands.

"What the hell are you doing? Not here." She glanced over, saw Hudson and went pale, though her hand did reflexively close over what Hudson could now see was a thick wad of folded bills.

"Hey, look at me when I'm talking to you." The man grabbed her chin and swiveled her head, forcing her to face him.

Hudson sighed. He set the bag with his cold medicine on the hood of his car and pulled his cell phone out of his pocket. In a matter of seconds, he had summoned backup.

Acutely aware of the fact he was unarmed, he approached the confrontation. "Excuse me, is there a problem here?"

"Mind your own business," the man barked. Then he saw the badge Hudson had casually slipped out of his pocket.

That was when Jazz cut and run. She let go of the money in her hand, and several twenties fluttered to the ground.

"Hey!" The man took a couple of steps in the direction Jazz was fleeing, sprinting faster than a girl in four-inch heels ought to be able to run, but Hudson snagged the man's arm.

"Sir, I'm going to have to ask you to put your hands on this wall, here."

"What for?" he asked haughtily.

"I'm arresting you for solicitation of a prostitute."

"Are you out of your mind? Do you know who I am?"

Great. Another entitled rich guy who thought he deserved a pass because he wore a suit and had a family.

"Don't know, don't care." With that he pushed the uncooperative suspect against the wall. "Now put your hands against the wall and *spread 'em*. Unless you want me to add resisting arrest to the charges. You have the right to remain silent…"

As Hudson continued the Miranda warning, the man finally complied, but not silently. "You are going to be very sorry. I'll have your badge."

"No, you won't," Hudson said in a bored voice. "You'll be

too busy hiring a lawyer and trying to hide your little indiscretions from your wife and your boss and your golf buddies."

"I was not paying that girl for sex!"

"Those twenty-dollar bills all over the ground say differently. Oh, and by the way, you're overpaying. In addition to being a dirtbag, you're a sap."

Hudson probably shouldn't have added that last part. Baiting a suspect who was not cuffed was on that list of things cops learned not to do. But Hudson was really sick and really annoyed that he was probably going to have to spend his morning filling out a report.

Without warning, the man swiveled around and took a swing at Hudson. It was a clumsy punch, but the man had some heft, and a strength born of outrage on his side. His fist landed in Hudson's solar plexus.

Then the idiot made a break for his car.

Hudson didn't think—he just reacted. He lit out after the man, tackling him in the parking lot before he'd got ten steps. They both went down, hard.

A Montgomery County Sheriff's Department squad car pulled into the parking lot just then and came to a stop mere feet from Hudson and his suspect, who was still struggling. Deputy Allison Kramer got out, shook her head, then held out a pair of cuffs.

"Need some of these?"

Hudson took them without comment, flipped the man onto his stomach and cuffed him, then hauled him to his feet with Allison's help. The man's face was now scraped and bloody, his nose possibly broken. He'd lost his hat and sunglasses in the scuffle.

"Holy crap," Allison said.

"He bolted," Hudson said in his defense, thinking she was reacting to the suspect's condition.

"No, it's not that. Do you know who this guy is?"

"Franklin Mandalay III," the suspect replied haughtily.

"Young lady, I want to file a formal charge of assault. I was minding my own business when this scruffy, disreputable individual attacked me. I was committing no crime. I had no weapon—"

"Save it," Hudson said impatiently. "Allison, I'll meet you at the station."

But despite his best attempt at indifference to the name Franklin Mandalay, Hudson's stomach felt queasy. If he had to get into a scuffle with a suspect, why did it have to be one of the most influential attorneys in Houston? Especially since his only witness had flown the coop.

CHAPTER ONE

HE ARRIVED LATE to the wedding reception, but that was par for the course for Hudson Vale. He would probably be late to his own wedding, in the unlikely event he ever got married.

A young valet with frizzy brown hair and big black glasses took the keys to his Z, whistling in appreciation. "Awesome. You restore it yourself?"

"Every square inch."

Ordinarily, Hudson took pleasure when someone complimented his ride. But these days, it was hard to take pride in anything. He'd been officially stripped of the one thing he was really proud of. Without the gun and the badge, he was just another guy. No, not just another guy. Another *suspect*. Scum, in other words.

One week after his scuffle with Franklin Mandalay, Internal Affairs was still investigating.

Hudson headed for the massive front door of Daniel Logan's River Oaks mansion, which looked like the manor house of an English village, not an oil billionaire's home smack in the middle of Houston. He hadn't really wanted to come to the wedding. He barely knew the bride, Daniel's former assistant Jillian, and had only met her groom, Conner, once. But his friends at Project Justice had wangled him an invitation. They'd also made him promise to come, knowing he needed to get out of the house. Knowing he needed distraction.

Now he wished he hadn't listened to them. He wasn't fit company. He'd quickly pay his respects to the bride and groom, say hi to his friends, then make his escape, thereby convincing everyone he was doing okay.

Which he wasn't.

The front door opened by itself, and a butler-type person gestured him inside a cavernous foyer every bit as opulent as Hudson had heard. A trickling fountain that would have been right at home in ancient Rome echoed against the marble floor and walls, and a stained-glass window cast colored bits of light like confetti over the far wall. From somewhere in the distance he heard faint strains of a country-and-western band, but this room was an oasis of quiet and dignity.

A plump young woman sat at an antique side table guarding the doorway leading to the rest of the house. She silently handed Hudson a pen adorned with a big white feather and pointed toward the guest book. The book was almost filled.

He smiled at the girl out of habit, because he always smiled at young women. She looked down and blushed. He wondered what her story was; had she been stuck behind the guest book because she was the awkward ugly duckling, or had she chosen this job because she wouldn't then be forced to mingle?

Hudson felt a fleeting urge to ask her. But his insatiable curiosity about people—especially women—often got him into trouble he didn't need.

Case in point: when he saw two people arguing in a parking lot, when he was sick and off duty, he could have looked the other way. But no, he just had to get involved. Not that he could see himself reacting any differently. He couldn't stand to see a woman being bullied, and as a cop it was his job to uphold the law, on or off duty.

He bit his tongue and walked past the girl into a living room that could have housed a couple of Sherman tanks. A few people sat on plush white sofas and chairs in this serene room, talking in low tones, but live music beckoned from outdoors. A roving waiter with a tray of full champagne glasses offered Hudson his choice, but champagne wasn't his deal, so he passed and headed through a Spanish-tiled solarium to the flagstone patio, where most of the guests had gathered to eat, drink and dance.

"Hudson! Over here!" A cool blonde in a pale turquoise dress waved madly at him.

Grateful not to have to wade through oceans of strangers trying to find someone he knew, he quickly made his way to an umbrella table where Dr. Claudia Ellison sat with her husband, Billy Cantu, a Houston cop.

Hudson hoped Claudia didn't have matchmaking in mind for tonight.

She threw her arms around Hudson and kissed him on the cheek, a rather effusive show of affection from the normally reserved psychologist, but since his suspension she'd been trying extra hard to show him and everyone else that she was on his side.

"How are you feeling?" she asked.

"The cold's gone." He didn't comment on anything else, because everything else sucked.

Billy stood and shook Hudson's hand. "Glad you could make it."

"I knew you'd want to see this place," said Claudia. "Isn't it amazing?"

"I guess. Listen, I'm going to find the bride and groom, pay my respects, then—"

Claudia put a melodramatic hand to her forehead. "No, you can't leave so quickly. We haven't even had a chance to catch up."

"You don't really want to know."

"Of course I do."

Billy pulled out a chair. "Have a beer. They got the biggest selection of microbrews I ever saw. Not that I'm really into designer beer, but this Dogfish Head Chicory Stout is pretty good stuff."

"Look, y'all don't have to be so nice. I'm not falling apart.

I'll get through this just like I've gotten through every other damn thing in my life, okay?"

Claudia waved away his diatribe with a careless hand. "Get over yourself. We're not being any nicer than usual. Now sit down, shut up and drink heavily of free booze. Logan has limos lined up for anyone who overdoes it."

Hudson was about to object again. That was when he saw *her,* the stunning brunette standing near the edge of the pool with a martini glass in her hand. She was tall, made taller still by silver stiletto heels. Her dress shimmered like liquid silver, clinging sinuously to her curves. Her black hair was piled on top of her head in an artfully casual way that had probably taken hours to achieve.

Hudson might not have paid her that much attention, except that she was looking right at him.

Without meaning to, he sank into the chair Billy had offered moments ago. *Who is she? And why is she smiling at me like that?*

"See something you like?" Billy asked.

Hudson forced himself to break the almost-hypnotic stare-off with the woman. Her eyes were a deep ocean-blue—he could tell even at this distance.

Claudia took an immediate interest in the object of his attention. "She's a friend of Jillian's, a sorority sister, I think. Can't remember her name."

Hudson stole another glance at her. She was on the move now. Walking. Toward him.

Billy punched him on the arm. "Dude, she's coming over here."

And she did. She came right to their table, striding boldly like a runway model. But she switched her gaze from Hudson to Claudia. "Hi, you're Claudia, right? I remember you from the bridal shower. I'm…Liz."

"Hi, Liz, it's good to see you again."

"Would you all mind if I joined you? My date seems to have gone missing."

"Sure, here's a chair," Billy said, nearly spilling his special beer as he pulled out the fourth chair for her. A waiter stopped by to see who needed drinks, and Billy insisted he bring Hudson a Fishhead, or whatever the hell the beer was called.

Hudson would have objected. But the woman had so gob-smacked him, he'd been struck speechless.

"This is my husband, Billy," Claudia said, "and our friend Hudson."

"Pleased to meet you, ma'am," Hudson said with his best polite Southern-boy manners.

The brunette took a sip of her martini, then somehow fished the olive out with just her tongue in a way that was totally sexy and classy at the same time.

Hudson's mouth went dry.

When the waiter brought his beer, he chugged down a third without even tasting it.

"You knew Jillian in college?" Claudia asked, trying to get the conversation rolling.

Hudson wasn't that interested in conversation. He just wanted to look at Liz, though her voice was a pleasing blend of smooth honey over six miles of rough road.

"I did, but we weren't good friends until more recently when we worked on a charity event together."

So, Liz obviously came from high society. Ivy League college, sorority, charity events. She oozed class. So not his type. Or rather, not the type who gave a sheriff's-department detective a second look. A suspended detective, accused somewhat convincingly of police brutality.

So why was she staring at him?

"Have we met?" he asked bluntly.

"I don't think so. I'd remember."

Then she'd probably seen his picture in the paper or on

TV. His case had drawn much too much unwanted publicity. The Mandalay name had a lot of cachet in the Houston area.

Claudia gasped. "Oh, Billy, I love this song. Let's dance."

Hudson recognized a ploy to leave him and Liz alone, but he didn't object. He'd just keep staring at her until she got tired of it. It wasn't as if he had anything to lose. He'd probably never see her again after this night.

"How about it, Hudson. Want to dance?" Liz raised one eyebrow playfully.

"Me? Not much of a dancer."

"Oh, come on. Anybody can dance."

"Sure, right." He let her drag him to his feet. What the hell. Didn't matter, really, in the grand scheme of things, and holding her in his arms didn't sound like such a bad deal. All he had to do was move his feet a little, or at least pretend to try to dance.

A parquet floor had been laid out over the flagstone patio for dancing in the shadow of the band, which had switched from country-western to big band. Hudson dredged up some long-ago memories of a ballroom dance class he'd taken to please an old girlfriend. He'd forgotten her name, but maybe he could at least remember how to get into hold.

He took Liz into his arms. As other couples twirled and dipped around him, he shuffled his feet back and forth.

Amazingly, she moved right along with him, graceful as a swan. In her tall heels she met him eye to eye. Now he could examine those amazing inky-blue eyes up close. Little gold flecks shimmered in the irises like rays of sunshine on the surface of the ocean, and a pleasurable tingle wiggled down his spine.

"Are you a friend of the bride, or the groom?" she asked.

"I know both of them, but only slightly. I guess Claudia got me the invitation. She thought I'd be interested in seeing the Logan place."

"It's pretty amazing. And if there's one thing Jillian knows how to do, it's throw a party. What do you do for a living?"

He knew the question would come up. "Cop. You?"

"Social worker."

Not what he expected. If she worked at all, he'd been guessing something glamorous—fashion editor, commercial real estate. "Enjoy it?"

"Immensely. You?"

"Usually."

"Aren't you scared?"

"Most of the time I'm just too busy to be scared."

"Ever been shot?"

"No. That sort of thing is very rare."

"Ever shot anyone?"

"Also very rare. I've hardly ever unholstered my weapon, much less shot at someone."

"Still, it's got to be dangerous at times."

"I imagine your job has its dangers, too. You probably deal with all segments of society. Lowlifes."

"Well, pretty troubled people, anyway. I wouldn't call them 'lowlifes.'"

The song switched to a slow number. Hudson thought the dance would be over, but she made no move to leave the dance floor. He pulled her close, resting his cheek against her hair and inhaling the scents of something clean and fruity. This was ridiculously pleasant.

But odd.

An unwelcome thought appealed to him. "Are you trying to make your date jealous, by any chance?"

She laughed. "Hardly. I think he's in the cabana banging one of the bridesmaids. It was just a casual date. I don't care."

"You need a ride home?" The words slipped out.

"I might." She tickled the back of his neck with her fingertips.

Was this exotic creature coming on to him? He wasn't

exactly a troll; he knew some women found him attractive. Some liked the whole idea of dating a cop—it was a power thing. Others liked his surfer-boy looks, or they found out he had a house at the lake and a boat and thought he had money.

But not *this* kind of woman.

He asked himself if perhaps he was being played, but he couldn't figure out her angle. Yeah, this encounter felt…off somehow. Yet he couldn't bring himself to put an end to it.

He didn't like games. But something compelled him to find out how this one would play out. He would call her bluff.

"I wasn't planning to stay long," he said. "We can leave whenever you want."

She put her lips close to his ear and whispered, "I can go anytime. But first, I think you should see the garden."

The song ended and they pulled apart. He had no interest in flowers, but the idea of strolling among fragrant roses with Liz was oddly appealing.

"I love gardens," he lied. "Lead the way."

She wobbled a bit on her high heels as they made their way around the enormous pool illuminated by dozens of floating candles. Maybe she'd had one too many martinis. He didn't want to hook up with her if she was going to regret it. And really, he had no business getting entangled with anyone, let alone a mystery woman, when his life was such a mess…no matter how alluring she might be.

They were just going to look at flowers, he reasoned. They hadn't reached the point of no return. Either of them could still bow out gracefully.

She took his hand, pulling him along, wanting to go faster in a suddenly childlike way. "It's the most amazing garden. The Logans' gardener, Hung Li, is a world-renowned rose cultivator. He has some prizewinning varieties that were developed right here."

She escorted him off the patio through a fancy gate in a redwood fence. A charming path of flagstones meandered through what had to be an herb garden, given the scents of sage and lavender greeting Hudson's nose.

"The Logans' chef, Cora, uses as many homegrown fruits and vegetables as she can," Liz continued as if she were a tour guide.

Stone benches were scattered here and there, along with pieces of huge marble columns strewn about, an echo of the ancient Rome theme inside the foyer. More statues, too.

He'd heard that Daniel acquired archaeological antiquities from private collectors all over the world, and he'd made provisions in his will for the items to be donated to appropriate museums in the items' countries of origin.

It took some kind of ego to do that.

They passed an enormous greenhouse, where Hudson caught glimpses of hothouse tomatoes through the windows. Row upon row of empty garden space, waiting to be planted, surrounded them.

Finally they reached another fence, a quaint white-picket affair that called to mind a country garden in rural England. On the other side, a small plot fairly burst at the seams with roses. Houston's mild winters meant you could have flowers year-round, if you worked at it. Apparently someone here did.

Rosebushes climbed fences and trellises grew out of huge urns and directly from the ground. The garden overflowed with red and pink and white roses, peach ones, yellow ones, roses in colors Hudson had never seen before. Even in the falling dusk, the colors were so vivid they hurt his eyes.

Hudson would be the last person to expect the sight of a bunch of flowers to move him, but the explosion of color took his breath away.

Or perhaps it was the woman standing next to him, whose beauty outshone even the most stunning of these roses.

"See this one?" She pointed to a bright yellow rose with orange-tipped petals. "It's called Texas Sunrise. And that one over there?" She pointed to a peculiarly shaded purplish-pink rose. "That's the Houstonian."

"You sound like you know a lot about roses."

"Well, I know what I learned on the tour Mr. Li gave earlier." She winked one long-lashed blue eye at him, and swear to God, he almost swooned.

"What's that over there?" he asked, pointing to another small, fenced-in area that sported a very different look from the carefully cultivated and pruned roses. Flowering shrubs, trees and vines grew in untamed profusion. A small brass plaque on the gate read Hummingbird Garden.

Hudson quickly realized why. The moment they entered the space, small winged creatures could be spied zooming all about the place, sampling nectar from both flowers and the feeders. There must have been at least fifty of them. Some had bright red throats, the color visible only when they turned a certain direction.

"Good golly." Liz barely breathed the words, she was in such awe. With that one decidedly unsophisticated expletive, the polish of wealth and privilege dropped away, revealing something of the little girl she must have been.

Tearing his eyes away from the sight of the tiny birds, Hudson chose to look at her instead. Liz's mouth was open slightly, her eyes bright as her gaze darted around the secluded garden.

One of the little critters stopped midair about six inches from Liz's face, seeming to look into her eyes in a curious way, then abruptly zoomed off.

She laughed in surprise and delight. "I've never seen so many at once." She kept her voice low, so as not to disturb the hummers. "And I've never seen them this close. It's like we stepped into a magic storybook." She turned then to look at him, and she must have seen something of what he was thinking—that he'd never been so close to such a beautiful woman, and that her naked sense of wonder was surprisingly erotic.

Hudson felt privileged—as if he'd seen a side of her few ever saw.

Whatever she'd seen in his face, she must have liked it, because when he leaned in to steal a kiss, she didn't object. She sipped a quick breath before their lips met.

She tasted of the martini she'd recently drunk, and he wondered idly how many she'd had. Only one or two drinks could lower inhibitions. He suspected Liz wasn't the type who picked up strange men at weddings; then again, he didn't know her at all.

Her lips also tasted of strawberry lip gloss, and when he ruffled her hair, he caught another whiff of that fruity scent— apple, maybe.

Unable to resist, he placed a series of light kisses along her jawline, then dipped his head to nuzzle her neck, pressing his nose against her soft skin.

Mangos. Her skin smelled like a ripe mango right off the tree, like the ones he'd had in Mexico. The woman was a veritable fruit basket of sensations. Even her breasts reminded him of ripe fruit, and he suddenly realized he had one of them in his hand. Her nipple peaked, pressing against his palm through the silky-thin material of her dress.

Liz moaned, soft and low.

Boisterous laughter drifted from the pool area, reminding Hudson that they were still in a public area, that anyone could happen upon them. He wouldn't really care, but she might.

"I want to take you someplace more private," he said, his lips close to her ear.

"Do you live alone?" she asked, not bothering to play coy.

"Yes. But my house is at Lake Conroe." He didn't want to drive all the way out there. An amorous mood sometimes had a way of evaporating during an hour on the road. "How about we find an empty room around here somewhere?" Surely some place in this monstrous house they could find a room with a lock and a bed or a sofa.

"Too many people around. Let's go." Without waiting for agreement, she grabbed his hand and dragged him out of the hummingbird garden, the magical little creatures forgotten. Hudson hadn't paid his respects to the bride and groom, but he doubted he would be missed.

He and Liz entered the house through a side door, making their way through a mudroom, then the huge granite-and-stainless-steel kitchen, which was bustling with activity. A champagne cork popped. A tray of hors d'oeuvres came out of the oven. No one paid two interlopers any attention.

Under other circumstances, Hudson would have wanted to gawk at the opulence of Daniel Logan's home. But his attention was too firmly fixed on the siren who had, for some questionable reason, culled him out of the herd of men in attendance at the society wedding.

Maybe his luck was turning.

CHAPTER TWO

ELIZABETH DOWNEY HADN'T meant for this to happen. As she sat in the passenger seat of Hudson Vale's classic 280Z, her gaze fixed on his firm profile as he deftly wove the sports car through traffic on I-45, she considered speaking up, changing the course of her actions. She could tell him she'd changed her mind. She had no doubt he would promptly turn around and take her back to the wedding or to her own apartment.

She'd never met Hudson until today, but she knew a lot about him. When she'd seen the headline about a Montgomery County sheriff's detective allegedly beating Franklin Mandalay during a bogus arrest, she'd been consumed with curiosity—about the incident and about the cop who'd stood up to a powerful and wealthy attorney. She had learned everything she could about Hudson, even paying a private investigator to suss him out, find out his story.

There wasn't much. Other than one incident during his rookie year when he'd been reprimanded for punching a wife-beater, Hudson Vale had an exemplary record. Prior to becoming a cop, he'd led a completely normal life. Two parents, a brother, middle-class suburbia. His dad had been a Houston cop, retired now. The Vale boys had gone to public school, then community college. The younger brother, Parker, was also a cop.

Hudson had never been arrested. He'd never been married. His only debt was a sizable mortgage on his house.

Elizabeth's eyes had nearly popped out of her head when

she'd spotted Hudson at the reception. She had stared at him rudely, she knew, but she'd had to be sure it was him. His photos certainly hadn't done him justice. In two dimensions, he was uncommonly good-looking. In three, he made her skin tingle and her mouth water. He made her think of sinful things.

She'd just wanted to meet him, that was all. Share one harmless dance. Size him up. But within five minutes of meeting him, she knew one or two dances wouldn't be enough. She sensed a lot going on behind those hazel eyes and the easy smile that faded when he thought no one was looking.

While his attention was on his driving, she took a leisurely inventory of his features. He had a strong jaw and a slightly hawkish nose—those were her first observations. His hair, worn a little long for cop standards, was wavy and streaked by the sun. It would probably curl if he let it get much longer.

His eyelashes were way longer than any man's ought to be. His lips were full, and whenever a car slowed in front of them, he teased his lower lip with his teeth, a gesture that did strange, squiggly things to her insides.

She cracked the window, drawing a rush of fresh air onto her face.

"Want me to turn on the AC?" Hudson asked.

"No, this is fine." She focused on his hand, which rested casually on the gearshift knob. He had a couple of healing scrapes on his knuckles. Souvenirs from his violent encounter?

They lapsed into silence, but it wasn't uncomfortable or awkward.

Again, she thought about telling him she'd been hasty. She could stop this now. End the encounter. But the little she'd learned about Hudson only made her want to know more.

"What made you become a cop?" That was a legitimate thing for her to ask. Any new acquaintance might pose a similar question.

"My dad was a cop. I admired him—still do. My brother's a cop. My uncle's a cop. Guess it's in the blood. What made you become a social worker?"

I knew it would drive my father crazy. "Long story."

"We're not on a tight schedule."

"Like a lot of people, I didn't know what I wanted, so I just gravitated toward classes that interested me. Ended up with a bachelor's in sociology and a master's in psychology. Social work was a good fit, and I like helping people."

"How do you help people? I mean, what sort of social work do you do?"

"I work at a free clinic. People who come to us aren't just physically sick, they're often in very bad situations—bad relationships, substance abuse, prostitution. I counsel them on how to escape those situations and create better lives for themselves."

Hudson nodded. "Hmm."

She couldn't be sure, but she sensed a slight note of disapproval. He could join the crowd. A lot of people thought she could have done better, and didn't hesitate to tell her so. Others thought social work coddled criminals and the lazy.

Maybe she could have been a doctor or a lawyer. Certainly her father thought so. But she liked her career just fine.

"Don't you get frustrated?" Hudson finally asked.

"How so?"

"Dealing with the dregs of society. Seeing the same people making the same mistakes over and over."

"First off, I don't think of them as dregs. More like, people who started life at a disadvantage, maybe made some bad choices." It was true some people never learned. But she firmly believed she helped others.

"You must have a kind heart. Seems whenever I try to help people, I get the shit kicked out of me one way or another."

"But you keep trying, right?"

"Sometimes I don't know why. Have you ever tried to rescue a cat from a tree?"

"No, actually."

"Damn thing will scratch you to shreds every time."

She wanted to argue that people weren't cats. They were basically good, if you gave them half a chance to be. But Hudson was clenching his jaw. She'd accidentally hit a nerve. Maybe she'd better back off. She wanted to know more about him, and antagonizing him probably wasn't the best tactic.

Suddenly he looked at her and smiled. "Sorry. You have no idea what a rough couple of weeks it's been."

Actually, she did. And she should tell him. Honestly, she'd thought he would recognize her, or that someone would tell him who she was. But he couldn't know, or he'd have never let her into his car.

She pushed the whole mess out of her mind. She was riding down the freeway in a cool car with a hot guy. She had nowhere to be, nothing else to do. For once in her life, she would stop worrying about all the consequences. She'd never indulged in a one-night stand before. Maybe it was time. She listened to a lot of the women she counseled talking about getting carried away, unable to control themselves enough to make sensible decisions. She'd always assumed she was above such behavior.

Maybe not.

Hudson's house was at the end of a cul-de-sac on a double-sized wooded lot. Like many waterfront homes, it stood on stilts, with only the garage on the ground floor.

He pulled his car into the garage and parked it; they got out, but they had to go back outside and climb a set of wooden stairs to a wraparound porch.

She fell in love at first sight. The house was small, probably only two bedrooms, but a wall of windows looked out on the lake, making the living room seem huge. He flipped on some lights. The place was furnished simply with a couple of low sofas and two chairs, rattan, clean lines. The wood floors were covered with slightly threadbare rugs.

What she really loved about it was, it wasn't a man cave. No huge TV or stereo system. No cast-off shoes littering the floor or spent pizza boxes stacked on the coffee table.

"Have a seat," he said as he headed into the kitchen. "I'm going to get myself a Mountain Dew." He stuck his head in the fridge. "I have other soft drinks, beer and, um, orange juice."

"I'm good, thanks."

He popped the top on his own soft drink and took several swallows as he joined her in the living room. She'd chosen one end of a sofa, inviting him to make his move.

He sat across from her, set his can on a coaster on the coffee table and propped his elbows on his knees, leaning forward. "You can relax, you know. I'm not going to jump you."

She realized she was sitting stiffly, her back straight as a fence post. Leaning back against the cushion, she crossed her legs. "Really? I thought that's what we came here for."

"Thought we'd talk first."

Uh-oh. She didn't like the sound of that. And he suddenly looked a lot more like a cop conducting an interrogation than a potential boyfriend eager to make a conquest.

She tucked one foot under her leg. She could brazen this out.

"Why were you staring at me? At the wedding?" he asked.

"'Cause you're cute."

"A woman like you must have 'cute' guys lining up to have sex with you. You don't need to pick up a strange one at a wedding."

"You must think I'm pretty shallow, that I'd just settle for any cute guy to satisfy my raging libido."

"You don't seem shallow," he admitted.

Maybe she ought to be afraid. He was accused of police brutality. Some really violent guys became cops so they could have a socially acceptable outlet for their…urges. He'd been accused of beating suspects twice…enough to form a pattern.

Maybe the P.I. she'd hired hadn't done a thorough enough job. Maybe Hudson Vale wasn't as nice a guy as he appeared on paper.

Then she had to laugh at herself, silently at least. The Logans' valet had witnessed them together. Even if Hudson had violent urges, she doubted he was stupid enough to assault her when they'd been seen leaving the wedding arm in arm.

Anyway, how could a man who was charmed by a bunch of hummingbirds be anything but a good guy?

"Something just seems a little bit off, that's all," he said almost apologetically. "I've learned over the years not to ignore my instincts. I thought at first you were trying to make someone jealous."

"I'm not, trust me. My date was just a date. In fact, it was a fix-up," she admitted. "When he went after one of the bridesmaids I was totally relieved."

"Now I know you're fibbing. You can get your own dates."

"I guess I can. I got you." Of course he was suspicious of her. He was a cop, one who'd faced off against a powerful, ruthless man who would stoop to any means to prove Hudson had assaulted him for no reason. "But is it so hard to believe I saw something I liked and went for it? I'm sure I'm not the first woman to make a play for you."

"No. But definitely the only one who looks like a supermodel."

"Now who's full of bull?" But she smiled. She liked it that he thought she was pretty. She knew she was reasonably attractive. And she was tall. But *supermodel* was a real stretch.

"It's like I won the lottery or something."

"The lottery? How much did you have to drink at that wedding?"

"I only had half a beer, or I wouldn't have gotten behind

the wheel. You were the one guzzling a martini when I first saw you."

"I do not guzzle. And if you're implying I was drunk, you're wrong. No false courage needed." She matched his steamy look with one of her own.

He drained the last of his Mountain Dew, then crushed the can in one hand.

The macho show of strength made her heart flutter faster than the hummingbirds' wings they'd so recently witnessed. He cavalierly threw the can over his shoulder. It sailed through the pass-through into the kitchen and sounded as if it landed in the sink. Then he came out of his chair, skirted around the coffee table and landed next to her.

"Hi, there."

"H-hi."

"Wanna make out?"

She very much did. She'd predicted Hudson would be a stand-up guy, but the boyish charm was a surprise, and it melted her jaded heart. She couldn't resist him, especially because he wasn't pushing her straight to the bedroom. The hungry look in his eyes told her he wanted her, but he didn't pressure her. His attitude was refreshing.

Elizabeth looped one arm around his neck, drawing him closer. He exuded warmth and an electric tension that her body responded to. Her skin prickled with heightened awareness, her chest tightened and she felt hot between her legs, hot and tickly, as if she was being brushed with rose petals. All from him touching her shoulder.

They took their time getting to that next kiss. She looked into his eyes, wishing she could dive right inside him, his delicious warmth enveloping her like a safe blanket. She parted her lips slightly, needing more oxygen. They shared the same air for several heartbeats before he finally closed that small gap between them and claimed her mouth with his.

He tasted like citrus, and she realized it must be the Mountain Dew. But the electric tingle of his mouth, the firm brush of lips on lips, tongue on tongue sizzled through her body. She would never be able to think about that beverage again without associating it with Hudson.

He shifted her onto his lap. His erection pressed against her thigh, and he adjusted her slightly so it nudged between her legs. His groan was more like a growl of pleasure.

They kissed for a long time. She learned everything there was to know about his mouth and what it could do to her, unable to stop herself from imagining how it would feel to have his talented tongue employed elsewhere on her body. She wanted him to lick her from head to toe like a giant Popsicle, and then she wanted to do the same to him.

He smelled good, like soap and leather, citrus and sunshine. His skin tasted incredible. She ran her tongue along his jawline, exploring the slightly sandpapery texture. He teased her ear with his tongue, which caused her to go very still so she could concentrate on every sensation. When he nipped her earlobe with his teeth she was sure she would spontaneously combust.

He hadn't even touched her breasts, but she was ready to skip over the rest of the foreplay and get him inside her. She was afraid she would climax before they were joined, and while that wouldn't be all bad, their first time she wanted them to come together.

Their *first* time. The thought set her back on her heels. As if there would be more. She knew how impossible that was, but she was already fantasizing about seeing him again.

"Condoms?" she asked between kisses, because that was the only word her sex-fogged brain could manage.

"Bedroom."

She clamored off his lap and grabbed his hand, pulling him off the sofa. Like eager children, they raced toward the back of the house.

He didn't turn on any lights, so she received only a few

fleeting impressions of his bedroom—bigger than expected, with a king-size bed on a platform. Some kind of dresser or chest in the corner. A ceiling fan overhead; that would be nice in the summer.

The bed was made, another unbachelorlike detail she filed away. Unless he'd planned to make a conquest at the wedding and had cleaned up in anticipation, she could conclude that Hudson was a good housekeeper, and that he didn't need a lot of stuff around him to make him happy.

Hudson yanked back the covers, raising the faint scent of vanilla.

He didn't press her onto the mattress immediately; instead he took her in his arms and kissed her again, deftly lowering the zipper at the back of her dress. He smoothed the silky fabric off her shoulders and it slithered down her body and pooled at her feet.

Feeling uncharacteristically shy, she was glad to be in semidarkness. She didn't fixate on her body like some of her friends. She was lucky to be naturally slender, so she didn't fight her weight, but she didn't spend hours at the gym or taking Pilates classes. She wasn't ripped and toned. In fact, she might be considered too thin, and the push-up bra she'd bought to help her A-cups fill out the dress was a bit of false advertising. When he unhooked and removed it, she had to resist the urge to cover her breasts with her arms.

He inhaled sharply. "I'm going to turn on the light."

"No." The single word sounded abrupt, so she softened it by caressing his arm and reaching for the buttons on his shirt. He'd taken his tie off in the car. Though he'd worn his lightweight suit well, she bet he looked unbelievable in a pair of faded jeans.

"No?"

"I like the dark. Moonlight is…romantic."

"Whatever you say." He slid two fingers of each hand inside the elastic of her panties and slowly slid them down her legs. She shivered, though she was anything but cold: her entire body burned from blushing.

She wasn't like this. She'd always been careful in relationships, careful about sex, watching for hints that a man was becoming too obsessed with her. She'd been the object of one man's obsession, and that was enough to cure her.

But this…encounter didn't feel dangerous or sleazy to her. It felt just right. Even if they never saw each other again after tonight—and, fantasies aside, they couldn't—she wouldn't feel bad about this. They'd come together with no pretensions, no false promises or cajoling on either of their parts. Only the rather peculiar circumstances that had brought them together stopped her from enjoying herself without hesitation, and she'd managed to stuff those reservations to the back of her mind.

Hudson peeled off his clothes with a grace and economy of motion that was a turn-on all by itself. What little light that came into the room from a sliding glass door played over the curves and angles of his body, revealing the hint of a muscled biceps here, a rippled abdomen there.

And the evidence of his desire, jutting forward without apology. Elizabeth's mouth went dry.

He came at her like a big, lazy tomcat with anticipation in his gaze, eyeing a mouse. Her own anticipation was about to leap out of her body, a tangible thing. *Touch me. Touch me.*

He put his hands at her waist and tried to span her in his grasp. "You're tiny," he said with a sense of wonder.

She'd never thought of herself as tiny. Skinny, maybe. But her height had sometimes made her feel like a giant. Now that she'd shucked her shoes, Hudson stood at least a few inches taller.

"You're just big," she countered, and they both knew she wasn't just talking about his muscular shoulders.

He grinned, proving no man was immune to a woman praising his equipment. "I'm glad you approve."

"Let's see if I approve of how you use it." Elizabeth wasn't normally one for saucy quips, especially during sex, but something about him brought out her playfulness. She slowly sank onto the bed, pulling him with her.

He kissed her in earnest now, wrapping her in his arms and rolling on his back so she lay atop him. His erection pressed against her abdomen, and the heat between her legs threatened combustion. Her womb ached for him to complete her.

She spread her legs and straddled him, rubbing herself against his erection.

He growled again. "Oh, man. You're making me crazy, you know."

Enough foreplay. They could fondle and tease and seduce later, perhaps during round two. She could only hope she would be lucky enough to get to round two. Right now, she needed to finish this or she was going to implode.

Hudson reached for a drawer in the nightstand and fumbled a bit in the dark. She heard the rustle of plastic. Once he got the condom out of its wrapper she took it from him.

"Turn around while you put that on me," he said.

"Excuse me?"

"I want to look at your bottom."

She laughed. So outrageous. And she did as requested, turning around to face the foot of the bed, sitting on his ribs as she smoothed the latex over his swollen member. He was hard as a hunk of rebar and three times as thick.

While she worked, taking her time, enjoying every moment, he put his hands on her bottom. "I knew it. You have the cutest little ass I've ever seen."

"You're impertinent," she said in her best schoolmarm voice. But she wasn't immune to praise, either. His approval warmed her blood in a way mere strokes and caresses couldn't.

She turned back around to face him. Their eyes met. The

moment seemed suddenly hugely significant. They were about to join their bodies and become one for the first time.

The only time, she reminded herself sternly.

"Do you want to be on top?" he asked.

She wasn't used to being asked for a preference. If she stayed on top, she could maintain better control. But control wasn't what she was after tonight. She wanted him to conquer her…at least for the moment.

She shifted her position yet again, sliding up next to him. She put her mouth right next to his ear. "I want you to take me."

He needed no further urging. In one second he was on top, the conquering hero. She opened her legs and welcomed him.

She'd thought he'd just thrust inside her, but he took his time, letting her get used to the feel of him filling her up, stretching her in a way that wasn't painful, yet she was very aware of his size and power. If he ever wanted to hurt her, he certainly could. And she knew he could be violent.

No. She wouldn't think about that now. The man she was getting to know wouldn't hurt someone smaller and weaker than him just because he could. Some cops were off on a power trip, but she was sure he wasn't that kind of cop no matter what the newspaper had said.

"You okay?"

"Never better."

"You went far away there for just a minute."

"I'm right here."

"You'd tell me if it was too much, right?" Even as he said this, he started to move. Every nerve ending in her vagina screamed with the pleasure of it, and it was all Elizabeth could do not to scream. Incredible.

She wanted to draw out the pleasure, but she found she had no self-control. She let the ecstasy overwhelm her, and she held nothing back, nearly weeping with the intensity.

"Oh, man." Hudson was obviously trying to hold back, but he couldn't, either. "Oh, yeah. Here it comes."

Still in the throes of her own climax, she watched his face as he came. His pleasure was a beautiful thing to behold. He gave himself over to it totally. She couldn't imagine him looking any happier if he really had won the lottery.

It was over quickly, yet Elizabeth couldn't imagine sex being any more perfect. As he lay on top of her, breathing hard, his skin slightly damp with perspiration, a glow of contentment settled on her.

"I usually can last longer," he assured her when he could talk.

She laughed. "Men and their egos. I wasn't timing you."

"I just wanted it to be good for you."

"It was, trust me."

"Give me a few minutes to recover. I think with you I could have a go every half hour all night long."

"You're quite the optimist."

"It's just that you're so pretty and sexy."

"I...well, I probably should be going." She didn't want to go, and since tomorrow was Sunday, she had nowhere to be and no one would miss her. Still, she didn't want to overstay her welcome.

"What? No way. I mean, of course I'll take you home if you really want to go, but I'm not one of those guys who makes a conquest, then can't get rid of her fast enough. I want you to spend the night, to get to know you better...and not just in bed." He shifted, separating their bodies. She missed him already. "I make killer banana pancakes."

"I have to work tomorrow." It was a lie. But she did have to make the break clean and decisive. This could not be the start of something, much as she wanted it to be.

When he found out who she was—and he would—he was going to be one pissed-off dude.

"Still, you don't have to run off. It's early yet."

He was right about that. It wasn't yet ten o'clock. Though the longer she stayed, the harder it would be to leave, she couldn't make herself get out of bed and put her clothes on.

"I'll stay awhile."

She snuggled up against him, still feeling the effects of her sexual haze. How sweet it would be if she could fall asleep here with her head on his shoulder, lulled by the rhythm of his deep breathing. Not that she could. Not with what she was keeping from him.

He, on the other hand, fell asleep almost instantly, which made her smile. Men were so predictable. She knew it was a physiological reaction, but it was amusing how he could be revved up in a frenzy one minute and a minute later sawing logs.

After a short while, she surprised herself by falling asleep, too.

When she woke sometime later, she was slightly disoriented. Hudson had an old-fashioned clock radio on his nightstand. Once she got her eyes to focus, she discovered it was almost 2:00 a.m.

She couldn't stay until morning. There was no way she could hide her identity from him—it was getting harder and harder to be deceitful.

She was hunting around in the dark for her dress when she heard a strange noise outside. That was what had awakened her, she realized.

The wind? An animal, perhaps a raccoon? There were a lot of trees around, and critters liked to hang out near lakes.

She listened. There it was again. Footsteps. Someone was on the balcony. And it sounded as if they were trying to jimmy a window somewhere else in the house.

She sat up and shook Hudson. "Hudson!" she hissed. "Wake up. Someone is trying to break in."

CHAPTER THREE

HUDSON WOKE INSTANTLY, sat up and listened. He heard it immediately—the sound of a window rattling from the other bedroom. And it wasn't the wind.

He leaped out of bed and grabbed his pants, jumping into them commando style. His gun was in the safe in the closet, damn it. He'd seen no need to take it with him to a wedding, and he would never leave it where a burglar could steal it. Too many stolen guns were on the street.

"Go into the bathroom," he said in the take-charge voice he used when he intended to be obeyed. "Take your cell phone and lock the door in case you have to call for help." He slid open the door of his closet and quickly worked the combination, then grabbed his backup weapon, a sturdy Glock.

He noiselessly opened the sliding glass door that led out to the balcony, which completely encircled the house. As he stepped out onto the wooden decking in his bare feet, he realized Liz was right behind him. And damned if she didn't have his Louisville Slugger gripped in both her hands. She'd obviously thrown on the first item of clothing she'd found, which happened to be his dress shirt. She'd buttoned only one button.

Some other time that would be really charming.

He wasn't going to waste time and breath trying to get her to obey orders. She obviously wasn't the hide-in-the-bathroom type of woman.

"Just stay behind me," he whispered. He walked to the corner of the house and peered around it.

Sure enough, a guy in a ski mask was halfway through his window.

The ski mask told him a lot. This wasn't a simple burglary. The intruder knew the house was occupied, and he didn't want to be identified. The other thing that told him a lot was the gun in the guy's hand.

Hudson raised his weapon. "Police! Freeze!"

The guy didn't follow orders. He pulled himself out of the window, pointed his gun straight at Hudson and squeezed off a shot.

Liz screamed.

Fortunately, Hudson pulled back around the corner, and the shot wasn't too well aimed to begin with. He heard the bullet whiz past his head and sail off into the trees behind the house.

Hudson would have been well within his rights to shoot the guy, but he didn't return fire. Maybe it was because he was already in so much trouble; if he added deadly force to the mix, even justified, his career was over. Or maybe it was simply because he didn't want to take the life of some scrawny drug addict.

If the burglar had raised his gun again, Hudson would have shot him. But he didn't. He turned and vaulted over the balcony railing. It was a long drop, but the guy landed on his feet. Hudson watched him hightail it out to the street and away like a jackrabbit on fire.

"Are you okay?" Liz asked, coming up behind him.

"He missed me by a mile. Not even sure he was really trying to hit me, though he ought to know better than to draw down on an armed cop."

"Maybe he didn't know you were a cop."

"I identified myself." The more he thought about it, the more disturbed he became.

He'd never had any crime problems here before. His house

wasn't an attractive target for burglars; he didn't have any fancy electronics or silver or jewelry. And if a burglar were simply choosing a house at random, there were plenty of unoccupied vacation cabins around.

"We should call the police," Liz said.

"I am the police."

"Well, yeah, but shouldn't you report this? Maybe he's still in the area."

"You kidding? The way that guy was running, he's halfway to Louisiana by now."

"What about evidence? Fingerprints and such."

"They wouldn't send out CSI for an attempted burglary."

"Attempted murder more like it," Liz argued. "He could have killed you."

"He wore gloves. He didn't leave behind any evidence."

"What about his tattoo? Did you see that?"

Now that he thought about it, Hudson did remember seeing a tattoo on the man's forearm. Something like a big fish. Now, that could be useful.

"I'll call it in tomorrow," he said, "but it's the kind of almost-crime that makes most cops shrug." Not to mention, he didn't want to have any contact with his fellow cops right now. Most of the guys he worked with didn't believe he'd beaten up Franklin Mandalay for no reason. They knew him better than that. But he couldn't take their well-meaning pity.

Hudson took the bat out of Liz's hands. "You could have been killed. Next time I tell you to hide in the bathroom, hide in the bathroom. And by the way, that's a fetching outfit you have on."

He couldn't be sure, because it was too dark, but he thought he saw the hint of a blush as she turned and went back inside.

"I wasn't going to let you go out there alone."

"I'm a cop. You're not. But…thank you." He tossed the bat aside, put the gun in the drawer of his nightstand, handy in case the guy came back. When he refocused his attention on Liz, she was shrugging her way out of his shirt.

Hudson went instantly hard, ready to go again. Judging from the look on Liz's face, she was ready, too.

"Oh. My," she said when he shucked his pants. "I've heard adrenaline sharpens one's libido, but here I have some rather convincing proof."

"Adrenaline's got nothing to do with it, sugar. It's all you." He playfully wrestled her down to the bed and kissed her—hard and fast, then slow and soft.

"Liz," he said before the lovemaking got so involved that he lost any ability to think or speak. "There's something you probably should know about me."

"I know all I need to know."

"Maybe not. I was suspended last week. A guy I arrested claims I beat him up for no good reason. Unless Internal Affairs clears me—and really, I have no way to prove the guy's lying—I might be out of a job."

"You're telling me this now…because…?"

"Because I want to see you again. But I figured you ought to know the worst before you decide if that's gonna happen."

For a moment she looked unbearably sad. Had he disappointed her that thoroughly? But what she said next surprised him.

"I already knew."

"What?"

"I saw it on TV. That's why I was staring at you at the wedding. I recognized you."

"Oh." He rolled away from her, trying to wrap his mind around the implications. "Please don't tell me you're turned on by the idea that I'm violent."

"No," she said quickly. "It's not that at all."

"Then what's this about?" Some women were attracted to notoriety, even the negative kind. "You like bad boys? 'Cause I'm not one."

"I know you're not. I confess I was a bit curious, but after spending a very short time with you, I was sure you couldn't have done what you're accused of."

"Really? That seems a little naive." All those doubts he had about why she'd come on to him reared their ugly heads. He should have listened to his gut when it told him something was off-kilter. His gut was always right. "Did Mandalay send you? Or his lawyer?"

She sat up, pulling the sheet up to cover her breasts. "Good God, no."

"That would be a good ploy. Send the pretty girl to seduce the sucker. Set up a fake burglary. Maybe coax the disgraced cop into yet another violent act, conveniently witnessed by said pretty girl—"

"You can't think I had anything to do with that."

"I don't know what to think. Most women would have cowered behind a locked door. But you were right behind me, where you could clearly see everything that happened."

"I'm not most women."

He wished she didn't look so damn fetching wrapped in a sheet. Even while he suspected she might be trying to finish trashing his career, he wanted her with an acuteness that stole his breath away.

Hudson scrubbed his face with one hand. Maybe he'd made a mistake. "Okay. Okay, I'm probably wrong."

"Maybe I should go home now."

"Liz, you don't have to leave."

"Oh, I think I do. Don't stir yourself. I'll call a cab."

"No, I'll take you home." Maybe she'd cool off on the drive to her home. Maybe he could undo what might have been the worst mistake of his life. "Just let me jump in the shower. I won't be five minutes." He needed a shower in the worst way. A cold one.

He didn't wait for her to agree. He scooted off the bed

and trotted to the bathroom. He'd be done by the time she was dressed.

He scrubbed down quickly, then dried off and brushed his teeth. He'd be damned if he'd force her to deal with his morning breath. In the unlikely event she let him get close enough that she could smell his breath.

A quick swipe of deodorant, and all that was left was to throw on some clothes. He exited the bathroom.

"Liz?"

Nothing. He checked the kitchen, living room and second bathroom.

Her things were gone.

She was gone.

"I couldn't do it."

"What the hell? Couldn't find him? Couldn't pull the trigger?"

"He had a woman with him."

"So?"

"You think I should have plugged her, too? Or left her behind as a witness?"

"You were wearing a ski mask. She wouldn't have recognized you. It would have been written off as a burglary gone bad."

"I don't leave loose ends like that. And I don't kill women. Nuh-uh. You didn't say anything about a woman."

"Christ, do I have to do everything myself? You realize if I go down, so do you. Hudson Vale got a good look at Jazz. If he finds her before we do, it's all over. She'll sell us out like day-old fish. It will all come out—do you understand me? We'll all go down."

"We'll get him another day."

"Time's running out." The man paused, thinking hard. "You know, never mind. I shouldn't have asked a boy to do a man's job."

"Oh, go screw yourself. You think it's so goddamned easy to kill someone, you do it."

The man hung up. It was remarkably easy to kill someone. Establish an unshakable alibi. Pay in cash. Leave no evidence behind, including no body.

His muscleman had outlived his usefulness. He was going to have to take care of him. Tonight, before the idiot got drunk and blathered to someone what he'd been up to. Then he'd take care of the others. He'd find Jazz and finish her off. Himself.

ELIZABETH FELT AWFUL for the teenage girl huddled in her office. Tonda Pickens was in a terrible situation, no doubt about it.

"If Jackson finds out I'm pregnant," she said tearfully, "he'll kill me. He will."

The fear was not ungrounded. When a woman was pregnant, she was much more likely to become the victim of violence from the very person who was supposed to love and protect her. Plus, in Tonda's case, her boyfriend-slash-pimp had hit her before.

"What about going home to your mother?" Elizabeth asked. "You haven't talked to her in a while. Maybe the fact you're having her grandchild would improve her attitude."

"Hah, you kidding? This is what she did to me for just kissing a boy." She lifted her hair off one side of her face, revealing a jagged scar. "I can't even imagine what she'd do if she found out Jackson and me..." She looked out the window, swallowing convulsively. "I have to get rid of it. I got no choice."

"Yes, you do have a choice." Elizabeth wouldn't counsel a nineteen-year-old prostitute to have a baby and keep it. But neither would she advise her to "get rid of it." Her job was to lay out all the options and let the girl make her own decision. It was the only way, because Tonda was the one who had to live with the physical and emotional consequences. "You do not have to go back to Jackson or your mother. There are shelters for women in your situation. Safe havens."

"If you're talking about one of those homes for unwed mothers where they make you pray and then make you give up the baby for adoption, no way. I won't carry a baby nine months and give it away. I've seen girls do that. It racks 'em up bad."

Elizabeth had, indeed, been thinking about a place similar to what Tonda described. It was a godsend for some girls, but not suitable for everyone.

"There are a number of places you could go. We could look into them together, find the one that suits you."

"What if I wanted…to keep the baby?" Tonda asked cautiously.

"If that's what you want to do, you have that right. No one can make you give it up. I won't lie to you—it won't be easy. If you want to keep the baby, you'll have to find some way to provide for it and yourself. Jackson would be legally obligated to pay child support, but I'm guessing that forcing him to do that would be a challenge?"

"I'd rather not even tell him."

Elizabeth would rather she didn't, either. What kind of father figure would a pimp be?

"I shoulda been more careful."

"You're not the first person to make a mistake, or the last. It happens. The thing to focus on now is making good decisions going forward."

Tonda placed a hand on her abdomen. "I know I said I wouldn't go for adoption, but what if I changed my mind? Could I find a good home for the baby?"

"We can certainly try. If you do a private adoption, you get to approve the adoptive parents. Just say the word, and I'll get you into a women's shelter—a temporary place until we can figure something out. But you don't have to go back to Jackson."

Tonda shook her head. "No. I'm not showing yet. Jackson won't know. I have to think. Maybe I'll call Mama. Give her some time to get used to the idea before I see her in person."

Elizabeth hated to let Tonda go home to her unhealthy situation. If she was still prostituting herself, she risked illness not just for herself, but the baby. But they'd discussed that already. Tonda wouldn't be pushed into anything—she had to make the decision herself.

"Just remember one thing, Tonda. No one has the right to hit you. Whether it's Jackson or your mother or a customer, if tempers start to flare, get out. Call the police. Call someone. Don't just think you have to put up with it because you have no choice. There are always choices."

Tonda nodded. "Thanks. I won't let anybody hit me, don't worry. I have more to worry about than just myself now."

That was a mature attitude, and Elizabeth was glad to see it. She walked Tonda to the door of the clinic. "You take care, Tonda."

"I will. Thank you, Ms. Downey." She gave Elizabeth a quick hug—something she'd never done before. The gesture warmed Elizabeth's heart. Tonda shouldered her backpack, which had a picture of a kitten on it, and pushed the door open.

Although Elizabeth tried to maintain a professional distance from her clients, she'd always had a soft spot in her heart for Tonda, who'd been coming to the clinic for almost a year now.

As the door closed behind Tonda, Elizabeth turned. That was when she saw two people standing in the lobby, watching her. The clinic manager, Gloria Kirby, stood awkwardly beside them. She motioned for Elizabeth to join them.

"Elizabeth," Gloria said, "these are detectives with the Montgomery County Sheriff's Department. They'd like a word with you."

What? "Oh, no, did something happen to one of my clients?"

The two cops regarded her gravely. One of them was a fortyish man, tall, thin and pale with a shaved head. The other was a humorless-looking Hispanic woman, who could have been twenty-five or forty-five, with her hair pulled back in a severe knot.

"Is there somewhere private we can talk?" the man said.

"Sure." She led them to her office, which was hardly more than a glorified closet, furnished with a battered wooden desk, an ancient metal file cabinet and two mismatched armchairs. She thought about offering them refreshments. She kept a cooler with water and soft drinks behind her desk and a stash of peanut-butter crackers in a bottom drawer. Often her clients arrived hungry.

But these two cops didn't look as if they wanted to eat or drink. She sat down behind her desk, and each of them took a chair.

"What can I help you with?" she asked, her stomach tying itself into knots.

They both looked uneasy. "I'm Detective Sanchez," the woman said, "and this is Detective Knightly."

"Ms. Downey," Knightly said, smoothly taking over, "can you tell us where you were Saturday night?"

This did not sound good. It was how the cops began every interview with someone suspected of a crime, at least if she could believe what she saw on TV.

"I was at a friend's wedding," she said.

"Until about what time?"

"I'm not sure. Seven? Eight?"

"And then where did you go?"

I went home with a man I just met and had mind-blowing sex. She was so not saying that. "I went home."

"Alone?"

"Yes." Lying to cops was getting to be a habit with her.

The two cops exchanged a glance. The woman, Sanchez, took notes.

"C'mon, why are you asking me this?" Elizabeth prodded. "What's going on?"

"It's about your father," Sanchez said. "We found him… well, there's no easy way to say this. We found him in Lake Conroe."

"Oh. Oh, Jesus." Every drop of blood drained from Elizabeth's head, and she was glad she was already sitting down. "Dead? He was dead?"

"Yes," Sanchez confirmed. "The M.E. puts his time of death sometime between the hours of 11:00 p.m. Saturday night and 5:00 a.m."

"My father was murdered?" she asked, just to be sure that she hadn't misheard something. The reality of those words tasted strangely sour in her mouth. She'd always assumed she'd be indifferent to the man's death. But hearing the news, she felt an odd sting of sadness.

"We're very sorry for your loss," Sanchez said in a perfunctory way. "His housekeeper told us you were his next of kin."

She nodded. "What should I do now? Do I need to identify him? Maybe there's a mistake." She grabbed on to that thin thread of hope. She wasn't ready for her father to be dead just yet.

"We identified him through his fingerprints," Knightly said.

"Oh." Elizabeth swallowed back tears. Why was she crying? Her father had been a thorn in her side for years now. She hadn't even spoken to him in months.

"Can anyone verify when you arrived home?" Sanchez asked. Back to business.

She hoped not. "I doubt it. I live in a big building—people come and go a lot." She paused, then realized where the questions were leading. "You think I had something to do with my father's murder?"

"These questions are just routine," Knightly quickly said. "We always check on the whereabouts of family members of any murder victim."

Any grief Elizabeth might have felt was quickly pushed aside in favor of fear. This was *not* routine. Anyone close to her or her father—including Mrs. Ames, the housekeeper— knew he and Elizabeth were estranged. She had even taken her mother's maiden name so that people wouldn't associate her with him. And now she was a suspect.

And if she gave them Hudson's name? The one man more likely than she to be the killer. Dear Lord. That was going to look very, very bad.

She shrugged helplessly. Had she used her cell phone that night? No. Her phone had been out of juice, and she'd used Hudson's landline to call a cab.

"When you went home," Sanchez asked, "did you make any phone calls, check your email?"

She shook her head. "Sorry. I went to bed with a book."

"It's all right," Knightly said soothingly. "I'm sure there'll be no problem. Again, we're sorry for your loss."

Sanchez didn't look so sure. She snapped her notebook closed. "I guess that's all for now. Don't leave town."

Elizabeth sighed quietly in relief. Maybe this would all blow over. They'd find who did this, and they wouldn't scrutinize her any further.

Sanchez stood, but Knightly remained seated, looking troubled. "Ms. Downey, do you know anyone who would want to hurt your father?"

"Detective, my father was a high-powered attorney who made his money by taking advantage of people in vulnerable situations. I imagine many of the people he dealt with hated him. I suggest you look there for a suspect."

"We'll do that. Again, sorry for your loss."

Elizabeth didn't take another full breath until the detectives were gone. Of all the lousy times for Franklin Mandalay to get himself murdered, why had he done it on the night the two prime suspects had been together?

CHAPTER FOUR

DETECTIVE CARLA SANCHEZ said nothing to her partner until they were back in their silver LTD.

"You went awful easy on her," Carla said as she slid her key into the ignition and started the engine. She turned the AC on full blast and angled one of the vents on her face. Hot day for October. She wished she'd taken off her jacket, like Knightly had.

"I don't think she did it," Knightly said. "Her reaction seemed pretty genuine. Those were real tears."

"Some people can cry on cue. Especially beautiful women who manipulate people to get their way. *Especially* if they think they're going to jail."

Knightly seemed to mull this over. He opened his notebook and glanced at his notes. "She does have a helluva motive."

"Yeah, like about seventeen million of them."

"Do we know for sure she inherits?"

"She's his only child. Only close relative."

"Who cut herself off from him and hasn't accepted a dime from him in seven years. That doesn't sound like someone motivated by money."

"You're letting your gonads sway you. Just because she's pretty and bats her eyelashes at you doesn't mean she can't pull the trigger on a gun."

Knightly nodded. "Point taken. It's too early to rule out anyone. But we *do* have other suspects."

"You mean Hudson."

"I know he was your partner, but we have to talk to him."

"I know." Carla and Hudson had been partners for a couple of years, and she knew him pretty well. He was smart, and he closed a lot of cases, but he was way too casual about rules like dress codes and properly filling out paperwork. And he was constantly on the prowl for women.

Okay, *prowl* wasn't the right word. He was just…aware. He flirted with every female he encountered and made conquests where he could.

Carla was one of those conquests.

After their one night together, he'd been ready to move on. She'd acted as though it was no big deal, but he'd hurt her feelings more than she would ever admit.

Yeah, she knew him pretty well, and though she pretended reluctance, she actually relished the thought of seeing him wiggle helplessly like a worm on a fishhook.

"I hate to even consider a fellow cop," Knightly said, "but we have to. Two weeks before Mandalay's death, Vale beat him up. The incident became very public and Mandalay was pressing charges. They go away with him dead."

"I won't argue with you."

Carla well remembered when she'd first met Hudson Vale. She'd been still in uniform. He'd been a green recruit. She'd thought he was the most charming man she'd ever met, not to mention sexy. Drinks after work had led to a crazy backseat encounter. But after that, he hadn't looked at her twice. She'd watched as he'd moved on to conquest after conquest—that blonde skank from Dispatch, then a stacked redheaded lawyer, then others.

Carla had no longer interested him.

She'd learned to work with him, even considered him a friend. But she hadn't forgotten.

"We might as well go question him now," Knightly said.

"Not if you're going soft on him. I don't want anyone accusing us of taking it easy on him just because he's one of us." She tried not to smile.

"Not soft, but I hope he has an alibi." Knightly opened his window. "Damn, Sanchez, you got it like a meat locker in here. You know that air-conditioning dries out my contacts, right?"

"Not too many people have an alibi for the middle of the night. I mean, most people go home and go to sleep, and who can verify that?"

"Huh. When was the last time you think Hudson Vale spent a Saturday night alone? Sleeping?"

"Good point," Carla conceded. "Guess we'll find out."

"Exactly," Knightly agreed.

HUDSON WASN'T USED to having so much leisure time. His first two weeks on suspension, he'd painted his house, sealed his deck, washed his car twice and made repairs to the dock.

Yesterday, Sunday, he'd been in a blue funk. Between thinking about the burglar he'd almost shot, and the abrupt disappearance of Liz early that morning, he hadn't summoned enough energy to do more than stare out at a great blue heron fishing along the lakeshore.

That Monday morning, he'd started in on gardening.

Not really his thing. Usually he trimmed a few bushes, kept the lawn mowed, raked leaves in the fall, and that was it.

A car had turned down his street; Hudson recognized the growl of a powerful engine, and knew almost before he turned his head that a police vehicle was coming his way. A silver LTD. Were they coming to arrest him?

Hudson's stomach whooshed even as he straightened and arranged his face into a neutral expression. He'd known this might happen. His word against that of a powerful, rich attorney, and the only witness to the incident, Jazz the prostitute, couldn't be found.

He relaxed slightly when he recognized his partner, Carla

Sanchez, get out of the passenger side. He and Carla weren't exactly warm and fuzzy with each other. They would never be drinking buddies or confidants. But she was smart, and he felt certain she had his back.

He tensed when he saw whom she was with. Todd Knightly, Mr. Rules-and-Regulations. Were they partners now? Did that mean Knightly was working Major Crimes?

Hudson tried to read their faces. Sanchez had her best poker face on. She wasn't giving him a clue. Knightly had a determined glint in his eye, but also appeared slightly worried.

"Mornin'," Hudson greeted them in his best good-old-boy demeanor. He stood up and brushed the dirt from the knees of his jeans, expecting Sanchez to make some crack about his disreputable appearance. She was always giving him grief about the way he dressed. She thought his loud Hawaiian shirts were juvenile.

She said nothing.

Last he heard, Carla hadn't believed Mandalay's story about an unprovoked assault. Had something changed her mind?

"I'm guessing," he said, "this isn't a social call."

Knightly didn't engage in any small talk. He never did. When he was on duty, he was all work, all the time. "Vale, where were you Saturday night between 10:00 p.m. and 5:00 a.m. Sunday morning?"

The question actually brought to mind a series of very pleasant memories. "I was here. At home." Though the evening hadn't ended as he'd wished, he couldn't help a slight smile as he recalled the beautiful siren who had shared his bed two nights ago.

"Alone?" Knightly said.

"As a matter of fact, no."

Knightly cut his eyes toward Carla and nodded, as if saying, *I told you so.* He took out his notebook. "Can you give me the name and contact information of the person or persons you were with?"

"Come on, what is this?" Hudson asked impatiently.

"Just cooperate, for once," Carla said.

Perspiration broke out on Hudson's forehead. Something was really wrong here. "Liz. Her name was Liz."

"Last name?"

Hudson rubbed his chin. "Ah, there's the problem. I didn't get a last name."

"Typical," Sanchez muttered.

Knightly ignored her. "How can we find this woman?"

"She's a friend of a friend. Of a friend. I'm sure I can track her down if there's a need. But might I ask why there's a need? Last I heard, I was off duty Saturday night. A guy is allowed to have a little fun, isn't he?"

"Franklin Mandalay." Knightly watched Hudson carefully, as if expecting some kind of reaction.

"Jeez, what's that bastard accused me of now?"

"He didn't accuse you of anything," Sanchez said. "He's dead. From a bullet through the heart."

"Dead?" He waited for someone to burst out laughing. Nobody did. "Holy crap, you're serious."

"He was found in the lake," Sanchez said.

Hudson immediately went into detective mode. "Time of death?"

"This isn't your case," Knightly said. "We'll ask the questions. You provide the answers."

Hudson sighed. Knightly had been watching too many episodes of *Dragnet*. "You can't honestly think I had anything to do with it."

"You had a beef with him," Sanchez said. "His body was found less than two miles from your house. And you don't have an alibi."

"I do have an alibi."

"Whose name you've conveniently forgotten. Do you take so many women to bed that—"

"Her name is Liz." Wow, Sanchez was certainly in a mood. So much for having his back. "I met her at a party. We came back here. She stayed until about four, then she had to leave because she worked in the morning." That was sort of the truth.

"What kind of car did she drive?" Knightly asked, all business.

Sanchez, on the other hand, was getting personal. Years ago, long before they'd been partners, they'd slept together. Once. She'd wanted more; he'd realized it was a mistake. She'd been angry at the time but claimed to have put the matter behind her. Still, she never missed an opportunity to rag on him for his "indiscriminate sleeping habits," as she called them.

"We took my car," Hudson explained. "And she took a taxi home. Look, I'll ask around, track her down. Give me a day or two. If I can't find her, break out the rubber hoses and the hot lights and have at me."

"In a day or two you could be on the other side of the world," Sanchez said.

Knightly shook his head. "He isn't going to run, Carla, or he would have done it already. He had to have known he'd be a suspect."

"I didn't know anything until five minutes ago," Hudson couldn't help but point out.

Knightly took off his mirrored sunglasses and pinched the bridge of his nose. "Look, Vale, we have to clear you from the suspect list. You understand that, right? People are going to ask questions, and we'll have to have good, solid evidence that you couldn't have done this. Give us a real alibi and we'll get our job done."

Hudson nodded. "I totally get that. And I will find the

mystery woman. So unless you're prepared to arrest me on the spot, y'all best back off and let me get to work."

Knightly considered him for a few more seconds. "All right. Two days." He turned and strode back to the car, jerking the driver's door open.

"Hey, Sanchez," Hudson said softly as his former partner turned away. "How long did it take for them to promote Knightly into my job?"

She lowered her voice. "The transfer to Major Crimes was already in the works. I requested to work with him. He might be a little humorless, but he's a good cop. He knows the law. He follows protocol."

Hudson knew he'd just been put down. But now was not the time or place to argue.

"You better go, before Mr. Rules-and-Regulations reports you for consorting with a suspect."

"If I were you, I'd forget about Knightly and focus on finding the girl. If she exists."

Hudson's jaw dropped as Sanchez slid into the passenger seat. Did his own partner actually think he might have killed a man? Did she actually prefer working with that pompous ass?

Knightly had about a year's seniority over Hudson. In fact, when Hudson had first made detective—assigned to juvie and missing persons—Knightly had shown him the ropes with a sort of big-brother attitude that was only slightly annoying. Hudson had assumed he was well-meaning.

But after a few months, Hudson had realized that Knightly relished his superior attitude. He had the state and local penal codes memorized word for word and wouldn't hesitate to complain to the lieutenant if he thought any of his colleagues weren't following the rules. He always wore a suit with razor-creased pants. He was always perfectly clean-shaven, his head freshly shaved every day to minimize the impact of his receding hairline.

When a position opened up on the Major Crimes squad,

both Knightly and Hudson were considered. When Hudson got the nod, Knightly congratulated him and appeared to be a good sport, but Hudson always suspected Knightly felt cheated.

Hudson took a deep breath to steady himself. He couldn't afford to let emotion cloud his thinking. This had gone way beyond salvaging his career. He was now a murder suspect.

His story about a woman with no last name who'd disappeared into the night with no trace did sound fishy. Hudson wouldn't have bought it if some other suspect had told it to him during an investigation.

But she was real. He simply had to find her and get her to make a statement to the police. It might be embarrassing for her. But even as little as he knew about her, he believed she would do the right thing. She wouldn't let him swing in the wind to save herself a little embarrassment. Or a lot of embarrassment if she turned out to be in a relationship. Which, he realized, he really hoped she wasn't…and not just to make his alibi stronger.

Liz was a friend of Jillian's. He didn't have Jillian's number, but Claudia would have it. Or someone at Project Justice, where she worked, would know how to get in touch with her. He pulled his phone out of his pocket and called Claudia, but only reached her voice mail, which meant she was probably in a session. He told her succinctly what he was looking for, confident his problems would soon be solved.

Thirty minutes later she returned his call. By then, he was sitting on his deck with a can of Mountain Dew in his hand, trying his best to let the view of the lake calm his nerves.

"I can give you Jillian's number, but it won't do you much good," Claudia said. "She's on her honeymoon."

Crap. He could still try to call her. Maybe she would answer. It wasn't cool to bother someone on their honeymoon, but getting Liz's contact information would take only a couple of seconds.

Claudia already knew what he was thinking. "Even if you called her, it's doubtful she'd pick up. They went to Patagonia."

Double crap. "The only thing I really know about her is that she's a social worker, and she works at a clinic of some kind. I guess I could call every clinic in the city and ask for her." But if that was his only recourse—

"You should talk to Mitch."

"Delacroix? The computer hacker at Project Justice?"

"We don't call him that. He's a computer data analyst. Tell him everything you know about Liz. Anything at all you remember. I bet he can find her for you in less than an hour. You've helped out Project Justice in the past. Now let them help you."

It took less than an hour. In fact, it only took about seven minutes. With some prodding, Hudson had remembered that Liz had said *free* clinic. That narrowed down the possibilities considerably. With a little bit of fancy online footwork, Mitch had come up with three urban clinics in the Houston area with employees named Elizabeth.

Hudson decided to visit them in person, rather than try to get Liz on the phone. As skittish as she was—and as angry as she'd been with him when she'd fled his house—she might refuse his call or try to make him think she was the wrong Elizabeth. It would be easier to confront her in person and convince her she needed to come forward with her statement.

With addresses for the three clinics in hand, Hudson set out to find his alibi. It took a few minutes for him to realize that the tightness in his chest had little to do with his thorny predicament, and almost everything to do with the fact he couldn't wait to see Liz again. He only wished his excuse for tracking her down wasn't what it was.

Houston City Clinic was the first stop. It was a depressing storefront office crowded between a run-down bodega on one side and a pawn shop on the other. Hudson had a hard time picturing Liz spending every day at a place like this. It would say something about her character if she wanted to help people *that* badly.

He walked through the crowded waiting room, filled with snuffling adults, screaming toddlers and feverish babies and thanked God for the great health coverage he got through the sheriff's department.

At least, for a while longer.

"Excuse me," he asked the harried receptionist, "I'd like to see Elizabeth, please."

"If you mean Dr. Eliza Eldridge, that's you and everybody else in here." She looked him up and down. He'd put on some decent-looking khaki pants and a polo shirt, wanting to appear his best when he encountered Liz again. He supposed he looked a little too well-heeled to be patronizing a free clinic, but people could fall into unfortunate circumstances anytime.

Or maybe the receptionist had simply pegged him as a cop. Some people had a sixth sense when it came to spotting law enforcement.

"Take a number," the woman said.

"Maybe you can help me."

"No cutting in line," she said without looking up. "Take a number."

"I just want to ask a question. Is Dr. Eldridge a tall brunette with dark blue eyes?"

"She's five foot two with brown eyes and a 'fro."

"Then I have the wrong Elizabeth. Thank you for your time."

She didn't look up.

One down, two to go.

The second clinic was in a better neighborhood. But it shared the same air of hopelessness as the first. "Elizabeth" was easy to find; she actually worked at the front desk, according to a nameplate. She wasn't Liz, either.

"Can I help you?" she asked with a friendly smile.

"Are you Elizabeth?" he asked, just to be sure. Liz had said she was a social worker, not a receptionist, but he had to be thorough.

"Yes, that's right."

"No other Elizabeths work here?"

"No, just me," the pretty Latina woman said, still smiling. "You aren't a bill collector, are you? 'Cause I made my car payment yesterday."

He smiled back. "No, nothing like that. Just trying to find an old friend."

"Good luck."

One to go. His heart lifted as he turned into the parking lot of the third clinic, Los Amigos Family Clinic. Despite the sadly depressed condition of the neighborhood overall, this clinic was clean and bright, and the entire block on which it sat was free from trash and graffiti. The small, freestanding building was painted in bright colors, and the windows were clean. A sign in the window advertised Free Flu Shots.

Inside was bright and fresh, too. There was still a crowd of people waiting for care, but they didn't seem quite as desperate as the patients at the other clinics.

The receptionist sat behind a glass partition. Hudson rang the bell, and the frosted-glass door slid open. A young man in a nicely pressed shirt greeted him with a polite smile. "Help you?"

"I'd like to see Elizabeth, please."

"I'm so sorry—Ms. Downey had to cancel her appointments today. She had a death in her family."

"Oh, no, that's terrible." Hudson's heart went out to Liz. He wanted to be there for her, to comfort her, give her a shoulder to cry on. Which was ridiculous, because he barely knew her. "Just to be clear, is this Elizabeth tall with dark hair and dark blue eyes?"

The young man nodded. "That's her. Can I give her a message?"

"I don't suppose you could give me a phone number, could you?"

"Ah, no. We can't give out our employees' personal—"

"Yeah, no, I get it. That's okay." He had a last name now. Downey. If nothing else, Mitch could find a phone number and home address. For that matter, he could tell Sanchez, and she could track Liz down. But he'd much rather talk to Liz first.

"Thanks." As he exited the clinic, he was already redialing Mitch.

AFTERNOON WAS WANING as Hudson approached the front door of the posh apartment building in Houston's downtown historic district. Who knew there were 28 Elizabeth Downeys living in the Houston area? Mitch was able to eliminate most of them based on identifying factors like race and age, but there were four who had shielded their privacy enough that he couldn't rule them out. Mitch had offered to hack into Department of Public Safety records and peek at their driver's-license pictures, but Hudson couldn't condone Mitch breaking the law on his behalf.

He'd find her. In fact, he was almost positive he had. This building just *looked* like someplace Liz would live—a red-brick 1800s building right off Market Square. Secure—but not behind the walls of some sanitized gated community where no one knew their neighbors.

Now he just had the security desk to contend with.

"I'm here to see Elizabeth Downey," he told the official-looking man who watched all who came and went through the lobby. He didn't wear a uniform, just a nicely pressed suit, but Hudson had no doubt the man could stop anyone who tried to gain entrance to the elevators or stairs without his okay. At least he'd try.

"Your name?" the guard asked as he picked up the phone from the antique desk.

He considered lying, but Elizabeth would probably refuse entrance to someone she didn't know. "Hudson Vale." God, he hoped she was home.

The man spoke softly into the phone. Though Hudson was standing right next to the desk, he couldn't understand what was said. That was a talent. The guard cast a suspicious eye at Hudson, then concluded the conversation and hung up.

"Fifth floor. Apartment 524."

Relief flooded through Hudson's whole body. She was here. And she'd agreed to see him. It had taken him half a day, but he'd found her.

Belatedly, he wished he'd brought flowers. She was undoubtedly still angry with him for the accusations he'd thrown at her Saturday night. That had been stupid of him.

The elevator couldn't move fast enough to suit him. When he finally alighted on the fifth floor, he practically sprinted down the hall until he found her apartment number. Taking a deep breath to steady himself, he knocked. Decisively. Twice.

The woman who opened the door was hardly recognizable as the sultry vixen who'd taken his breath away Saturday night, seducing him so shamelessly. She stood before him in sweats and an old Bryn Mawr College T-shirt, her face pale and devoid of makeup, her hair pulled back untidily in an elastic band.

She was still achingly beautiful.

"Liz." Somehow, that was the only word that would come out of his mouth.

She turned, leaving the door open, and he followed her into her apartment. It was an expensive-looking space, open and airy. The walls were painted in soft pastels; the furnishings looked classy but not formal or pretentious. The only item that looked out of place was a huge bouquet of orchids

on the dining-room table, wilted and turning brown. Everything else was clean and well-maintained.

"I can explain," she finally said.

"There's no need." He felt a little off-balance. *She* was the
one apologizing? "I don't blame you for bailing out on me. I
said some awful thing, things I didn't mean. If I'd bothered
to use half a brain before I spouted off…"

She looked at him curiously, as if an apology wasn't what
she expected, either.

He closed the door. "I'm sorry for your loss."

Her expression changed rapidly from guilt to suspicion.
What had he done now?

"I stopped at your clinic first," he explained, figuring she
didn't appreciate his intrusion into her privacy. "Someone
there told me you'd had a death in your family."

"Dear God, you still don't know."

"Uh…guess I don't. Pretty clueless here. Liz, I don't
mean to intrude on your grief. But I'm in a difficult situation here, and you're the only one who can help me. Believe
me, I wouldn't have bothered you otherwise. I mean, I did
want to see you again. And I'm kind of glad I had an excuse
to track you down—"

"I can't help you. You have to leave." She strode toward
her front door, obviously expecting him to vacate.

"What? I haven't even told you what the problem is."

"I already know. You want me to vouch for your whereabouts on Saturday night."

"Well, yeah. How do you know about that?" Then he
slapped his own forehead. "Duh. It's probably been in the
news." He hadn't turned on a TV in days. "Look, I understand if you don't want to see me again, or if you don't want
the whole world to know you picked up some strange guy at
a wedding. But there's no need for anyone to know. Just talk
to a couple of detectives. Tell them you were with me, that I
couldn't possibly have killed Mandalay."

She paused at the door, her hand hovering over the knob. Finally she turned and looked at him with something approaching honest regret. "I would help you if I could. I'm not embarrassed. It's just that using me as an alibi won't do you much good. Because if there's one person in the world who had a better reason than you to kill Franklin Mandalay, it's me."

Oh, God. This did not sound good. "Maybe I better sit down."

"No, no, you have to leave." The urgency had returned to her voice. "We can't be seen together."

"We've already been seen together. Your security man downstairs knows I came to see you. The valet at the wedding saw us leave together. You think cops won't figure that out?"

Her face fell. She returned to the living room and more or less collapsed onto that comfy-looking sofa. Hudson sat in the chair opposite her.

"Maybe you better tell me everything," Hudson said. "Why would you want to kill Franklin Mandalay?"

"Because he's my father. And we're estranged. He is manipulative and controlling and a liar. And I'm his sole heir." With that, her eyes filled with tears. "Jesus, I have no idea why I keep crying. He was not a very nice man."

Mandalay was her father? Hudson's head was spinning like a gyroscope. "I knew there was something off about that night," he murmured. Then, louder, he said, "Tell me everything. All of it, Liz. If I get even a whiff of deception from you I'm going straight to the police."

CHAPTER FIVE

LIZ MASSAGED HER temples and looked as if she was collecting herself, rounding up her thoughts. "Our meeting *was* accidental," she began. "Well, sort of. I already told you I recognized you from the newspaper. I wanted to meet you. I actually admired you for standing up to my father, and I knew you hadn't done anything wrong."

"Hmm." Should he believe her now? He had no idea.

"When I saw you at the wedding, I planned to just talk to you. But then one thing led to another and I completely forgot why I'd wanted to meet you in the first place."

"Hmm," he said again.

"Hudson, I really liked you. But I knew if you found out who I was you'd be freaked out, and I just didn't see any happy ending if the truth came out. That's the real reason I left your house so fast. I saw my opportunity, and I dashed. I didn't want you to know anything more about me—I was afraid you'd try to find me."

"Guess your fears came true." He pondered the situation for a few seconds. "So, you called a cab?" Her cell phone would have a record of that call, he realized.

"Using your phone. My cell was out of juice."

Okay. That was probably good news. "And you went straight home?"

"Hudson, of course! Jesus, don't tell me you think I did it."

"The time-of-death window goes until 5:00 a.m. That's more than an hour after you left my place." At her stricken expression, he changed tacks. "No, Liz, I know you didn't do it. But the cops are going to ask you that. They're going to ask you a lot more. You better be prepared for it."

"The cops already talked to me."

Oh, hell, of course they had. She'd probably been notified first thing after the body was identified, then asked at least a few preliminary questions. "When?"

"Yesterday afternoon."

"What did you tell them?"

"That I went straight home from the wedding. I didn't talk to anyone or see anyone. I went home alone, and no one can corroborate my whereabouts."

Hudson jumped up and started to pace. "You lied to the police?"

"You think I should have told them I was with you? How would that look?"

"You should *never* lie to the police. They always find out, Liz."

"They don't have to find out. What did *you* tell them?"

"I said I was with you, of course. How the hell was I sup- posed to know you would be the other main suspect?" He thought some more. "There's only one thing to do. You have to go to the Montgomery County sheriff's office and tell them the truth. We'll go together."

"No! Hudson, no, we can't do that. It'll look so bad that I lied. For me *and* for you. Because if they think I did it, and they know we were together, you'll go down with me."

She had a point. Still... "I don't know how we can keep it secret. The cabdriver who took you home—"

"I didn't tell the police anything about a cab."

"Yeah, but I did."

She squeezed her eyes shut, then opened them again. "We'll deal with that if we have to."

"They'll ask people at the wedding. The valet, for instance. He saw us leave together."

"I can't tell them I lied, Hudson. I won't."

Great. If he tried to claim she was his alibi, and she denied his story, he would look even worse. The valet might not recall seeing them together; the place had been a zoo. If he could find which cab company she'd called...

"Hudson, there must be something else we can do."

"We could fly to the Bahamas, but they probably already have our passports flagged."

"Really?"

"Liz, focus. We aren't going to flee the country. Let's think this through. You didn't kill your father. And I didn't kill him. Ergo—"

"Someone else did. We just have to find that person!"

Easier said than done. He prided himself on being a good, thorough detective. But without his badge—without the authority of the Montgomery County sheriff behind him—his efforts would be severely hampered.

"Any ideas who could have done it?"

"One of his desperate clients. Or someone he swindled." She shrugged. "He wasn't a part of my life anymore. I have no idea what was happening in his world."

Hudson had a hard time understanding that. His parents were his rocks, and he loved them both fiercely and saw them on a regular basis. "How long have you been estranged from him?"

"Since I was eighteen. I got an academic scholarship to Bryn Mawr. He refused to let me go, insisted I go to Rice University and live at home."

He glanced at her sweatshirt. "Guess Daddy didn't get his way that time, huh?"

"No. He took my car away. I went anyway."

"You haven't seen him since then? That's, what, ten years?"

"Oh, I've seen him. He pops up periodically—here or at work, or we sometimes attend the same functions." Her gaze darted to the dying orchids, then back. "But no matter how hard he tries...tried...he can't engage me. I ignore him. And he goes away."

"So the estrangement was one-way."

"If you mean I wanted it and he didn't, yes, that's exactly right."

Only one more question came to mind at the moment. "Why? It was a long time ago, and it sounds like maybe he just didn't want his daughter to be so far from home."

"It wasn't just that. I had my reasons."

"That answer isn't going to wash with the cops when they question you again." And something told Hudson they would. Though he hadn't seen it the first time they'd met, Liz fairly reeked with deception. Maybe he simply hadn't wanted to see it last Saturday.

"I'll tell the cops if they ask. But you're not the cops."

He wasn't...but he was. They could take his badge and gun away, but inside he was still a cop. He always would be. It drove him nuts that he didn't have his usual resources at hand. He couldn't simply call up DMV records or look up someone's criminal history.

"Hudson...what about the burglar?"

"Yeah. Kinda suspicious—a guy with a gun in close proximity to where the body was found."

"Was my father killed with...? Was he shot?" She realized she'd never asked how he'd died, and she'd deliberately not watched the news or read a newspaper. "They told me he was found in the lake, and I guess I just assumed he'd drowned."

Hudson nodded. "He was shot."

"So the creep that broke into your house was connected to my father?"

"I think he was there to kill me," Hudson said flatly. "I think if you hadn't been there, that's what would have happened."

"My father wouldn't have had you killed," she said reasonably. "I'm sure he was angry over being arrested, but I can't see him going that far."

"I can." Hudson still shivered when he remembered Mandalay's cold eyes. "Something was going on in that parking lot. Something other than a simple business transaction. Whatever it was, maybe he wanted it to stay hidden—at any cost."

"Okay, so let's assume the burglar was there to kill you. He fails. Reports back to my father. They get into an argument. Gun comes out…" She swallowed convulsively.

"It's okay to grieve, Liz. Whatever happened that caused the feud between you…I'm guessing you have some fond memories, as well."

She nodded. "He used to be the center of my universe."

Hudson had to admit, he was consumed with curiosity about what all had happened. But she wasn't ready to tell him yet. She would be. Someday.

"Okay, I'll make a deal with you. Knightly and Sanchez think my alibi lady doesn't exist. I'll continue to tell them I can't find you."

"Oh, thank you, Hudson—"

"Wait, wait, I'm not done. They only gave me a couple of days to produce you as my alibi. I doubt they have enough to arrest me. But if they do…then I'll have to come clean." He hated lying to cops—to his own partner especially. But he had to agree with Liz on this one. Once they knew the two prime suspects had been together Saturday night, he and Liz would probably find themselves in jail and unable to conduct any kind of investigation of their own.

"Okay… And during this grace period?"

"I'll find the real killer. There's simply no other choice."

"I'll help."

"We're dealing with a ruthless person or persons here. I can't put you in danger."

"I'm already in danger. What if I get convicted of murder? Sentenced to death? Anyway, I've got something you might need."

"Really. What might that be?"

"Money. Lots of it. Getting information out of people can cost. Speaking of which…how did you find me? Money also buys privacy. Jillian was pretty much the only person at that wedding who knew me. And even if you managed to get hold of her in Patagonia, she would never tell. She knows better."

"I called in a favor at Project Justice. And I did some leg-work," he added, unwilling to give Mitch all the credit.

"Project Justice. So maybe we should get them to help us find the real killer. That's what those people do, right? Help people who have been unjustly accused?"

"Usually they help people unjustly convicted and imprisoned. We haven't even been arrested."

"So, they'll get a jump start on our case. Anyway, I have an ace up my sleeve. I serve on the board of directors of the Logan Charitable Trust."

"You're friends with Daniel Logan? The billionaire?"

"You were at his house. You don't know him?"

"Not well enough to just call him up and ask him for a favor like that."

"Leave it to me. I'll let you know once I've set up a meeting. Meanwhile, you better go. The less we're seen together, the better. It's only a matter of time before some enterprising reporter puts it together."

"Damn." He shook his head. "I've never been the subject of media scrutiny before. I don't like it. Not at all."

"You get used to it."

"So I take it you've dealt with this kind of thing before?"

"When I was fourteen, my mother disappeared. Poof." Liz spread her fingers wide, outlining an imaginary cloud of dust. He couldn't help noticing that her immaculate man-icure from Saturday had deteriorated; she'd been chewing on her nail polish.

"Given who my father was," she continued, "the media went crazy over the story. Reporters camped out in the street in front of our house for literally months. I didn't leave the house, not even to go to school. My father hired a tutor. I became a prisoner in my own home."

"That sounds brutal. Did you find out what happened to her?"

"There was some evidence she had a lover. The police decided she must have run off with him, but I never bought it. She wouldn't have left me without a word. Dad, yeah, she'd have left him. They hadn't been happy together for a long time. But not me. We were tight." Liz paused, reflecting. "I know she's dead. Realistically, that's the only possible answer. Beyond that, I don't know, and I'm not sure I want to know. That way, I can fantasize that it was quick and painless, you know?"

Hudson didn't really understand that attitude. If something happened to one of his parents, or his little brother, he'd want to know, no matter how unpleasant it was for him.

"Reporters still call me about it, wanting to revisit the case, since it was never solved."

"Have you tried to find her? Recently, that is? In Montgomery County, we have a cold-case squad. There are new techniques, or maybe just looking at an old case with fresh eyes…"

"Anytime anyone tried to look into it, my father stonewalled them. He said he didn't want to open old wounds. No investigation ever got very far."

"Was he ever considered a suspect? Your dad?"

"Briefly. But he was out of the country when it happened. That theory never got much traction."

"It's easy enough to create an ironclad alibi if you hire a hit man…." Then Hudson remembered himself. "I'm sorry. I shouldn't vent my sordid theories in front of you."

"Let's not get distracted. One parent's homicide at a time, okay?"

"Sorry." He pulled a card from his wallet and handed it to her. "That's got my cell number. Let me know... No, don't call me directly. When you set up something with Project Justice, have someone there contact me. The less direct contact between us, the better."

ELIZABETH HAD TO admit, the Project Justice office was impressive. Not the outside, so much. The historic, three-story brick building in old downtown Houston, not far from her apartment, was distinguished, but nothing dramatic stood out. In fact, only a very small plaque in the wall advertised that the foundation was housed here.

Inside, however, it was a different story. The brass double doors opened into a soaring lobby with walnut-paneled walls and a gray marble floor, polished to a high sheen. You could have fit a bowling alley in that lobby, but it was empty, except for two rather uncomfortable-looking straight-back chairs against one wall. In the center of the room, toward the back, was an enormous circular desk behind which an extremely formidable woman sat surveying her territory like a hungry vulture.

Elizabeth approached the woman confidently, her heels clicking loudly against the floor and echoing off the walls. The woman's nameplate identified her as Celeste Boggs.

"Good morning, Ms. Boggs," Elizabeth began. "I'm here for a meeting with—"

"I know who you are. Sign in. I'll need to see some ID, make sure you aren't an impostor."

Elizabeth obliged and Celeste handed over a visitor badge.

After Celeste summoned someone on the phone, a young woman who must have been an intern appeared from behind a frosted-glass partition.

"Ms. Downey? I'm Jax. I'll take you to the meeting room."

Elizabeth struggled with where to clip the visitor badge on her collarless shirt. She finally settled on her belt.

She followed the young woman down a series of hallways, all of them decorated with the care any River Oaks maven would use to decorate her house. Designer paint colors adorned the walls, while subtle lighting illuminated various pieces of original art. This place was almost as impressive as Daniel's house. She'd grown up with all the trappings of wealth, and she was still impressed.

If anyone could help Elizabeth and Hudson, it was Daniel Logan. Aside from the fact he was a billionaire, he was one of the most influential people in the whole state of Texas. He was a personal friend of the governor, and it was rumored he was on a first-name basis with the president.

Jax finally paused before a room labeled Conference and tapped softly, waiting until someone opened the door. She then stood aside and allowed Elizabeth to enter.

Elizabeth's eyes immediately sought out Hudson. He was there, looking delicious as ever, and her heart jumped and briefly tripled its rate. Each time she saw him, her regret for the most unfortunate circumstances of their first meeting grew sharper.

"Good morning, Elizabeth," Daniel's voice boomed. At first glance, she thought he was seated at the head of the conference table—until she realized his head and shoulders were being transmitted on a giant TV screen. She had heard that Daniel once suffered from an acute case of agoraphobia, making it nearly impossible for him to leave his house. Although he was much improved, he still did the majority of his business—whether it was running his oil company, his charitable trust or Project Justice—from the comfort of his home office.

"Good morning, Mr. Logan." She felt a little silly talking to the computer screen, but there was a small camera mounted just above the screen, so she supposed from his viewpoint it was as if she were really looking at him.

"Please, sit down. I think you're the last to arrive, so we can get started."

She glanced at her watch as she seated herself, worried that it was later than she'd thought. She prided herself on being punctual.

"You're not late," Hudson said. "The rest of us were just early."

Discussing her before she had arrived? Or was that paranoid?

The closest empty chair was beside Hudson, so she took it, though sitting next to him unsettled her nerves.

Daniel introduced her to the others in the room. Some of them she'd met briefly at the wedding, but fresh introductions helped her put the names and faces into their professional context. Joe Kinkaid, one of the lead investigators at the foundation, was a thirtyish, clean-cut guy with a boyish charm. But his demeanor suggested ex-military. His posture, maybe, or the bulky, complicated dive watch on his left wrist.

Mitch Delacroix, a slightly scruffy, laid-back man, greeted her with a good-old-boy "pleased to meet ya," revealing the traces of a Cajun accent. The only other woman in the room, a tall, glamorous brunette dressed to the nines in a turquoise suit, was Raleigh Shinn, the foundation's chief legal counsel.

The show of force encouraged Elizabeth; if Daniel was going to reject their request for help, he was pulling out some pretty big guns to do it.

"I'll just get right into it, if that's okay," Daniel began. He was a man of few words, but what he said was always important. "A lot of people need our services. I wish we could help them all, but though the foundation is growing all the time, we simply don't have the resources to take on every case."

"But—" Hudson started to object. He stopped himself

when he saw the quelling look on Daniel's face. Raleigh, too, gave him a stern look of reproach. He sank lower in his chair.

"That's why we have a protocol in place, so that the most urgent and deserving cases get our attention first."

Oh, dear. This didn't sound promising.

"That said, Hudson, you've been a friend to Project Justice on a number of occasions. You were a tremendous help with the Mary-Frances Torres case, and if not for you, our Jillian might have frozen to death in a deep freezer."

Elizabeth turned to look at Hudson with a fresh appraisal. She'd heard about the attempt on Jillian's life because the media had picked up the story. It was the type of situation that begged for headlines: beautiful young investigator working undercover gets locked in a deep freezer at her company picnic by the murdering CFO. She hadn't realized Hudson had taken any part in her rescue.

Hudson nodded acknowledgment but refrained from speaking, and who could blame him?

"I can't take resources away from cases we've already committed to working," Daniel continued, "and our investigators here are always stretched to the max. But I want to help. Just from the little I've learned so far about your situation, it seems highly unlikely either of you committed murder. But it also appears you've unwittingly put yourself in an extremely vulnerable situation."

To put it mildly.

"So here's what I propose. Hudson, you're a highly trained and decorated homicide detective. But since you're currently suspended, you don't have access to the tools you need to properly investigate."

"Exactly," Hudson agreed, unable to stop himself. "I've never been so frustrated."

"Well, we've got the most powerful computers money can buy and the most skilled...data analyst you'll ever find."

At the mention of his specialized abilities, Mitch nodded.

"We've got any kind of surveillance equipment you might need, including spare vehicles that can't be traced to us through any police department. We have experts on call—voice analysts, handwriting and ballistics experts. We have a top-of-the-line crime lab right on premises for DNA, fingerprint ID—"

"Wait a minute," Hudson said. "You need access to the national database for that. Only police departments—"

Elizabeth kicked him under the table.

"Ow. What was that for?"

So much for her attempt at subtlety. "It was to remind you that law enforcement isn't our friend right now. And if Project Justice has a way to ID fingerprints without involving the police, just accept it and move on."

Reluctantly Hudson nodded while everyone else in the room, Daniel included, tried not to laugh.

"We'll give you a desk, a phone, interns for grunt work. And for anything you need more help with, I'm assigning Mr. Kinkaid here to assist. Officially, he'll be overseeing your case, though for the most part you'll be given autonomy to investigate however you see fit. I figure you're your own strongest advocate."

"That's incredibly generous of you, Mr. Logan," Hudson said.

"Thank you so much, Mr. Logan," Elizabeth said at the same time. She couldn't adequately express the relief she felt just knowing the powerful Project Justice was on her side.

"Please, call me Daniel. We're not formal around here. Except for Raleigh." He gave his attorney a teasing smile.

"I have to appear in court later," she said.

"Now, I just have a couple of details I'd like to clear up before I turn my attention to other matters. And Hudson, Elizabeth, if this is embarrassing, I apologize, but I have my reasons for asking. How many people, outside this room, know that the two of you spent most of Saturday night together?"

"I told the detectives working on the Mandalay murder that I spent the night with a woman named Liz," Hudson said. "I never gave them a last name since I didn't know it at the time, and they're under the impression I made it up. Other than that, I've told no one."

"Elizabeth, how about you?"

"I haven't told anyone. But the valet at Jillian and Conner's wedding saw us leave together."

"Which one?" Daniel asked, keenly interested.

"Young, male, frizzy brown hair, big black glasses," Hudson answered without hesitation.

"That would be Dennis." Daniel scratched his chin and thought for a moment. "I believe he's due for a vacation. The Bahamas are nice this time of year."

Elizabeth nearly fell out of her chair. Daniel would just send someone on a Bahamian vacation to prevent him from being a witness?

"The doorman at my building let Hudson in, took his name and called up to me, so he can place us together."

"What's his name?" Daniel asked.

"Oscar Palacios. He has a memory like an elephant. Remembers every detail of what happens in that building."

"I'm guessing he probably needs a vacation, too. A nice, long one."

Elizabeth tried not to let her alarm show. "Um, you mean a real vacation, right? Not a nice long sleep with the fishes?"

Everybody laughed at her. "We skirt the law on occasion," Joe Kinkaid said. "If someone's life or liberty is at risk, we do what's necessary. Within reason, though."

"I didn't really think you would," she murmured, feeling foolish now. She apparently didn't understand the culture of these people. Hudson included. He seemed to fit in here, while she was the outsider, even though it was partly her influence that got them this meeting in the first place.

"I won't get into the nitty-gritty details of the investigation," Daniel said. "I'll leave that to you, Joe. I just have a couple of rules. The first is that Elizabeth not do any fieldwork on her own. She's not trained as an investigator, and I won't have her exposed to any danger."

"But I want to help!" Elizabeth objected. "I pretty much caused this mess. I should help with fixing it."

"You can help," Hudson said. "We'll work together, all of us. There are plenty of things you're probably good at—phone calls, combing through records, surveillance…"

"Whatever you need," she said with genuine enthusiasm. "Really. You need me to make a food run, I'll do that."

Joe grinned. "Maybe a shoulder rub when things get tense— Ow!"

Raleigh scowled. "Knock it off, Kinkaid."

"No offense taken," Elizabeth said. She wasn't part of this club, but that didn't mean she wanted to be treated like a delicate china doll.

Hudson seemed to think she needed protecting. He stared daggers at Kinkaid until the other man's grin faded. "Just trying to lighten things up," Kinkaid murmured.

"One more thing," Daniel said. "No one says anything to the press, under any circumstances. The less publicity this case receives, the better, because a media circus is not conducive to any investigation. Hudson, Elizabeth, you two need to avoid being seen together in public. Anytime you're out, be aware of who might be watching you or following you. In fact, if either of you ever wants a driver to come pick you up, just to make sure you're not followed, say the word. I don't have to tell you how relentless, and pitiless, the media can be. The Mandalay murder is huge news. It's been picked up by the national press, as well. Even a small amount of snooping will dig up you two as possible suspects, so brace yourselves."

"What should we say if we get a microphone stuck in our faces?" Hudson asked.

"You say, 'No comment,'" Daniel replied. "They'll try to provoke you. They'll push your buttons. You show no emotion. You say nothing except those two words. Don't give them anything they can use as a sound bite. And don't talk to the police without an attorney present.... That goes for both of you."

"Got it," Elizabeth said.

Hudson nodded his understanding.

Elizabeth couldn't deny the disappointment she felt that Daniel forbade her to take an active role in the field. In the back of her mind she'd pictured herself investigating closely with Hudson, riding around with him to interview witnesses, long nights with heads bent close, studying evidence. She probably had a highly romanticized image of how crimes got solved. Hudson had said she would still be included, but the more likely scenario was that she would be out of the loop, left at home wondering what was going on.

Daniel issued a few more cautionary remarks, then left things in Joe Kinkaid's purportedly capable hands. He seemed awfully young to be in charge. Then again, Hudson would run the actual investigation.

Mitch gave Hudson and Elizabeth cell phones. They were strange-looking, silver devices with no brand name visible. "Use these phones when communicating with each other and anyone at Project Justice," he instructed. "They're specially encrypted. No one can trace calls made with these or locate you through the phone's ping. They're already preprogrammed with everyone's number you might need."

"Holy cow." Hudson examined his new phone with a mixture of awe and disapproval.

Suddenly Elizabeth remembered something. "One other person saw us together, Hudson. The burglar."

"The burglar?" Kinkaid raised one quizzical eyebrow.

Hudson recounted the incident with the tattooed house-breaker.

"You didn't think that was important?" Kinkaid asked. "Some guy trying to kill you the night of the murder?"

"Agreed—we need to find him," Hudson said a little testily. "He had a gun, and he was in the area."

"So if he figures out who I am," Elizabeth said, thinking aloud, "we're toast. One anonymous call to the cops…"

"We gotta find him before that happens," Hudson concluded. Then he laughed. "Maybe Daniel could send him on vacation, too."

"The guy tried to kill you. He belongs in prison, not on vacation." She shivered, thinking about that moment. Hudson had dodged a bullet…literally. She'd been so scared she'd almost collapsed, her legs had trembled so hard. He'd downplayed the danger, but for the difference of a few inches Hudson wouldn't be sitting here today.

"So let's find this dude," Kinkaid said. "Can I get a description?"

"He's got a big fish on his arm," Hudson answered. "How hard could he be to identify?"

CHAPTER SIX

RALEIGH HAD SOME papers for them to sign. It was standard cover-your-butt stuff, promising that Hudson and Elizabeth wouldn't sue Project Justice if things didn't go as planned and absolving the foundation from any responsibility. There was also a confidentiality agreement. Raleigh explained that some of the foundation's methods were unorthodox, others involved proprietary information—confidential informants, things like that—and their clients had to promise not to divulge anything about how the operation worked to any third party. Hudson scribbled his signature without hesitation. Elizabeth read the documents through carefully first, but she also signed.

Raleigh took the contracts and left.

"What else do you have to go on?" Kinkaid asked. "I assume you'll start with the victim and move out."

"There's a prostitute," Hudson reminded everyone. "Her street name is Jazz, but I don't have a last name. I arrested her maybe eighteen months ago in a sweep, but I cut her loose before she was booked. We were after the johns, not the prozzies. If she's in the system at all, it's not under that name. She might not be a direct witness to the murder, but Mandalay had some business with her. They were arguing, and he was pushing some cash on her—more than a normal amount a street ho would earn."

"Don't call her that," Elizabeth said sharply.

Hudson, Kinkaid and Mitch all looked at her funny.

"Would you prefer 'lady of the evening'?" Hudson asked. "'Fallen lamb'?"

"*Prozzie, ho*—they're derogatory terms implying judgment. Most of the prostitutes out there aren't there by choice. They're victims of poverty and abuse and exploitation. They're often dragged into that life as children. Then they get hooked on drugs, or they have a pimp who takes over their lives and they can't get away—"

"Elizabeth," Hudson said. "They're breaking the law. And they do have choices. This is America, not some third-world country. If they're on drugs they can get rehab. And if their pimps are holding them prisoner, they can flag down any police cruiser and get help."

"You are so completely clueless." She shook her head.

"How do you know so much about prostitutes?"

"I talk to them every day at work. They come in because they've got an STD, or because they're sick and their pimps won't pay for a doctor. Do you have any idea how hard it is for a girl in that life to even talk honestly to a doctor or therapist? They're scared to death. Their pimps keep them scared of what will happen if they try to leave. And with no other authority figure to turn to—"

Hudson held up a hand to halt her tirade. And it was a tirade, she realized. He'd hit one of her hot buttons.

"If I agree to stop using the word *ho,* can we move on?"

"Sorry." She could worry about saving the world some other day. Today she needed to worry about saving herself.

"Whatever was going on in that parking lot," Hudson said, "Mandalay was pretty keen that the police stay out of it. The accusations against me might have been more than an attempt to get out of being arrested."

"Maybe I can find this girl," Elizabeth said. "I can ask around, talk to some of my clients—"

"Daniel said to stay out of the field," he reminded her.

"He can't stop me from chatting with my own clients at

my own place of business. I do it all the time. Speaking of which—" she glanced at her watch "—I should get to work soon." Though she would have liked to take a few more days off, the Los Amigos Clinic really needed her, and she'd promised to return that afternoon. "I can take time off if you think I can be helpful, but if you're going to just pat me on the head and reassure me that the big boys are taking care of things and I shouldn't worry my pretty little head, I'll leave it to you. I have clients who need me."

"Actually, there's something you can help with. Do you have access to your father's house?"

"Yes." She'd spent last night at the house, in fact, beginning the process of tying up the loose ends of a life ended suddenly. She had reassured the staff that they still had jobs, for the moment. Her father had insisted she be a cosigner and beneficiary on his bank accounts so that she could take care of things if anything happened to him. Despite the fact Franklin Mandalay was gone, there were still bills to pay and decisions to be made involving the running of a large estate.

"Can you take me there?" Hudson asked. "I'd like to look around."

"Sure. Meet me there this evening, around seven, if that's convenient. The housekeeper, Mrs. Ames, is off tonight, so no one will see you there. But I don't know what you think you'll find. The police were already there. They tore the place up pretty good looking for evidence." Elizabeth had been shocked at the mess the cops had left. They'd gone through her father's home office like a horde of barbarians. They took the computer and had removed the contents of every drawer. They'd sprayed chemicals all over the place, hoping to find blood evidence, she guessed. When they were done, they'd carted off boxes and bags of supposed evidence, and they hadn't even issued an apology.

This was the victim's home. She couldn't imagine how

much worse it would be if they decided to tear up the home of a suspect—*her* home.

"You never know what they might have missed," Hudson said. "Anyway, they were looking for evidence to implicate me. Or you. I'll be looking for evidence that points to someone else."

"Do cops really do that? Come up with a theory early on, then only search for evidence that supports that theory?"

"We're not supposed to. We're supposed to keep an open mind. But it's human nature to look for answers that support what you already believe. If you have a strong suspect, you look for evidence relating to him. You tend to attach more significance to the clues you like and less to the ones that don't fit. The Project Justice files are filled with cases of people arrested and convicted despite evidence that strongly suggests their innocence—evidence that wasn't discovered because no one was looking for it, or was discovered but overlooked and dismissed, or out-and-out covered up because the cops were positive they had the right guy."

At least he had the good grace to appear disturbed by such frequent miscarriages of justice.

"I like to think I'm not like that," he said. "But, like I said, human nature is human nature. Mistakes get made."

"Which keeps this foundation in business," Kinkaid added. Elizabeth had almost forgotten he was in the room. The air was so thick with tension between her and Hudson that she'd telescoped out everything else. With Kinkaid's words, the tension broke. Elizabeth breathed a small sigh of relief. She needed to put some distance between herself and Hudson, so she stood, clutching her shoulder bag in front of her like a shield. "I'll see you tonight. Let me know if I can help in any way. And if there's more news—good or bad—let me know that, too."

"See you tonight, then." Hudson's promise sounded almost

like a threat—as if he wanted to deal with the unfinished business between them that he couldn't address with witnesses.

HUDSON DID HIS best to shake off the residual effects of Liz's proximity as he followed Mitch and Kinkaid down a long hallway and through a door that opened up to a large room. A dozen desks were situated here and there, some in cubicles, some out in the open. It reminded Hudson of the bull pen at the station where he worked, which shouldn't be surprising. A lot of the investigators at Project Justice were former cops; a setup like this probably made them feel right at home.

These people weren't cops, though. They were a private police force with the resources his department would have if treated to an unlimited budget. He got the idea that anything these people wanted, within reason, could be had. Frankly, he was a bit jealous. And not quite sure how he felt about so much money and talent used to free the people his department, and others like it, worked so hard to put in prison in the first place.

Not that Hudson thought anyone should be jailed for a crime they didn't commit. God knew if he hadn't felt strongly about that before, he sure did now. Clearly, police made mistakes.

But what if Project Justice was wrong? What if they freed someone who really belonged behind bars? He recalled a well-publicized case from several years ago where the foundation proved a man—a hardened repeat offender—was innocent of murder. A week after that man was freed from prison, he had assaulted and nearly killed an old woman. Daniel Logan, as well as the original investigator on the case, had quickly issued public statements of regret, but Daniel had still maintained that just because someone *might* commit a crime was no reason to imprison them for something they didn't do.

Hudson didn't see it that way. That scumbag should have been behind bars.

"The first thing we should focus on is the armed house-breaker with the tattoo," Kinkaid said. "Mitch has access to a tattoo database."

"Really?" Hudson's own department had a tattoo database. These days, when someone was arrested, they took his fingerprints and mug shot as well as photos of any identifying tattoos. The tattoos were good and bad news; they could be used to identify someone, but they also could be altered or removed. You got a witness on the stand swearing up and down the person who shot him had a tattoo of a swastika on his arm, and lo and behold the suspect now had some kind of flower where the swastika once was. "Is this the foundation's private database?" he asked.

Mitch didn't reply, which meant he'd probably hacked into police computers. No wonder Daniel was insistent on the confidentiality agreement. With a well-placed phone call, Hudson could shut this place down, and a lot of district attorneys would be thrilled.

"Where was this tattoo located?" Mitch asked.

Hudson pictured the scene in his mind. "Right forearm."

"And it was a fish, you said?"

"It was dark, and I couldn't see it real clear. But Liz and I both thought it looked like a fish."

Mitch typed for a bit, narrowing down the possibilities. In the end, he had four candidates for Hudson to inspect. He was able to eliminate the first three without blinking.

When Mitch clicked on the link for the fourth one, nothing happened at first.

"What the hell?" He took off his glasses and peered more closely at the screen, as if he had missed something. Then an error message came up.

RECORD DOES NOT EXIST

"Huh. That's weird."

"What?"

"The record doesn't exist? If it doesn't exist, why is there a link to it?"

"Well…" Hudson thought about it. "Maybe it was just a blip. Things vanish on my computer all the time. Usually I just pushed a wrong button."

"I don't push wrong buttons." Mitch said this not with any sense of vanity, but as if simply stating an irrefutable truth. "No, it's just gone."

"Well, sometimes we remove something from the database if it's bad information or if a guy's status changes. Like, he dies or something."

"Then wouldn't the record reflect that? No." Mitch shook his head. "This smells fishy, pardon the pun. This is the shadow of a hacker. A bad hacker. And believe me, I know what bad hacking looks like."

"So someone suspected we'd come looking for fish man and made sure we wouldn't find him?"

"Yeah, but he failed to erase all the links back to the photo."

"How many people have the skills to hack into the police computer?"

"Not many. Unless they have an in."

"You mean they know someone who works there and borrow or steal their password?"

"Exactly."

Hudson didn't like the implications—that someone in law enforcement was involved in this mess.

"Hell, it sucks to get that close to the guy, then not even learn his name."

"I'll keep looking." Mitch resumed tapping on the keyboard, his fingers flying so fast, they were a blur.

"I'll talk to some of my contacts on the street, see if they've heard of the guy."

"You might talk to Billy Cantu at the Houston P.D. Guy's got an awesome number of contacts. And be careful out there.

If someone really is anticipating your moves, they might predict that you'd talk to your snitches. They could plant fake info, set a trap, intimidate the snitches or pay them more than your going rate to mislead you. All kinds of things."

"Yeah, good point. I'll be careful." Hudson held out his hand. "Thanks, man. You have no idea how much I appreciate having somebody in my corner. I never thought about what it feels like to be a suspect."

"Been there, done that. It's about the worst feeling in the world."

"That's right. You were accused of killing some guy, like, back in the '90s?"

Mitch nodded. "I was sick to my stomach the whole time. You know you didn't do it, but you don't have proof."

Hudson nodded. The only other person he knew who might understand what he was feeling was Liz. But so far they'd failed to reestablish the rapport they'd enjoyed Saturday night. He still didn't like that she'd deceived him about her true identity. The whole evening had been based on falsehood. She'd been *curious* about him, she'd said.

Her idle curiosity had landed them in a lot of trouble.

"If you want someone to go with you—you know, watch your back—I don't have anything else hanging. I've never been a cop or anything…"

Hudson laughed. "No, you're just a mixed-martial-arts champion. Weren't you on the Olympic team or something?"

"No. No. Well, maybe. The judo team is looking at me, but the next Olympics is a long time from now."

"I'd be pleased to have you watch my back."

"Let's go, then." Mitch packed up his laptop in about five seconds flat. "I'll take my work with me, in case we have some downtime. Or in case you need some quick research."

ELIZABETH HADN'T FUSSED so much since the first time she had a boy over when she was thirteen. What was his name? Oh, yeah, Hank. Hank Balducci. She'd made sure the house was immaculate, she'd worn her cutest new summer shorts outfit, brushed her hair out long and loose rather than plaiting it into its usual braid, and she'd laid out a selection of videos for them to watch, movies she thought Hank might like, with sports themes or car chases. She'd even asked Mrs. Ames to help her bake brownies.

She'd imagined she might get her first kiss that night. But her father had imagined something completely different. From the moment Hank arrived, her father had watched them like a tiger watching a couple of young zebras playing together. He'd glowered at Hank until the poor boy could barely string two words together coherently.

There'd been no movies, no brownies. After thirty minutes he'd mumbled some excuse about his mother needing him at home and he'd sprinted for the door.

Elizabeth had been furious with her father, but he had soothed her by explaining that he'd only been trying to protect her, that she was at a vulnerable age and boys would always be trying to take more than she wanted to give and that this boy, in particular, was not good enough for her.

"His father works at the DPS," her father had spat out, as if a civil-service job were on a par with being an ax murderer. "His mother works, too. Retail." Again, as if that was a bad thing. "I send you to school with the kids of the most prominent families in Houston, and you make friends with the scholarship student? Someday, Elizabeth, you'll marry a senator's son. You can't go wasting yourself on the Hank Balduccis of the world."

He'd offered to take her out for ice cream, but she was still mad, and she stayed mad for weeks. Her anger hadn't brought Hank back, and it hadn't stopped her father from interfering again, although the next time, he'd done it on the sly.

Although circumstances were nothing like when she was thirteen, and Hudson was coming over not for any social reason, she felt that same silly sense of giddiness. When she arrived at her father's home after work, she'd finished cleaning up the mess left by the cops. Mrs. Ames had been working on it, too, returning items to the drawers where they belonged, replacing cushions onto the furniture. But she'd left early today—and who could blame her? Elizabeth swept, vacuumed and dusted.

When the house was immaculate, she changed out of her stale work clothes into a cool sundress and sandals, telling herself she wasn't primping, merely getting comfortable. But then, why had she spent so long in front of the mirror, giving her hair that casual "I just quickly pinned it up" look that took twenty minutes, thirty pins and a curling iron to produce?

God, what was she thinking? Hudson Vale might be a tasty morsel, but that train had left the station. She'd seen the way he'd looked at her when she'd admitted lying to the police, and it wasn't the way a man looked at his lover.

From the start, she'd shown him her worst side. First, she'd acted like a trashy, easy pickup who'd dumped her own date and who couldn't even bother to exchange last names before jumping into bed. Then she'd run away without saying goodbye, and on top of everything else, she'd been lying to him the whole night. Her explanation had sounded lame even to her—as if she'd viewed Hudson as an interesting case study, a fascinating specimen. Her attraction to him was real, but would he ever believe that?

One strand of her hair kept falling in her face—not in a good way—and she finally gave up on it. This was ridiculous.

She'd instructed Hudson to enter the estate from the rear alley entrance, because a couple of news vans were parked outside the front gate.

At precisely seven her cell phone rang; she'd programmed the back gate buzzer to signal her phone. She pushed the appropriate code, then walked downstairs, through the living room, kitchen and out to the garage to greet her guest.

Her intention was to be friendly but professional. No sense him knowing how much she regretted her recent actions. How much she wished they'd met under different circumstances. No sense looking more pathetic than she already did.

Hudson's now-familiar 280Z swung into view along the back driveway, then whipped into an empty slot in the four-car garage. Her own car and her father's Range Rover occupied two more slots. His Cadillac Escalade, which had been found not far from where his body was discovered, was still being processed by the police.

She'd have to dispose of his two vehicles somehow. Who would want to buy a murder victim's car? She supposed there were car liquidators who could find a buyer.

Hudson climbed out from behind the wheel and she waved a greeting. That was when she realized he wasn't alone; Mitch was riding shotgun.

Good, that was good. She'd been dreading the inevitable awkward alone moments between herself and Hudson. With Mitch as an unwitting chaperone, she could relax a bit.

"I brought Mitch in case there's any computer stuff," Hudson explained as Elizabeth led them into the house.

"Oh, dear, I might have saved you a trip, Mitch," she said. "The CSI guys took Dad's computer."

"He only had one?" Mitch asked.

Elizabeth shrugged. "How many does one person need?"

"At least two, if he's involved in criminal activities," Hudson replied. "It's like having two sets of books. One is the official record, kept squeaky clean. The other houses the real details, and it's kept somewhere safe. Most likely with instructions given to a close confidant that it be destroyed if anything happens."

"I'm not sure my father had any close confidants." Elizabeth led them back through the kitchens, retracing her steps through the dining and living rooms to the other wing of the house, where her father's office was located. "He didn't trust anyone. Well, maybe the housekeeper. But I can't see Mrs. Ames destroying evidence. She's painfully honest."

When they arrived at the office, Hudson whistled low. "They really did a number on this place."

"How can you tell?" she asked. "I thought I'd straightened up pretty well."

"I can smell the fingerprint powder. Obviously used with abandon." He ran his index finger along the edge of an open drawer, pulling back a smudge of black powder. "Okay if I look around?"

"That's what you're here for."

Hudson examined the contents of a few drawers, opened the credenza. He turned the office chair upside down, peered under the desk and peeked under the mouse pad. He methodically searched every corner of the room, even going so far as to examine the undersides of the potted plants' leaves and inside the globes on the chandelier.

He paused in front of a small, freestanding safe next to a file cabinet where her father had kept important papers. He'd given her the combination years ago.

"I opened it for the cops," she said. "They took everything, but I think it was just stuff like his passport and birth certificate, maybe some papers related to my mom's disappearance. I know he always kept that stuff where I couldn't see it."

Hudson frowned at the safe. "Is this it? The only safe?"

"Again, how many safes does one man need...? Oh, I get it. One to keep the innocent documents, another to store the stolen jewels and securities."

"Your father stole jewelry and securities?" Hudson obviously still hadn't figured out her sense of humor, which could erupt at odd moments, usually when she was nervous.

"That was just a figurative example, but I personally wouldn't be too surprised. He had very little respect for the law. He cheated on his taxes, fixed speeding tickets for his buddies, frequented prostitutes—"

"He what?" Hudson almost exploded.

"He hired call girls. They used to come to the house all the time. He thought I wouldn't figure it out—claimed they were regular dates, you know—but it was kind of obvious."

"That would have been some valuable knowledge to have," he said. "When he was questioned after his arrest, he claimed he would never pay for sex."

"Ha! If I'd known that was his defense, I would have come forward."

"Really? You'd have sold your old man up the river?"

She paused a fraction of a second before answering. "No, maybe I wouldn't have. I talk a good game, but in the end, despite his character flaws, I didn't hate him."

"But you really didn't get along with him."

Mitch had wandered into another room, so he couldn't hear their conversation. Otherwise, she might not have been quite so frank. "We barely spoke. I hung up when he called, and I publicly snubbed him. It was the only way I could keep him from trying to run my life." She didn't sugarcoat her feelings in front of Hudson. He had a vested interest in protecting her from prosecution; if she went down, so did he.

Hudson looked as if he wanted to pursue the matter, but she didn't. He must have sensed her reluctance, because he moved on to other matters. "There's no other safe in the house?"

"Well, there's the quintessential wall safe behind a painting."

"I wish," Hudson said. This time he thought she was kidding when she wasn't.

"No, really. We have a wall safe behind a painting. It was there when my father bought the house, and unfortunately, the combination was lost even before that. We've never used it." She led Hudson into the living room, where Mitch had already pulled back the oil painting of a ballerina to reveal the old-fashioned safe—with what looked like the modern addition of an electronic keypad of some sort.

"Oh, very good, Mitch." Hudson nodded his approval, then turned to Elizabeth. "Do the cops know about this?"

"I saw no need to mention it, since I…I didn't think there was any way to get it open. But that…" She leaned closer. "That keypad doesn't look old at all."

Hudson and Mitch exchanged a look.

"Oh, come on, there's nothing in there. Are you going to tell me you guys know how to crack a safe?"

Hudson grinned. "I bet you a dollar Daniel knows a safe-cracker."

"No need for that. Not yet, anyway." Mitch fetched his suitcase full of goodies, then sifted through various esoteric-looking electronic devices until he found the one he wanted. "This might take a while. Y'all can carry on about your business."

Taking the hint, Hudson and Elizabeth wandered into the kitchen. Elizabeth mindlessly went to the fridge, hunting for something to drink. "Before you ask, I'm afraid we don't have any Mountain Dew."

Hudson laughed. "I am capable of drinking something else. But that's okay—I'm not thirsty."

She settled on a bottle of mineral water for herself. She unscrewed the top and didn't even bother with a glass, just chugged right out of the bottle.

Elizabeth couldn't deny she was a bit shaken by the discovery that her father had been using the old safe. "I don't know why I'm surprised about anything my father did at this point." She leaned against the island, resting her elbows on the cool marble top. "What do you suppose we'll find in there?"

"Evidence of some criminal enterprise is my guess. Maybe he was blackmailing someone, and they killed him rather than paying up."

"I can't see my father blackmailing someone. I mean, he's ruthless enough to do it, but it's not like he needed the money."

"Are you sure? A lot of rich people lost a lot of their wealth in the recession. How did your father get rich, anyway? Just from lawyering?"

"He inherited a good chunk of it. Then, in the eighties during the telecom boom, he started investing. He owned the majority of a small high-tech company that hit big, eventually got bought by a huge conglomerate. He liked to brag that he got out at just the right time. Since then he's dabbled in different ventures, but mostly he bails out companies in trouble in return for a huge ownership stake. He saves the company then forces a sale. It's a nasty business."

"Is he a tech guy? He knows computers and such?"

She shrugged. "He always bought the latest and greatest, most powerful computers. Whether it was a prestige thing, or he really knew how to use them, I'm not sure."

"Does he have high-tech friends?" Hudson seemed to be more than casually interested in this aspect of her father's life.

"I don't know. Why is this important?"

"Something weird happened a little while ago. Mitch hacked into a police database, and we found what looked like the tattoo of the guy who shot at me—a tiny thumbnail photo. But the actual record was missing, and Mitch said it looked like the work of a hacker."

"My father didn't have any real friends, but he knew a lot of people. Whatever had to be done, he always found the right person and hired them. Unfortunately, the cops took everything that had his contacts—his address book, computer. If he had a cell phone when they found him, they probably took that, too. They even took the landline phone on his desk, in case it had some phone numbers stored in its memory."

"Got it unlocked," Mitch called from the living room.

"He *is* good," Elizabeth marveled as she and Hudson rushed to see what Mitch had uncovered. He stood in his sock feet on the white sofa, his hand on the safe door, looking like a magician about ready to reveal his best illusion.

"I haven't opened it yet. I thought we should all do it to-gether. Chain of custody and all that."

Hudson nodded. Elizabeth held her breath. And Mitch slowly swung the heavy safe door open.

"Bingo," Hudson said softly. Sure enough, sitting inside the safe were a laptop computer and several stacks of paper money, rubber-banded into bundles. Hudson slid his arm around Elizabeth's shoulders. "Liz, baby, we might be look-ing at our salvation."

CHAPTER SEVEN

MITCH TOOK PICTURES while Hudson removed the laptop computer and placed it in a paper bag. None of their careful treatment of the evidence would carry any weight from an official standpoint, of course. Anything he or Elizabeth got close to would be tainted, even with Mitch as a witness.

But that wasn't the purpose of this exercise. They needed leads that would point them in the right direction. Once they figured out who had really killed Mandalay, Hudson could take it to his lieutenant or the captain. The photos would document his version of events, at least.

Next, with gloved hands, Hudson removed the stacks of cash and placed them in a second bag. Once those were gone, several other items became visible—two passports and a couple of small boxes.

The passports were interesting. One was Venezuelan, for a man named Enrique Zuckas. The picture, though, was of Mandalay. A second passport was from the Cayman Islands. The name was John Weland; the picture was Mandalay's.

Liz stood by silently watching, her hands locked together, her face pale. She said nothing until Hudson brought out a third passport. This one was also Venezuelan, but the name was Antonia Zuckas. The picture was undeniably Liz. "Oh, my God."

"I take it you don't know anything about this?" Hudson asked.

"Of course not!"

"It looks like your dad was preparing to flee the country—with you."

"Well, he would have had to hog-tie me and drug me. I wouldn't have gone."

"Maybe he was just hopeful," Mitch suggested. "The estrangement with your father—your idea, right?"

"Completely mine," she answered. "He never understood why I cut him out of my life. He had a peculiar blind spot."

"Why did you?" Hudson asked. "I don't mean to be nosy, but I'm trying to understand his mind-set. You said it was more than his refusal to let you go away to college."

"Was he abusive?" Mitch asked softly. "That's something I understand."

"Not in the way you mean. He never laid a hand on me. It was more a case of him wanting to possess me, like a pet or something. He insisted on controlling every aspect of my life—my friends, my clothes, my hair, my diet, the books I read. I mean, right down to the toothpaste I used. No amount of reasoning or arguing could change his behavior, so I left home as soon as I could manage it."

"You been close to him since then?" Mitch asked, which was the same thing Hudson had asked when he'd learned of the estrangement.

"I've seen him. I tried a couple of times to let him back into my life, just a little. But if I gave him an inch, he started trying to take control. One time, he decided he didn't like the apartment I lived in. So while I was at work, he hired a moving company to relocate all of my belongings to a luxury condo, then acted like he'd done me this big favor. I actually had to get a lawyer involved to get my stuff back. And you can't believe how hard it is to get a lawyer to go after another lawyer, especially *him*."

"Jesus," Mitch murmured.

Hudson felt for her. He'd always enjoyed a warm relationship with his parents. They were supportive, but never interfering. They were proud that both of their sons had followed in their father's footsteps but had never pushed them to make that choice.

"Let's see what's in those boxes," Liz said, seeming to shake off the memories.

There were three small white boxes. Hudson set them on the glass coffee table and opened them one at a time. He heard Liz's sharp intake of breath. She sank next to him on the sofa, as if her legs were no longer strong enough to support her.

The boxes contained jewelry—an antique gold locket, a dainty Rolex watch and a gold charm bracelet.

"You recognize these?" Hudson asked.

She nodded. "They were my mother's—things she wore every day. The locket belonged to her grandmother. The charm bracelet was her mother's. The watch was a gift from my father to her."

"And your mother…disappeared, right?" Mitch asked.

Liz nodded. "When I was fourteen. Everyone said she'd run off with a lover, but I never believed it."

They all stared silently at the jewelry, pondering the implications. Hudson picked up the watch and studied it more closely, turning it around and around in his hand. He spotted something that looked like rust on the band. But surely a Rolex watchband wouldn't rust.

"If she did run off," he said, "it might make sense that she would leave the jewelry behind. Aside from wanting to start with a fresh slate, the jewelry might have been used to identify her. So if she was trying to disappear…"

Liz shook her head. "No way."

"It happens, Liz," Hudson said gently. "People get to a breaking point. Maybe she saw the act of disappearing as the only way she could be truly free of your father. If he controlled her the way he controlled you…"

"What you say makes sense," Liz said, "and I might be persuaded, except for one thing. I have a specific memory of my father giving the detective a description of this jewelry. He claimed it went missing right along with her. When he's had it the whole time. What do you make of that?"

Hudson couldn't possibly say aloud what was going through his head. *Your father killed your mother, but then he couldn't bring himself to dispose of such valuable jewelry right along with the body.*

Instead, he said something that might also be true. "He kept these items safely tucked away for a reason. Maybe when he looked at them, they made him feel closer to her memory. Maybe the items turned up long after the police stopped investigating the case. We'll probably never know."

Liz narrowed her eyes. "I know what you're thinking. You think he killed her."

"Well…it did cross my mind."

She shook her head vehemently. "No. He wasn't perfect, but he loved my mother. He worshipped her. He would never hurt her."

"Even if she threatened to leave him? Even if that was the only way to prevent her from—"

"Stop it." Liz's cheeks flamed pink as her emotions flared. "That's not what happened. Why do you always see the worst in people? Like you said, my dad probably found her jewelry later. Maybe he even told the police. I was only a child, and my dad shielded me from details of the investigation."

Hudson nodded, not at all satisfied with that explanation. Of course Liz would have a hard time believing her father would kill his beloved wife, the mother of his child. But Hudson had no problem with the concept. He'd looked into Mandalay's eyes when he issued those threats against Hudson.

The man had been evil.

Now that Hudson had seen the fake passports, he realized Mandalay's out-of-the-country alibi for the day his wife went missing might have been a sham. The man could have crossed the border at will, no one the wiser.

Mitch cleared his throat, reminding them both that he was still there. "Maybe we should focus on one mystery at a time, huh?"

Hudson nodded. "Right. We can't afford to get distracted. But, Liz, I promise you, when this is over, I'm going to look back into this case, and I'm going to find out what happened to your mother."

He wanted to do that one thing for her.

She gave him a sad little smile. "I'd really rather you didn't. It won't bring her back."

"No, but I think you'd probably like to know the truth, wouldn't you?"

She shrugged noncommittally.

Mitch stood, seeming uncomfortable with the intense emotion in the room. "Let's get this stuff back to the lab. Soon as Beth pulls fingerprints from the computer, I'm going to dig in. Within a couple of days I'll have a hundred new leads." He packed up his bag of toys.

Liz stood, too, and smoothed the skirt of her pretty sundress. Earlier she'd had on something different—a conservative blouse and pants. Hudson couldn't help wondering if she'd changed into something attractive and feminine for him.

Probably not. Clearly she hadn't fixed her hair for him; she'd just wadded the thick, brown mass on top of her head and put a stick through it to get it off her neck. For some reason, he found the hairstyle sexy as hell, especially with that strand falling across her face. His fingers itched to smooth the stray piece of hair behind her ear.

"Let's touch base again tomorrow," Hudson said. "Is it okay if I take the jewelry? Just temporarily."

"Sure." She didn't ask him why, for which Hudson was grateful. She wouldn't like his answer.

"Wait, I'm going to leave with you two," she said. "I don't want to stay here alone."

She collected a few things, and the three of them left

through the garage door. Liz set the security alarm and locked the door.

As Mitch loaded his bag and the evidence into the Z's miniscule trunk, Hudson helped Liz with a small box, which she'd packed up with a few mementos that had belonged to her parents, things she wanted to keep safe.

"You can call me, you know. If you just want to talk. It's a lot to take in, all this stuff we're finding out about your father. I know you weren't close, but—"

"I guess I still loved him, despite everything," she said. "Why else would I keep crying? And why would I keep those stupid flowers he sent me sitting on my dining-room table, even though they're dead?"

"Ah. I wondered about that."

"It's hard to completely hate someone who loves you as much as my father loved me. He truly wanted the best for me. He used to say to me, even when I was a little girl, that he was going to see to it that my life was perfect, that I always had the best schools, the finest clothes, the most handsome and successful husband—that I would always have every single thing I wanted." She shook her head sadly. "He didn't understand that all I ever really wanted was to be free to pursue my own dreams—not the dreams he had for me. That all he had to do was love me, and my life would have been fine."

Hudson shrugged. "Every parent does what they think is best. Sadly, you don't have to pass any kind of test or get certified to have kids."

"What about your parents? Do you have horror stories?"

"It's almost embarrassing, but no. I had a great childhood. No complaints about how I was raised. The only thing my mother nags me about is getting married and giving her grandbabies."

Crap. He wished he hadn't mentioned that. Because the moment he said it, he pictured Liz as a bride; Liz holding an infant, his child.

Hudson turned away from Liz, afraid she could somehow see his thoughts reflected in his face, and opened her car door for her. "Be safe. Remember, there's a killer out there somewhere who doesn't want us to find the truth."

She gave him a quizzical look. Then, just before ducking into her Prius, she kissed him. It was quick, intense, and it made him see fireworks. By the time his senses cleared, she had the engine started and she was backing up.

He waved weakly.

Hoping Mitch hadn't witnessed the kiss, he slid behind the wheel of his car.

"Did Elizabeth just kiss you?" Mitch asked.

"Well…yeah. I think she just wanted to, you know, connect with somebody. She was pretty shook up about finding the stuff in that safe. I'm sure it was just an impulse."

"You two can't get involved, you know. Not until Franklin Mandalay's murderer is caught and charged, at least."

"We aren't involved. It was a one-night stand." Maybe if he said that enough times, Hudson would believe it. But right now, he felt involved up to his neck.

"Ms. Downey? You okay?"

"Hmm? Oh, jeez, I'm so sorry, Tonda."

"That's okay—I'd be distracted, too, if somebody shot my old man." At Elizabeth's surprised look, Tonda smiled slyly. "What, you think I can't read a newspaper?"

"I shouldn't bring my problems to work with me. We're here to talk about your situation. You were telling me about Jackson?"

"Yeah, I broke down and told him about the baby. He reacted just like I thought he would. He said he'd pay to get rid of it."

Elizabeth felt herself flinch. She'd like to lock up Jackson in a closet with a rabid pit bull, but she knew Tonda had feelings for the scumbag. A prostitute often developed an attachment for her "manager," because he "took care" of her.

"He yelled a lot. Said I better not try to tap him for child support or I'd be sorry. But then, actually, when I told him I was gonna keep it and there was nothing he could do about it, he calmed down. Said we'd work something out." Tonda laughed. "You know, I think he was really surprised I wanted to keep his kid. And all that yelling was just, you know, bluster. Is that the right word?"

Elizabeth nodded. "Still, you need to be careful. When a woman is pregnant, it's the most dangerous time of her life in terms of domestic violence."

"I don't think he'd hurt me. Not bad, anyway."

Famous last words, but Elizabeth didn't want to argue about it. They'd covered the same territory in previous sessions; Tonda refused to think ill of Jackson. Most women didn't want to consider that the father of their child would hurt them or the kid.

"I told him I wasn't gonna work no more, 'cause I don't want to give the baby some disease. He said he'd kick me out on the street. But I don't think he will. 'Cause later, he kept grinning when he thought I wasn't looking."

"Well, Tonda, I'm proud of you for how you're dealing with all this. You've come a long way since I first met you."

"I'm healthier, anyway."

Elizabeth had seen Tonda sporadically at the clinic for the past year. When she first came, she'd been malnourished and depressed. Gradually her outlook had improved, and she gained some weight and started taking care of herself more. Though of course it would be a good idea for her to leave "the life" altogether, no one was going to talk her into it. The change had to be her own idea. She had to see an alternative, visualize a different life for herself. Elizabeth was trying to give her the tools to do that.

"Say, Tonda, this is a long shot, but have you ever heard of a call girl named Jazz? Latina, long black hair, really pretty?"

"Jazz? No… Oh, wait…Yazmin?" She gave the name a Spanish pronunciation.

"Maybe. You know her?"

"I heard of her. If it's the same girl, she used to be with a dude named Carlos—went by 'King C.' Then she got all full of herself and decided she didn't need a manager. Went strictly call girl. Internet, credit cards, the whole deal."

"Do you know her last name?"

"Mmm, no."

"What about a guy with a big fish tattoo on his arm? The tail is on his hand and then his whole arm is fish scales."

"That sounds kinda familiar…. I can ask around, if it's important. What you want to know for?"

"Apparently Jazz knew my father. I'd like to talk to her. She might have been one of the last people to see him alive."

"I'll find out for you."

"Oh…no, wait, Tonda, just forget it. It could be dangerous. I'll tell the police what you told me already. That could help."

Tonda laughed. "Okay, whatever you say." She glanced at her phone. "I better be going. Gotta buy groceries. The doc said I need to watch my salt, so no more pizza and Taco Bell every night."

Elizabeth hugged her favorite client, and Tonda departed, leaving Elizabeth to ponder. She had two new names to give Hudson—Yazmin and Carlos. Carlos might know the prostitute's last name.

She dug the silver cell phone from her purse and started to dial Hudson's number, then stopped herself. This wasn't exactly stop-the-presses information. She just wanted an excuse to talk to him, to hear his voice.

She still couldn't believe she'd kissed him in her dad's

garage. She hadn't planned it at all; he'd just been standing there looking so cute, so sexy, and he'd been so concerned about her feelings even if he had accused her father of murder. And she'd just done what came naturally.

Hudson hadn't exactly kissed her back, but then, it had all happened so quickly, he really hadn't had a chance. He'd just stared at her with a stunned expression. And she'd retreated to her car before she could ruin the moment by talking. She was dying to know what he thought about the kiss, or if he would rather pretend it never happened.

She hadn't felt this goofy about a kiss since David, her high-school boyfriend. Unlike with Hank, that relationship had progressed to making out. Until her father got wind of it. David had broken up with her in a most abrupt and unexpected way; then, a few weeks later, Elizabeth had seen him driving a brand-new Mustang she was sure he couldn't afford.

Quietly she set the phone down. Hudson had said he'd touch base with her sometime today. She would wait until he called, instead of behaving as if she had a teenage crush on him. Even if she did.

CARLA DOWNED THE dregs of her herbal tea she'd made earlier and grimaced. Vile stuff, and worse cold, but her stomach just couldn't take it anymore. Then she focused her attention on her computer screen again. This was some interesting information. But how to inform Knightly? He wasn't going to be thrilled with her methods.

She sensed a presence behind her and stifled a curse.

"What are you up to?" Knightly asked suspiciously.

They were the only two detectives in the bull pen; everybody else had gone home or was out in the field.

"Checking on a lead." That was suitably vague. Knightly wasn't a computer-savvy guy, not that she knew of, anyway. Maybe he wouldn't question her methods too closely.

"It seems our suspect paid a visit to Franklin Mandalay's home last night."

"How do you know that?" he asked. "Did you—did you put a tail on Hudson?" He sounded scandalized, and she couldn't totally blame him. He was lead on this case. If she was out doing stuff on her own, she ought to at least keep him informed.

"Vale would spot a tail in two seconds flat," she finally answered. "But I did something better."

Knightly leaned over her and squinted at the computer screen. "You planted a tracking device on his car." His voice fairly dripped with disapproval. "You do know you need a court order for that, right?"

"Only if we want to use the results as evidence. I just want to find out what he's up to during his enforced vacation."

"He's doing exactly what I would do under the circumstances," Knightly said. "He's investigating the crime himself. He thinks we've rushed to focus on him as a suspect—which some of us have," he added pointedly. "You know I hate investigating one of our own."

"You don't think he'd turn on you in a second if your roles were reversed? He's not your biggest fan, you know."

"Maybe he would, but that doesn't mean we have to sink to his level. Anyway, he could have gone to the Mandalay house to talk to servants, maybe search for evidence our team missed."

"He was there for over an hour, and get this. Elizabeth Downey was there at the same time. He met her there. You know what I'm thinking? Elizabeth. Liz. She's Hudson's mystery woman."

Knightly appeared intrigued despite Carla's questionable tactics. "So you think our two chief suspects know each other."

"I think it's highly probable that they not only know each other, but that they were together the night of the murder.

Elizabeth was at the society wedding. Hudson said he met his sexual conquest at a party, but a wedding is a party, right?"

Knightly shook his head. "Maybe Elizabeth just happened to be at her father's house when Hudson arrived. I'm sure she has lots of things to take care of following her father's death."

"According to the report, they left at exactly the same time."

"Now wait a minute. Let's be logical about this. If Hudson and Ms. Downey were together the night of the murder, why would he even mention it to us? He has to know she's a suspect. And if he does decide to mention it, why doesn't he just tell us her name instead of inventing some mystery woman named Liz? Either he wants us to know he was with her or he doesn't. And if he doesn't, he wouldn't mention a woman at all."

Why did Knightly have to be so damn logical? "I don't know. But I'm going to find out. Hudson would spot a tail, but Elizabeth Downey won't."

"Last I heard, Captain Hodges won't authorize the overtime unless we have a more compelling suspect."

"I'll tail her myself. And I'll do it on my own time." She would borrow her cousin's car, just in case she *was* spotted. "Want to join me?"

Knightly wavered. He probably didn't trust her to handle this on her own.

Finally he nodded. "Let me go home, grab a shower and a bite to eat, and I'll go with you. But, Carla, why didn't you just tell me what you were doing? With the tracking devices? I'm your partner now. You have to trust me."

"Let's just say I was protecting you, okay?" Carla congratulated herself on coming up with a plausible reason. "I know what I'm doing isn't strictly kosher. If I get caught, I don't want you to get in trouble, too—not when you're so new to Major Crimes."

"But now you bring me in?"

"Because I've observed something relevant. C'mon, Todd, this is weird, the two of them getting together."

He nodded.

"I'll pick you up at nine," she said.

CHAPTER EIGHT

"Mom, this is the best pot roast I've ever had."

Hudson's mother, Binnie, giggled. "You say that every time you eat it."

"It's true every time I eat it."

"Which is, like, every week," Hudson's brother, Parker, said. "Why did you make his favorite dinner, anyway? I thought we were celebrating my birthday."

"Don't you like pot roast, Parker?" Binnie asked.

"Sure, but…it's not my absolute favorite."

"Oh, I'm sorry." Binnie looked embarrassed. "I guess I don't know what your favorite dinner is."

"Now look," Hudson chided his brother. "You embarrassed Mom. What is your favorite dinner, anyway?"

"You see? See there? That's exactly my point. Everybody knows Hudson's favorite meal is pot roast with potatoes and green beans. And apple pie for dessert. What are we having for dessert?"

"Well…apple pie," his mom said.

"For the record, since you asked, my favorite meal is fried catfish and collard greens. And cheesecake for dessert."

"Well, on Hudson's birthday, that's what we'll have, and the slate will be clean," Binnie said. "But tonight…well, you're not the one who might end up in Huntsville eating prison food."

There it was. Hudson had been hoping to avoid talking about his supposed crimes. It was bad enough when he'd only been suspected of using excessive force. The possibility of her eldest boy being convicted of murder had made his mother come unglued, and he didn't want a repeat performance. "Mom, they haven't even taken me in for formal questioning."

"Well, have you seen the newspaper or watched TV lately? They've got you tried and convicted."

"Don't read the papers. Mom, I've told you that. They're full of it. Long as it's shocking, doesn't matter if it's true." And what could be more shocking than a police officer, sworn to uphold the law, killing someone?

"Have you hired a lawyer yet?" Parker asked.

"Project Justice has a lawyer assigned to look after my interests. I'm following her advice." Hudson had provided his family with only the barest of facts about the case. He wouldn't have told them anything—except he felt it was necessary to reassure his mother that he wasn't letting his own police department steamroller him into a life sentence—or worse.

Parker, who looked a lot like Hudson except with shorter hair and a slightly rounder face, swallowed a huge bite of potato, then gestured with his fork. "Yeah, but she's looking out for everybody, not just you. She's also protecting the chick, the victim's daughter, right? That's what the paper said."

"Don't call her a *chick*. It's disrespectful. She and I are in this together."

"The way I see it, you two have completely different goals. If she goes down, you're off the hook. And vice versa."

"That's not the way this works. We both know it was some third party. We're trying to help each other."

"Hudson." His mother looked at him sternly. "How do you know she didn't do it? Is it because she's so pretty?"

"Yeah, not to mention she's a bazillionaire now that her old man is dead," Parker added.

"I just know." He really didn't want to get into this, especially not with his mother. And definitely not with his father, who had his head down and was shoveling in the food, pretending not to be involved, though he was for certain taking it all in.

None of his family knew the reason his fate was tied with Liz's, and he didn't enlighten them.

"You're not usually so trusting," Parker said. "When it comes to criminals, you're just as suspicious of a pretty face as anyone else."

That was when a phone rang, thankfully distracting everyone from the argument. No one moved.

"Mom?" Parker said. "Isn't that ringing from your apron pocket?"

"Oh, I guess it is." She pulled what looked like a very cheap phone from her pocket and stared at it, perplexed. "I haven't even given this number to anyone, so I don't see how it could be for me."

"Have you used it to call anyone?" Parker asked.

"Well, of course."

The phone went silent. She shrugged and stuck it back in her pocket. Although she liked the idea of having a mobile phone, so she could talk to her friends and relatives while she was in the garden or out shopping, she'd never truly embraced the technology.

"Whoever you called has the number to your phone," Hudson pointed out.

"Oh. Well, if it's important, they'll call the home phone. Anyway, the minutes are almost gone on this one. I bought a new one this afternoon."

"Wait," Parker said. "When you run out of minutes, you buy a new phone?"

"Well, you get a ton of free minutes with the phone," she said defensively. "I thought they were meant to be disposable. Is that not right?"

Parker rolled his eyes. "Any more potatoes, Mom?"

"On the stove."

Parker got up and headed for the stove.

"Bring enough for me, too, please," Hudson said.

His mother hopped up. "Here, I'll get them for you, dear." She whisked Hudson's plate away and scurried to the stove. Parker just stood there holding his empty plate, staring in disbelief at their mother playing blatant favorites.

"Don't worry," Hudson said in a loud stage whisper to his brother, "it's only temporary. She doesn't really like me better. Remember when you got accused of cheating on a test in junior high? Remember how Mom put extra cupcakes in your lunch sack and bought you new jeans when you didn't even need 'em? I was lucky she didn't forget to take me to school. She'll get over it. Soon as I'm cleared."

"*If* you're cleared."

Everyone froze. Hudson gritted his teeth and looked at his father, who'd finally decided it was time to speak up.

Rusty pushed his chair back and stood. "Hudson, forget the potatoes. Walk with me."

This wasn't a good sign. His father, whom everyone called Rusty for the fiery red hair he'd once possessed, didn't invite a private conversation unless he had a pretty strong reason. The last time he'd done it, it was to inform Hudson that he was pulling the plug on his son's surfing career unless he enrolled in college.

Four years earlier, Rusty Vale had retired from the Houston Police Department, where he'd risen to the rank of captain. His bum knee had made it impossible to continue in that capacity. He'd taken early retirement and bought a few acres in Rosenburg, southwest of Houston. He had a garden, a few chickens, a few goats and leased the rest of the land for cattle grazing. Between his pension and selling eggs, honey and goat's milk, he made a fair living. And the whole family ate really well. Whatever Rusty didn't grow, he bartered for with his neighbors.

Rusty wordlessly headed out the door, expecting Hudson to follow. Which he did.

Rusty said nothing until they reached the end of the long gravel driveway. "You're sleeping with that girl, aren't you." It was a statement, not a question.

Now, how the hell had Rusty heard about that? Hudson played dumb, just in case his father was talking about something else. "What girl?"

"The daughter."

"I slept with her. Once. I had no idea who she was."

"Did she know who *you* were? That you'd beat up her father?"

"Yes. She claims she admired me for standing up to Franklin Mandalay. She says her own father was a terrible bully."

"And you believe her?"

Hudson wavered. "I've tried to figure out her angle. But it doesn't make sense. She didn't do herself any favors by getting tangled up with me. Best-case scenario, I was some kind of thrill lay for her, and we just had the bad luck to get together on the worst night possible."

He hated to state it in such bald terms. But he could not afford to get sentimental where Liz was concerned. What if she was playing him? What if she'd been in cahoots with her father that night? What if she'd gone to his house to look for something Mandalay could use as leverage against Hudson?

Hudson didn't want to think these things about her. But if his job had taught him one thing, it was that however bad you believed people were, they could be even worse.

"Who else knew you were together?"

"No one! Unless someone saw us dancing at the wedding and followed us. Then decided to off Mandalay to… I don't know. Create irony? It makes no sense."

"What's your take? You have any idea who did it?"

"Mandalay was involved in something illegal. When I arrested him he was handing over a pile of money to a prostitute—way more than any ordinary john would pay a hooker. He was involved in something fishy—and he was willing to go to great lengths to protect it."

"I always knew he was dirty."

"You know something about Mandalay?"

"Yeah. He killed his wife."

Hudson couldn't believe his ears. He stopped walking, just stood shaking his head in the dusty street. "You investigated Holly Mandalay's disappearance?"

"Not me, personally, but a buddy of mine who worked in Missing Persons, Homer Vilches. We all figured Mandalay was good for it. But someone from up high—I mean, really high—said to leave it alone."

"You think Mandalay had the Houston chief of police in his pocket? Or the homicide captain, maybe?"

"Or the mayor. Who knows? Lot of corruption going on back then."

Hudson told his father what he'd found in the wall safe. "There was something brown and crusty stuck between the links of the watchband. I think it was blood. I'm having it tested."

"Why?"

Hudson shrugged. "If he murdered his wife, maybe the crime came back to haunt him. Maybe there's a connection. I'm grasping at straws." He didn't mention that he also wanted to find out what had happened to Liz's mother. For her. Despite her pretended indifference, it must eat her alive inside not to know, to wonder if she'd been abandoned by the woman who was supposed to love her more than anyone.

"I got a few folks owe me some favors," Rusty said. "Homer Vilches died a few years ago. Cancer. But I know a couple of other old-timers who might remember something about that case."

"Thanks, Dad."

"And you... Could you for the love of Pete be more careful who you take to your bed? Your brother does a complete background check on every woman he dates—before he asks her out."

"It's a weakness. I admit it. But honestly, even if I'd known who she was, I'm not sure it would have made a difference. We didn't know her old man was gonna get himself offed."

"And you're positive she didn't do it?"

"Yes. Well, pretty sure. She left my house at four. Time of death could have been as late as five—but she didn't even have a car. She would have had to take a taxi…."

"Did you see the taxi? Maybe Mandalay picked her up from your house…and something happened."

"No." He was the first to believe the worst about his fellow human beings. But his cynicism wouldn't stretch far enough to accommodate his father's theory. "She's not capable of murder. I might be an easy lay, but I'm also a good judge of character. If she gave a crap about money, she wouldn't be working at a free clinic counseling teenage mothers and prostitutes."

"If you say so, then I believe you. I'll let you know what I find out."

Hudson's phone rang. The silver one, from Project Justice.

"Hold on, Dad. I have to take this." He clicked the phone on. "Yo."

"It's Mitch. I've been looking at the call history on that phone we found in Mandalay's safe. Almost all of the calls are to throwaway cell numbers—a sure sign of criminal activity. No way to trace the owners of those phones, but I was able to figure out where one particular number—one he called on a regular basis—was usually located. It's in the Barrio. I've narrowed it down to about a four-block area."

"That's fantastic, Mitch." Four blocks was a big chunk of real estate, but still, he was going fishing tonight.

ELIZABETH JUMPED WHEN her cell phone rang. No, not her regular phone, she realized. It was the encrypted phone Daniel had provided. She pulled it out of her purse and fumbled with the unfamiliar screen, finally finding the talk button. "Hello?"

"Liz. It's Hudson."

As if she couldn't recognize his voice by now, or the fact that he was the only living person in the world who called her by a nickname. She still wasn't sure why she'd chosen to introduce herself as Liz. Her mother had called her that, but nobody else. "What's up?"

"I got a lead. That cell phone we found in the safe? Mitch traced several calls to a certain location in the East End. The number he was calling was a throwaway, no way to determine the owner. But Mitch was able to figure out a physical location—well, within a few blocks. It's a place where a lot of hook—I mean, ladies of the evening—hang out. I thought I might drive around, see if I spot either Jazz or Fish Tattoo man."

"Hudson, are you sure? Your car—it's so recognizable."

"Oh, I'm not gonna be in my car. Daniel gave me a loaner. The license plate will trace back to someone totally unconnected to me or Project Justice. And I have no intention of stopping or confronting anyone. I just want to see what's going on down there."

"If you're sure it's safe."

"I'm so sure that I want you to come with me."

She looked down at herself. It was only eight o'clock, but she was already in her jammies. She'd planned to go to bed early and watch some mindless TV. "Hudson, we can't be seen together."

"And we won't be. My loaner car has tinted windows. I'll pick you up at ten sharp in front of your building…okay?"

Elizabeth knew she shouldn't. But driving around with Hudson sounded a whole lot more appealing than watching reruns of *The Rockford Files*. Being at her father's house yesterday, seeing those items that had belonged to her mother, had stirred up a lot of uncomfortable memories—things she didn't want to think about or talk about. She didn't feel like calling any of her friends; she couldn't talk about what was going on, and Daniel had stressed that she might be in danger if the real murderer was someone trying to get to her father's money. She found that unlikely, but she didn't yet know what her father's will contained. She was reasonably certain he'd left the bulk of his estate to her, but he'd probably left sizable bequests to other people, too, like Mrs. Ames.

"Liz?"

"Yeah, okay, I'll go. See you at ten."

Ten seemed a long time away. Elizabeth washed her dishes—she hadn't eaten much of her dinner of pasta with sauce from a jar, so she saved what was left in a plastic container. After the kitchen was spick-and-span, she wondered what wardrobe would be appropriate for surveillance, or whatever it was they were doing. Reconnaissance, maybe. She settled for jeans and a beige knit shirt with a zipper down the front, one of her favorites because it was so comfortable, although she couldn't help thinking about Hudson tugging on that zipper. She topped the outfit with a lightweight navy hoodie for warmth. She wore her running shoes—just in case she had to run, she thought with a laugh.

Surely Hudson wouldn't put her in any danger.

A new doorman had taken Oscar's place while Oscar and his family were in Aruba, or wherever Daniel had sent them. He believed he'd won a contest, which was logical, since he was always entering sweepstakes to keep the boredom at bay while he sat at his desk.

Daniel had known that, somehow. He thought of everything.

Elizabeth had no desire to make casual conversation with the new guy about her plans, or have him see her leave, so she departed through the garage entrance, walked out through the security gate and strolled casually toward the front of the building. At the stroke of ten o'clock, a ruby-red Lexus pulled up to the curb and the passenger window slid open.

"Hey, there, baby, goin' my way?"

She quickly opened the door and slid inside the climate-controlled interior. "Wow, when Daniel gives you a loaner, he doesn't skimp." Though in all honesty, Hudson himself was way more interesting than the car. Dressed in faded jeans and a gray T-shirt with the name of a gym on the front, a baseball cap pulled down low, tonight he was all bad boy.

She'd pictured him in faded jeans that first night they met; the reality was even better than her fantasy. The denim molded to his thigh muscles and cupped his equipment. Her mouth went dry.

"This puppy's got a 380 V-8 under the hood, eight-speed automatic transmission, sport-tuned air suspension, variable gear-ratio steering and teleios alloy wheels."

"How do you know so much about it? Are you some kind of Lexus expert?"

"I looked it up. It's also got heated seats, moon roof, on-board GPS, and it syncs with my iPod." To prove his point, he switched on some music.

She was surprised to hear one of her favorite bands' music surrounding her. "You like the Gipsy Kings?"

"Love flamenco music. I'm kind of shocked you even know who the Gipsy Kings are."

"Saw them in concert last year. Hey, this isn't some ploy to make me think we have something in common, is it? I mean, those Project Justice guys can probably find out in ten minutes which teeth I have fillings in and what brand of nail polish I prefer."

Hudson laughed. "I swear I don't have any inside information about you. I really do like flamenco music. I like guitars in general—rock, blues, everything from Clapton to Hendrix to B. B. King."

"Do you play?"

"Sadly, I'm tone-deaf. I can listen and appreciate, but I can't sing or play a note." He slid the car smoothly into the sparse evening traffic. "Do you play?"

"I wanted to play guitar when I was a kid. You know, I wanted to form a group like Josie and the Pussycats. But my father didn't think that was dignified enough. So it was piano lessons for me. Six years' worth. And when I didn't excel, I was moved to the violin and then the clarinet. I can play all of them, but not well."

"I bet you're just being modest."

"No, I'm not. If I'd been any good, my father never would have let me quit."

"I was so bad, they kicked me out of the church youth choir."

Now it was Elizabeth's turn to laugh. "Sorry, but I just don't picture you as a choirboy."

She expected him to join her in laughing, but suddenly he got very serious. "I think someone's following us."

"Really?"

"No one was following me before I picked you up—I made sure."

"Which means I'm the one under surveillance?" That did not sit well with her. Despite the initial questioning by the police, she didn't believe she was truly a suspect. It was only if they found out where she'd been Saturday night that she risked turning mild suspicion into an arrest warrant. "Can you tell who's following?"

"It's a white Subaru. Not a typical cop car."

"I don't know whether to be relieved or more worried."

"Who else might be following you?" he asked. "Any jealous boyfriends in the picture?"

"No! Of course not. I live a very quiet life."

"What about your clients? Any of them have a beef with you?"

Her thoughts flitted briefly to Tonda's pimp, Jackson. He'd

confronted Elizabeth once, about a year ago, when she'd first started counseling Tonda, trying to convince her to give up "the life" and get a legitimate job. He hadn't appreciated Elizabeth interfering with his livelihood. But he hadn't bothered her since then, and Elizabeth had finally realized that she couldn't *make* Tonda quit. Of course, with the baby coming, Jackson might be more worked up than usual, especially if he thought Elizabeth had talked Tonda into keeping the baby.

Still…Jackson wouldn't be caught dead in a Subaru. He leaned toward Lincoln Continentals as big as a barge, with custom chrome wheels. "I don't think anyone from work would bother me. But I just remembered something I wanted to tell you.

"One of my clients thinks she knows Jazz, your mysterious prostitute. Or at least knows of her."

"Liz. Daniel said you shouldn't investigate on your own, and I agree."

"Who else is going to question my client? You? You think she's going to open up to a cop, a former cop, a lawyer or anything that resembles any of the above? Don't even think about it. Anyway, it's not like I'm running around with a gun knocking on strangers' doors. She's my client, someone I've known almost a year. She would never hurt me."

"Yeah, but if she mentions your conversation to the wrong people— Let's just say, we don't want to tip our hand. We could scare our killer away, as well as any witnesses. We could also provoke the killer into doing something rash. Something else rash."

Elizabeth hadn't thought of it that way. "I told her these were dangerous people and not to mention the matter to anyone else. I trust her." But Tonda was only nineteen and not always prone to the wisest decisions.

"So…what did you find out?"

"Jazz might actually be Yazmin. She used to work for a

pimp named Carlos, or King C, but then, according to Tonda, she broke away. Went on her own. Internet call girl."

"Hmm."

Elizabeth had expected a more positive reaction than that. "That's not helpful information?"

"It's just that I've been poring over internet sites, looking for her, making calls. I haven't seen or encountered a Jazz or a Yazmin or anyone who looks or sounds like her."

"Maybe she's lying low."

"Maybe. Or something happened to her. Your father could have been attempting to bribe her, buy her silence. When that didn't work…"

"You always go for the darkest explanation. My father didn't kill her."

Hudson didn't argue. He pushed a button on the steering wheel. "Call Mitch."

Using the sync, the car dialed his phone.

Mitch's voice came over the speakers almost immediately. "What's up, Hud?"

"My missing prostitute might be going by the name Yazmin…. The spelling?" He shot Elizabeth a questioning look.

"*Y-A-Z-M-I-N,* I think," she supplied.

"She might have a pimp, or former pimp, named Carlos or King C," Hudson said.

"I'll get on it."

"Also, can you run a plate? White Subaru. Victor Alpha Charlie 288."

"Sure."

Hudson was silent awhile, his brow furrowed as if he was working something out. Finally he asked, "Doesn't it bother you, associating with prostitutes?"

"It's not like we go out drinking together. I counsel these women. I know exactly what their lives are like, and no, it doesn't bother me."

"When I was in Vice, I talked to them all the time."

"I'm sure you did. But the women *trust* me. They know they can tell me anything and I won't get them in trouble."

"Do you try to get them to quit? I mean, I get how young girls might be victimized, but adult women—surely they can make better choices."

"Not if they're hooked on drugs. Their pimps control when and how much of the drug they get. In return they have to do what he tells them to do. And even if they're not drug users, a lot of them have kids, and turning that next trick might allow them to feed those kids the next day."

"Yeah, yeah. I've heard the same arguments from defense lawyers and social workers a zillion times. But that's not my concern. I'm supposed to arrest people who commit crimes, thus making our community safer for all those people who do manage to raise their kids without breaking laws. It's *your* job to help them fix their lives, not mine."

"I do try to get them into better situations," she said. "Most of them have tragically low self-esteem. It's difficult to convince them they're worthy of a better life. They're brainwashed to believe they deserve to be abused, degraded—"

"Okay, okay, I get it. I guess I just see things from a different perspective. I see this whole continuum of crime, everything from graffiti to burglary to drugs to murder, and most of it I can lay at the feet of the gangs. Prostitution is just another cog in that big crime machine. It's not that I don't feel for those women. I do. But I can't spare too many tears when any day they could walk into a police station and provide evidence that would help us put away their pimps, their drug dealers."

"Yeah, and get them killed." No matter what he said, he really *didn't* get it. But then, most law-and-order types didn't.

"I'd rather spend my energy protecting the real victims—the convenience-store worker who gets shot in a robbery, the little kid that gets killed by a stray bullet in a drive-by. Not to mention you and me. You lost your father, who some part of you loved even if he was a bastard. And now some dirt-bag is out there running free while you and I are suspects."

"It's not like I feel sorry for the murderer."

"Are you sure? Maybe he came from a broken home. He could have been trying to rob your father for money to feed his starving children, and the gun went off accidentally—"

"Look, just because I show some compassion for people who make mistakes doesn't mean I think murderers shouldn't be caught and brought to justice. You're deliberately skewing my beliefs for your own amusement. Stop it."

He said nothing more, but she could tell he was biting his lip.

She turned to look out the back window. They were on busy Gowan Street; all she could see were lots of headlights. "Is the Subaru still back there?"

Hudson glanced in the mirror. "Yeah. I could lose him, but if it's a cop, and I start driving like I've spotted the tail, he'll know *I'm* a cop. Which pretty much narrows down my identity."

"I guess I see what you mean."

"If we just act oblivious, as civilians would, our friend doesn't know who I am. You're just out on a date with some anonymous guy named Lester."

"Lester?"

"That's who the car's registered to. Lester Holmes."

"Is he a real person?"

"I don't think so. Project Justice has a few fictional constructs. A casual background check won't raise any red flags."

Elizabeth just shook her head. She'd been around wealth and power her whole life, but Daniel Logan's influence knew no bounds. At least he tried to accomplish something meaningful with his wealth. Unlike her father, whose only goal was to accumulate more, more, more of everything—money, possessions, people, power, influence, whatever.

Still, he'd donated a lot of money to charity. He wasn't all bad. No one was all bad.

"So we just keep letting this dude follow us?" she said. "It creeps me out."

"I bet you anything it's a reporter."

"Well, isn't there some way to lose him without looking like we're trying to lose him?"

Hudson thought for a minute, glanced at the GPS screen. "Oh, I know. Perfect timing."

They'd been driving the surface streets out of downtown, through the pleasant Midtown, a thriving, mixed-use urban area with some of the most prized real estate in the city, but he made a sharp turn onto McGowan and zoomed under the freeway.

"What are you doing?"

"There's a busy railroad crossing on Lawndale—it's sort of on the way to where we're going. If we time it just right…"

Elizabeth didn't like the sound of this. Her fears must have shown plainly on her face, because Hudson tried to reassure her.

"I won't put you in any danger. Promise. I used to do this all the time when I was a teenager."

"Oh, *that* reassures me."

CHAPTER NINE

ELIZABETH WASN'T QUITE sure where they were; somewhere south of downtown. As they approached the crossing, there was no sign of any train. Hudson slowed down and pulled over to the curb. Elizabeth glanced nervously behind her. The Subaru pulled past them—then quickly pulled into a parking lot. Hudson looked at his watch again. "Wait for it…wait for it…" He watched the warning lights, then cracked his window and listened. "That's it."

He pulled back into traffic at the exact moment the red warning lights started flashing and the bell clanged. Just as the gates started to drop, he whipped into the left lane and zoomed across the tracks, missing the dropping crossbar by inches.

Moments later the train rushed past behind them.

Hudson whooped in victory and Elizabeth hyperventilated. "Was that really necessary?"

"Awwww, it was textbook! He'll never know we spotted him—he'll just think I'm a bad driver."

"You could have gotten us killed."

"Nonsense. Didn't you ever play chicken as a teenager?"

"Correct me if I'm wrong, but isn't it against the law to ignore railroad warning lights? Doesn't that put us in this criminal continuum you mentioned?"

"It's not the same," he mumbled, but she knew she'd scored a point.

She craned her neck and peered out the back window.

The train still blocked the intersection, while Hudson left the Subaru far behind. He turned left on a random street, under an overpass, then right again onto another well-trafficked avenue. They were in the Third Ward now, an urban neighborhood known for its high crime rate.

"If you didn't play chicken," Hudson asked, "what *did* you do for fun when you were a kid?"

"I went to movies. I used to go swimming a lot in the summer. My friends and I used to…" What did they do? Usually organized activities, well chaperoned by parents who'd been thoroughly vetted by her father. "You're right. I didn't have much fun." Suddenly she smiled. Maybe she wasn't in the best situation of her life at the moment, but this was an adventure. When else would she ride in the passenger seat of a luxury car with a dashing rogue at the wheel, evading a determined reporter or maybe even a cop?

She tried to stop grinning, but she couldn't help herself. Hudson's exuberance was infectious. They were Burt Reynolds and Sally Field in *Smokey and the Bandit*.

"What's so funny?" he asked.

"Oh, nothing."

He sobered. "We're in our target neighborhood now. We better keep our eyes open."

"What, exactly, are we looking for?"

"Jazz. Or Yazmin, whatever. Also Fish Tattoo man."

Hudson's phone chimed over the car's speakers, and he pushed a button on the steering wheel. "Yo."

"Hudson. I think I found her. I'm forwarding you a picture." It was Mitch's voice.

The screen on the dashboard, where the GPS had its map, suddenly filled with the image of an attractive Hispanic woman with long dark hair. It was a mug shot, but her natural beauty shone through despite her smeared makeup and sullen expression.

"That's her!" Hudson was as excited as a little kid at his first baseball game. "You got an address?"

"Her name is Yazmin Cortez. Address is more than a year old but I'll give it to you. I did some cross-checking, and a lot of other names are associated with that same address—including one Carlos De Lugo, who has a long record that includes some pandering charges." He paused before delivering the zinger. "Street name King C." Another picture flashed on the screen next to Yazmin's, of a tall, thin Hispanic man with a shaved head. The long scar on his cheek could only have come from a knife.

Elizabeth shivered. Could this be the man who had killed her father? He looked like someone capable of murder, though by now she ought to know better than to judge someone's character strictly by a photo.

"Thanks—I owe you," Hudson said. "I'll check it out."

"You shouldn't go by yourself," Mitch warned. "Call Kinkaid."

Hudson grinned. "I think I can handle a pimp. What about the plates?"

"Registered to a Michael Sousa. Elementary-school teacher. No record."

"Hmm." Maybe the car hadn't been following them after all. He thanked Mitch again and ended the call.

"He's right," Elizabeth said. "You shouldn't confront any of these bad boys alone."

"I used to patrol all the time by myself. Sometimes the budget just wouldn't stretch far enough for us all to have partners. It's no big deal."

"You're not going now, are you?" she asked with some alarm. She might have sympathy for some of the hard cases she encountered, but that didn't mean she wanted to meet them face-to-face in a bad part of town.

"We're just gonna drive by the address. Maybe pull over and watch for a while."

"I'm not sure you should park this car in this neighborhood."

"It'll be fine."

Elizabeth had a bad feeling about this. Sure, Hudson was used to this type of situation. But before, he always had the power of the badge behind him and backup just one radio call away. Bad boys didn't mess with cops. Right now, she and Hudson looked exactly like the kind of clueless, wealthy people who made perfect targets—cruising in a really nice car into a bad part of town. She could already feel people on the street watching them, curious.

"Hey, you think this Carlos guy could be the Fish Tattoo man?"

"It says he's six-two and one-eighty. The housebreaker seemed more short and dumpy, but it was dark and I was scared."

"Sometimes baggy clothes can make someone look shorter and dumpier."

"Then I guess if we find him, we should look at his arms."

"ARRIVING AT ADDRESS 3447 Bellows Street," the GPS voice cooed.

Hudson turned off the device, but he left the screen on with the pictures of Jazz and Carlos, so Liz could refer to them if needed. He didn't have to; he had both of their faces memorized.

His first pass, he just looked over the building, driving by at a normal speed. The apartment once leased to Carlos and/or Jazz was typical of this neighborhood, a boxy, beige brick building sitting on a half-acre plot of dirt—no grass, no plants, and only one lonely tree that had lost most of its leaves.

"That's grim," Liz commented.

"Look. On the corner."

"Couple of working girls."

One was blonde and fair, one possibly Hispanic. "Check out the dark-haired one."

"It's not Yazmin."

Neither woman paid much attention to the car. They knew better. There were fine lines the working girls wouldn't cross if they didn't want to get busted. They let the customers come to them; they let the customers make the first mention of cash for sex. A cop wouldn't do that because it was considered entrapment. They could only arrest a prostitute if he or she actively "solicited" money for sex.

"I don't really expect to see her here," Hudson said as he turned a corner and rejoined traffic on a busier street. "Your client said she was a call girl. Since she was last seen in Conroe, that's probably where she lives now."

"She could be anywhere," Liz reasoned. "She probably knows you're looking for her, and she doesn't want to be found, so she won't be where you'd expect."

Hudson made a few more turns. "There, at the Quikki Market. Two more." One prostitute lounged against the wall talking on a cell phone; the other was leaning into the passenger window of a souped-up Mustang. "If only I had some flashing red lights, I could scare that guy to pieces. Or do you think the johns are victims, too?"

"You don't have to agree with me on everything," she said hotly. "But I don't appreciate being ridiculed. No, I have no sympathy for the johns." She shuddered, recalling a dozen stories she'd heard from her clients of violence and depravity. "Arrest as many of them as you want. Post their pictures in the newspaper. Make sure their wives and girlfriends know what they're up to so they can have themselves tested."

"I'm sensing a double standard." At her outraged expression, he had to laugh. "Sorry, I'm just giving you a hard time. We're on the same page regarding the johns."

"Oh, my God."

"What? Do you see Jazz?"

"Stop. Stop the car."

Hudson slowed down, but he didn't stop all the way. "Liz, what's going on?"

"That's Tonda Pickens." At his blank look, she added, "My client." She rolled down her window. "Tonda!"

A slim African-American woman, who looked way too young to be selling herself on a street corner, stared at their car in surprise. "Ms. Downey?"

"Hudson, stop the car!"

He knew he shouldn't, but Liz's command was so compelling, he did it anyway. "Liz, what are you doing?"

She ignored him and motioned for Tonda to come over.

The girl drew closer. "You're gonna get me in trouble."

"Pretend you're talking to a customer."

Tonda closed the distance between them and leaned on the car door. "Ms. Downey, what're you doing here? This isn't a safe neighborhood, especially in a car like this."

"Then it's not safe for you, either! I thought Jackson said you didn't have to work."

"I'm not doing the full...you know. Just..." She pantomimed an activity with her hand and her mouth that was unmistakable. "The baby can't catch anything that way."

"Well, it could, but I'm not going to argue that. Just—get in the car."

She looked over her shoulder, a frightened expression on her face. "I better not.... Jackson finds out I been talking to you... He's right over there, across the street. He takes down the license plate of any car I get into, for my safety."

"It's okay—this car won't trace back to me. Just get in. I'll pay you for whatever time you've lost."

Hudson finally couldn't contain himself. "Liz, this isn't part of the plan."

"Tonda, meet Hudson. Hudson, Tonda."

The girl reluctantly climbed into the car and Hudson put it in gear. "Who's he?"

"He's the one looking for Yazmin. Tonda, what if we took you someplace tonight where you'd be safe?"

"No. Ms. Downey, really, you shouldn't interfere."

"I could take you to a women's shelter. From there, we could relocate you to a different city. Help you find a real job, an apartment…"

"You're talking crazy. Jackson would kill you."

"Jackson won't know I had anything to do with it."

"Then he'd kill me. No. No way. You better give me my twenty bucks and drop me back where you found me."

"I just want something better for you, Tonda." There was a pleading note in Liz's voice. "For you and your baby."

"It's gonna be better. Jackson's gonna get us our own apartment, just the two of us. We're gonna be a family."

Poor deluded girl, Hudson thought.

Liz slumped in her seat. She reached into her purse and pulled out a stack of bills. "Here. Give Jackson a twenty and keep the rest for yourself."

Tonda took the money and stuffed it down her bra with a well-practiced move. "You tryin' to get me killed? Jackson finds out I'm holding out on him, I'll be in a world of hurt— Hey, that's Yazmin."

"What?" Hudson and Liz said together, peering out the windows and turning their heads.

"Not out there—on the screen."

"Oh," Liz said, sounding disappointed.

"If you're looking for her around here, don't bother. I heard she and Carlos aren't on good terms. He was really mad, said he was gonna cut her. She wouldn't dare show her face here." Tonda didn't wait for Hudson to return to the block where he'd picked her up. When he stopped at a light, she got out. "Thanks, Ms. Downey. But you're getting in too deep, coming 'round here."

She slammed the door and walked off in her platform shoes without a backward glance.

"Way to line her pimp's pockets," Hudson commented as they drove off. "I know you're trying to help her, and that's very admirable, but you need to be more careful. What if she goes back and tells her man about this? He could come gunning for you."

Liz waved away his concern. "She wouldn't rat me out."

"You can't know that for sure. If her man starts sweet-talking her… I mean, let's face it—she didn't get to where she is today because she's immune to a man's persuasive tactics."

Liz shrugged. She apparently wasn't willing to concede the argument, even though he was right.

Hudson returned to the address on Bellows Street that Mitch had provided, slowing down at the adjacent block. He found a parking spot and pulled the Lexus between a pickup truck, held together mostly by Bondo, and a brown '76 Monte Carlo missing all its hubcaps. In fact, every car on the street was missing its hubcaps.

Hudson retrieved his binoculars from the glove box. From here he had a good view of the apartment building. He was pretty sure he knew which door was apartment D.

"This might be kind of boring," he said.

"I'll just check phone messages."

"No, don't. In fact, you should keep your phone turned off. If a cop is following you, they can locate you from your cell-phone ping."

"Don't they need a court order or something?"

She was so naive in some ways. "We won't be here too long, promise. I just want to see if anyone is coming and going from that apartment."

He didn't have to wait long. After about five minutes, a woman in short-shorts, a tube top and thigh-high white boots approached the apartment building on the arm of an older man, probably in his sixties, dressed in khakis and a neatly pressed shirt.

"You horn dog," Hudson groused. "You should be ashamed of yourself."

"What?" Liz placed a hand on his arm as she leaned over, trying to see what he saw.

"Hold on. I got my sights on a working girl, and she's heading for our building with a john."

The couple paused at the bottom of the stairs. The man looked around in a paranoid manner, then reached in his pocket and pulled something out. That was when Hudson realized there was a third person, lurking in the shadows. The prostitute's manager. Hudson could just make out the glow of the tip of his cigarette, but nothing else.

The john handed the anonymous man something, then headed up the stairs with the hooker. They turned right and headed into apartment D.

"Bingo," Hudson said softly. "That apartment is still being used as a love nest. And I see someone who might be Carlos."

Hudson was itching to talk to the guy. He could pose as a john. With his sunglasses and baseball cap, he wouldn't be recognizable. He just wanted to size this guy up, maybe inquire about Jazz. He could claim to be one of Jazz's former customers, trying to hook up with her again.

Yeah, that would work. He'd played this role many times when he worked undercover stings on the Vice Squad.

Hell, what was he thinking? He couldn't leave Liz in the car by herself, and he sure couldn't take her with him. He put the car in gear.

"Wait, where are you going?"

"To take you home. I shouldn't have brought you here."

"Wait. Aren't we going to talk to that guy?"

"Another time."

"He might not be here another time." She unfastened her seat belt. "Let's just ask him if he knows where to find Jazz."

"You're not going anywhere!"

"Then you go. I'll lock the doors. I'll keep my phone in my hand. You'll be there and back in two minutes. It'll be fine."

His suspect was just a few feet away. He'd never be out of sight of the car. "Are you sure?"

"Of course I'm sure. I'm not a 'fraidy-cat when it comes to bad neighborhoods or scary characters. The bad boys aren't interested in victimizing anyone who doesn't make themselves an easy target."

He would never call Liz an easy target. "The car alarm has a panic button. Right here."

She nodded. "Go. Now."

Still feeling uneasy, he got out and locked the door with the key chain, gave her a little wave, then sauntered across the street as casually as he dared, keeping his eye on the man at the bottom of the stairs. He'd melted back into the shadows, but Hudson could see the top of his hat silhouetted against the lone porch light that still worked on the apartment building.

However, Hudson pretended not to see the man. He approached the staircase, then stopped and stared up at the second story, scratching his head as if he were confused.

"Can I help you with something?" The question was more of a challenge than a polite query.

"Oh. Hi. I was just looking for a girl named Jazz. I think she lives around here somewhere."

"Lot of people lookin' for Jazz," the stranger said, stepping closer. It was definitely Carlos. He wore a black leather blazer over his white T-shirt and jeans. In person he seemed taller than in his picture. His build was slender, but what there was of him looked solid. His hands were covered in scars, probably from fights. In addition to the scar visible in his mug shot, he had another one that split his lower lip, and yet a third on his neck. Guy obviously liked to get into knife fights.

"This is the right building, then? It's been a year or so since I saw her. The phone number I had for her is no good."

"Jazzy's not here. She took off coupla months ago, owin' me money."

"Damn, that's too bad."

"If you're looking for company, I know lots of ladies. Accommodating ladies. If you like Spanish, my friend Lola is just your style. She looks a little like Jazz. But younger." Carlos winked.

How to gracefully extricate himself? Any normal horny guy looking for a good time would gladly consider a substitute. "Party girls?"

Before Carlos could answer, a car alarm shrieked so loud Hudson jumped about a foot. At the same time his phone vibrated. He looked at the screen, then took off at a dead run. Liz was calling for help!

A guy was stooped down, stealing the rims off the Lexus, but all Hudson could think about was Liz. If she was hurt, he'd kill the son of a bitch.

"Hey, you!" The gun was in his hand before he realized it. He'd tucked it in the small of his back as he'd got out of the car, using a little sleight of hand so Liz wouldn't see it and get wigged out.

The guy grabbed the rim and ran like a weasel. That was when Hudson realized the thief had two confederates; each of them had a rim.

Hudson didn't waste time chasing them. It wasn't as if he could shoot them for jacking his rims, and they could have friends nearby. Besides, he was more concerned about Liz. He reached for his keys, but the door clicked unlocked before he could get them out. He yanked it open.

"Liz. You okay?'

"They surrounded me like piranhas." Her eyes were wild with fear. She grabbed on to his arm as he slid behind the wheel. "I'm sorry, Hudson—I hope I didn't spoil your investigation."

"Who the hell cares? I'm worried about you!"

"I'm fine. Really." She seemed to be making an effort to calm herself, but her movements were still frenetic as she checked all around them, trying to spot any imminent threats. "I just panicked. There were six or eight of them—"

"Six or eight? I only saw three."

"All but three disappeared the second the alarm went off."

"Jesus. I never should have left you here alone. What the hell was I thinking?"

"It's okay. Hudson, it wasn't your fault—"

"Of course it was my fault. I'm responsible for you. I should have trusted my gut. I'm so sorry. If anything ever happened to you I don't know—"

"It's okay. Nothing happened."

With every word they exchanged, they'd leaned in closer, speaking more and more softly until they were whispering. Finally there was nothing left to do except kiss her, and he did.

He'd forgotten how hungry her kisses could be, and how quickly she could produce a response in his body. He forgot what they were doing there; his universe shrank to the few cubic feet of air in the car and the feel of Liz's lips on his, her hand gripping his arm, his fingers tunneling through the silky strands of her hair.

They kissed for who knew how long until Hudson came to his senses and remembered where they were. They needed to get out of that neighborhood; in his current state of distraction, that gang could come back and lift out the whole engine and he probably wouldn't notice.

Reluctantly he pulled away from Liz with one final nibble to her upper lip. "We need to get going."

"Oh, um, right." She put on her seat belt while Hudson pushed the start button. The engine roared to life; that was good. Once they'd made it back to the main thoroughfare, Liz pulled down the visor and turned on the lit mirror. Hudson had to struggle to keep his eyes on the road rather than watching her repair her lipstick; every move she made was imbued with sex, and he couldn't figure out why. She couldn't touch him, even innocently, without calling to mind wrestling between the sheets, her fingernails pressing into his naked back. She couldn't clear her throat without his remembering the cute little noises she made when she was having an orgasm.

"How are we going to explain to Daniel about the missing rims?"

"I'll take care of it. I didn't even tell anyone you were coming with me tonight."

"Really? Why not?"

"I'd rather ask for forgiveness than ask for permission."

"Oh? You think Daniel, or Joe, would have nixed the idea?"

"No good reason for me to involve you. Despite what I said earlier, it's a risk every time we get together that someone will put two and two together."

"So then, why are we doing this?"

"I think that kiss said it all." He chanced a glance at her, but he couldn't quite read her expression. Anger? Irritation? Confusion?

"Adrenaline caused that kiss," she finally said, her voice prim.

Convenient explanation. But that didn't explain away any of the other times they fell into each other's arms. He could tell she didn't buy it, either. She was grasping.

"I just wanted to see you," he finally said, opting for honesty. They'd played enough games. "I can't stop thinking about you."

"You know, sometimes, when two people are involved in a high-stakes or dramatic situation, they bond. But once the situation is resolved…" She shrugged.

"Oh, okay, I get it. This is your social-worker mumbo jumbo for 'Once this mess is resolved our…mutual interest will disappear.'"

"I'm just saying we don't have a lot in common, other than we're trying to keep ourselves out of jail."

"You'd rather date someone from your own socioeconomic background."

"How in God's name did you reach that conclusion from what I said? Are you deliberately trying to provoke me?"

"Just trying to understand. You know, the mutual-interest thing happened before we knew we were in the same hot water. Unless you were pretending to like me."

"I wasn't pretending, then or now."

"But you never intended it to go longer than one night."

She didn't deny it. "It can't work in the long run."

"How do you know? Do you have a relationship crystal ball?"

"I know because I've studied hundreds of relationships. I even worked as a marriage counselor. I see what works and what doesn't. Two people who look at the world in completely different ways can't possibly make it work."

"Never? Not ever? There's never been a single healthy relationship where the two people looked at the world differently?"

"Well…I'm sure there might be exceptions. One or two."

"So who's to say we can't make it three? I'm not asking for a commitment here. But you're anticipating trouble that doesn't exist yet."

"Doesn't exist? All we do is argue."

"That's not all we do. In fact, I thought we got along pretty well that first night."

"Why are you doing this? Have you ever had a long-term relationship? Been married or lived with a woman?"

"Not yet. Haven't found the right woman."

"Well, I'm certainly not her."

How could she be so sure? He found their arguments oddly…stimulating. Maybe she'd intended last Saturday to be a one-night stand, a walk on the wild side. But he had a feeling it could be so much more.

Hudson kept driving, letting her stew. After a while, the silence grew awkward.

"You hungry?" he asked. "We could grab something to eat."

"I'm starving. I couldn't make myself eat much dinner, but now I'm ravenous."

"Adrenaline surges will do that. Burn up all your energy reserves, I mean. Let's go somewhere. Italian? Mexican?"

"We can't. You know we can't be seen together. How about if we go to my place and grab something?"

"You can cook?"

"No, I'll have my live-in chef whip up something." She laughed, breaking the tension. "Of course I can cook. Nothing fancy, but I can manage pasta or a frozen pizza."

"Sounds great." Now things were looking up. If Liz was inviting him into her apartment for dinner, chances were good he'd spend the night. No matter what sort of psychobabble she tried to throw at him, she couldn't hide that hungry look in her eyes. And she wasn't just hungry for pizza.

CHAPTER TEN

WHAT HAD ELIZABETH just done? Why had she invited him to come into her apartment? A late-night dinner, a glass of wine—she was definitely having a glass of wine after tonight's adventure—it was practically foreplay.

There were so many reasons she should stay away from Hudson Vale, and really only one for keeping him close: she was crazy about him. Even if they didn't have much in common, and even if the attraction would fizzle once they cleared their names and no longer had a common goal, she couldn't bring herself to tell him to stop with the kisses and keep things on a professional level. They might soon find themselves imprisoned for the rest of their lives, or even condemned, if the county prosecutor decided to throw in a conspiracy charge and turn it into a capital case.

Which reminded Liz of why they'd come here tonight. "Did you find out anything from the pimp?"

"No. He doesn't know where Jazz is, either. He said she owes him money. He also said other people have been looking for her, but I didn't get a chance to find out who."

"Ugh. All that for nothing."

"That's how police work goes. You talk to a zillion people, ask ten zillion questions—most of it goes nowhere. You just have to hope that lucky break is around the next corner."

"What about my dad's computer? Mitch said he'd get a ton of leads from it and I haven't heard a thing."

"He's still trying to break the security. Apparently it requires fingerprint recognition before it will open. Beth picked up some of your father's prints from the case, and the two of them are trying to make up a facsimile that will fool the computer."

"Sounds like James Bond stuff."

When they got to her building, she gave him her passkey to get into the parking garage. "Do you see anyone hanging around that might be watching my building?" There were cars parked up and down the street, at least half of them with dark-tinted windows.

"Could be anybody. At least I don't see the Subaru."

He parked his car in the space belonging to a neighbor who was out of town. He got out first, checking to make sure no one was lurking behind parked vehicles or one of the concrete support columns. Then he opened Elizabeth's door and took her hand as she exited the car.

He didn't let go of her hand. She used her passkey again to get them onto the elevator and they ascended to the fifth floor. This reminded her of when she'd been a teenager, sneaking around with her high-school boyfriend because she knew her father didn't like him. David had come to the house only once, when her father was traveling on business and the servants had gone home or retired to their quarters for the evening.

She'd thought they were being so clever. She hadn't realized then her father routinely reviewed the home's security-camera footage. The oddly sudden breakup had happened shortly after that night.

Elizabeth was embarrassed when they entered her apartment because those dead orchids still sat on her dining-room table, droopy and brown, dropping petals everywhere. She set down her purse, then moved to stand in front of the sad arrangement.

"It's time I retired these," she said decisively.

"You don't have to on my account. Grief has its own timetable, and I'm not judging."

"No, it's time."

"Why don't you go see about dinner. I'll take care of this for you. Okay?"

She liked that he didn't simply bulldoze over her wishes, that he waited for her to agree before he started stuffing dead flowers down the trash chute.

"Sure. Thanks. Pasta or pizza? Or I could bake a couple of chicken breasts."

"Whatever's easiest. I'm not picky."

She turned toward the kitchen. "Wine? I've only got white. That's probably not your drink of choice."

"I guess I'm easy to predict, huh?"

"You were drinking beer at the wedding."

"I'll take wine. I need to broaden my horizons."

Elizabeth actually found herself humming as she got out two wineglasses and opened a bottle of Pinot Grigio she had chilling in the fridge. Hudson had followed her to the kitchen, but only to get a trash bag.

He rejoined her a few minutes later, found the glass she'd poured for him on the breakfast bar and took a sip. "Not horrible. I bet this is some superexpensive wine, huh?"

"You have the funniest ideas about me." Deciding her leftovers wouldn't be enough to feed both of them, she'd put a pot of water on to boil. Now she opened a bag of rotini noodles and dumped them into the pot. She'd already put some seasoned meatballs from the freezer into the microwave. Now she added those to jarred sauce in a pan. "I get that wine at the grocery store. It's about five dollars a bottle."

"Oh. It's nice."

He was probably just being polite.

An awkward silence settled over them as she poked at the pasta with a wooden spoon. This was so wrong. He shouldn't be here. The stakes were higher than when she was in high school. She wasn't just risking getting a lecture from her father. Their lives hung in the balance.

Yet she couldn't bring herself to ask him to leave, to request that he contact her only through Project Justice. She craved him—and not just his body. For the first time in her life, she truly understood some of the urges that her clients claimed they couldn't resist, urges that got them into hot water.

Elizabeth's glass of wine disappeared in record time as she stood over the boiling pot, willing the pasta to be done. Hudson refilled her glass and then his own. Finally the timer beeped and Elizabeth turned off the burner and poured the pasta into a colander. She served up the rotini in large, shallow bowls with a generous portion of sauce and a sprinkle of Parmesan. Salad greens from a bag and bottled dressing completed the simple meal, which they carried into the breakfast nook, where a window afforded them a view of the city at night.

Hudson took a bite. "Mmm. Not bad."

"It's better than a frozen dinner and not much trouble to fix." She sampled the pasta and nodded appreciatively. She was glad to be putting some food into her stomach; the wine was already going to her head. Or maybe it was Hudson making her woozy. No meal was going to fix that.

"You like living in the city?" He gazed out the window at the festive display of urban lights outside.

"Yeah, I do. I like the energy of it. I have my privacy, but I also have people all around me."

"I can see the appeal. I mean, you're so close to everything. But I can't imagine living so far from trees and water."

Yet another thing that made them incompatible.

"I see the appeal of your place, too. But I'm not sure I could get used to listening to crickets all night long. I'm so used to sirens and trucks and helicopters."

He smiled at that. "Sometimes it's too quiet at the lake," he agreed, surprising her. "I never thought that until I had to spend a week there off work. I got pretty stir-crazy. There's only so many nature walks a guy can take before he goes bonkers. I even thought about getting a dog."

"I love dogs," she said wistfully. "I've thought about getting one, too, but it wouldn't be fair to leave it home alone all day."

"What kind would you get?"

"Something small, probably."

"One of those little dust-mop things?" He wrinkled his nose.

"Oh, I suppose you'd want a pit bull. Or a big, slobbery Labrador retriever."

"Actually, I think I'd get a boxer. We had a boxer when I was a kid. Her name was Dixie." He smiled fondly as he stared out the window, obviously revisiting his long-ago furry friend in his mind.

Elizabeth's heart flipped over. How could she resist a guy who liked dogs?

"You've got tomato sauce on your chin," she said.

"Hmm? Oh." He swiped at his face with his napkin, missing the spot altogether.

"Here." She took her own napkin, reached across the table and started to dab at the small spot of sauce. But before she could actually do it, the strangest urge overtook her. She stood and moved to stand directly in front of him, then slowly leaned down and kissed the sauce from his chin, perilously close to his mouth.

She heard and felt his sharp intake of breath. He was probably as surprised as she was by what she'd just done. But it didn't take him long to get over the shock. He pulled her into his lap and locked his mouth over hers.

The wine couldn't hold a candle to the intoxication of Hudson's kisses. It was even better than she remembered, being in his arms, sharing body heat, sharing the same breath. She could feel his pulse everywhere she touched him—his neck, his chest. It seemed as if their pulses were synchronized.

The kiss went on and on, and when she pulled away to gasp in some air, he kept kissing her, moving to her jaw, tickling her ear with his tongue.

"You are playing a very dangerous game, missy," he said in a voice that was oddly strangled.

"It's no game." Nothing she'd done in the past five minutes was calculated, and she couldn't bear it if he thought that. "I just seem to lose all self-control where you're concerned."

"I'm a little short on control myself." He grabbed her ponytail to hold her steady and kissed her again. Though he stopped short of hurting her, she couldn't miss the command in his gesture. She had awakened a potentially dangerous sexual animal. Turning back now was out of the question. Pandora's box was wide-open and all sorts of trouble had just come flying out.

Hudson moved his chair back from the table, and Elizabeth repositioned herself to straddle him. The pressure of his erection between her thighs sent currents of electric pleasure coursing through her whole body. He slid the zipper down on her shirt—just as she'd fantasized—and pushed it off her shoulders, then brushed his lips against her collarbone. Even that simple gesture was ridiculously thrilling.

"I'm betting," she said between kisses, "that you're a man with a condom in his pocket."

"Why do you think that?" He didn't confirm or deny.

"Because if a guy senses even the smallest chance that he might get laid, he does whatever he can to up the odds."

He made no reply to that, choosing instead to dip his head and press soft, warm lips against the tops of her breasts. Her nipples tingled in response, hardening inside her bra so that she wanted to rip the garment off. She almost did.

"So, do you?" she prompted. Truth was, she had condoms, too. She'd bought some the day after her fling with Hudson simply because she never wanted to be caught without any protection, though she hadn't seriously dated anyone in a long time.

When she'd made the purchase, she'd fantasized about finding herself in just this situation. But she didn't want Hudson to know that. This thing between them, whatever it was, was too new, and she would be the first to admit she was too inexperienced to know how to handle it.

Case in point: an hour ago she'd told him she wasn't interested in continuing their relationship—or whatever it was. Yet here she was.

"What if I don't?"

"We'll cope— Oh, do that again."

"What, this?" He brushed his fingertips along her nape, soft as a dragonfly's wings.

Her whole body went liquid. "That's the thing." Without meaning to, she pumped her hips back and forth, increasing the friction against her clit. If she wasn't careful, she would come apart right here at the breakfast table, fully clothed. Well, almost fully clothed. The shirt was gone, though she didn't remember him taking it off. She sat there in a sinfully sexy, shell-pink bra she'd carefully selected because it always made her feel feminine.

And because it had matching panties that were held together at the hip with nothing but tiny satin bows. Oh, Lord, maybe she hadn't consciously planned this, but on some level she must have known it was going to happen.

Warmth pooled between her legs, and if she didn't get her clothes off in the next thirty seconds they were going to combust.

He pulled the elastic band out of her hair, his actions gentle despite his obvious impatience. Once her hair was free, she shook her head and it fell around her shoulders. He pressed his face into it.

"You smell like a fresh-fruit stand—did you know that?"

She took that as a compliment.

"Bedroom?" she squeaked.

"Now you're talking." With what seemed like very little effort he stood, carrying her with him. She wrapped her legs around him and locked her ankles and kissed him the whole way to the bedroom. He didn't require directions; it wasn't a big apartment, and knowing Hudson, he'd probably scoped it out while she was busy in the kitchen.

He nudged the bedroom door open with his foot and moved through the darkened room as if he'd been there before. Two more steps and she found herself on her back on the bed with Hudson a welcome weight on top of her. Her senses were filled with him—the smell of his skin, the feel of his demanding mouth on hers, the soft, springy texture of his hair as she dug her fingers through it.

Quickly he found the front clasp of her bra and brushed the garment aside. Just enough ambient light streamed through her window that she could see the contours of his face and neck, and she knew he could see her, as well. She wanted to be naked for him. With a wantonness that shocked her—still—she wanted him to see her head to toe. She wanted to see appreciation and raw lust in his eyes, the way he'd been the first time they were together.

Apparently he had the same thought, because moments later he was tugging her shoes off, unzipping her jeans. She accommodated him by lifting her hips off the mattress as he slid jeans and panties down her legs. So much for the matching lingerie; he'd have to appreciate that some other time.

Would there be another time? No, she couldn't worry about that now. They were together in this moment, and though she had no guarantees he wouldn't walk out the door in an hour or two never to return, she was going to give this her all. No playing it safe.

She shrugged out of her bra while Hudson peeled off his own clothes lightning fast, hurling them all over the place, though his gaze never left her. He was breathing hard by the time they were both finally naked.

"Liz…"

"What?" She wasn't sure what she wanted him to say, but she wanted to know what he was thinking.

"Nothing. I just… I'm overwhelmed by this, by you. I never expected…"

"I know—me, too. Try not to overthink it."

"Making love to you is like standing in a hurricane-force wind and trying to grab on to it."

She reached up to caress his face. Who knew the tough cop with the surfer-boy looks could be so poetic? "Ride it out," she said with a grin.

He grinned back. "I will. Don't rush me."

"A hurricane can last for hours and hours."

Hudson lay down next to her and pulled her on top of him. He kissed her until she was dizzy and gasping for air; he ran his hands from the top of her head to the tops of her thighs, pausing to grasp her bottom and squeeze her cheeks, then tried to span her waist with his hands.

"You feel fragile," he said between long, insistent kisses. "I'm surprised you don't break, the way I manhandle you."

"I'm stronger than I look." And he'd been nothing but gentle with her. Insistent, commanding, but always gentle. To prove she was no china doll, she rolled over and pulled him on top of her, relishing the feel of his whole body, hot and hard, in contact with the length of her, his impossibly hard arousal pressing against her belly. Her womb contracted, sending ripples of pleasure up and down her body, a precursor to the pleasure peaks she craved.

Where was that condom? Had he left it in his pants pocket? Then she spied it next to the pillow. She reached to the side and grabbed it, then tore open the package behind Hudson's back as he nuzzled her neck and nibbled her earlobe.

"What're you doing?" he asked, sounding mildly curious

but unwilling to be distracted as his kisses moved toward her breast.

"The condom. I'm ready."

"Don't rush me." He locked his mouth onto her right nipple and suckled, swirling his tongue until he brought the rosy bud to an almost-painful peak. But not truly painful. The sensation made her squirm with delight.

Wasn't it the man who usually rushed? It was, at least in her limited experience. How novel to make love with a man who knew the meaning of foreplay. The whole nature of this evening was different than their first time, when they hadn't known each other. He was letting her see more of his personality, and she was far less guarded. She'd been a brazen hussy at the wedding, but that was something of a facade, giving her the false courage she needed to seal the deal with what she was sure would be a one-night stand. Tonight she was less on guard, and her enjoyment had at least doubled.

He might not want to rush, but she needed to feel him inside her. She was going to burst into tears if he didn't fulfill that need pretty damn snappily. With that in mind, she reached down and grasped his erection.

His gasp of momentary surprise was gratifying.

"Remember, I'm the hurricane," she said with a wicked grin.

"You sure as hell are."

"If you want to play some more, you can do it after you see to my pleasure."

"I thought I *was* seeing to your pleasure."

"You're driving me insane is what you're doing." She playfully pushed him off her and onto his back, then quickly sat up and straddled his thighs. He laughed at her antics as she poised the condom over him, but the laughter died into a groan as she slowly sheathed him, taking her time despite her own impatience. When all was properly in place, she raised up on her knees, intending to lower herself onto him.

"Uh-uh, I get to ride the storm." Before she could blink he had her on her back again, proving any advantage she thought she had over him was pure illusion. He inserted his hands between her thighs and opened her like a flower, dipping his head to give her one feathery kiss and a flick of his tongue, a simple gesture that stole all the air out of her lungs.

He was good.

Hudson took his time entering her. She was beyond trying to exert any control. He was firmly the master of this dance now, and she was the one along for the ride, letting him take or give pleasure however he saw fit.

She felt every delicious inch of him as he buried himself inside her, and she gloried in the tense expression on his face as he fought for control—not of her, but his own body. She wrapped her legs around him, pulling their bodies even closer, and he kissed her long and hard once again.

Then he started to move.

Every thrust was a revelation. Just when she thought it couldn't get better, it did. She was genuinely high, as if she'd taken a powerful drug. The whole room spun like the craziest amusement-park ride ever. She was vaguely aware that she cried out, but she had no control over that at all. She was exploding in a warm, syrupy orgasm like nothing she'd ever imagined. Wave after wave of pleasure crashed over her.

When Elizabeth finally opened her eyes again, Hudson was drooped over her, perspiring as if he'd just run eight blocks to catch a bus during the height of a Texas summer. She was damp, too, their skin slicking together.

"Oh…my…" she finally managed. It seemed some kind of profound words were called for, but she couldn't begin to find them.

"Guess I should have taken that storm warning a bit more seriously."

They were like a couple of survivors, except instead of a

disaster, they had weathered the most pleasurable thing she'd ever experienced.

Hudson slowly withdrew from her—even that felt good to her ultrasensitized flesh—and rolled onto his back. He slid one arm behind her and drew her against him into a sweet snuggle. Neither of them said anything else for a long time. There really didn't seem to be any words that could sum up what had just happened. Maybe it was because they both knew this might be their swan song, that nothing lasting could occur between them for so many reasons. Or maybe they were just uniquely, biologically matched to produce the most intense earthquake of a sexual experience in the world. Whatever, Elizabeth didn't try to analyze or compare or predict. She just pressed the side of her face against Hudson's chest and listened to his heart as it gradually slowed to something close to normal.

Curious, she pressed two fingers against her own carotid artery. Their heartbeats were perfectly in sync. She smiled, wondering if it meant anything or if it was just coincidence.

He ran his palm against her upper arm. "What?"

"Hmm?"

"You're smiling."

How could he know that? He couldn't possibly see her face from where he was. "It's silly," she said. "But I was noticing that our hearts are in sync."

"Entrainment."

"What?"

"When two people sit near each other and stare into each other's eyes, their hearts will start to synchronize. It's called entrainment."

"All it takes is staring?"

"That's what I hear."

They'd gone way beyond staring. No wonder they were entrained. "How long does it last?"

"I don't know. I just heard something about it on NPR one time."

"You listen to NPR?" She thought National Public Radio would be too cerebral for a cop to be interested.

"You have the strangest ideas about me," he said, echoing what she'd said earlier to him. "I like flamenco, but sometimes I listen to NPR. Sometimes I listen to country music and sometimes hard rock and sometimes the shock-jock-du-jour."

"I am learning not to pigeonhole you." She closed her eyes, reveling in this sweet, lightweight postcoital banter. It seemed so incredibly...normal. If she could make love to Hudson every night and talk to him like this for ten minutes afterward, she'd be the happiest woman on earth.

Wow, where had *that* come from? Dangerous thought. Good sex and banter did not a healthy relationship make.

"You hungry?"

"What do you think? I barely ate two bites of the nice dinner you fixed, and now it's probably stone-cold."

"I have a microwave."

She grabbed a satin robe from the closet while Hudson dragged on his jeans, going commando. She quickly heated up their dinners, and they sat on the floor in front of the TV with their plates on the coffee table and watched a hilariously stupid '80s sitcom.

The whole scene was so blessedly mundane, Elizabeth wanted to capture it and trap it in a jar, where she could take it out and examine it whenever she wanted. But the nature of such moments was fleeting; perhaps that was why they were so special.

Once their stomachs were full, they stumbled back to the bedroom, shed their clothes, fell back into bed, and Hudson made good on his intention to take his time. She felt no impatience this time; she was content to let him explore the terrain of her body any way he liked. Every once in a while she gave him a languid caress along his rock-hard thigh or muscular back, but mostly she was lazy and let him play. He seemed to enjoy giving her pleasure in imaginative ways—licking, kissing, blowing, squeezing—and all of it was good, so good.

When they made love again, it was a slow, sensual dance rather than a race to the finish, but no less satisfying. The only moment of tension Elizabeth felt—besides the expected, good kind—was when they were done and she waited for that inevitable moment when he made his excuses and left her bed. It was no less than she deserved after the way she'd acted their first night together, though she doubted Hudson was spiteful that way.

It probably would be better if he left under cover of darkness—less chance he'd be recognized as he slipped to his borrowed car.

But he didn't leave.

She fell asleep as content as she'd ever felt, idly wondering if this was that thing human beings chased after, this sense of completeness.

It wouldn't last. It couldn't, and she was as prepared for that likelihood as she could be. But for now, it was enough.

CHAPTER ELEVEN

HUDSON WAS DRAWN out of a deep sleep by the annoying song from his Project Justice phone. He opened his eyes, felt a moment of panic when he didn't know where he was, then remembered and relaxed. Dawn was just beginning to break, and the soft morning light through the unshaded windows revealed Liz sprawled in the bed like a true hedonist, on her stomach with her limbs pointing out in four opposite directions, her face in the pillow, her gorgeous mop of hair a cloud of silk around her head and shoulders.

His phone was in his jeans pocket. He got out of bed carefully so as to not wake Liz. By the time he got to his phone it had rolled to voice mail, but he saw who was calling—Beth, the scientist who ran the lab at Project Justice. She was also Mitch's wife.

His gut tightened, and he tiptoed out of the bedroom before returning the call.

"Beth? Did you call?"

"Oh, right, I did just call you." She sounded a little sleepy and distracted, as if she'd been up all night working in the lab.

"Is something wrong?"

"You said you wanted to know right away when I got results on that watch."

Hudson rubbed his eyes and glanced at the antique mantel clock. "At six in the morning?"

"Oh. Sorry, I didn't know it was that early."

"You've been working all night?"

She paused before answering. "It's how I foil morning sickness. I stay up all night."

That made him smile. "Congratulations."

"Thanks." She lowered her voice to a whisper. "No one else here knows yet. Anyway, I didn't realize it was quite that early. No windows in the lab."

"So what did you find out?"

"Well, the material you spotted is definitely human blood."

The tightness to his gut returned. "Did you test it for DNA?"

"It was a pretty small sample, but yeah, I got a partial profile. It's pretty close to Elizabeth Downey's...but not an exact match. It probably belongs to a close female relative."

"Like her mother, for instance? She doesn't have any sisters that I know of."

"Yes, it could be her mother. But it was a tiny amount of blood. It could have come from something as innocent as a scratch on the wrist, even a mosquito bite."

Or it could have got on the watch when Holly Mandalay was murdered by her own husband. It was a dark, horrible thought, not one Liz would welcome. But didn't she deserve to know what had happened to her mother?

"Does this have a bearing on the Franklin Mandalay murder case?"

"Not directly. At least, not that I know of. I know I shouldn't use Project Justice resources for something unconnected to the case, but I can't help feeling it might be relevant."

"I won't tell if you won't. Daniel's not chintzy with resources. He's always saying that the clue that solves the case can come from an unexpected source. What do you think is going on here?"

"Elizabeth's mother disappeared when she was a teenager. Officially, it looked like a case of abandonment. Money was withdrawn from her bank account, her purse and her car disappeared." Hudson had learned that much by reading old newspaper articles found on the internet. "But personally, I think that bastard Mandalay murdered her. Maybe she was threatening divorce, maybe she wanted to take Liz away from him. I don't know. But if she'd abandoned the family, she would have taken her watch with her. Instead, it was locked in a wall safe."

Hudson heard a noise. He looked up to see Liz standing in the doorway, stark naked, with the most awful expression on her face.

"Thanks for calling, Beth. I'll get back to you."

"You're wrong," Liz said.

"You weren't supposed to hear that."

"He didn't kill her. He couldn't have done that. I know he did some bad things, but he loved his family. It tore him to pieces when she left."

"Forget I said it, okay? It's probably not true. I'm a cop, and my mind likes to work itself around crimes. I'm probably wrong."

"You don't think you're wrong at all. You're just saying that to placate me."

He started to deny it, but he could see in her eyes that she'd pegged him perfectly. He couldn't lie to her; it would only compound the problem.

"It's something I have to look into," he said.

"Why? It has nothing to do with my father's murder."

"We don't know that. We don't know what's significant and what's not."

"You decided to follow a meaningless clue because you're morbidly curious. And you have some ridiculous idea that you'll give me closure by finding my mother.

"Well, I don't want closure. I don't want to know what happened to her, okay? Just leave it alone." She turned and disappeared into the bedroom, slamming the door.

Hudson scrubbed his face with his hand. Damn. That hadn't gone well.

Maybe he *was* morbidly curious. But figuring out the Mandalay family history might help him learn more about what made a man like Franklin Mandalay tick. What motivated him? What sort of criminal elements would he mix with, and why?

No matter what Liz believed, he was going to pursue this lead. He simply wouldn't do it around her.

He heard the shower going a few minutes later. Though he'd fantasized about joining Liz under the warm spray, he guessed that wasn't going to happen. This was his cue to find the rest of his clothes and put them on. He'd worn out his welcome.

Liz made an appearance a few minutes later, dressed in jeans and a sweatshirt bearing the logo of the clinic where she worked. She still looked incredible, even with no makeup.

Hudson was already dressed and had spent a good five minutes trying to figure out how to use her complicated coffeemaker. Surely some caffeine would ease this awkward situation.

"I tried to make coffee, but I don't have a doctorate in nuclear physics."

That brought a slight smile to her face. "It's a ridiculously complex machine, but it does make good coffee."

He stood aside as she proficiently added beans to the grinder, then filtered water. She adjusted levers and dials, and soon lights began blinking and the thing started hissing. She set a mug under the spigot just in time to catch the dribble of coffee the wicked machine produced. He had to admit, it smelled good. But he'd probably imposed on Liz enough.

"I really should go."

"I don't mind fixing you coffee," she said. "I went a little sideways for a minute there, but as you can probably tell, the subject of my parents pushes a lot of my hot buttons."

She was making quite an effort on his behalf, and he appreciated that. But that guarded look in her eyes hadn't been there last night. She'd lost confidence in him because he'd suggested the unthinkable. She wanted to believe the man whose DNA she carried had some goodness in him; Hudson, on the other hand, seemed anxious to discover the worst.

That must be how it looked to her. Hudson would be hard-pressed to earn back her goodwill.

Well, hell, it had been nice while it lasted. He never should have tasted the forbidden fruit. Until last night, he'd never known he could feel such happiness. And until this morning, he hadn't known he could feel such disappointment—with the world at large, and with himself.

She set the mug in front of him, along with a small carton of half-and-half. He creamed the coffee and took a sip. "Good stuff. But I probably should go."

She didn't argue. "I'll walk you down. You need a key to get into the garage." She found her purse and dug around for the passkey. "Whenever you're ready."

He nodded. He wasn't exactly ready, but now was probably better than later, before he gave in to the temptation to defend his actions. She didn't want to hear his theories. She didn't want to hear anything that contradicted her fantasy version of her mother's fate. He would give her that…for now.

After checking that the hallway was empty, they walked to the elevator, but it appeared to be stalled somewhere above them.

"Probably someone moving in or out," Liz said. "Let's just take the stairs."

"Are you going to work today?" he asked as they trotted down five flights of concrete steps.

"Yes. It's best for me to keep busy."

"Be really careful, okay? We're rattling cages. The real murderer could be getting nervous. In fact, why don't you call in sick?"

"No. That's cowardly. I've done nothing wrong and I won't hide. I figure I'll just go about my business, and whoever is watching me will get bored." At his worried look, she added, "I'll keep my office door locked. I'll be fine."

When they reached the door to the garage, Liz slid her passkey through the card reader.

"Wait. I don't like how this feels."

"Me neither, Hudson, but you can't take it back. You found my mother's blood on that watch, and you can't undo that."

"A goodbye kiss, at least?" he wheedled.

She wavered. "You know what that can lead to."

"In a parking garage?" Sensing surrender, he leaned in to kiss her. She melted against the door. She tasted of coffee and some kind of sweet lip balm, and he sank into the kiss, wanting to prolong it as long as possible. He pressed his body against hers, and he could feel her heart beating against his.

Together. Entrainment.

The door opened suddenly and she lost her balance; Hudson held her and kept her from falling. Just then a bright light shone right in his face and a strident voice demanded, "Sergeant Hudson Vale, did you spend the night with the murder victim's daughter?"

HUDSON JUST STOOD THERE, frozen like the proverbial deer in headlights, but Elizabeth went into action. She yanked Hudson back inside and pulled the door closed as fast as she could, nearly smashing a helmet-haired TV reporter and her cameraman in the process.

"No comment!" Hudson yelled just before the door snicked closed. For a few moments, he and Elizabeth just stared at each other in stark terror, gasping for breath.

"How did they know?" he demanded of no one in particular.

"It doesn't matter. They know." She turned and retraced

their steps through the basement. What else could she do except bring Hudson back upstairs to her apartment? She couldn't throw him to the media wolves.

"We'll claim mistaken identity," Hudson said decisively. "If I can get out of here somehow, Project Justice will create an alibi—"

"The camera was three feet away. You weren't even wearing the hat and sunglasses, and I was in your arms. There is no way out of this. We can't deny it."

"Well, don't get mad at me."

"I'm not mad at you. I'm mad at the world, the fates, and I'm mad at my father for getting himself killed at such an inconvenient time. If I didn't know better, I'd think he did it on purpose just to get us in trouble."

"I know he was a major manipulator, but not even Franklin Mandalay would go that far just for spite."

Halfway up the stairs, Elizabeth ran out of steam and sank onto one of the steps, leaning against the wall. "Hudson, what are we going to do? However bad things looked before, they look a hundred times worse now."

"We'll call Daniel Logan."

"Are you kidding? He specifically told us not to be seen together. He's going to be furious, and I wouldn't be surprised if he dumped the case."

"He wouldn't do that. Once he commits the foundation to seeking the truth in a case of injustice, he sees it through to the end."

"Until today," she muttered. "Look, don't call Daniel. Call Joe. See if he can defuse the situation."

"Yeah. Yeah, that's a good idea."

Once they were back in her apartment, Hudson used his silver cell phone to call Joe. Elizabeth needed to keep her hands busy, so she toasted some bagels while listening with one ear to Hudson's conversation. He outlined the situation in the least inflammatory terms possible, leaving out any particulars as to why, exactly, Hudson had been in Elizabeth's apartment at seven in the morning. She had no doubts Joe would draw his own conclusions.

"We can do that," Hudson said. "Sure. Right. Thirty minutes. Got it." He disconnected, then took a long sip of the coffee Elizabeth had set in front of him on the dining-room table.

"What did he say?"

"How do you feel about leaving the building in a garbage container?"

"Seriously?"

He grinned. "No. We need to be down in the parking garage in thirty minutes. Joe will make sure it's cleared of reporters, then we'll get in a car and he'll take us out of here. You need to pack a bag with whatever you might need for a few days, but don't sweat it too much. If you forget something, it'll be provided."

"Where are we going?"

"Daniel's house. It's secure and comfortable, and you'll be safe there until…"

"Until the police come for us?"

Hudson's mouth thinned into a grim line. "I'm trying really hard not to consider that."

She handed him a plate with a bagel smeared with cream cheese, and he leaned up against the kitchen island to eat it. "Thanks."

"It's no trouble."

"I feel like I should buy you some groceries. You've been feeding me—"

"Please."

He shrugged.

Elizabeth took a bite of her own bagel. It tasted like cardboard. She forced herself to chew and swallow. "They're going to come for us. They're going to haul us in and question us. I'm frankly surprised they haven't already." She took a sip of her own coffee, then carried it toward her bedroom. "I'm going to pack."

"They can't haul us in and question us if they can't find us."

"I don't intend to evade the police."

"I do." He followed her, but paused at her doorway. She didn't blame him—everything in this room screamed that they'd had wild sex—the rumpled sheets, Elizabeth's clothes from last night still on the floor. Even the scent of sex lingered in the room.

As quickly as she could, she dragged an overnight case from her closet and stuffed it with a few underthings, some shirts, a pair of black jeans and a nightgown, one dress, just in case. In the bathroom she grabbed a toothbrush and at the last minute a bottle of Advil. She had a feeling she was going to need it.

She called work and told them she had to take the day off for personal reasons. Gloria didn't even question her. Elizabeth didn't like shirking her duties, but if the cops *and* the press were stalking her, she couldn't bring that kind of scrutiny to the clinic. Even if she wasn't there, reporters might try to get information out of Gloria and other coworkers. She warned Gloria not to talk to anyone asking questions about her.

"Of course not, sweetie," Gloria said in her best mother-hen voice. "You know we take privacy seriously around here."

While she'd been on the phone, Hudson had stood next to the picture window in the breakfast nook, staring out at the city coming awake.

"Liz, who would your father confide in?"

"He never was one to have close friends. I don't recall him being chummy with neighbors or golf buddies—nothing like that."

"What about staff?"

"He always treated the staff like, well, like servants. Underlings. I can't imagine him… Well, except for Mrs. Ames. She's the only one who's been around a long time. Since before my mother died, actually. I think he had a bit of a soft spot for her."

"And how did she feel about him?"

"She used to urge me not to think badly of him, that he was under a lot of pressure."

"So she made excuses for his bad behavior?"

Elizabeth nodded. "She didn't hate him or anything. Maybe she even understood him a little."

"A servant like that probably would be the soul of discretion, yes?"

"Absolutely. Mrs. Ames would never talk to the press."

"What about the police?"

"She probably wouldn't lie to the police outright. But if it involved my father's public image or reputation, she might not be completely truthful."

"Would she be more forthcoming with you?"

Elizabeth thought about that for a few moments. "Possibly."

"You need to talk to her, then. Domestic workers know a lot more than most people give them credit for. They overhear conversations. They see what's in the trash, the mail. They see who comes and goes, and when."

"So I need to find out who my father was talking to, who might have come to the house, when he was coming and going…right?"

"And if anything at all unusual was going on, even if it seems unimportant."

She nodded. "Okay. I'm sure she'll help me if she can. She's a good woman, and I don't think she wants me to go to prison for a murder I didn't commit."

Hudson's silver phone rang. He answered briefly, then nodded. "They're in the parking garage."

"They?" Elizabeth's stomach swooped and she envisioned Daniel joining them, and what his reaction might be.

"Not sure who Joe meant by *we*. Guess we'll find out."

Joe met them at the parking-garage door. "Coast is clear. There aren't any security cameras in the garage, though given the rent you're paying, Elizabeth, there should be." He led them to a Lincoln Town Car with tinted windows, where two strangers leaned against the doors. Strangers who bore a striking resemblance to Hudson and Elizabeth, at least in terms of their height, build, hair and skin tone.

Elizabeth barked out a laugh. "Seriously? You're going to pull a switcheroo?"

"You get in the car and change clothes with Mandy," Joe said, as if he did this kind of thing every day. "When you're done, Hudson will change with Matt. We'll send your doppelgängers out the front door and into a limousine. They're going to claim they were the ones the reporters saw earlier today."

"How did you find the doubles so quickly?" Elizabeth asked. "How is this going to work? They don't even live in my building."

Joe grinned. "They do now, at least temporarily."

"I've learned it's best not to question how Project Justice makes things happen," Hudson said. "Just accept it and be grateful."

Elizabeth had no choice but to go along, though she feared she was digging herself deeper and deeper with every deception she perpetrated. She should have just been honest with the cops from the beginning. This was her fault. Her fault for playing her little game with Hudson in the first place; her fault for thinking she could sleep with him with no one being any wiser. She should have known better. Like her father used to say, there was no free lunch. Everything had a price. She just wasn't sure how high this price was going to rise.

CARLA ENTERED THE station, feeling gritty-eyed and slow despite having drunk the majority of a venti latte—never mind doctors' orders. She and Knightly had stayed out late last night—first, following the Lexus Elizabeth Downey had climbed into. Then, when the driver had lost them at the train tracks, Carla had insisted on parking near Elizabeth's apartment building again and waiting until she reappeared.

They hadn't waited for long. The Lexus had returned in little more than an hour. It had swung into the parking garage, disappearing beyond the reach of their curious eyes. Carla had tried to follow, but the guard at the entrance gate hadn't been impressed with her badge.

"Private property," the Goliath of a guard had pronounced. "Sorry, Detective, but you'll need a warrant."

So Carla and Knightly had watched. And watched. And watched some more. They'd stayed until after midnight, when Knightly had insisted they give it up. She'd reluctantly agreed. Her kids were pretty responsible, but she still didn't think it was right to leave them home alone late at night.

Carla had tried to find someone to take over the surveillance, but budget cuts being what they were, no one was available. So Carla had called someone else—someone who came in handy when she wanted a certain tidbit leaked to the public without anyone knowing where it came from.

Knightly was already at work, of course. She doubted he'd ever been late a day in his life. He was staring at his computer, his eyes bugged out.

"What's up?" she asked as she dropped her suitcase-sized purse on her desk.

"You were right."

"What? Who?" She moved to stand behind Todd and look over his shoulder. He was watching one of the local channels' internet feed.

"Vale. And Downey. Apparently we weren't the only ones keeping an eye on those two."

"Reporters?" She tried to screen the delight out of her voice. Her ploy had worked better than expected.

"So it really was Vale in the Lexus?"

"You'll see. They're about to run the story again—I just saw a teaser."

Carla didn't have long to wait. During the next segment, they played a short film clip of a couple sort of falling through a metal security door, then quickly pulling back through again. The reporter said with a deep voice of authority that the two people were, in fact, Hudson Vale and Elizabeth Downey, two "persons of interest" in the Franklin Mandalay murder case. Two people who had no reason to know each other.

"That was awful fast," Carla said. "And kind of blurry. Are we sure it was them?"

"I'm sure." Knightly sounded really sad. Poor idealistic schmuck. He'd never liked Hudson. In fact, he'd been just as annoyed as Carla with Hudson's laid-back attitude, and probably a little jealous of the way women fell all over him. But apparently Knightly was serious about the police brotherhood, the "blue line" and all that macho stuff. He actually felt bad that one of their own was dirty.

Knightly had got up to refill his coffee cup from the department sludge pot when the "special report" slug-line appeared.

"Hey, Todd, you better come back and watch this."

He was beside her in an instant. "What the hell?"

A new film clip, being broadcast for the first time, showed a couple emerging from Downey's apartment building who appeared to be Downey and Vale. At first. They wore the same clothes as the couple who'd been briefly filmed in each other's arms through a gap in a metal security door. But on closer inspection… "It's not them."

"No way! It was Vale in the earlier footage. Hell, you saw him. He was your partner…. Didn't you recognize him?"

"It did look like him," she conceded. "But the clip was so short and I only got a glimpse. I couldn't say for sure, a hundred percent."

"It was him. I'm not crazy, and I don't want it to be, but it was."

"Then let's subpoena the footage from Channel 4 and get a better look at it to find out."

"Why don't you just ask him?"

"Who, Vale?"

"Yeah. He'll tell you if it was him or not."

"And you'd believe him? Just like that? A guy who probably killed someone? To protect his own skin, a man will lie, Todd. But that film clip will tell us the truth."

Carla's phone rang, and she returned to her desk while Todd kept watching the news, scowling. Hudson's cubicle was across from hers, a visual reminder of his absence.

On the fifth ring she picked up the receiver. "Sergeant Sanchez."

"Hi. It's Mina."

Mina was one of Carla's confidential informants. Over the past couple of days, she'd put some feelers out. Fingers crossed, but one of them was about to pay off.

"Yes, how can I help you today?"

"I know where Jazz is holed up. What's it worth to you?"

A lot. But she was only authorized to offer twenty. "Forty." Hell, she'd kick in twenty of her own. She'd been looking over the alleged police-brutality case against Hudson, and she was intrigued by this character, Jazz, whom Mandalay had, according to Hudson, been talking to in the convenience-store parking lot.

Mandalay had tried to downplay it, but the mystery woman had dropped the money and run. The money had been collected as evidence. All indications were that Hudson had been telling the truth about what he'd seen. Which meant everyone knew Mandalay had been involved in something shady.

Carla intended to find out who knew what. Talking to Jazz would be enlightening.

A few minutes later she concluded the conversation, pleased with herself. This information was golden.

Todd was on the phone, apparently trying to get some judge to issue a subpoena that would compel the TV station to hand over that video footage. She waited until he was finished talking, then tapped him on the shoulder.

"Todd. I have a lead on Jazz."

He looked at her blankly. "Who?"

"Jazz," she repeated patiently, recalling that her partner wasn't as familiar with the excessive-force case as she was. "The woman Mandalay was paying off when Hudson arrested him?"

"Oh." Todd waved his hand dismissively. "Doesn't matter whether Hudson was telling the truth or not—he still has a motive. So, disproving his story is a waste of your time."

"Waste of my time?" Was he joking? "She's a potential suspect. Or a witness. Don't you want to know why he was paying her off?"

"He was talking to her a week before the murder. I'm just not sure it's connected."

"But it could be. I thought you'd be interested in something that might lead away from Vale. Anyway, we can't let anyone think we've rushed to judgment where Vale is concerned. We have to be open to all evidence."

He thought about that. "Yeah, okay. Let's talk to her. I'd give anything if we didn't have to arrest one of our own. His behavior reflects badly on the whole department. But we can't delay arresting him much longer. We have a duty to the community."

Please. She was pretty sure she'd never been that idealistic.

Carla collected her gun, holster, jacket, purse and the rapidly cooling latte. "Let's roll."

CHAPTER TWELVE

HUDSON BELIEVED HE now knew what it felt like to be "kept." He'd been given a room at Daniel Logan's estate that was nothing short of luxurious—inch-thick carpeting, an antique bed with a down comforter, and…was that a gilt chandelier? He felt like the proverbial bull in a china shop. He was afraid to touch anything.

A change of clothes had been provided, too. They fit perfectly.

He had no idea where Daniel had stashed Liz, but it was probably on some other wing of this massive house. Hudson hadn't seen Daniel face-to-face since the press debacle, but he didn't look forward to it. He'd known seeing Liz was a risky proposition, but he'd gone over it in his head, and at the time it had seemed as if there was only an infinitesimal chance anyone would witness them together.

Now the risk he'd taken seemed foolhardy, putting both himself and Liz in a terrible position. He'd also risked losing the support of Project Justice, though the fact that Daniel had brought them here was a good sign. If only Hudson didn't have to face the formidable billionaire.

A discreet knock sounded on the door. Hudson opened it to find Elena, Daniel's long-legged personal assistant, standing in the hallway.

"Daniel said to tell you lunch would be served on the sun porch in ten minutes." Her husky voice had the barest trace of an accent. Hudson thought he remembered that she was from Cuba. "Thanks, Elena."

She turned and walked smoothly down the hall in her stilettos, her hips swaying invitingly beneath her snug skirt. Before he'd met Liz, Hudson would have pursued Elena, or at least flirted with her. But Liz had spoiled him for all other women. He'd always been a major flirt; he wondered if he'd ever get that back. Maybe after Liz was out of his life for good.

Hudson ran his fingers through his hair and called it good enough. It would take the better part of ten minutes to find his way to the sun porch in this labyrinthine house.

When he finally found the right porch, Liz and Joe were already there, sipping lemonade and chatting amiably. A surge of jealousy pulsed through Hudson's body. Joe was a good-looking guy. He had that clean-cut, Special Forces look that made Hudson seem scruffy by comparison.

And Joe wasn't a murder suspect.

Knowing he was blowing things out of proportion, Hudson tamped down the jealousy, pasted a neutral expression onto his face and strolled in, pulling out a chair that was neither too close, nor obviously far from Liz and straddling it. "Hey."

"You get situated okay?"

"Yeah, sure."

A woman around forty with short red hair entered with a fruit platter and set it in the center of the table. The arrangement of berries, kiwi and melon was a work of art; everyone stared at it, but no one touched it. What Hudson really wanted was a burrito from his favorite Tex-Mex hole-in-the-wall bulging with shredded pork, cheese and spicy chorizo. He'd eaten half of the bagel at Liz's, but that hadn't scratched the surface of his hunger.

Liz finally spooned a few berries into a crystal bowl and nibbled at them, to be polite, Hudson guessed.

"Did you let them know at work you won't be in for a few days?" Joe asked Liz.

She nodded. "My boss was very understanding."

The redheaded woman returned with another platter, this one piled high with tortilla wraps—roast beef, turkey, cheese, vegetarian, chicken salad. Hudson grabbed one of the beef ones. He poured himself a glass of lemonade. The sunny, cheerful room, with its tall windows and colorful Saltillo tile, should have been relaxing, but Hudson felt tense as a cat. Maybe involving Project Justice was the wrong thing to do. He wasn't accustomed to someone else calling the shots, especially when it came to saving his own neck. He had leads to check out.

Finally, when the redhead brought in a delectable dessert tray with everything from double-fudge brownies to tapioca pudding, Daniel made an appearance. Dressed in khakis and a soft blue golf shirt, he still looked intimidating.

"Sorry to make you all wait," he said affably. "I've been talking to the sheriff."

Hudson had already grabbed a brownie and taken a bite; now he almost choked on it. "Sheriff Brooks?"

Daniel nodded as he took a seat and examined the dessert selections, finally choosing one of the puddings. "Although we often butt heads with law enforcement, I don't deliberately antagonize them. We depend on their cooperation and goodwill. Besides, Mark Brooks is a friend of mine."

Meaning Daniel probably made a generous contribution to his campaign fund.

"I just wanted to give him a heads-up. Didn't want him thinking you were purposely evading police scrutiny, Hudson. I explained that you were my client, and that I'd brought you here to prevent the press from dogging your every step."

Hudson's stomach knotted at the thought of the sheriff—a stern, uncompromising man—having Hudson's difficulties waved in his face. "So Sheriff Brooks knows that Liz and I…"

"Not at all. Liz's name didn't come up."

"How could he not know?" Liz asked. "I'm sure that clip of us at my apartment building has been on the news by now."

"It has been," Daniel confirmed. "So has the other clip of our stunt doubles."

"All due respect, Mr. Logan," Hudson said, "but even if you've created some momentary confusion with the look-alikes, it's a short-term solution at best. Knightly and San-chez are probably getting a warrant for that video footage as we speak. The county lab has ways to analyze the footage, blow it up six feet tall frame by frame. They'll compare it to my picture, and that'll be that."

"Not if the footage has been accidentally…misplaced." Daniel flashed a slight smile as he let that sink in.

Hudson was astounded at the man's sheer gall. Daniel could be charged with obstruction of justice. As a cop, Hud-son would be furious. As a suspect, he was…relieved. Grate-ful. Sanchez and Knightly might suspect Hudson and Liz were in cahoots, but they couldn't know for sure that they knew each other. Or at least, they couldn't prove it…yet.

"Okay." Hudson took another bite of his brownie.

Something tickled his foot. He drew back reflexively, his reptilian brain thinking a cat, or some other animal, had brushed up against him. Then he saw the gleam of danger in Liz's eye and realized with a start that it was her. She wasn't playing footsie with him, much as he wished that were true. She was warning him to chill out.

Unfortunately, her actions were having the opposite effect. Seeing her only a few feet away, so elegant even dressed down as she was, and all he wanted to do was touch her, hold her. Kiss the hollow of her neck like he'd done last night. Provoke her into crying out with pleasure. The fact that he couldn't was torture. Now the simple pressure of her bare toes against his instep had him squirming in his chair.

"So what else is happening?" Daniel asked. "Can I get an

update? I'm aware that Mitch is trying to break the encryption on the laptop you found. In fact, he's downstairs in my office—he wouldn't even stop for lunch. We were working on it together, but so far we haven't found a way in."

Hudson pulled himself together enough to tell Daniel about his encounter with Carlos the previous night, carefully leaving out Liz's participation. "So the address we have for Jazz is old."

"Is that when the Lexus lost its wheels?" Daniel asked, more curious than angry.

"Um, yeah. Sorry about that."

Daniel shrugged. "I'll get new ones."

"So, we've got leads on the prostitute, Jazz, or Yazmin," Hudson said. "We're looking for a man with a fish tattoo on his arm. Liz is going to talk to her father's housekeeper, Mrs. Ames, to see if she noticed any events out of the ordinary. I'd like to sit in on that. All due respect to Liz, but she's not trained in interrogation."

"I'd like that, too," Liz put in.

"Okay." Daniel regarded him expectantly. He wanted more, and unfortunately, Hudson didn't have much else to report. The investigation was stalled in the water.

"Once Mitch gets into that laptop," Hudson added, "I'm sure we'll have a lot of new leads. And, well, my father is talking to some old friends, retired cops who might know something about the, um, Holly Mandalay disappearance."

Daniel squinted. "That happened, what, ten years ago?"

"Fourteen," Liz said in a clipped voice. Her foot had been lightly resting on his. She withdrew it.

Hudson hadn't wanted to mention the matter again in front of Liz, but he felt he needed to justify himself to Daniel.

"You think there's a connection?" Daniel asked.

"Without elaborating, yes. Call it a hunch." He glanced quickly at Liz and back to Daniel. Daniel seemed to get it.

"Okay." Daniel didn't force Hudson to explain further.

"I'm sending a team with metal detectors to your house. I'll need you to show me on a map where you think your house-breaker's stray bullet might have gone. He fired at you with a handgun?"

"Yeah. A thirty-eight or a 9 mm," Hudson said, irritated that he hadn't thought of this route himself. If they could find the bullet, and match it to a weapon stored in the police ballistics database—he wouldn't ask how that was done—it could help them identify Fish Tattoo man. He was the closest thing they had to a viable suspect in Franklin Mandalay's murder.

"You have a car at your disposal. Joe can drive—he's former Secret Service, trained in protection, marksmanship, evasive driving. If he starts throwing orders around, I suggest you follow them."

Hudson nodded, though again, it irked him not to be calling the shots. But if he wanted the benefit of Daniel's expertise and billions, he had to give up some of his autonomy. He recognized that, but that didn't mean he was happy about it.

Liz nodded, too.

"I don't want to tie your hands, but it would still be better if the two of you aren't seen together. That would add fuel to the media fire. You do see why I cautioned you not to appear together in public?"

"Yes, Daniel, we get it," Liz said. "Really, we do. I'm sorry we did something so stupid."

Daniel shrugged. "Everybody makes mistakes. Live and learn." He'd taken two bites of the pudding and set it aside; now he chose an apple from the dessert tray and started peeling it with his pocketknife.

The tightness in Hudson's chest eased. They were getting off easy. From now on he would take Daniel's warnings seriously.

Mitch chose that moment to appear, his arms full of what looked like enough electronic bits to build a robot. "Daniel, you won't believe—" He skidded to a stop, blinking owlishly behind his glasses at Hudson and Liz. "Oh, y'all are still here?" he drawled.

"I did mention they were staying here indefinitely," Daniel said mildly. "What won't I believe?"

"Huh? Oh. The—"

"Is that my father's laptop?" Elizabeth asked with some alarm.

Mitch looked embarrassed. "Oh, yeah. Don't worry, Ms. Downey, I'll put it back together good as new. Except—it won't have anything on the hard drive."

Daniel appeared a tad impatient. "What are you saying, Mitch?"

"I have tried every low-down dirty trick I know to crack this encryption. Then I tried one of your gadgets, and it worked. Or I thought it did. I thought I was in, till I got this black screen that said Unauthorized Access in flashing letters."

"Is that the same thing as the blue screen?" Hudson was familiar with the dreaded blue screen from the computers at work. It meant the computer had suffered some kind of meltdown and it would take a genius from IT to bring it back.

"This is worse," Mitch said. "The data self-destructed. The drive wiped itself clean. So did the backup drive. I can't bring it back. I can't get anything. I'm sorry."

He looked so crestfallen, Hudson almost laughed. He guessed Mitch wasn't used to failing when it came to outsmarting computers. But then the implications hit him, and the urge to laugh abruptly left him. He'd been counting on something from that computer providing a solid lead. Now they were back to square one.

Liz looked as if she wanted to cry, and Daniel pinched the bridge of his nose. "All you can do is try, Mitch. You gave it your best shot, working on it all night. Why don't you find a bedroom upstairs and get some sleep? Take the rest of the day off."

Mitch nodded glumly.

Daniel continually surprised Hudson. The press portrayed him as a driven businessman, determined to always get what he wanted. Hudson had expected someone more ruthless. With a temper, maybe. But Daniel seemed to him exceedingly fair-minded, respectful of his employees' time and energy. He could have blown his top over the debacle with the photographers this morning, but he hadn't raised his voice. Although Hudson had to admit, a single, quelling look from those dark, penetrating eyes could freeze his blood faster than any tirade.

AFTER LUNCH, ELIZABETH and Hudson went to her father's house to talk to Mrs. Ames. Joe drove them in one of Daniel's many spare cars—another Lincoln Town Car with heavily tinted windows. Hudson sat up front with Joe, talking to him about guy stuff, for which Elizabeth was grateful. She wasn't sure how to deal with Hudson anymore. Her body still tingled from the memory of their unbridled lovemaking. Yet now a huge gulf separated them.

It had to do with her father, and what Hudson thought he'd done. That alone was enough to make her tense with anger. But it was only symptomatic of the real problem. Hudson had a dim view of humans as a species. He apparently thought people would devolve to their most base instincts if laws and cops weren't in place to keep them in line. Elizabeth felt just the opposite; she believed people were basically good, and they wanted to be good. It was often terrible circumstances that drove them to commit crimes.

Not that she would make excuses for whoever killed her father. Nothing could excuse that, except perhaps self-defense, but her father wouldn't actually physically assault anyone.

No, he would send one of his shady goons for that.

All this made her head hurt.

"So," Hudson was saying, "Daniel said we'd have drivers

who were, like, trained in high-level security and evasive driving. Is that you?"

Joe shrugged one muscular shoulder. "I'm former Secret Service. I guess that's me."

"Presidential detail?"

"First Lady. Spent a lot more time than I ever wanted to at tea parties and library luncheons and charity fundraisers."

"Still, it must have been something, carrying that responsibility. Were there ever any threats?"

"More than I can count. Most of them bogus—bomb threats, usually. I was tense all the time and bored at the same time. Job gave me an ulcer. I like working for Project Justice better."

So the Secret Service explained his clean-cut look and disciplined demeanor. But she recognized a broad streak of mischief and humor in him, too. Though Daniel didn't enforce any particular dress code, today Joe wore a sharp blue suit, crisp white shirt—and a tie festooned with neon-pink flamingos. He couldn't do *that* at the Secret Service.

Soon enough they arrived at her father's estate. Elizabeth exited the car and punched in the code, and the wrought-iron gates swung open.

Sadness engulfed her again as she climbed back into the car and it glided down the driveway. It was so weird, knowing her father wasn't inside the house. He'd driven her insane with his obsessive need to control her life when he was alive, but now that he was gone, she found herself missing him. They hadn't even released his remains for burial; she couldn't imagine what the police were waiting around for. It wasn't as if his cause of death was in question.

She hadn't given much thought to what she might inherit from him. It was too overwhelming to imagine herself the master of all his money and business interests. In a way, she hoped he'd left it all to charity, but what were the chances of that?

"You grew up here?" Joe asked as Elizabeth let them in the front door with her key.

She swallowed back the tears that threatened and tried to appear normal. "Yup. I had a pretty skewed view of the world until I got out on my own."

"Mmm, I smell cookies," Hudson said. "Unless I miss my guess, peanut butter."

"That would be Mrs. Ames. She's been cooking and baking nonstop since my dad died. She says she wants to use up the groceries before they go bad, but I think it just keeps her mind off things when she stays busy. Mrs. Ames?" Elizabeth called out. "We're here!"

She'd called earlier to warn the housekeeper they were on their way to talk to her about her former boss. That alone had probably been enough to prompt a frenzy of baking.

"In here, sweetie," Mrs. Ames called back in a wavery voice. She wasn't old—maybe in her late fifties or early sixties. But she dressed in the manner of an earlier generation, and her demeanor was that of someone older. She'd been working for the Mandalay family since she was a teenager, first for Elizabeth's grandparents, then her parents.

Today she had on a cotton dress with a full skirt that reached almost to her ankles and a pair of what looked like orthopedic army boots. A frilly white apron protected her clothing. Her hair, a mixture of once-fiery red and dull gray, was gathered into a tight bun at her crown. She wore rimless glasses that habitually slid down to the tip of her nose when she was working.

"Hello, sweetie. I'd hug you but my hands are all floury." She wiggled white-coated fingers in the air. She was clearly in the process of baking more cookies.

"I'll hug you, then." Elizabeth walked over to the housekeeper and slid an arm around her shoulders for a squeeze. Mrs. Ames hadn't exactly been like a mother to her when her own mother disappeared. She hugged a lot, but there were clear boundaries between servant and employer that she wouldn't cross. She'd been a sympathetic listener but never tried to tell Elizabeth what to do, other than the cautious advice to cut her father some slack.

"Introduce me to your friends," Mrs. Ames said. "Then you can all help yourself to those cookies on the rack. They should be cooled down by now."

Elizabeth performed introductions, leaving out any reference to titles. If it was easier for the older woman to believe Joe and Hudson were merely friends, Elizabeth would humor her.

"Oh, man," Hudson said, his mouth half-full of cookie, "these are outstanding. Is this your recipe?"

"My grandmother's, actually," Mrs. Ames said with a twinkle in her eye.

Honestly, Elizabeth thought, *some advertising agency could make millions hiring Mrs. Ames to sell cookies.*

"All of the women in my family are bakers."

Hudson covertly nodded to Joe that he should eat a cookie, probably wanting him to get on Mrs. Ames's good side. Reluctantly Joe grabbed one of the morsels and took a bite. "I'm training for a marathon and I'm not supposed to be… Whoa, these are good."

Elizabeth ate one, too. Although her problems were too complex to be fixed with a cookie, the way they could be when she'd been a little girl and skinned her knee, the sweet-and-salty taste threw her back to a time when things were so much simpler.

Still, she couldn't afford to wallow in sentimentality. She had a job to do.

"So, Mrs. Ames, I told you on the phone that we wanted to ask you about my dad."

"I'm happy to cooperate any way I can, but I can't see how it could help. The police already asked me lots of questions. So many questions." She leaned against the counter for a moment, the weight of her grief etched in the lines of her face. "I can't imagine there's anything we didn't cover."

"I'm sorry," Elizabeth said. "I know this is painful."

"For you, too, I'm sure," Mrs. Ames murmured.

"It's just—you know the police think I had something to do with Dad's death."

"Ridiculous. That's why I don't watch TV or read the paper. Those reporters are just looking for a sensational headline."

"It's not just the reporters. I really am a suspect. Hudson is, too. Our only hope is to find out who really killed Dad. And to do that, we have to find out what he was involved in."

"He certainly didn't confide in me about his business dealings or personal life."

"But you were in a position to see who he met with, or who he talked to on the phone—"

"I'm not a snoop," she said indignantly. "I have an impeccable reputation. I was once offered a job at the governor's mansion.... Did you know that? But I stayed here. Your father treated me very well, and what kind of person would I be if I betrayed his trust?"

"Mrs. Ames," Hudson said, "we understand that you wouldn't intentionally violate Mr. Mandalay's privacy, but surely you don't want his daughter wrongly accused of his murder while the real killer walks free. You must have let in his guests sometimes, didn't you? As part of your job?"

"Yes, of course. It was my job to make his guests feel welcome." Her cookie sheet was full of little mounds of flour-covered dough. Shortbread cookies. Elizabeth's mouth watered.

"So who came to see him? Your answers don't violate his privacy. He's in a better place now where he doesn't have to worry about what anyone thinks of him. And your answers could help us bring his killer to justice. You want that, right?"

Mrs. Ames frowned. "Of course. Mr. Mandalay didn't en-

tertain a lot, but he did have a guest now and then. His lawyer, Mr. Pine. The occasional, um, female friend."

"These female friends," Hudson said, smoothly taking
over the questioning, for which Elizabeth was grateful. She
had no idea how to ask these questions in a way that wouldn't
be offensive to someone who'd changed Elizabeth's diaper
when she was a baby. "How many were there, in the past
year, let's say? Did he have one particular girlfriend, or a
bunch of them?"

Elizabeth wouldn't have believed a woman Mrs. Ames's
age could blush, but she did. "Well, more than one. But not
more than five."

"Five?" Elizabeth couldn't help saying.

"Were these young women?" Hudson asked. "Or more
women his age?"

"Always younger," she said with a disapproving frown. It
was the closest Elizabeth had seen to the housekeeper criticizing her boss.

"And was there one in particular that he seemed to favor?
One that came more often than the others?"

"I only saw one of his dates more than once. Very pretty
girl. Spanish. Dark eyes and hair. I think he liked her because
she looked a little like his late wife. Mrs. Mandalay, God rest
her soul, had an exotic look about her, too, though I'm not
sure where that came from."

"Would you recognize this lady friend if I showed you a
picture?" Hudson asked. He was already digging through the
messenger bag he'd brought with him.

"I imagine. But surely you don't think a sweet little thing
like her could commit murder."

"People can surprise you, Mrs. Ames." Hudson pulled out
a picture of Yazmin and showed it to Mrs. Ames.

"Oh, yes, that's her, though I must say it's not a very flat-
tering picture. She should have gone to Glamour Shots."

"That's because it's a mug shot," Hudson said. "Your boss's girlfriend was a prostitute."

Elizabeth flinched at the bald truth. Why did Hudson have to state it so harshly? But Mrs. Ames just thrust her chin out and looked Hudson in the eye.

"That's patently ridiculous. Mr. Mandalay would never date a prostitute. With his money and good looks, he was an attractive catch for any girl. Why would he pay for companionship?"

"Some men find it easier than working on a real relationship," Hudson answered as he reached for another cookie.

Fast as a mousetrap, Mrs. Ames grabbed the cooling rack and moved it out of his reach. "That's enough cookies. I'm donating these to the homeless shelter. You wouldn't want to take food away from hungry, homeless people, would you?"

"No, ma'am." Hudson had clearly got on her bad side. She wasn't going to be very forthcoming with information if he continued to rub her nose in the fact that her beloved employer was engaged in some pretty slimy activities.

"Let's move on," Elizabeth said briskly, shooting Hudson an I-dare-you-to-stop-me look. "Besides the lawyer and the girlfriends, who else came to the house? What about workers? You know, gardeners, repairmen."

"Oh, well, I know all of the people who do the maintenance. There's Rosa, the girl who helps me clean, and several gardeners—Bill, Paolo, Ramon and…oh, that one I don't like. He's rude and he smokes when I've told him a number of times that smoking isn't allowed anywhere on the grounds."

"Can you give us full names for the ones you do remember?" Hudson prompted.

Mrs. Ames complied. The first three she'd named had been working on the estate for years. "I wish I could remember that fourth one's name. He's only been around for the past few months. Actually, I haven't seen him since Mr. Mandalay passed. But I knew when I first laid eyes on him that he was a shifty type, that he wouldn't be around long."

"Do you have payroll records?"

"Mr. Mandalay handled that himself. He was very particular about how the grounds were kept. He personally hired and paid the gardeners."

"This other gardener whose name you can't remember," Hudson said. "What did he look like?"

"Dark. Short. Very stocky, but a little bit gone to fat. And all those tattoos—revolting."

"What kind of tattoos?" Hudson was suddenly on edge.

"On one arm he was just covered all the way to the wrist with odd images—writhing serpents, devils, a human heart with a knife in it." She shivered with revulsion.

"And the other arm had this big mermaid. The tail started on his hand and then it was scales all the way up until... Well, she was bare-breasted. Right on his upper arm. You could see it when he wore a tank top to mow the grass."

Hudson looked at Elizabeth, but she wouldn't meet his gaze. Mrs. Ames had just identified Fish Tattoo man. Which meant her father undoubtedly had some connection to the break-in and possible attempted murder.

Elizabeth didn't want to know this, damn it.

CHAPTER THIRTEEN

IT WASN'T LIKE Elizabeth to stick her head in the sand, but couldn't they discover who killed her father without digging into the sordid details of his life? When they brought this unknown perpetrator to justice, the details would all come out. Her father's reputation would be ruined, and he wasn't even here to defend himself.

"Elizabeth," Mrs. Ames said, "is something wrong? You look like you just took a bite of a bad apple."

Elizabeth shook off the bad feelings. "No, I'm fine." No sense tarnishing the man's image in Mrs. Ames's eyes. That would come soon enough.

Impulsively, Mrs. Ames grabbed a tin of cookies she'd packed up earlier and handed it to Elizabeth. "Here. Take these to work with you," she said gruffly. "I know a lot of your patients are poor and they might like some home-baked goods to munch on— Oh." Her eyes opened wide. "Munch. I remember hearing someone call the gardener by that name."

Hudson flashed a big grin. "Thank you, Mrs. Ames. You've been very helpful." And that was their cue to leave. It was clear what needed to be done now; Jazz and Fish Tattoo man, aka Munch, *had* to be found.

"I'm not going in to work for a while," Elizabeth said, sliding the tin of cookies back toward their maker. "You should probably just give these to the food bank."

When they got back to the car, Hudson climbed into the backseat with her. "Are you okay?"

"No, I'm not okay. My father tried to have you killed."

"If this Munch character had wanted to kill me, he easily could have," Hudson reasoned. "He was ten feet from me."

He was humoring her. "Then why was he there?"

"We'll have to ask him when we find him. And we *will* find him."

And when they did, what other horrible facts would be uncovered?

"Look, just because your dad was involved in some criminal enterprise, it doesn't mean he was a murderer," Hudson said.

"What about my mother? You think he killed her."

"I'd like to know why he had her jewelry when he reported it missing. Maybe it was something as simple as insurance fraud. But I'm not going to jump to the conclusion that he killed her." Not out loud, anyway.

"I don't want to know. In fact, I think I should go back to Daniel's and… I don't know. Paint my nails and get a massage. You and Joe can do the detective thing. I'm clearly not cut out for it."

Hudson didn't argue with her. Instead he took her hand and pressed it between his, letting her know in a way more powerful than words that he understood her pain.

"If my father did send someone to kill you," she said, "or even just rough you up, I shouldn't be surprised. There's something about his history you should know."

"Okay."

"The reason we're estranged—the reason I cut him out of my life—is that he wouldn't stay out of my personal life. He scared away every boy who tried to date me. The first one, he just glared at. That was enough.

"The second one, he paid off. The third one…" She could hardly bear to admit this, but Hudson should know. "He was tougher. It was my first year of college. My dad tried to pay

Darren off, like he did the boy in high school. But Darren had family money. A bribe didn't tempt him.

"Then a couple of thugs attacked Darren in the street, beat him up. They broke his arm. Darren reported it as a mugging. But next thing I know, he's blocking my calls and moving across the country.

"I refused to admit it to myself at the time, but somewhere deep inside, I knew. I knew my father had sent those men to beat up poor Darren."

Elizabeth's phone rang. She didn't want to talk to anyone, but she checked to see who it was anyway.

Tonda.

Suddenly she could hear her own heartbeat in her ears. Though Elizabeth had given Tonda her personal number, the young woman had never called her before. It had to be something important.

"Tonda. What's wrong? Did Jackson hit you again?"

"No, no, it's nothing like that. I'm fine. But I… Are you alone?"

"Yes." She hated to lie, but she sensed Tonda wouldn't tell her what the problem was if she thought someone else might overhear.

"I found Yazmin."

"Tonda. I told you not to get involved—"

"I didn't do it on purpose. I saw her. She was in a coffee shop wearing sunglasses and a big hat, and I knew it was her."

"Where was this coffee shop?" Yazmin would be long gone by the time they got there, but at least Tonda's tip might narrow down the area of town where she was hanging out.

"That don't matter. Do you want to talk to her or not?"

"Well, yes, I do, but—"

"She's scared. I told her you might be able to help. She said she would talk to you. But only you. You can't bring anyone— not that cop you're hanging with, for sure."

"Wait a minute. Is Yazmin with you now?"

"Yes."

"Where are you?"

"Only if you promise you'll come alone."

"I promise." She would figure out how—somehow.

"We're at the Galleria Mall. Come up the escalator near the cinnamon-bun shop. When you get to the top I'll call you back and let you know where we are."

Damn. Tonda was serious. No chance of showing up with Hudson and Joe in tow. Jazz would bolt.

"Okay. It'll take me a half hour or so to get there. Please, please wait for me."

"We will."

When she hung up, she found Hudson looking intently at her. "What was that?" He'd apparently been able to tell, just from her demeanor, that it wasn't a run-of-the-mill phone call.

"Tonda."

"The one we talked to last—"

"Yes. She's with Yazmin. Jazz."

"That's great! Where are they?"

"She wants to talk, but only to me. No cops. No anybody."

"What? Oh, come on."

"Tonda trusts me. I guess that's good enough for Jazz."

"Too bad. She has to talk to us."

"No, she doesn't."

"Just tell us where she is. We'll scoop her up."

"Not to put too fine a point on it," Joe said, proving he'd been listening despite trying to look as if he wasn't, "but we have no authority to 'scoop her up,' as you put it. About the best we could do is call the cops on her. She is a person of interest in the Mandalay murder."

"And trust Sanchez and Knightly to question her? Knightly would probably start quoting the penal code at her. Then he would lecture her on the evils of prostitution. And if he hadn't bored her to death by then, he *might* ask her what her business was with Mandalay."

"What about the other detective? Sanchez."

"I thought Carla had my back. But she hasn't done me any favors. I don't…" This was hard for him to admit. "I don't trust her. I think she wants to see me behind bars."

"No matter how evil or incompetent the cops are," Joe said, "we can't illegally detain Jazz. Project Justice skirts the law sometimes, but Daniel draws the line at kidnapping."

"It *sucks* not having a badge," Hudson grumbled.

"So I'll go talk to her. It's in a public place—nothing will happen to me."

Hudson shook his head. "People are killed or kidnapped in public places all the time."

"I appreciate your wanting to protect me, Hudson, but this is my life we're talking about as well as yours. I have to go talk to this woman."

"Over my dead body will you go talk to her alone. God only knows what she's involved in—"

"You can't order me around! Where do you come off—"

"Have you forgotten that there's a murderer out there who might just be trying to stop us from finding out the—"

"I'm very aware, thank you very—"

"Children, children," Joe interrupted. "Simmer down back there. I think I have a solution. Elizabeth, I'd be okay with you talking to Jazz in a public place, provided you wear a wire. And you let Hudson and me stick somewhere close by."

Elizabeth mulled this over. "Okay, I can deal with that." She was betraying Tonda's trust in her—a little bit. But her intention wasn't to double-cross Jazz or get her in any kind of trouble. They needed information—that was all.

"Where are we going to get a wire?" Hudson asked. "Do they have that kind of stuff just lying around at Project Justice?"

"As a matter of fact, yes. But we don't need to worry about that. Elizabeth, do you still have your silver phone?"

"Yes…"

"It's preloaded with an app that allows you to leave an open channel while the phone appears to be off. It also has a supersensitive microphone, as good as any dedicated mic you'll find the police using. Just stick your phone in a pocket. We'll hear and record every word that's spoken."

"I don't like this," Hudson said.

"Stop being a mother hen," Elizabeth groused as she dug around her purse for the silver phone.

Hudson raked his fingers through his already-tangled hair. "She needs a code word. Something she can say that will let us know she's in trouble—if she sees a gun or something."

"I'm really scared," Elizabeth said.

"You should be."

"No, that's the code. Something I might naturally say if I sensed trouble. If I go shouting 'Mayday' or 'Rumpelstiltskin,' they'll know I'm signaling someone. If you hear me say, 'I'm really scared,' you have my permission to burst in with guns blazing."

"That'll work," Joe said. "Now. Where are you supposed to meet Tonda and Jazz?"

She told them. She just hoped she could trust them both not to betray that trust. If Joe and Hudson were humoring her with this phone-app business, she was going to strangle them both.

"I'm at the top of the escalator now," Elizabeth said, though she was pretty sure Joe and Hudson could see her. They'd entered the mall about three minutes after she did. Hudson had on his sunglasses and baseball cap that made him look like a drug dealer, but at least he wasn't immediately recognizable. When she'd seen that they were inside the mall, she'd headed for the escalator.

Her phone rang—her regular cell phone. "Hello?"

"We're in the Saturday's restaurant. At a booth in the back."

Elizabeth oriented herself, spotted the popular chain restaurant. "Saturday's, I see it." She wanted to be sure Hudson and Joe heard her destination. "Be there in a minute." She turned the phone off and hid it in the bottom of her purse, then stuck the silver phone in her jeans pocket.

They'd tested the microphone app briefly in the mall parking lot. The results were amazing.

Elizabeth slid past the hostess, waving as she spotted Tonda. At last, she was going to meet the elusive Yazmin, aka Jazz. Tonda moved over to make room for Elizabeth.

"Yazmin, I'm Elizabeth Downey. Thank you so much for talking to me." She extended a hand to the tall, painfully thin woman who hid behind a huge floppy hat and sunglasses. Despite the disguise, Elizabeth recognized her from her mug shot.

Yazmin didn't accept her handshake. "I know who you are." She sounded just this side of hostile.

Elizabeth supposed she couldn't blame the woman for being so distrustful. She'd probably been taken advantage of her whole life by people in power, people who were bigger, stronger and richer than she was.

"I appreciate you agreeing to this meeting." Elizabeth tried again. "It's so important—the police think I might have killed my father. I'm just trying to find out what really happened to him."

Yazmin peeked around the side of the booth. "You swear you came alone?"

"It's just me." Sort of. Elizabeth would pay penance for her lies later.

"Before I tell you anything, why are the cops looking for me? I didn't do anything."

"Cops are looking for you?" Maybe Hudson had underestimated his former colleagues' intentions. Maybe they really were turning over all stones.

"Someone named Sanchez. Mina, who used to be a friend,

told this Sanchez person where I was staying. But another friend tipped me off to what Mina had done. I got away."

"No one's trying to railroad you, Yazmin," Elizabeth said gently. "Everybody—us, the cops—are trying to find out who killed my father. So unless you did it, you have nothing to worry about."

"I don't know anything." It seemed like something automatic that Yazmin would spout when she felt threatened.

"But you did have business with Franklin Mandalay, right? You were seen arguing in a parking lot a week before he died."

"We was just doing business. You know."

"There was more to it than that. He was trying to give you money. You didn't want to take it."

Tonda raised her eyebrows. "You didn't want him to pay you?"

Elizabeth put her hand on Tonda's knee, trying to quiet her. This interview was difficult enough without interruptions.

"I guess that cop saw everything."

"He's my friend. We're both in trouble."

"What do you need from me?"

"You knew my father. You've been to his house. He was involved in some criminal activity that might be connected to his murder."

Yazmin took a long time before answering. "Okay, but you didn't hear this from me. Got it?"

Elizabeth nodded. "I have no intention of getting you in trouble. Not unless you pulled the trigger. You didn't, did you?" As if she would say, "Yes, I did."

"Would I be here if I'd killed him? I'm terrified."

"Why? Is someone threatening you?"

"There's some cop looking for me. Isn't that enough? Wouldn't they just love to pin a murder on someone like me? Easy sell to a jury."

Elizabeth couldn't argue with her.

"Look, here's the deal," Yazmin continued. "Your papa had a lot of girls on his payroll. Girls like me."

Elizabeth nodded her understanding while swallowing down bile. She'd known her father hired prostitutes; she hadn't known he managed them.

"He all but ruined King C, my...manager. Lured the girls away with promises of medical insurance, protection, credit-card processing, legal help—but in return he was asking for a lot—complete control of all of our money. He controlled everything—our work hours, what we wore, where we worked, our customers. Anybody who didn't fall in line got a visit from Guido."

"Guido?"

"That's what we called him. I don't know his real name. Had a big tattoo on his arm of a—"

"A mermaid?" Elizabeth finished for her.

Yazmin nodded. "You know him?"

"Trying to find him. He tried to kill Hudson."

"Oh, my Lord," Tonda murmured, her eyes big as quarters. "I seen that guy talking to Jackson not a month ago."

"The day Guido broke a girl's ribs, I decided to call it quits. I didn't want to work for Frank and I didn't want my ribs broke. That's when I moved out of Carlos's crib. Went to Conroe. Got most of my business through the internet, though when times were slow I still could work a corner with the best of 'em. Thought I was safe, but he found me."

Elizabeth was sick. She didn't want to know this about her father, but she knew she had to stick with this interview. It might be their only chance.

"Conroe was a whole new territory for Frank. That's when he hooked up with a partner. And if I thought Frank was controlling, this supposedly silent partner of his was ten times worse. I could not do business—he made it impossible. And the girls who gave in to him—they were treated worse than dogs. I heard he was mean just for the sake of it—you know the kind of man I'm talking about."

"Like my dad," Tonda said under her breath.

"And I didn't even have Carlos on my side. I was all alone. I finally told this partner that I was done. If he didn't leave me alone I was going to the police and telling them everything I know. I figured he'd either back off…or kill me. That was when Frank stepped in. He kinda liked me, I think. Didn't want to see me hurt. He met me at the Quikki Market, tried to sweet-talk me into falling in line. But I wasn't going for it. Then he tried to pay me to leave town, but I'd already uprooted and moved once. I have a kid in Houston, you know? I only see her once a month. If I moved away, I'd never see her."

Elizabeth's heart pounded in her ears. This was great information—if only she could stomach it.

"So who is this partner?" Elizabeth figured whoever he was, he'd just become her Suspect Number One.

"Nobody knows who he is. He's like a ghost. Appears out of nowhere, usually in the dark. He's a voice in your ear, that's all."

"So you never saw him?"

"Not clearly. He's tall. That's about all I remember."

"What race?"

Yazmin shrugged. "I don't know. There were a couple of girls who were using Frank's death as a chance to break away, go back to being independent. One of them got mugged and beat up pretty good. The other disappeared."

"Disappeared?" Tonda repeated. "As in, permanently disappeared?"

"Maybe. I don't know. Her name was Maggie. White girl, red hair. I only met her once."

"I don't blame you for being scared, Yazmin. If you want protection, I can get it for you. It might take a little time." She would have to convince Daniel to take the woman in temporarily or put her up in a hotel or hire a bodyguard for her. But Daniel was a reasonable man, and he might just do it.

"No, I don't think so. I'm tired of trusting other people. I'd rather watch my own back."

"I understand." She reached into her purse and switched off the microphone app. She was in no danger, and she wanted to talk privately to the two women. She grabbed a business card and handed it to Yazmin. "If you ever want to talk to me—just talk, you know, about problems—I work at a free clinic in Houston. I'm hoping to be back at work next week sometime." If she was lucky. She wrote her cell number on the back of the card. "Meanwhile, if you think of anything else, you can call me anytime day or night. If you're scared or you find out anything about this silent partner—please let me know."

"I will." Yazmin tucked the card into her shoulder bag. "You're okay."

Tonda beamed. "Told you she was."

Elizabeth caught a movement out of the corner of her eye. She peered across the restaurant to the hostess stand. "Oh, crap."

"What?"

"Is there a back way out of here?"

Yazmin nodded. "That's why I wanted to meet here."

"Go. Now. Use it. I think I was followed." It would take too long to explain what was really going on.

Yazmin didn't hesitate. She scooted out of the booth and bolted for the ladies' room.

"There's a maintenance exit in the hallway near the bathrooms," Tonda explained.

"We're about to have company," Elizabeth whispered. "Tonda, please understand. They brought me to the mall. But they promised I could meet with you alone."

Tonda looked horrified. She placed her hands flat on the

table, as if this was the only way she could keep from lunging for Elizabeth's throat. "You lied to us?"

"I'm afraid I did. It was the only way they'd let me meet with you at all."

"Cops?" she said warily. "Maybe I better go to the ladies', too."

"They're not cops. Exactly."

"Oh. Your buddy Hudson."

"Not my buddy right now," she murmured.

It seemed as if they were going to sit the next booth over. Didn't they trust her? Maybe she shouldn't have turned off the mic, though she didn't think that was the reason they'd come. They'd appeared too quickly.

She waved to them. "Hello, boys." Her icy tone belied the friendly greeting. "'Fraid your cover is blown."

"Oh," Hudson said. He looked at Elizabeth, then Tonda, then back at Elizabeth. "Where's Jazz?"

"Bathroom," Elizabeth said.

Hudson shot a panicked look toward the restroom hallway while Joe didn't waste time; he headed in that direction. "You let her go alone?"

"She's not my prisoner, Hudson. She came to me willingly."

"She's a treasure trove of information. You've barely scratched the surface. You can't just let her walk away like that."

"Well, I just did, didn't I?"

Joe returned from the bathrooms. "She's gone."

Elizabeth was incensed. "Thanks to you. You didn't have to come barging in here. Did you hear the code phrase? No. You had no right—"

"The mic went silent. That's reason enough."

Jeez. They must have been waiting right outside the restaurant door.

"I needed to talk to her confidentially. I couldn't do that with you two listening in."

Tonda looked outraged. "You're wearing a wire?"

"I had to, Tonda. I'm sorry."

"Yeah. Whatever. Let me out."

"Tonda—"

"I said, let me out."

Reluctantly, Elizabeth slid out of the booth. Tonda threw five dollars on the table. "Don't want to stick you with the check for our coffee." She strolled out of the restaurant like a queen.

Though Elizabeth was devastated to have disappointed Tonda like that, she was proud of the girl for standing up for herself, not being cowed by the two rather intimidating men looming over the table.

Hudson took a couple of steps after Tonda as though he was going to stop her.

"Let her go, man," Joe said. "We're not going to get anything out of either of them now."

Hudson blew out a breath and heaved himself into the booth. "If I just could have questioned her—"

"You could have. Eventually." Elizabeth put as much starch into her voice as she could. "I was building rapport with her. She was starting to trust me. But maybe that's something you don't understand. Trust?"

"I did trust you. Until you warned Yazmin. That's why she took off, right? You saw us and warned her?"

She shrugged. "I wasn't going to betray those women any more than I already had. You may be a great cop, Hudson. But I know these women. I talk to them every day. If you'd tried to strong-arm her, she'd have shut down. You wouldn't have gotten one more bit of information."

"We won't anyway."

"She's got my number. I did her a favor. She might return it. You never know."

"So what did we learn?"

"We learned what my dad was involved in," Elizabeth said bitterly. "And we learned there was a partner."

"Yeah, a nameless, faceless partner who might have been tall. Sounds like the boogeyman. Give me a break."

"Hey, it's more than when we started," Joe said.

"Let's just go," Hudson said, standing again. "I told you this wasn't going to work."

NONE OF THEM said anything on the way home. Just as they reached the gates of Daniel's estate, Elizabeth's phone rang. She was shocked to see that it was Tonda.

"Tonda. I'm so sorry."

"I just got a minute. Jackson would rip me a new one if he knew I was calling. But that guy with the fish tattoo on his arm?"

"Yeah?"

"Jackson said he lives at the Bella Breeze apartments on Cherry Blossom." Tonda hung up.

So, Elizabeth didn't know how to get information, did she? "Wait. Don't open the gate."

"Why not?" Hudson turned to look at her, pulling his sunglasses off so she could see his hazel eyes.

"I just found out where Munch lives."

Joe pulled a U-turn.

CHAPTER FOURTEEN

JOE DID A search on the GPS for the Bella Breeze Motel. In moments, they had a route. Twenty minutes. "We should drop her off first," Hudson whispered to Joe.

Liz leaned forward from the backseat. "No way. I'm in this as deep as you are."

"Earlier, didn't you say you wanted to leave the investigating to the detectives?"

"Well, yeah. But this is my source's information."

"Liz. This guy is dangerous."

Of course he was. What was she thinking? "Then none of us should go. Maybe we should call the cops."

Hudson was an inch away from saying *I am a cop* before he clamped his mouth closed. "And tell them what?"

"This guy tried to kill you."

"You want to know what happens if we call the cops? Either they blow us off completely, or they check this apartment building when they get around to it, or they show up with three squad cars, sirens blaring, and Munch goes out the fire escape and disappears."

"You don't have a lot of faith in your fellow cops."

"This is Houston. Harris County. If we were in Montgomery County I could call... Hell, I wouldn't trust them to do it right, either."

"The original crime is their jurisdiction," Joe pointed out. "You *could* call them."

"Don't bother, Joe," Liz said. "He wants to be in control."

Hudson raised one finger, intending to argue, but before he could formulate a denial, he realized she was right. He wanted to be in control, in charge. As a cop, he always had a stake in solving a crime, bringing a bad guy to justice.

As a victim, that stake was a lot higher. Of course he wanted to control every aspect of the investigation. It was too important to trust to anybody else. Kinkaid had skills, for sure, but Hudson was the only real detective here.

"Don't worry," Joe said. "She can stay in the car. We lock her in, nothing short of a nuclear blast will get in here."

Liz grumbled something, but Hudson couldn't quite understand it. He tapped on the car window. It looked like normal glass....

"Bulletproof," Joe said. "At least unless someone's shooting with a sniper rifle or armor-piercing grenade launcher."

"Yeah, well, last time I left Liz in a car by herself things didn't go so well."

Liz looked slightly uneasy as she leaned back in her seat and refastened her seat belt. But even the reminder of the gang stealing hubcaps didn't cause her to back down.

"Can we lean on this guy a little?" Hudson asked. "He's not like those scared little hook—" he wished he'd stopped himself in time "—working girls, I mean."

Liz's eyes flashed dangerously.

Joe followed the GPS's monotone voice down a narrow, depressing street, past a used-tire shop and a bedraggled taqueria. "We don't have to treat him with kid gloves, if that's what you mean. We can give him some crap."

Not if Liz had anything to say about it. She'd probably insist Munch had issues and they needed to show him compassion. But she *was* going to stay in the car. "Does this thing have a panic button?"

"Right here." Joe pointed to a big red button on the dash. "Liz, if you feel like you're in trouble, push the button. This thing will put out a siren shrill enough to burst eardrums. We'll only be a few feet away."

"Does someone stealing hubcaps qualify as trouble?" she asked drily.

"You can't remove the hubcaps on this car. You can't even flatten the tires without a great deal of effort and tools most street thugs don't carry. We won't go far. You'll be fine."

Hudson watched Liz with his peripheral vision. Her lips were firmed into a grim frown. "What if *you* get into trouble?"

"Call 9-1-1 and lay low till someone gets here," Joe replied, choosing to take her question very seriously, though Hudson had gone into bad neighborhoods hundreds of times to question witnesses or suspects, and no one had ever tried to kill him. He still wasn't sure Munch was trying to kill him the night he broke in. That single shot, so far off target, had been meant to scare him, slow him down and give Munch a chance to escape.

But then, what had he been doing there? Obviously it hadn't been a random B and E.

Liz continued to look unhappy with the status quo.

"Cheer up, Liz," he said. "I got a feeling. This guy is gonna have the answers."

"And if you find him, and he does have some answers— who located him?"

"You. And Tonda." He had to give her credit where it was due.

"And why did she take the time to help us out?"

"'Cause she trusts you. And she doesn't trust me."

"We're just lucky I didn't completely destroy the relationship I've been building with her for over a year. She's so close to quitting the life. So close."

"I'll believe that when I see it." Tonda probably said whatever Liz wanted to hear.

Liz cleared her throat. "She's pregnant, you know."

"No. I didn't know that."

"She says the father is stepping up, taking responsibility, treating her right. Then he sends her out on the street to give blow jobs, telling her she can't catch any diseases that way. Stepping up my... Okay, I'm done. Off my soapbox."

Hudson didn't really understand where she was coming from, but he admired her dedication. He would try harder to be supportive of the work she did and the attitudes she displayed.

If he ever got the chance. She was still pretty angry with him for breaking up her meeting with the prostitutes.

The possibility that, after they'd exonerated themselves, he and Liz would go their separate ways seemed wrong. He caught himself every few minutes visualizing some scene in the nebulous future when he was free from this cloud of suspicion, enjoying some simple pleasure like eating barbecue or fishing on the lake...and there would be Liz in his vision, laughing with him, getting barbecue sauce on her chin, sunning in a bikini.

They'd shared so much. They'd...okay, they'd bonded. Yeah, they looked at things differently sometimes, but they also saw things the same. Like hummingbirds. And sex. And flamenco music. And sex. How could they just walk away from that without at least trying to make it work?

"There it is," Liz said, breaking into his anguished thoughts. "The Bella Breeze Motel. It's not exactly *bella,* is it?"

The motel in question was a small, two-story L-shaped building that might once have been white, with trim a sickly shade of pink. One of the apartments had boarded-up windows. A black, sooty stain billowing out along the roofline suggested there had been a fire. The pitted blacktop parking lot was mostly empty except for a couple of beater Chevys and a multicolored El Camino. One lonely bicycle was chained to a post, its front wheel missing.

Joe pulled the car into a parking space in the farthest corner of the lot. "Hudson, maybe you should wait in the car with Liz. Munch knows your face."

"I'm wearing shades and a hat. And I'll stand behind you. Liz, you keep an eye on us while we try to find this joker."

"Are you just gonna knock randomly on doors?" she asked.

He shrugged. "We'll try the manager first."

Joe and Hudson exited the car. Hudson got a strange feeling in his gut as he walked away. Logically, he knew Liz would be okay. The car was a damn fortress.

"She'll be fine," Joe said, obviously sensing Hudson's unease.

They headed for a door with the word *Manager* in English and Spanish crookedly written in what looked like Magic Marker. They knocked. Inside, a TV was blaring on a Spanish-language station. After a few moments, the door was yanked open by a Hispanic man in a sweaty work shirt. He said nothing, merely glared at them.

"Sorry to bother you, but I'm looking for someone who lives here named Munch?" Joe asked politely. Hudson stood behind and slightly to the side, keeping his profile to the manager to lessen the chance he'd be identified.

"You cops?" the manager asked suspiciously.

"No, sir. Actually, I'm his new lawyer. Trying to keep him *out* of trouble."

"Who's he?" The manager jerked one thumb toward Hudson.

"My paralegal."

It was all Hudson could do not to laugh out loud. Joe was a smooth liar. With his clean-cut looks, anybody would believe he was an attorney.

"Munch is in the last unit upstairs, on the right," the man said indifferently. "If you get him to answer, tell him to clean his place up. Guy never takes his trash out. Neighbors are complaining about the smell."

Joe and Hudson exchanged a meaningful look.

The queasiness in Hudson's stomach kicked up a notch. Was Munch a hoarder? Or something worse?

As they made their way up the metal staircase to the up-stairs walkway, Hudson heard a *thunk thunk* noise behind him. He whirled around and Liz ran right into him.

"Sorry," she said automatically, backing up a step.

"Liz. You're supposed to be—"

"I'd rather be with you guys. It's creepy by myself in that car. Everybody's staring at it."

She was right. A group of young men who'd been walking by with their basketballs had stopped to ogle the car, which did stand out.

"Just stay behind me, Elizabeth, okay?" Joe had paused at the top of the stairs to put in his two cents. "You have your phone handy?"

"In my hand. I've already dialed the nine and one of the ones."

Hudson ushered her ahead of him so she'd be sandwiched between the two men. But the manager had said Munch wasn't answering his door. Sensing the noose tightening around him, he'd probably gone into hiding. If Hudson had killed some-one, he wouldn't just sit around his apartment, waiting for the cops to show up.

Hudson detected the smell in the air before they even reached the door. Oh, God. He knew that smell.

Joe stood before the door, took a deep breath and knocked decisively. "Munch? Hey, Munch, it's your lawyer. Open the door—we gotta talk."

"Lawyer?" Liz looked back to Hudson.

"Project Justice doesn't condone kidnapping or beating people up," Hudson whispered, "but lying is apparently fine."

Joe pressed his ear to the door. "I don't hear anything."

Hudson didn't, either. "I say we go in anyway. Search the place."

Joe took a quick look over both shoulders to make sure no one was watching. "You two shield what I'm doing."

"Are you going to pick the lock?" Liz asked as she and Hudson moved to stand between Joe and the balcony railing.

"I'm not that patient." With that, Joe took one step back and kicked the door. The wood splintered, and the lock broke and the door bounced open.

"Damn," Hudson said, "they teach you that in Secret Service school?"

"Special Forces," Joe answered matter-of-factly. Then no one spoke for a few moments, because they were too busy gagging. A hideously fetid stench billowed out of the apartment, along with a cloud of flies.

"Sweet Jesus," Liz said, her eyes huge. "I'll just wait out here."

"If this is what I think it is," Joe said, "none of us is going to stay long."

HUDSON BRAVELY ENTERED the apartment and Joe followed, dragging a reluctant Liz with him. He didn't particularly want her to see whatever was dead in here. But they couldn't leave her standing outside by herself. The men who'd been admiring the car had shifted their attention to her. Liz's stunning looks provoked attention wherever she went, but even in jeans and a sweatshirt, she really stood out in a place this mean and ugly.

Liz pulled the hem of that sweatshirt up and over her nose and mouth. "I'll just wait here by the door," she said.

"Okay, but don't touch anything," Hudson warned her. He wanted no chance that any of their DNA would be found here.

"Not to worry."

"Don't shed any hair or leave a footprint in anything, either."

Munch's apartment was piled high with junk—boxes full of God knew what, broken furniture, stained rugs, holes in the walls. Still, in all that mess, it was easy to find the dead guy—just follow the flies. He was in the bathtub, along with a lot of congealed blood and decomposing body fluids. The maggots had done a pretty good job on him. Hard to even tell what had killed him. But the remnant of a fishtail could be seen on the back of the victim's hand.

"This him?" Joe asked.

"Pretty sure it is." Shit. There went their best hope of finding out what Mandalay had been mixed up in. "He's been here awhile, too. Days, maybe a week."

"Whoever killed Mandalay might have done this, too," Hudson said. "Some kind of business deal gone awry?"

"Or Munch could have killed Mandalay, and some third party—an ally of Mandalay's, perhaps—killed Munch," Joe said. "Can't rule that out."

A short shriek from Liz had Hudson sprinting back to the main room.

"Liz. What's wrong?"

"There, on the coffee table." She pointed at the table, covered with old newspapers, empty beer cans and petrified pizza, as if a snake might be lurking there. Frankly, he wouldn't be surprised in this mess. "What is it?"

"That gold watch."

Sure enough there was a gold watch. Hudson couldn't believe he hadn't spotted it at first. He leaned down to inspect it more closely. "Looks old. Looks like real gold, too."

"It's both. A vintage Hamilton Barton nineteen-jewel watch in a fourteen-karat-gold case."

Finally Hudson figured it out. "It was your father's?"

"Yes. Used to be my grandfather's. Dad was obsessive about that watch. Is there— Did you find a dead body?"

He nodded grimly. "It's Munch. Probably murdered. We're waaaaay too late to get any information from him. We're just going to take a quick look around and then get out of here."

"Shouldn't we call the police?"

Hudson grimaced. "It won't look good, us being here. We'll call it in anonymously. Or get the manager to call."

"Hurry and finish looking around. If I don't get out of here pretty soon I'm going to hurl." She put the sweatshirt hem over her face again.

Joe returned from the bedroom. "I took a quick look around. Didn't see anything except some overdue phone bills. It's possible our guy's real name was Calvin Bean."

No wonder he'd taken a nickname.

Hudson made a quick sweep of the kitchen, dining room and living room, snapping pictures with his phone as he went. It wasn't the thorough, methodical search he wanted to do, but they couldn't disturb the scene any more than they had without risking an obstruction-of-justice charge.

Finally they left the apartment. Hudson closed the door behind him as best he could.

The apartment manager was striding down the balcony toward them, his eyes stormy with anger. "Who's gonna pay for that door, huh?"

Guess he and Liz hadn't hidden Joe's entry method well enough.

Joe reached into his back pocket, extracted a wallet and pulled out several bills, handing them to the angry man. "That should cover it, along with the cleaning bill. And…" He pulled out a few more. "You got a dead guy in the bathtub. When you call the police, I'd appreciate it if you don't remember us being here. We didn't do anything wrong, but we don't want to get involved."

The man made a quick count of the money and smiled. *"Madre de Dios!"*

"Next time an apartment starts to smell, check on it sooner."

The manager watched them walk away, looking as if he had mixed feelings about the way his day was going.

None of them said anything for a good five minutes, until

they were back on a main road and headed for a better neighborhood. Hudson had got in the backseat with Liz, sensing she might need someone to hold her hand or at least make eye contact with her. She looked pretty shaken.

"Why was my father's watch there? Did this Munch person rob him?"

"We're gonna find out, Liz," Hudson said. "I promise you."

"Maybe someone was blackmailing him," she said. "He got tired of it, confronted them, and…it didn't go well."

"That's a possible scenario," Joe said. Without asking, he pulled into a Pepe's Tacos drive-through and ordered a dozen tacos.

"How can he even think about food?" Liz whispered. "I'm pretty sure I won't eat for a week. Ugh, I can still smell it. And you guys *saw* him."

"You do get used to it after a while," he said. "You just have to find a way to tune out the emotions, to forget about the smell and the gore and the maggots—"

"Oh, thank you—you had to mention maggots?"

"—and look at the case clinically. You want to have compassion for the victim and family, of course, but you have to get past being horrified. I still remember my first dead body, though. I was a green patrol officer. Guy tried to cross the freeway on foot. The results weren't pretty. I lost my breakfast."

Joe laughed.

"Stop talking, both of you. I don't want to hear another word. And for God's sake, keep those tacos away from me."

Hudson felt bad for Liz. It was awful enough to lose a parent, even if he'd been a bastard. Liz had probably pictured his death in her mind a hundred ways. But to come face-to-face with violent death, then to see undeniable evidence that her father had been mixed up with the dead man—to be standing in the apartment where he might have been killed—had undoubtedly brought the crime to life for her.

She'd been ashen-faced on the ride home, hadn't said a word after yelling at Joe to keep the tacos away from her. Hudson's attempts to distract her had been disastrous. He supposed what was funny to people in law enforcement didn't necessarily translate to a civilian.

Once they'd reached Daniel's house, she'd excused herself, leaving Joe and Hudson to explain to Daniel about finding the body.

The news hadn't exactly thrilled Daniel. The three of them were sitting out on the flagstone patio, the sparkling blue pool and landscaped greenery a stark contrast to the ugly subject of conversation.

"How long do you think he's been dead?" Daniel asked.

"A long time," Hudson replied, and Joe nodded. "It's going to be hard to pinpoint. Maybe a scientist can figure it out based on insect larvae or something like that. But my guess is, he didn't live long after he tried to break into my house."

"Did you call it in?"

"We asked the apartment manager to do it," Joe said. "And I called Billy Cantu, gave him the whole story. He said he would keep our names out of it if he possibly could."

"If it gets out that you were there," Daniel said, "Montgomery County is going to go after you for messing with their investigation."

Hudson shrugged. "I can't help it if my own colleagues are incompetent. *They* should have been looking for Munch. They should thank me for doing their damn jobs. I have a right to try to prove my innocence."

Daniel nodded. "Your actions are entirely defensible. I'm not criticizing. Just saying, cops sometimes get unreasonable when they're trying to defend their position. Knightly and your partner are going to look foolish for pursuing you as a suspect when we prove who really committed the murder."

Hudson knew how he would feel if he were in Knightly's or Carla's shoes. He supposed he couldn't totally blame them for butting heads with him.

"Is Elizabeth okay?" Daniel asked. "Did she see the dead body?"

"No, but what she did see was bad enough. And what she smelled was worse. We told her to stay in the car, but she wasn't keen on that idea. She was pretty shook up, especially when she spotted her father's watch. Almost certainly her father's killer was in that apartment at some point. Munch might have killed him, or whoever killed Munch might have done the deed."

"I sent you some pictures," Joe said. "We didn't touch anything, but I took a lot of pictures with my phone. I figure you could blow them up and go over them inch by inch."

"My specialty." Daniel looked as if he relished the prospect. He was a master at pattern recognition—and finding that one detail that didn't fit.

The French doors opened, and Elena stepped out looking her usual stylish self. "Daniel, I just went to check on Elizabeth like you asked me to, and she's not in her room. I checked all the public rooms, too.

A frisson of alarm shot through Hudson. He'd assumed that she'd gone to her room to rest. He was relatively sure nothing bad could happen to her behind the protective gates and fences of Daniel's estate, but in her current state of mind, what if she wandered off? Injured herself or went for a walk and became lost?

Daniel didn't look too worried. "She probably just went for a walk. Nothing like spending time in nature to soothe jangled nerves."

"Do we need to cover anything else right now?" Hudson asked, eager to take his leave. He wanted to find Liz. He wanted to know for sure she was okay.

"My metal-detecting team did find a bullet in the leaf litter, in that little group of trees near your house."

"At least that's some good news."

"I'm working on getting it entered into the ballistics database. It takes some creative favor-calling, but we might know something soon."

With that, the meeting was over. Hudson tried to imagine where a distraught woman might go on this enormous estate to clear her head. Then it hit him. What was the most idyllic spot on the grounds?

"A walk sounds like a good idea," he said to the others.

"Dinner's at seven," Daniel announced.

That would be plenty of time. Maybe. Hudson knew he ought to be out there, shaking the bushes, trying to find a crazed killer. But right now, he could think of nothing more important than finding Liz. If he was going away for a long time, he needed to make things right between them. He had to tell her... He wasn't sure what to tell her. He just didn't want her to be mad at him anymore.

The rose garden didn't look quite as spectacular as it had for Jillian's wedding. But maybe that was because he was looking at it without Liz. She had made the place more special, and she definitely wasn't here. He plucked a soft peach bloom from one bush, managing to prick his finger in the process.

He pushed through the picket-fence gate into the lush, untamed growth of the hummingbird garden, and his heart almost stopped. There she was, sitting on the stone bench.

Liz was the picture of grief. She'd changed out of her jeans and sweatshirt into a simple dress that flowed over her body like water. Her hair was loose, her face was in her hands and her shoulders trembled every so often. Her sobs were silent—and more heart-wrenching because of it. She didn't want anyone to hear, didn't want to be found.

He should just creep away and not violate her privacy. But

he couldn't see someone in that much agony and not try to ease the pain.

"Liz." He spoke softly so as not to startle her, but she jerked her head up anyway.

"Oh. What are you doing here?"

"I came looking for you. Thought you might come here."

"I wanted to see the hummers again. But they aren't here."

"Maybe they went south for the winter or something."

"I thought, 'How could I think about death and sadness while watching one of those precious little birds?' They're so incredibly alive."

"I'm so sorry, Liz. I keep forgetting that you're grieving. I don't mean to say things that hurt you. I don't mean to be disrespectful regarding your feelings. I know you see things differently than me, but I'm going to try harder to respect your worldview." He sat down beside her, half expecting her to jump up and flee. But she didn't. She seemed in a listening frame of mind, so he kept going.

"I'm sorry for getting you into trouble with your client, too. I never would have come into the restaurant like that if I hadn't been worried about you. You went silent."

"I would have let you know if the situation wasn't safe."

"And I didn't trust you. I know."

"Tonda can be emotional. She's been mad at me before. She'll get over it."

"You want me to talk to her?"

"No, I don't think that would help. I'll give her a little time to sulk, then I'll try to make it up to her. A year ago, she wouldn't have stood up to me. She had no backbone. No identity beyond what others assigned to her. Now she's her own person. It's actually gratifying to see that growth."

"She's a tough cookie."

"No, she's not. She puts on a brave front, but she's barely nineteen." Liz looked down self-consciously. "I shouldn't even be talking about her to you."

"Talking about who?"

That got a watery smile out of her.

He held out his hand. "Friends again?"

She took his hand, her touch tentative at first, then firmer. God, her skin was soft. He realized he was still clutching the stolen rose in his other hand. He offered it to Liz. She smiled again but didn't take it from him, instead folding his hand between both of hers. He tucked the rose behind one of her ears, careful that no thorns would jab her.

They sat like that for several heartbeats, and Hudson could almost feel the frayed ends of their connection meeting again, becoming enmeshed. He became suddenly more aware of her in a sexual way, too. Not that he wasn't always aware of how beautiful she was, but now visions of naked flesh and the sound of heated breathing flashed through his mind's eye. His mouth became dry and his jeans too tight.

"Liz…"

"Hudson…"

They'd spoken at the same time. He was almost glad that he didn't have to continue, because he wasn't sure what he wanted to say anyway. He leaned in closer. It felt just like a first kiss, but with someone he'd known his whole life. He already knew the texture of her lips, the scent of her skin, the feel of her body wrapped around his.

When their lips actually met, Hudson went all light-headed. He wanted to laugh. He hadn't blown it totally with her.

He allowed his hand to wander over her slender back, noting the sharp contours of her shoulder blades, the frailness of her shoulders. He circled her upper arms with his hands. She was so slender—stronger than she looked, maybe, but still no match if any man wanted to overpower her, hurt her. No wonder he felt so protective of her.

Suddenly Liz broke the kiss, pulled away, a look of torture on her face.

"Liz. What? What's wrong?"

"We can't do this."

"No one can see—"

"It's not that. We shouldn't let ourselves… There's no point…"

"No point?" he repeated incredulously. If there was no point in *this,* was there a point to anything?

"I can't see a future in this." She indicated with her hand the connection that ran between them. "I get my hopes up, and then—"

"And then I blow it by saying something so totally insensitive that you're sure there's no hope for me."

She shrugged. "You're not hopeless. You're just…you. And I'm me, and we are so different."

Just then a hummingbird appeared, leisurely sipping from the flowering bush behind Liz's head.

"Look behind you," he said softly. "Turn your head real slow."

She did, then gasped. "They're not all gone."

"Maybe we are different," he said. "But we have this in common."

She looked back and smiled sadly. "I'm not sure hummingbirds are enough to save us."

His heart sank. He wanted to argue. He wanted to demand that she think harder about what she was throwing away. People who were different fell in love all the time. Look at Daniel and his wife, Jaime. She spent her life putting criminals behind bars. Daniel spent his getting innocent people out of prison. Yet somehow they found common ground and by all accounts were insanely happy.

But he could tell Liz wasn't in the mood to be convinced of anything. She wasn't in a good space, emotionally. Maybe she couldn't bring herself to be happy. On some level, she might feel guilty for not being there for her father. There was probably nothing she could have done to prevent his death, but she might not see that.

He kissed her on the cheek, then stood and walked away, feeling hollow. At that moment, he didn't care if they put him in solitary confinement for the rest of his life.

CHAPTER FIFTEEN

LIZ DIDN'T COME to the dinner table. Elena reported that she wasn't feeling well and had asked that a tray be brought to her room.

Hudson felt both relief and disappointment. He craved being close to her. But her nearness was also torture when he knew he couldn't touch her, couldn't take her to bed. "Is she okay?" he asked Elena.

"She is fine, just a little tired. She said she is not fit company."

Hudson begged to differ; even out of sorts, Liz was fine company.

Joe had gone home; the table was set for only two—Hudson and Daniel. Cora entered as if on cue, setting a plate in front of each of them bearing a juicy sirloin steak and baked potato. Another servant placed a big bowl of green salad on the table and a silver gravy boat filled with dressing.

Hudson cut into his steak and checked the doneness; medium rare, just the way he liked it. How had Cora known?

"Isn't Jaime going to join us?" Hudson asked after thoroughly appreciating his first bite. He knew the district attorney had arrived home from work; he'd been sitting outside on an upstairs terrace that overlooked the front driveway when her Land Rover had come through the gates and pulled into the massive garage on the far side of the house.

"It's probably best if Jaime doesn't have any close contact with you," Daniel said apologetically. "You're now a material witness in a murder that took place in her jurisdiction. She's very conscious of anything that might appear as impropriety."

"I wouldn't tell."

"She's scrupulously honest. People already look askance at her because of my job."

"I'm sorry I've prevented you from having dinner with your wife, Daniel. I'll go eat in my room if you'd rather—"

"Jaime and I will see each other later. Trust me—we arrange our schedules in such a way that we have plenty of quality 'us' time. Anyway, I wanted to talk to you. Alone."

A chill of trepidation swept up Hudson's spine.

"Did you ever do any target practice near your house?" he asked. "Maybe with your partner?"

The piece of steak Hudson had just swallowed stuck in his throat. He made an effort to force it down, then took a few sips of water. "What? No. It's not even legal to discharge a firearm that close to Lake Conroe."

"We got a match on the projectile we found behind your house."

"Don't tell me. It traces back to my gun. Which means I shot at myself. If someone's trying to frame me—"

"Hudson. Hold on. It wasn't your gun. It was…it was a gun registered to Carla Sanchez."

It felt as if someone had just dumped a bucket of ice water over Hudson's head. "Carla? *My* Carla? Wait a minute, that must be a really common name—"

"Your Carla Sanchez," Daniel confirmed. "Address and date of birth matches up."

"Daniel, that doesn't even make sense. Carla would never be mixed up in something like this." Or would she? He'd believed she didn't still hold a grudge over their ill-fated liaison, but what if he was wrong?

"She's a single mom, two kids to raise, trying to figure out how to pay for their college on a cop's salary. She starts out maybe just looking the other way once or twice. Then it escalates—"

"Carla has her issues, but I've never seen any sign of corruption."

"People can surprise you. My own chef tried to kill me, a guy I'd known since college. I would have sworn he couldn't do that, either."

The carefully prepared dinner, worthy of a four-star restaurant, now didn't tempt Hudson in the slightest. No, what he wanted was a drink. He'd never been one to drink until he passed out, but suddenly he understood the appeal.

"I should talk to her."

"That's probably not a good idea. Even if she's not responsible, someone might get nervous if they find out we're closing in."

"I'm sure she has a simple explanation."

"I'm sure she does, too," Daniel said placatingly. "Let's sit on the information at least for a day or so. You're way too close to her to do any kind of adequate investigation, so Joe's taking care of that."

Hudson felt nauseated at the thought of anybody digging into Carla's private life. But still…how could one of her bullets have got into that woods? Either she'd loaned her gun to a lowlife like Munch, or… "Maybe someone planted that bullet there. Trying to railroad Carla, just like they're doing me."

"I suppose it's not out of the question. A cop hater. Did you and Carla have a beef with anyone lately? Did you arrest anybody who might be nursing a grudge?"

"Just Mandalay. But how would he get access to Carla's gun or a bullet fired from it?" Hudson searched his memory. Could he be overlooking someone? But he continued to draw a blank. "I can't remember anything out of the ordinary. No threats, no weird phone calls, even. Most of the homicides we deal with are pretty straightforward. Guy shoots another guy in front of ten witnesses, that sort of thing."

Hudson's phone vibrated in his pocket. He checked the screen. "Sorry, Daniel, I have to take this."

Daniel nodded. "Of course, go ahead."

Hudson stepped away from the table. Then, when he saw that Daniel was checking messages on his own phone, he moved all the way out into the hallway so they could both talk in private.

He answered his phone just before it went to voice mail. "Dad. What's up?"

"I have an appointment with Homer Vilches's widow, Nellie. I thought you might want to go with me."

Hudson had heard the name before, but he couldn't quite place it. "Who is Homer Vilches?"

"My old buddy? The one who investigated Holly Mandalay's disappearance?"

"Oh. Oh, right. Tonight? It can't wait until tomorrow?" Although he was anxious to learn more about the disappearance of Liz's mother, he was exhausted down to his marrow, and Hudson really didn't want to do anything else to antagonize Liz right now.

"Nellie's in the hospital. Very ill, kidney failure. Frankly, she's deteriorating rapidly. Tomorrow she might not be able to talk, or remember."

Hudson took a deep breath. Sounded as if he really had no choice. "Okay. I'll meet you there. Which hospital?"

His father gave him the particulars. Now he just had to tell Daniel what he was doing—and ask to borrow a car. Nothing like feeling sixteen again.

HUDSON MET HIS father in the lobby of Memorial Medical Center. Daniel hadn't balked when Hudson wanted to go alone. He'd given him the keys to a Land Rover, told him to be sure he wasn't followed and turned him loose.

Rusty Vale shook hands with his son. "When I heard Nellie was sick, I wasn't going to bother her. But I spoke with

Nellie's sister, Judy. She said something strange happened shortly after Homer Vilches died. A cop showed up at Nellie's door, wanting to look at Homer's private files. Said it was an official matter but didn't elaborate."

"That sounds kind of fishy."

"I thought the same thing. I want to see what Nellie remembers."

Rusty already knew Nellie's room number. They headed for the elevator.

Nellie Vilches did not look good. A tiny, frail woman hooked up to more machines than NASA used for a space launch, she had decidedly yellow skin, and her breathing was shallow. Poor woman. And wasn't it just Hudson's luck that his best witness was dead, and another was dying?

"Hello, Nellie, it's me, Rusty Vale," Rusty said with exaggerated cheer as they approached her bed.

"Rusty?" Her eyes opened, but it didn't seem as if she could see. She didn't look in their direction. "After all these years, how good to hear your voice. How's Binnie?"

"Ornery as always. I've brought my son with me. Hudson."

"Pleased to meet you, Mrs. Vilches." He grasped her bony hand in his. "Although I think we met once when I was a little kid."

"Yes, I'm sure we did. You sound all grown-up now. What are you, twenty? Twenty-one?"

"Thirty-two, ma'am."

"Oh, how do the years slip by so fast?" She laughed, but the laugh turned into a cough.

"I should have come to see you before now," Rusty said gruffly. "You always figure you have plenty of time."

"Don't give it a second thought. Judy said you might be coming to see me. That you wanted to ask me something?"

Hudson was grateful that Nellie's mind still seemed to be sharp. He was also grateful to the sister for preparing Nellie for their visit.

"Nellie," Rusty began, "Judy said that shortly after Homer passed away, someone came to your house and wanted to look through Homer's personal records."

"Oh, that." She frowned. "He said he was working on one of Homer's unsolved cases, and he was desperate for any clue that might help him. But he wouldn't say what case."

A man, then. Not a woman. Not Carla. Hudson hadn't realized he was holding his breath until then.

"When was this?" Hudson asked.

"Oh, maybe three years ago? Well, there the man was," Nellie continued, "looking oh-so-official in his uniform, and of course I let him do anything he wanted. He spent some time going through Homer's file cabinet, and in the end he took one file with him. He thanked me and left. Later, though, I wondered. It just seemed…weird."

"Was he a Houston city cop?" Hudson asked. "Or from somewhere else?"

"I don't know." She sounded distressed. "I don't remember."

"Do you remember what he looked like?" Rusty asked.

"He was tall and thin, young, with glasses and dark hair. And a prematurely receding hairline—I do remember that."

Rusty looked at Hudson, but all Hudson could do was shrug. That description could fit a million people.

"You don't happen to remember what folder he took, do you?" Hudson asked.

"Why, yes. I was curious, so after he left I took a peek inside the file cabinet to see what was missing. I was familiar with his files. I'd gone through them myself, many times. Kind of silly, but it made me feel closer to him to see the notes he took. Like being inside his head."

She paused significantly.

"It was the Holly Mandalay case. That's the one that was missing, and it didn't surprise me. Homer was always funny about that case. Couldn't stop…talking about it at first, then one day…he just never said another word about it."

Whatever strength Nellie Vilches had mustered to speak her piece to Hudson and his dad was fading fast. Her eyelids drooped, and she was almost gasping for breath.

Rusty squeezed her shoulder. "I'm sorry, Nellie. We've tired you out."

"Oh, it's okay. I'm glad to be able to tell someone about this before… Well, whatever." She closed her eyes. "It won't be much longer."

"Thank you, Mrs. Vilches." Hudson gave her hand one last squeeze. "We really appreciate your time."

She said nothing else. Maybe she'd fallen asleep.

Hudson and his father remained silent until they'd exited the hospital. It was a fine autumn evening, cool but not quite jacket weather. Mrs. Vilches likely would never feel a fall breeze brush her cheek again.

"What did you make of that?" Hudson asked.

"I always got the feeling Homer was somehow pressured into putting that case in cold storage. Obviously I was right. Someone was interested. Didn't want anything Homer had learned to get into the wrong hands. Did you recognize the person she described?"

Hudson shook his head. "It was a little too vague."

"It might not have even been a real cop."

"But I can't rule that out. A guy took a potshot at me the other night. Some folks with metal detectors found the bullet. It traced back to a gun owned by my partner."

"The woman? Sanchez?"

"Yeah. But Nellie's visitor was male. Hell, maybe this has nothing to do with the whole Mandalay thing."

"Maybe." Rusty didn't sound convinced. "*Someone* put pressure on Homer Vilches to bury that missing-persons case."

"I can take a guess who that was. Pressuring law enforcement was something Franklin Mandalay knew how to do. He had a history of strong-arming anybody who opposed his wishes in any way. Even sent some thugs to beat up his own daughter's boyfriend."

"Hmm. Any chance the boyfriend murdered Mandalay?"

"Hell, who knows? All the people who hated him, you probably couldn't fit them into the Astrodome."

"And yet they're focusing on you."

"And Mandalay's daughter. It's that kind of detective work that keeps Project Justice in business. Happens more than us cops would like to believe."

ELIZABETH COULDN'T SLEEP. Every time she closed her eyes, she was assaulted by grisly mental images of the dead man. Even though she hadn't actually seen him, her imagination conjured up a host of horror-movie stills.

She tossed and turned for an hour, then decided she should get up. She could try drinking warm milk. Or maybe some physical activity would help. She hadn't worked out at the gym in ages.

The Logan estate had its own workout room with a whirl-pool and sauna. Elena had told Elizabeth it was in the base-ment, and that she was welcome to use it. She decided to throw on a robe and head downstairs—not to exercise, but to soak her feet in the whirlpool. Maybe it would relax her.

It wasn't hard to find. Elizabeth took the elevator to the B level, then wandered down a hallway until she found an open door.

Someone else had got the same idea, apparently. Her breath snagged in her throat as she caught an eyeful of Hudson run-ning on a treadmill. He wore only a pair of shorts and shoes; the rest of him was bare, his golden skin shiny with perspi-ration. Judging from how hard he was breathing, he'd been at this for a while.

Elizabeth wanted to slink away unnoticed, but she was rooted to the spot. He was so gorgeous, like a sleek wild animal.

Though she was sure she hadn't made any sound at all, Hudson turned and saw her. He was startled enough that he lost his footing and almost was thrown off the treadmill, but he righted himself and hammered the emergency-stop button.

"Jeez, Liz, you scared me to death."

"Sorry. I didn't think anyone else would be down here."

"You can't sleep, either, huh?"

She shook her head, suddenly very aware of how thin her robe was and how very little she had on underneath. If he kissed her right now, if he pressed that deliciously sweaty body against hers and pushed her up against the wall—

Suddenly her mind was filled not with visions of death and decay, but with images of her and Hudson in a passionate embrace—on the weight bench, the stair climber, and... oh, my, the chin-up bar.

She tried to summon some of the anger she'd been clinging to, but she couldn't seem to find it.

"Liz?" His look was one of concern, not lust, yet the slight flaring of his nostrils told her he was aware of her as a woman.

"Oh, um, yeah, couldn't sleep."

"Me, neither. It's pretty sobering to discover your own partner might be involved in murder. I don't know if you heard, but the bullet found in the woods by my house traced back to Carla Sanchez."

"Oh, Hudson. I'm so sorry." That had to be hard for him.

"I don't want to believe it. The whole idea of a dirty cop..."

"They could plant fake evidence, pay off witnesses to lie— God knows."

"Right."

Until now, Liz had avoided thinking about what would happen if they didn't find the real murderer. Arrest, incarceration, a trial, legal fees. They wouldn't let her use any inheritance to help with those fees, either. Her father's estate would be frozen so fast...

She folded her arms, belatedly realizing how the action caused her robe to mold to her breasts. "Deep down, I've always believed we could prove our innocence."

"Me, too." He pulled her to him, put his arms around her. The move felt so natural, his comforting embrace so welcome, that she made no move to stop it.

"Do you think they have enough to arrest either of us?"

"They must have something—but maybe not enough. I can't imagine why they haven't brought us in for official questioning by now. If they really think we did it, they should be trying to wrest confessions out of us. Get us to turn on each other. That's what I would have done."

"Maybe they have something strong enough that a confession isn't even necessary. Hudson, I'm scared."

"Me, too. You know what happens to cops in prison?"

She didn't want to think about that.

"Hudson?"

"Yeah?"

"What if we ran?" Suddenly that option sounded much more attractive than it had a few days ago. She had some money. They could make their way to Venezuela or some country without a U.S. extradition treaty.

"You'd do that? With me?"

Would she? Life as a fugitive wouldn't be any picnic. But if it saved Hudson from being murdered in prison... "I don't know. I'm confused. One minute I feel strong, the next I'm sure I wouldn't last a day in prison. But it's bound to be worse for you. You'd probably rather not be saddled with me, anyway. I'd just slow you down."

"I wouldn't leave you to take the rap alone."

"That's very noble." She sighed, feeling a false sense of contentment pressed up against Hudson's body, still hot from his workout. "I'd be too scared to run."

"Running would just make us look guilty. Even if they arrest us, even if the worst happens…Project Justice will keep working to exonerate us. Once Daniel believes someone is innocent, it takes a lot to change his mind. He'll stand by us."

That was only slightly reassuring. If their witnesses kept dying, their evidence disappearing, how could anyone, no matter how brilliant, no matter how many resources he had at his disposal, prove they were innocent?

"Hudson?"

"Yes, Liz?"

"If this is possibly our last night of freedom, don't you think we should do something special? Something we'll remember for a long time?"

"You mean, like, borrow a couple of Daniel's polo ponies and ride naked through the woods?"

She swatted him on his rock-hard backside, probably hurting her hand more than his butt. "That's not what I meant."

He laughed softly. "I know what you mean. Last time I wanted to go there, you shot me down."

"Because of the implication that it was leading somewhere. Somewhere I couldn't promise to go. Tonight, I just want to connect with something positive. I want to remember how good we are together. And I want to think about life, instead of death."

His answer was to tip her head up and kiss her. "We started things with a night of shallow, meaningless sex. It's fitting we end things that way, too."

She didn't take offense, though she considered nothing about their first night together shallow. She'd started caring for him from the moment they'd met, and her feelings had only deepened.

However, lasting relationships relied on more than caring. Everything had got messy. Their situation had brought them closer, but it had also highlighted their differences—core beliefs that wouldn't change overnight.

No point worrying about anything long-term. They could hardly work out their differences from separate cell blocks. Prison letters weren't going to cut it for them. The buck stopped here; tonight was probably all they had.

Hudson tugged at the belt of her cotton robe. The half bow she'd hastily tied a few minutes ago came loose and the robe fell open, revealing the barely there silk nightshirt, which was all she had on underneath. He traced the outline of her breasts with a delicate touch; her nipples rose into hard peaks clearly visible through the thin material.

"I've never seen anyone respond the way you do." His voice was thick, husky.

"You think that's fast, you should feel what's going on below the waist."

"I intend to."

It wasn't lost on her that his reaction to her was just as fast, just as visceral. Those teeny little shorts didn't hide much.

Suddenly he scooped her up in his arms. Both her slippers fell off. "What are you doing?" Lord, he was strong. He'd picked her up as if she was no bigger than a kitten. She might be thin, but at five foot nine no one ever accused her of being petite.

"Have you ever made love in a Jacuzzi?"

One door down from the workout room was a wet area with a whirlpool bath and ice plunge. The mosaic-tiled walls depicted underwater scenes in shades of blue and green. Just when she'd thought she'd seen it all, the opulence of this place surprised her. The whirlpool could have accommodated six or eight people. The glowing water steamed.

"Does he keep this thing hot all the time?" She couldn't help thinking about the energy waste.

"No, I turned it on when I came down. It should be about perfect." He set her down on the cool tile and quickly untied his shoes. Feeling self-conscious standing there in her jammies, she decided to get in. The water was perfect—just about body temperature. She descended the steps, not bothering to remove the nightshirt. As she submerged her body, the nightshirt floated up, becoming all but invisible.

So much for modesty.

Hudson was watching every move she made. "Nice look."

She pulled the now-useless nightshirt over her head and onto the tile deck, sinking to neck-deep in the water and finding a ledge to sit on. Hudson, now naked himself, joined her, but not before turning on the jets.

The water churned and foamed all around her, the bubbles caressing her already-supersensitive skin. She closed her eyes, relishing the sensation. Tonight was all about living in the moment.

"How's that?" he asked.

"Mmm." When she opened her eyes, he was standing before her waist-high in the water, looking like a sexy god of the sea about to ravish a mermaid. With a wicked grin he leaned down to kiss her, then wrapped his hands around her rib cage and lifted her up. Seeing his intention, she wrapped her legs around his hips and he moved his hands to support her bottom.

His erection teased between her legs but he made no move to enter her. "Now, let's see…" He moved around the hot tub until he found exactly the right spot. A strong jet of water and bubbles rushed against the most sensitive part of her body.

"Oh." So that was what he was after. "Oh, my. Wait, Hudson, I'm going to—" Too late. With almost no warning she climaxed with a sharp, semihysterical shriek while he laughed wickedly.

She bit his shoulder.

"Ow!" But he wouldn't stop laughing. His sheer delight was contagious, and once her body had stopped convulsing quite so wildly she laughed, too.

"That was so unfair."

"Want to do it again?" He maneuvered her just an inch or

two and then back so that wicked jet brushed between her legs for half a second.

"Oh, yessss— I mean, no." She sobered, and her eyes unexpectedly filled with tears. She leaned in so he couldn't see her face and whispered in his ear. "I want you inside me. I need to feel you, all of you."

"But we don't have—"

"I don't care."

If getting pregnant was the worst thing that happened to her, she would count herself lucky.

The thought shocked her. But there it was. Having Hudson's baby actually sounded attractive to her.

She didn't have time to think about it any further, because he was quick to obey, his erection pressing against her, seeking entrance.

Slowly he lowered her onto him. She'd never felt anything as good as filling herself with Hudson, with his essence, both of them cocooned in the warm, swirling waters.

He turned and sat on one of the underwater benches. She folded her legs, supporting herself on her knees in a position that might have been uncomfortable were they not nearly weightless. Widening her legs, she grasped his shoulders and pulled herself closer until she literally felt his hip bones on the backs of her thighs.

Since he no longer needed to support her weight with his hands, he busied them with other activities, like squeezing her breasts together and dipping his tongue into the cleavage.

With small movements, she could control their sexual dance, and she moved up and down, sliding him in and out of her, slowly, intending to drive him as crazy as he'd driven her. Since she'd just climaxed, she had more control. This was the first time she'd maintained any presence of mind when they made love, and she used it to the fullest, choreographing the rhythm, the depth, kissing him, taking the slight hint when he thrust his tongue into her mouth.

She brought him just to the edge of losing control, then slowed and let him cool slightly, only to repeat the process. The third time, he made a strangled noise in his throat.

"Have mercy, woman."

"Maybe you'll think twice before you make me come before I'm ready." But it was all good. She'd loved it.

"How about now, huh? Can I make you come now?"

"You don't need to do a thing."

She moved a little faster, just a little, and she felt the passion rising in her body again, a gallon of warm honey coursing through her veins, culminating in the most delicious crash of sensations.

As soon as her body began to pulsate with her second climax, he joined her with a triumphant cry.

Elizabeth let her tears flow this time. She couldn't even put a name to what she felt, only that it was intense and out of her control. He put his arms around her and held her tight.

"It's gonna be okay, baby. Somehow. We have to make it okay."

For a moment, she let herself believe him.

CHAPTER SIXTEEN

CARLA ARRIVED EARLY to work, hoping for a few minutes of peace and quiet to get her head on straight.

She used to love her job. Now every day was a chore as she did all the things necessary to build a case against a man she knew wasn't guilty of anything.

She'd just brewed herself a cup of herbal tea—nasty stuff—when Todd strode into the bull pen. She hadn't realized he was already at work, but she shouldn't be surprised. He was always punctual, always putting in the extra hours. Whether he was trying to impress the brass, or he really had a strong work ethic, she wasn't sure. But it was very different than Hudson, who sometimes skated in thirty seconds before their shift began.

She found herself missing Hudson's laid-back ways. She didn't like the way Todd questioned every move she made, the constant note-taking.

Everything about Todd Knightly grated on her nerves. She'd told the lieutenant she could stomach partnering with Todd for a few weeks. But if this partnership with Todd became permanent...

She shuddered. If that were the case, she'd have to put in for a transfer. She'd go back to working Vice if she had to.

Todd had his cell phone clamped between his ear and his shoulder, a doughnut in one hand, a mug of coffee in the other. He set his coffee down, finished his phone call, then turned to Carla with a triumphant grin. "That was the crime lab calling."

"What do they have to say?" Carla held her breath.

"Hudson Vale's DNA was found all over Franklin Mandalay's car. Since he claimed to have had no contact with the man other than when he arrested him, I do believe that gives me probable cause."

"You're going to arrest him?" Carla couldn't believe this was happening. She'd wanted Hudson to suffer...a little...but she'd never wanted it to go this far.

"It's not a pleasant duty, but it's one I take seriously. Yes, I'll take him into custody."

Carla decided right then she'd have no part of this. Hudson wasn't capable of murder. Did Todd have no instincts? Then again, Todd didn't know Hudson the way she did, and she hadn't exactly been defending him.

Todd brushed some doughnut sugar off his uniform. "He's staying at Daniel Logan's estate, you know."

"Yes, I know," she said drily.

"I hope that smug billionaire doesn't try to block us. Him and all his fancy lawyers."

Carla kind of hoped he did.

HUDSON WOKE THE next morning with a smile on his face, and it took him a few seconds to get up to speed and realize why.

Liz.

She hadn't spent the night with him. Much as he'd wanted her to, she'd decided to keep last night's events private, and he had to respect that. But the fact they'd had to part ways with a few heated kisses in a hallway didn't detract from all that had happened.

He hadn't imagined the unique connection between them. It was way more than physical; they'd connected clear down to the soul. There'd been no barriers between them, physical or emotional.

He knew why she'd done it. She thought this was good-bye. They both could feel the noose tightening around their necks. Though Knightly hadn't bothered them, hadn't de-manded they answer any more questions, they knew he was watching their every move.

It was only a matter of time before Knightly and Sanchez pounced.

Rather than feel resigned to his fate, Hudson got out of bed with a renewed sense of purpose. He was not going to let that son of a bitch get the best of him. He was close to figuring it all out, but he couldn't do it with his hands tied.

It might be time to cut ties with Project Justice. As much as he appreciated Daniel's generous help, Daniel had certain standards to maintain, certain lines he couldn't cross if he intended to preserve the foundation's reputation and continue to help other blameless people sitting in prison, waiting for someone to prove their innocence.

Hudson understood that. But he suspected his survival depended on his ability to cross those lines, to find out what he needed to know no matter what.

Someone at Munch's apartment complex had to have seen something. That was where Hudson intended to start. The cops were probably done processing the crime scene, so they wouldn't bother him.

Then he was going to find Jazz. Hudson was sure she knew more than she'd been willing to tell Liz. In fact, Hudson had been thinking about Carlos. He vaguely matched Nellie's de-scription of the man who'd paid her a visit. He certainly had a motive to kill Mandalay, if the millionaire lawyer was in-terfering with his business.

A text from Elena on his silver phone informed him that breakfast was at eight. Hudson showered and dressed, intend-ing to eat a huge breakfast. God knew how or when he'd eat in the coming days. It would be catch-as-catch-can.

Breakfast was on the patio. Although there was a slight

fall chill in the air, Daniel had one of those tall space heaters like restaurants used, so the area was perfectly comfortable.

Liz was already seated at the table, looking fresh as a new bar of soap. She wore jeans and a little white sweater with pearl buttons, and her face was relaxed, her hair loose around her shoulders.

She looked like a woman who'd been well loved.

As soon as she saw him she smiled, a secret smile just for him, and his heart bloomed inside his chest. Maybe they weren't totally compatible in every area, but what couple was? That didn't stop him from feeling something very deep for her, like nothing he'd ever felt before.

He'd stopped short of trying to tell her how he felt last night. That could wait until they'd dealt with this albatross around their necks. He refused to tie her to him with declarations if he was going to prison.

"Good morning, Liz. Sleep well?"

"Not at all," she said easily. "You?"

"Caught a couple of hours this morning." He sat across from her and poured himself some coffee. "What's on the breakfast menu today?"

"I heard something about a cheese-and-mushroom frittata."

Staying at Daniel's was like staying free at a four-star hotel. He thought about how nice it would be to take Liz to a fancy resort sometime, where they could do whatever they pleased, eat whatever they wanted and make love three times a day.

But unlike here, it would be just them, he thought as Elena showed Joe to the table. They all greeted each other uneasily.

"Do you have a plan for today?" Liz asked the two men politely.

"Actually, I have some good news," Joe said. "I went back to the Bella Breeze apartments and waited until the cops were done processing the scene—then I started talking to people."

Amazing. That was exactly what Hudson had been planning to do. Maybe he hadn't given Joe enough credit for his investigative skills.

"Did they talk to you?"

"Most didn't. Even though I told them I wasn't a cop, most still thought I was. But I did find one older woman who was willing to open up—the kind who spends most of her time peeking through the curtains to discover what her neighbors are up to. I knew she had to have seen something."

"I love those old ladies," Hudson said. "There's one in every neighborhood. What did she have to say?"

"Nothing, at first. But after I petted her cat for a while and told her about my own cats, she opened right up. She has no love for the police."

"And…?" Liz leaned forward, her eyes bright with anticipation.

"She heard gunfire in that upstairs apartment. She remembered it was very late on a Saturday night, about a week earlier."

"The same night my father was killed," Liz said.

Suddenly a look of concern came over Joe's face. "Elizabeth, are you sure you want to hear this part? It might be uncomfortable for you."

"We can go in the other room." Hudson was already pushing away from the table. He had no desire to cause her further emotional distress.

"No, please, I want to hear."

Joe looked at Hudson, and he nodded, pulling his chair back in. Though he wanted to protect Liz, she was a big girl. She probably knew what was coming.

Joe continued. "The woman heard two shots—a few seconds apart. So she watched out the window. She saw a man leaving Munch's apartment with…with a large, heavy-looking bundle, which he put into the back of his car and drove off."

Holy Mazola. "Can she describe the man?"

"Tall. White. Wearing glasses, a hat and a bulky jacket."

"Damn, that doesn't really rule me out, does it?" Hudson said. "Does she think she can identify him in a lineup?"

"She said probably not."

"What about his car?" Hudson asked eagerly. No way it was an old 280Z. You could barely fit a loaf of bread in the trunk, much less a dead body.

"Big SUV. Dark color. You don't own anything like that, do you? Either of you?" Joe looked at Hudson and Liz in turn.

"No," they said at the same time.

"Easy access to such a vehicle?"

Again, they answered in the negative.

"Elizabeth, it's possible—no, probable—that Munch's apartment was where your father was killed. Whoever took that body drove a long way to dump it. Probably intentionally, to set Hudson up as the prime suspect."

"Oh. Wait." Liz looked troubled. "Damn it!"

"What?" Hudson was pretty sure he wouldn't like what came next.

"Dark SUV. My father's Escalade. It was probably his car. The killer put my father in the trunk of his own car and drove him to Lake Conroe. Still—isn't this something positive? Why would Hudson go out of his way to make himself look guilty? Why wouldn't he just leave my father there?"

Joe nodded. "Good point. But we have to think hard before we go to the sheriff with this. The woman's description of the suspect looks superficially like Hudson. If a good prosecutor got hold of the woman, he could twist her words."

"The description could fit lots of people," Hudson said, "including Carlos De Lugo, Jazz's pimp. He makes a pretty good suspect. If Mandalay was involved in prostitution, and he knew Jazz, stands to reason he knew Carlos, too. His rap sheet includes some pretty nasty stuff."

Joe flipped through his notebook. "Yeah. Armed robbery, assault with a deadly weapon, impersonating a police officer, pandering—"

"Impersonating a police officer?" Hudson repeated.

"Yeah. Is that important?" Joe asked.

Hudson shrugged and took a gulp of coffee, scalding his mouth. He wasn't going to bring up the subject of Holly Mandalay around Liz unless he had to. Their truce was too fragile.

"At least we know something more about what happened that night," Liz said. "If my father was killed there, his DNA will be there, right? The police will have to concede that he was killed nowhere near where Hudson lives."

Joe nodded. "Very good point."

Cora, the chef, entered then with the promised frittata. It smelled like heaven. A plate of crisp bacon followed, as well as a bowl of fruit salad.

Despite the unappetizing nature of their conversation, they all served themselves hearty portions. If this was going to be Hudson's last decent meal for a while, he'd lucked out.

After a few bites of the frittata, Joe looked up. "Shouldn't Daniel be here?"

"Yes, he should," Liz said. "Normally Cora times things perfectly so that her boss's food doesn't get cold before he gets to the table."

As if on cue, Daniel appeared. He looked abnormally disheveled, as if he'd just thrown on his clothes. In fact…he hadn't shaved.

"Daniel." Hudson came out of his chair. "Something's wrong."

"Yeah, you could say that." He settled into a chair and poured himself some coffee. "I've been on the phone with a contact I have at the Montgomery County crime lab. They've been processing the items found in Franklin Mandalay's car."

"The Cadillac Escalade," Hudson said, just to be clear, though he knew that was the car Daniel referred to.

Daniel nodded. "Hudson, you're sure you've never been in that vehicle?"

"Absolutely not."

Daniel paused, as if not quite sure how to continue. "Your DNA was found in the car."

"What? No way." Hudson's head spun. This could not be happening. "Where was it found?"

"Tissues."

"You mean, like, Kleenex? I hardly ever even use tissues, unless I'm sick. Which…I was, couple of weeks back. The day I arrested Mandalay. I was at the Quikki Market buying cold medicine."

"So, someone could just dig through your trash," Liz said, obviously seeing what he already knew—that the evidence had been planted.

Hudson puzzled it out for a few moments. "I barely left the house while I was sick. So someone would have had to get into my garbage can."

"What about at work?" Daniel asked.

Hudson thought back. "I was at work when I first started sneezing… Hell. That was before I even arrested Mandalay. Two weeks before the murder. Someone would have had to do an awful lot of planning in advance to frame me for a murder that hadn't been committed."

"There was DNA found on one other item," Daniel said. "A baseball cap."

Even more puzzling. "What kind of baseball cap?"

"University of Houston."

"That's… It was in my desk at work."

Daniel nodded. "Still think it couldn't be Carla?"

"The witness saw a man moving the…" He didn't finish, still trying to shield Liz from grisly reminders of her father's death. "Not a woman. Jazz also mentioned a man. And Mrs. Vilches."

"More than one person could be involved," Daniel pointed out.

"A ton of people come in and out of the bull pen. No one would think twice if someone opened a desk drawer looking for a stapler or Post-it note or whatever." *Please, don't let it be Carla. But the bullet was from her gun....*

"This will all matter when it comes to building a defense," Daniel said.

The frittata sat heavy in Hudson's stomach. "So I should expect to be arrested?"

"No way around it. I've already called Raleigh, told her to be on alert. Of course I don't have to tell you not to answer any questions without a lawyer—"

"I'm not going to answer any questions, period." Even innocent people sounded guilty during an interrogation.

"I'm sorry, dude," Joe said. "I feel like I failed you."

"You did everything you possibly could. And, hell, I hope you're not done yet."

"No way. I'll keep digging. I'll talk to Carlos. Maybe someone you work with has money problems? A foreclosure imminent? You said your partner was a single mom—oftentimes they're up against the wall."

"I don't know. I can't think." The walls were closing in on him. He stood up. "I need to clear my head. I'm gonna walk outside for a few minutes, get some fresh air." Which was ludicrous; they were already outside. But he had to say something.

He didn't dare look at Liz. If he did, she would know what he was up to.

"Don't be gone too long," Daniel said, sounding like an overprotective dad, but the implication was clear. When the sheriff's deputies arrived, he should make himself available.

Hudson hated to betray the trust Daniel had put in him. But he had no choice.

When he'd been walking yesterday, looking for Liz, he'd noticed a twisting live-oak tree growing near the perimeter fence. That was when he'd first toyed with the idea of fleeing.

He hadn't been ready to do it then. But just in case... shielded from view of the house by the group of trees, Hudson had surreptitiously snipped a wire on one of the motion detectors set at intervals around the fence. If he was lucky, the malfunction hadn't yet been noticed by Daniel's security people; or if they had noticed, they'd attributed the problem to animals chewing on the wire, or a simple short, and it had been put on a list of repairs to be done.

He didn't check whether the wire had been fixed. He was due at least a little luck, wasn't he? He slithered up the trunk of the tree. With one last look over his shoulder, he made the leap to the ground on the other side.

LIZ DIDN'T KNOW what to do with herself. She wandered from room to room in Daniel's house, unable to enjoy the carefully decorated spaces, the priceless artwork on the walls. Daniel's golden retriever, Tucker, followed her around, pausing whenever she did to look up at her with his soulful eyes, as if he wondered what was wrong and wanted to help.

Every time she thought about Hudson being arrested, she wanted to cry. She felt even more frightened when she took it a step further, when she thought about being arrested herself. From the beginning, she'd seen that hers and Hudson's fates were tied together. They'd been together that night, and everybody knew it now despite their attempt at subterfuge. If the cops arrested Hudson, could her own arrest be far behind?

Maybe they wanted to continue watching her. See if she might try to cover her tracks while attention was focused on Hudson.

How would she be able to help him if she was behind bars herself?

Joe and Daniel were downstairs in Daniel's bat cave, where he had all the powerful computers and programs that would run simulations and recognize patterns. But while they didn't exclude her, she didn't feel welcome. She wasn't much help to them, other than when they wanted to get a more touchy-feely evaluation. And they had a psychologist on retainer for that kind of thing, as well as a former FBI profiler only a phone call away.

She wished Hudson would come back inside. She sympathized with his desire to see the sky and the trees, breathe fresh air, for as long as he could. But didn't he want to see her, too?

The look he'd given her when he left the breakfast table had confused her. His expression had been a mixture of fondness, sadness, regret…and guilt. Guilt because he felt he was dragging her down with him?

She was in Daniel's library, perusing the shelves of leather-bound volumes, when the doorbell chimed. Her whole body tightened. It could be anybody—a repairman, a friend or neighbor or someone Daniel had called in to consult. He had the most amazing network of professionals who could do anything. But she knew it wasn't any of those people.

Elizabeth peeked out the door of the library to see Elena rushing past, looking troubled. She watched as Elena headed down the staircase to the basement.

Moving to the windows, Elizabeth peeked through the blinds. Two Montgomery County cruisers sat in the driveway, doors left open, lights flashing.

Her trepidation turned to anger. There was no need for this show of force. All they had to do was ask Hudson to turn himself in and he would have.

Wouldn't he?

With a sudden surge of bravado, Elizabeth exited the library and made her way to the foyer. Detectives Sanchez and Knightly stood just inside the door, two beefy uniformed deputies right behind them. All of them looked ill at ease and out of place in the opulent, marble-floored room with its gurgling fountain, statues and stained glass casting rainbows all around them.

She strode in, intent on saying her piece before Daniel or Joe arrived and cautioned her not to.

"He didn't do it. You guys are making a terrible mistake."

Knightly smiled like a predator. "Ms. Vale. I thought you might be here, too. We'll see who made a terrible mistake."

"The murder occurred in Houston. We were miles away in Conroe."

"Oh? And how do you know that? Exactly?"

"There was a witness who saw someone moving the body."

Knightly appeared skeptical at best. "Really?" He whipped out his notebook.

Had she just said something that sounded suspiciously like a confession?

"Who is this witness? How did you find him?"

Elizabeth wasn't about to reveal anything about the witness. To do so might cause her to end up like Munch. "We found the witness because we're doing the investigation you *should* be doing."

Daniel and Joe swept into the room like a hurricane.

"Elizabeth," Joe said, "you shouldn't say anything more without an attorney."

"But they need to know—we have to make them understand that Hudson could not possibly—" She forced herself to shut up in the face of Daniel's quelling look.

"Elizabeth, don't worry. We will of course turn over anything we've learned to the police when they ask us to. How about it, Sergeant…Sanchez, isn't it? And Sergeant Knightly? Bring my investigator into your interrogation room and question him. Mr. Kinkaid is a former Secret Service agent with the highest security clearance and an impeccable reputation."

Joe nodded. "I would be happy to tell you everything I've learned—provided the entire interview is on the record."

Interesting, Elizabeth thought. With everything on the record, there was no way the police could sweep exculpatory evidence under the table, pretend it didn't exist.

"I assure you, our investigation has been very thorough." Knightly matched Daniel's ultrapolite tone. "We'll take you up on your offer, Mr. Logan, Mr. Kinkaid. But right now, I'd like for you to produce Mr. Vale. I have a warrant for his arrest and a search warrant that allows me access to your property and any buildings on it to locate him."

"Unfortunately, Hudson went for a walk. He's not my prisoner here, and he didn't say exactly where he was going or when he would be back. I've got people out looking for him now. I assure you, it's not my intention to hinder your investigation or conceal Hudson's whereabouts from you."

Sanchez looked directly at Elizabeth. "How about you? You must know where your lover is."

Lover. Talk about a loaded word. Should she deny it? But Sanchez knew the truth of it. She was looking at Elizabeth not as a cop, but woman to woman. Could Carla see it in Elizabeth's face? Were her feelings that obvious?

"I'm afraid I don't," Elizabeth finally said. "The last time I saw him was at breakfast, about two hours ago." She looked her directly in the eye, daring Sanchez to challenge her.

Sanchez said nothing. She looked supremely uncomfortable. Because she knew Hudson hadn't done it? Because she had firsthand knowledge of the crime? Or was she simply upset because her former partner was in this much hot water?

Knightly looked at his watch. "You've got five minutes to produce him. Then we look ourselves."

Joe took Elizabeth's arm and gently guided her away from the cops. "Come on, Elizabeth. Maybe we can find him."

She waited until they were out of earshot before speaking. "I'm sorry, Joe. I hope I didn't damage our case. I'm just so frustrated. Those detectives are so smug, and they're not going to listen to anything that doesn't build the case against their pet suspect."

"I'm afraid you're right. Listen, do you know where Hudson is?"

Elizabeth's stomach sank. "I honestly don't."

"Did he say he might run? Did he give you that impression?"

She thought back to their conversation last night. "He said cops don't fare well in prison, but that was the only indication he gave me that he might not go willingly. In fact, when I suggested we run—"

"You did *what?*"

"It was just a fleeting impulse. Anyway, he nixed the idea. You don't think he would run, do you? Really?"

Joe pressed his lips together. "I don't know. If I were in his shoes, if I felt like I'd been framed and I couldn't prove my innocence…" Joe shook his head. "I just don't know. If he doesn't cooperate, it won't help his case."

"I guess I can't blame him."

"If he's still on the estate, where do you think he might go?"

"The hummingbird garden," she said. "It's a special place. It's where we first… Well, it's special."

But when they went there to check it out, it was empty and quiet, an ordinary place holding none of the magic she remembered from previous visits.

They searched for an hour—the cops, Daniel's security people, Elizabeth, Joe and Daniel himself. There was no sign of Hudson.

He'd vanished.

"I don't know what to tell you," Daniel said, seeming genuinely flummoxed—enough so that Elizabeth concluded Hudson hadn't clued anyone in on his plan to bolt for freedom. "He's not answering his phone."

"I guess he's looking for more charges to be filed," Knightly said smugly, though there was a tone of frustration in his voice, too. "He was told to keep himself available, and he's deliberately flouting that request."

Daniel shrugged. "If he didn't know an arrest was imminent, I don't know how you can accuse him of that. I'm sure he just needed some time to himself. Have you tried his house?"

"Thanks for the advice," Knightly said with a note of sarcasm. "Don't worry, we'll find him. And if I discover you're hiding him, you'll be slapped with an obstruction-of-justice charge so fast—"

"I'm not hiding him." The animosity in Daniel's voice was enough to shut Knightly up. He motioned for the other cops to follow, and they left. Daniel, Joe, Elena and Elizabeth watched out the windows until both cars cleared the gates, then Daniel let out a long, pent-up breath.

"You don't know where he is?" Daniel asked Elizabeth one more time.

She shook her head. "I would tell you if I did." What she didn't say was that she hoped, if he was fleeing the law, that he got away with it. Maybe he would make it to South America, like they'd talked about, and stay there until Elizabeth and Daniel's team could prove his innocence. Because prison wasn't a safe place for him to await the slow wheels of justice.

CHAPTER SEVENTEEN

HUDSON SPOTTED HIS mom standing at the sink, washing dishes. There was no sign of any police presence. Knightly and Sanchez would look for him here eventually, but they hadn't arrived yet. Still, Hudson didn't know how much time he had.

After leaving Daniel's estate, he'd run at least four miles, keeping to back roads, trying to look like an ordinary guy out for a jog. When he'd got far enough away from the estate—well away from the ritzy River Oaks neighborhood— he'd found his way to a busier road and hitchhiked most of the way to his parents' house in Rosenberg.

He'd come around from the back side, in case someone was watching the front, though he doubted Sanchez and Knightly would have had time to set up surveillance quite yet. He moved through a hedgerow, keeping low to the ground, using shrubs and trees as cover, until he reached the safety of the screened-in porch.

It would be better if his mother never knew he was there. That way, there would be no need for her to lie to the cops when they asked if she'd seen him.

Hudson duckwalked across the porch, well below window level. The door to the inside was open, letting in the cool, autumn day. His mom liked her fresh air.

His parents kept their keys on a rack near the garage door, which was off the kitchen. There was no way he could get past her without her seeing or hearing him; he'd learned that as a teenager trying to sneak into or out of the house. But he had an idea.

He made his way to the front door, which also was open with just the screen door closed. He silently opened the screen door and rang the doorbell, then sprinted across the living room to the dining room, where he crouched behind the dining-room table.

"Be there in just a minute," Binnie called. She would have to turn off the water, dry her hands, then make her way to the front door. She walked right past his hiding place. As soon as her back was to him, he tiptoed into the kitchen, then made his way to the hallway leading out to the garage. She wouldn't see him here unless she specifically went looking.

"Hello," he heard her calling out, "anybody here?"

First, Hudson checked the hall closet, where his folks kept things like batteries and flashlights, a few tools, garbage bags, that sort of thing, to see if there was anything useful there. The first thing he noticed was a pile of cheap cell phones—his mom's stash of throwaways.

Thank God for his mom's quirky habits. Each of those phones would have a few minutes left and they would be untraceable. He also found a stack of paper shopping bags, the pretty kind with handles that came from high-end stores. His mom couldn't stand to throw those away. He selected one and shoved the cell phones inside. He took a crescent wrench, a screwdriver and some bungee cords, though he really had no idea what he would do with the stuff. He wasn't exactly MacGyver.

Time was running out. His mom could finish the dishes at any moment and decide to take the trash out.

The key rack was next. Hudson took a hasty inventory of the various keys hanging on the rack. His dad's were gone. His mom's were there, along with keys to the shed and another set of keys clearly labeled *Baumgartner*—the neighbors' keys. Finally he found both sets of keys he wanted. Likely they wouldn't be missed, at least for a while.

His only route of escape was out the garage. He waited until his mother returned to the kitchen and turned the water back on. Then he slipped out the door into the garage, which was unfortunately closed.

He thought he would just ease the door up a couple of feet, slide out, then leave the property the same way he'd come in. But he quickly saw the error in his plan.

When had his parents got an automatic garage-door opener? That thing was going to make a helluva noise and his mother would definitely hear it. But she would probably think it was his dad, coming home unexpectedly. She would only go to check after a minute or two when he didn't appear.

It was the best he could do. He pushed the button and scooted out under the door as soon as it had raised up three feet or so. Then he ran like a chicken being chased by a cook with a hatchet. He could only hope none of the neighbors saw, but this neighborhood was rather rural and sparsely populated, so he was probably safe.

He took the shortest route off the property and out of sight. Once he was on the street and half a block away, he slowed to a brisk walk—just a guy out for a walk on a beautiful fall day.

Next stop—U Store It. When his great-uncle had gone into a nursing home, Hudson's parents had ended up with his car, an ancient but sturdy green Buick. They kept it in a storage facility, always meaning to get rid of it but never quite getting around to putting an ad in the paper. The tags were expired, but with luck no one would notice.

Hudson needed a way to get around, and no one would be looking for that car. Even if his parents realized he'd taken it, they probably wouldn't rat him out. He hated to put them in that position, but he had no choice. If he was going to catch a murderer, he needed wheels.

The storage place was only a couple of miles away, so he

walked. No one seemed to notice him when he entered the property. He walked back to the unit, opened it and was relieved to see the Buick sitting right where it should be.

There was a lot of other stuff here, too—some old water skis, a floor lamp, various framed posters, some junk he recognized as having come from his and his brother's rooms. If he'd had the luxury of time, he'd have gone through it to see if there was anything useful. But he wanted to get the hell away before someone thought to look for him here.

Hudson slid behind the wheel, stuck the key in the ignition, held his breath and turned. Although it hesitated a couple of times, the engine finally turned over and the car started. Hudson checked the glove box to see if it still had its registration papers, in case he needed to sell it. He'd be doing his parents a favor, actually.

The registration was right where it should be.

He knew a guy who would pay top dollar for vintage cars, no questions asked. Liz's suggestion about South America flitted through his mind. With a couple thousand bucks, he could get there and have a little to spare. He could find work, rent a room, wait it out. Wait until Project Justice exonerated him.

But he would still have to deal with other charges, like fleeing to escape justice. He would never get his badge back. And chances were good he would never be free of the murder charge. He could never come back to the States.

He could never see Liz again.

Nope. That was the coward's way out. This flight from justice was temporary. He just needed a few more days. He would find Munch's friends, family. Find out if he'd talked about his involvement with Mandalay. It was the kind of thing a two-bit thug like Munch would brag about. Maybe one of them would know the identity of the tall man who'd disposed of Mandalay's body.

It was someone he worked with. Someone who had access to his desk at work. Someone who had an ax to grind. Someone *male.*

Oh, hell. The answer had been staring him in the face the whole time. Why hadn't he seen it before?

ELIZABETH COULDN'T STAND pacing around Daniel's house one minute longer. Despite the size of the house and grounds, she was feeling claustrophobic, like one of those animals in a wildlife park. They had fields to run in, plenty of food, but they weren't free.

She wanted to go home—to her tidy little condo, where not so long ago her life had been simple, if not perfect. She'd gone to work each day and come home every night feeling as if she'd done some good in the world. Her biggest worry was how to keep her father from taking over her life.

He'd been a pain, that was for sure. But she still missed him. Not her father the murderer, but the father she remembered from when she was little, who had spoiled her and told her over and over what a wonderful life she had ahead of her, how special she was, how she touched his life with magic.

True or not, his constant praise and encouragement had started her off in life with high self-esteem. She could at least be grateful for that.

Feeling the need for a female friend, Elizabeth sought out Elena, who was in the process of replacing faded flower arrangements with fresh ones. She caught up with her in the foyer. The flowers there were orchids, calling to mind the ones her father had sent. Elizabeth ruthlessly pushed the memory into the back of her mind.

"The arrangements are beautiful," she said. "Do you do them yourself?"

"Oh, goodness, no. I have no artistic talent whatsoever. Mr. Li, the gardener, does them. There are so many flowers growing on the estate and in the greenhouse, and he wants everyone to enjoy them, even if they don't have time for a walk outside."

"He seems passionate about his work."

"Oh, he is. Everyone should feel so lucky to have a calling like his. Or like you. It must be wonderful to help people work through their problems."

Elizabeth dug out a smile. "Most days I feel very lucky to be doing what I love. What do you love, Elena?" She couldn't help herself. Elena, while incredibly efficient and seemingly serene, was a puzzle to Elizabeth. She sensed a quiet yearning beneath the beautiful woman's calm facade.

"I don't know."

"Have you been to college? That's where a lot of people figure out what they love, by taking different classes."

"Yes. I have a business degree." Elena shrugged. "I like what I'm doing, for now. The pay is very generous, so I can send most of it back to my family in Cuba."

"How did you come here?"

Elena smiled self-consciously as she picked up the bowl of faded flowers and carried it into the kitchen, where presumably someone would put them in the compost and wash the container. She then headed for the patio, where the table they'd had breakfast on just a couple of hours earlier was now filled with a frenzy of bright colors, the exotic blooms arranged into the most creative bouquets.

"My story is complicated," Elena said.

Elizabeth scooped up one of the arrangements and grabbed another. She might as well help out.

"You don't have to do that," Elena protested.

"I'd like to feel useful."

They headed back indoors, to the living room this time. Elena pointed to a table where Elizabeth could set the heavy arrangement until Elena cleared a space for it.

"I'm a good listener," Elizabeth said.

Elena shook her head, and Elizabeth sensed sadness there.

"Another time, perhaps, when we can relax over a pitcher of margaritas."

"I'll hold you to that. Say, Elena, I'd really like to go back to my apartment. I can see the writing on the walls—I could be arrested anytime."

Elena stopped what she was doing and turned, going to Elizabeth and taking both her hands. "That would be so stupid of the police. Anyone can see you are kind, that there is no violence in you."

"Unfortunately, the police look at evidence, not emotions. And right now, the picture they've painted of me is pretty damning. I'd like to tidy things up—ask my neighbor to water my plants, pay bills, clean out the fridge—that kind of thing. Is there a car I could use?"

Elena frowned. "Daniel said you shouldn't go out by yourself. It's too dangerous—someone could be after you."

"Oh, I think they've accomplished what they want. With the sheriff focusing on Hudson and me as suspects, the real murderer can go on about his business. If he were to hurt me, it would only turn suspicion in a new direction."

"Unless he could somehow blame Hudson for that, too," Elena said practically.

Gad. Elizabeth hadn't even considered that. Maybe she *wasn't* safe.

"I'll get one of our security people to take you home so you can do these chores, okay?" Elena was already reaching for the phone.

Elizabeth would have preferred to get off by herself, but perhaps it would be safer to have company.

Thirty minutes later, Elizabeth was ensconced in the backseat of another cushy Lincoln Town Car with a nice, deceptively harmless-looking man named Toby at the wheel. Elena had assured her Toby could handle whatever threats came her way.

"We do have an escort," Toby said casually once they were on the freeway.

Elizabeth craned her neck to look out the back window. She saw a sea of cars.

"They're cops. I'm sure of it. Nothing you can do about that, really, so long as they stop short of harassing you."

"Whatever." She didn't care if they saw her visiting her own home.

"You should know, they might be listening to anything you say and watching anything you do, even when you think you're in private."

"You mean, they might have bugged my apartment? Or put in surveillance cameras?" Her skin crawled at the thought.

"Anything's possible."

"Well, it's not like I'm going to say anything incriminating."

"Even when you're innocent, conversation can be taken out of context. Just be aware. At the estate, your privacy is protected."

Except that Daniel always knew who she was talking to when she used the silver phone. She'd twice tried calling Hudson's untraceable silver phone with hers. But apparently Hudson wouldn't risk even that. The cops couldn't trace them through the phones, but Daniel could.

Toby pulled up to the curb and let her out, then instructed her to wait in the lobby with the doorman until he'd parked the car and joined her. He didn't want her entering her apartment without him.

Though it was late October, her building still ran the air-conditioning in the lobby. It was too cold, and she stood with her arms wrapped around herself. She said nothing to the doorman, whom she didn't recognize. Oscar was probably still on vacation, and this guy could be anybody—one of Daniel's people, an undercover cop or a legitimate temp worker. He seemed to pay no attention to her.

Toby reappeared a couple of minutes later, and they rode the elevator upstairs. He entered her apartment first, doing an exhaustive check for people and for booby traps. He even checked for surveillance equipment. He found nothing, but told her she should still be on her guard.

She dealt with her mail first, paid a few bills, doubling the amount on the check to cover the following month, too. She cleaned out the fridge, then went outside on her balcony to water the plants. She would leave a note for Jean, her next-door neighbor, asking her to water them, at least until it became clear Elizabeth wasn't coming back.

That was a depressing thought.

While she attended to business, Toby sat on her sofa reading a book.

She'd just finished watering when her cell phone chimed. Not the silver one, but her regular phone. When she saw that it was Tonda, she answered immediately. Maybe Tonda would have some new information.

"Tonda. What's going on?"

"I'm hurt bad, Ms. Downey," she sobbed. "Real bad."

Oh, dear God. "Tonda, what happened?"

"Jackson. He just snapped. Beat me up pretty bad."

"Is he there with you now?" Elizabeth had to first determine if Tonda was still in danger.

"No. He left."

"Then call 9-1-1 for an ambulance. I'll meet you at the hospital."

"No, no, no hospitals. They'll call the police!"

Of course. Tonda didn't want the police involved. It was something Elizabeth dealt with over and over, this mistrust of police from her clients who'd been treated badly by law enforcement or who were scared of going to jail themselves.

"We can sort that out later. The important thing is to get you taken care of. You and the baby."

"Will you come get me?" Tonda asked in a small voice. "Please, I'm scared."

"All right, I'll come. But you have to let me take you to a hospital."

"Yeah, okay. But you have to come by yourself. No cops. Nobody else." She was crying so hard, Elizabeth could barely understand her.

"No cops." She wondered how Tonda would feel about Toby, then dismissed the thought. Toby would never drive her to see Tonda. He would deem it too dangerous. He would insist on letting the authorities handle the matter, since technically it had nothing to do with the case. "Just tell me where you are."

"I'm at home. At the apartment on Cherry Blossom, 3322A. Please hurry."

If Elizabeth's cell phone was being monitored by the police, they might show up anyway. She couldn't help that. But what to do about Toby?

Her neighbor's balcony was right next door, separated only by a five-foot wall. Getting over it would be easy, and she knew her neighbor never locked her sliding glass door. With a quick glance inside to make sure Toby was still occupied with his book, she dragged a chair to the wall and clamored over. She was inside, through the apartment and out into the hallway in moments. All she needed was a few minutes' head start on Toby and he wouldn't be able to follow.

Her police escort might be a bit harder to shake, but maybe they wouldn't be watching the garage. They'd expect her to exit with Toby and get back into his car, right? If it was just one guy, he couldn't watch all the exits at once.

She had no purse, no money or driver's license, but fortunately, she'd stuck her keys in one pocket and both cell phones in the other. Her car was in its usual spot. She got in, backed out and was out of the garage and on the road as quickly as she dared.

The address Tonda had provided was familiar enough to Elizabeth that she could find it without using her GPS. Three minutes into her flight to freedom, the silver phone rang.

Her heart beating wildly, she answered.

"Elizabeth, what the hell!" Daniel exploded.

"It's not what you think," she said hastily. "I'm not meeting Hudson. I don't know where he is and I haven't heard from him. I'm going to pick up a client who's in trouble. She made me promise to come alone, and I can't break—"

"You're putting yourself in danger."

"This has nothing to do with my father's murder. One of my clients got beat up by her boyfriend. I'm taking her to the hospital. As soon as I'm sure she's safe, I'll come back to your place."

"There was no need for all this subterfuge," he groused. "You scared Toby to death."

"I'm sorry. I guess I just… I don't know. I needed to feel like I was in control of something."

"I promise not to interfere. But I'd like to at least know where to start looking for you if you go missing."

"I'm sure I'll be fine." Unless Jackson came back. After a moment's thought, she gave him the address. "If she sees anyone but me—on the street, in the parking lot—she'll run, and I'll lose her forever. Next time Jackson beats her, he might kill her. She might lose her baby. Please tell me you understand that, Daniel."

"I do. Be careful."

Tonda's neighborhood, in the Third Ward, wasn't very far from where Carlos and his girls did business. It was daylight, and Elizabeth's car didn't have expensive wheels or much of anything worth stealing, but she knew she still had to be careful.

At least she didn't have a purse or money to worry about.

There was the building. She cruised slowly past. It wasn't a horrible place. The small, Spanish-style building was prob-

ably an eightplex. The pink stucco was stained, and a few of
the red clay tiles were missing from the roof, but someone
had made an attempt to landscape the place. The grass was
patchy but green and had been mowed recently. A couple of
brick-lined flower beds featured a handful of sagging pansies.

Elizabeth found a place to park on the next block. She
glanced up and down the street; no one seemed to be about.
No sign of anyone following her, though she'd already proved
she was no good at spotting a tail.

Just as she got out of the car, the silver phone rang again.
She checked the caller ID and didn't recognize the number.
That was odd. The only people using these silver phones
were Project Justice people. Deciding it had to be a wrong
number, she almost let it go to voice mail but then impulsively answered.

"Liz."

Only one person called her that. "Hudson. Where are you?"

He didn't answer her question. "I'm sorry, Liz. I couldn't
let them take me to jail. We're so close to finding the real
killer."

"I know, but Hudson…" Hell. Tonda was waiting for her.
She might be bleeding, unconscious, in dire need of medical care.

"I wanted you to know I'm okay. Tell them I'll turn myself
in. In two days. I just want two more days. If I can't wrap it
up by then…"

"Okay, but I can't talk right now. Tonda's in trouble. Jackson beat her up. I need to find her and take her to the hospital."

"Oh, no. I'm sorry." He sounded genuinely regretful.
"Where is she?"

"At her apartment."

"Don't you dare go there alone. Tonda is a big girl. She's
tough and streetwise. If she can call you, she can call 9-1-1."

"She said Jackson left, and she's afraid—"

"I don't care. You're not going there alone, are you? Surely Daniel wouldn't let you."

She bristled a bit at the implication that Daniel had the last word on where she went and what she did. But then a surge of guilt coursed through her at the underhanded way she'd slipped out of her building and away from Toby. "I'm here already. I have to go to her. She said if I didn't come alone—"

"Liz, don't—" The line went dead.

She couldn't wait any longer. Tonda needed her. She made her way up the uneven brick walkway and five steps leading to a wide concrete porch that ran the width of the building.

Number 2 was on the ground floor, left side. A large picture window faced the porch, but the curtains were drawn and Elizabeth couldn't see in. Taking a deep breath, she knocked on the peeling brown door. "Tonda?"

Nothing. Had Tonda heeded her advice and called for an ambulance? Or was she even now lying inside, injured too badly to answer?

Elizabeth turned the knob. The door was unlocked. She pushed it open a few inches. It appeared dark inside. All was quiet.

"Tonda!" She called again, louder this time. "Are you here?"

Her heart pounding, she pushed the door all the way open. A coat closet faced the doorway, open. A couple of jackets hung among several empty wire hangers. She left the door open and ventured farther inside.

Maybe this wasn't such a good idea after all. What if this wasn't really Tonda's apartment? What if she'd misheard the address Tonda had given her and this was a crack house or something?

Then her eye caught movement. She reached for a light switch and flipped it.

Tonda half sat, half lay on the sofa. Her face was a bloody

mess, one eye swelled closed. But her other eye was open and full of fear.

"Don't be afraid. It's just me." Elizabeth strode to the couch, intent on checking Tonda's condition more carefully. Was she still bleeding?

Tonda's one good eye widened. She shook her head almost imperceptibly

The hairs on the back of Elizabeth's neck bristled to attention. Something was very wrong. She started to turn, but before she could, something heavy crashed down on her head, and everything went black.

CHAPTER EIGHTEEN

Out of minutes.

"DAMN IT!" HUDSON screamed impotently at the message blinking on the screen of his cheap cell phone. Each of his mother's discarded phones had less than five minutes. He grabbed another phone and powered it up. Two minutes. He didn't have time to mess around. He called Carla's cell. Thank God he had a talent for memorizing phone numbers.

"Who's this?" Carla answered suspiciously.

"Carla, it's me. Are you alone? Please, dear God, don't give me away. You know I didn't do it, right?"

She cleared her throat. She wasn't alone.

"I need an address. Tonda Pickens. In the Third Ward, somewhere. It's an emergency—a woman is injured there and I have to find her." It was at least part of the truth.

"Hold on."

He felt the seconds ticking by. Carla was probably in the LTD, looking up the address on the onboard computer as Hudson headed his car toward the Third Ward.

"I'm still looking," Carla said casually, as if having a normal conversation with a friend. "What's going on?"

No way was she guilty of anything. Not murder, not corruption. If she'd framed him, she'd be hanging him out to dry. She could be sending units to Tonda's address, and that would be okay, too. He had a very, very bad feeling about

Liz showing up at that address by herself. The timing was highly suspect.

"I need two days."

"Okay by me."

"Knightly's with you?"

"Not him. Right after we left the Logan place, he said he wanted to go talk to some Houston cops he knew regarding the Munch homicide. Man-to-man. Clearly he didn't want me interfering, so he dropped me at the station."

More alarm bells.

"Don't trust him with your back, okay? Don't trust anybody. Just so you know, whoever railroaded me is trying to do the same to you. The bullet Munch fired at me was traced back to your gun."

"What bullet? Where?"

"Remember, the prowler who shot at me? Daniel's people found the bullet. They checked it against the ballistics database—"

"Well, it's not mine!" she said hotly. "I never… Oh, my God."

"What?"

"My backup weapon was stolen! That first week you were out, somebody bashed my car window at a gas station and grabbed my purse."

"Carla, listen. I think Knightly's dirty. He knows Project Justice is getting closer to the truth, which means he's desperate. I have to go now." His minutes were about to run out anyway, and he only had one more phone after this. Anyway, he was getting close to the neighborhood. He knew vaguely where Tonda's street was. He just had to find it. "Do you have Tonda's address?"

"It's on Cherry Blossom. Thirty-three—" The phone cut her off. Out of minutes again, damn it.

He picked up the last phone from the passenger seat. Unable to resist the compulsion, he dialed Liz again. The phone went to voice mail.

His apprehension turned into a cold, hard ball of fear. He stomped on the gas pedal. He knew Tonda lived on the 3300 block of Cherry Blossom. He'd find Liz if he had to bash down the door of every house and apartment on that street.

CARLA STARED AT her phone. She had no idea what to make of all this. If Hudson had given her half a chance, she'd have begged him to turn himself in. She might have her issues with Hudson—and yes, she might have enjoyed his being a murder suspect just a little too much. But she didn't believe he was guilty. No amount of DNA found in Mandalay's car would convince her Hudson had killed the man. DNA could be planted. Tissues could be taken from the trash and placed anywhere. And that baseball cap—Carla remembered Hudson wearing it to the station earlier, during the summer, when he'd come straight from a softball game. Why would he have worn it at night, to commit a murder, then left it at the scene? He wasn't stupid.

"What's going on?" She'd rendezvoused with a deputy from Patrol, Ronnie, to help her with some routine neighborhood canvassing around the area where Mandalay's car had been found. Although she and Knightly had done this once, a lot of people hadn't been home and she wanted to follow up.

Now she had a new objective. "Head for 3322 Cherry Blossom. It's in the Third Ward."

ELIZABETH'S HEAD POUNDED. If she opened her eyes, she was going to throw up. Where was she? Was she dying? She couldn't remember anything. Wait. Wait. Tonda had called. She was hurt, needed help. Elizabeth had slipped out of her apartment building and away from Toby the bodyguard…but that was the last thing she remembered.

Her arms were twisted painfully behind her. The pounding

in her head now warred with a piercing ache in her shoulder. Had she been shot? Stabbed?

She had to open her eyes. Her thoughts were starting to align themselves, feel less chaotic. Something bad had happened and she had to figure it out.

The smell of stale cigarettes assaulted her nose. Her stomach roiled, threatening to revolt.

Open. Open your eyes.

She cracked one eye open then the other. She was half sitting on a ratty green sofa in a small, sparsely furnished living room. An old-style TV was on to some infomercial, but the sound was turned down.

Something stirred beside her. She slowly turned her head. Every small movement brought stabbing pain behind her eyes and a kettledrum pounding inside her skull.

Tonda. Tonda was sitting next to her, her face bloody and swollen.

Elizabeth gasped. "Oh, my God," she whispered. "Tonda, are you okay?"

Tonda wouldn't look at her. "I'm so sorry, Ms. Downey. He made me do it."

"No, honey, it's not your fault—" As Elizabeth tried to sit up, she realized her wrists were confined behind her back. She jerked her arms, trying to free herself, and found she was wearing metal cuffs.

"He made me do it," Tonda sobbed again, her voice barely a whisper. "He made me call you. He hurt me and he said he would k-kill me."

Elizabeth still wasn't clear what was going on, but she knew one thing. "It's not your fault. It's Jackson's."

"No, not him. It wasn't him. He made me lie."

"Who…who made you lie?"

Her eyes cut to the other side of the room. "Him."

Elizabeth jerked her head to look. She recognized the face that looked back, though she'd never seen it with such an expression of evil. "Sergeant Knightly." This made no sense at all. "How do you even know Tonda?"

"I know a lot of working girls. I've seen her around. Saw her at the clinic, in fact, that first day Sanchez and I came to talk to you."

Elizabeth felt even sicker, knowing her fondness for her client had put the girl in danger. "So this was a trap. Hudson said it might be, but I was too stupid to listen."

"You told Vale you were coming here?"

"Yes. He should be here any minute." No. She hadn't taken the precautions she should have. She'd been so sure this had nothing to do with the murders. "Your only chance to escape is to leave. Now."

He just kept smiling at her. He was holding a gun, she realized, though it wasn't pointed at them. He wasn't worried about either of them making a bolt for freedom or overpowering him. Elizabeth's hands were cuffed behind her back. She could run, but she couldn't fight, couldn't even open a door without a great deal of maneuvering.

Tonda wasn't cuffed or tied up, but she was hurt, possibly seriously, and so terrified she wasn't about to move.

"I've got it all worked out," Knightly said. "The fact you've called Vale here makes it easier. I had to get him here somehow."

"You *want* him here?" she asked incredulously.

"Someone has to be blamed for all the shooting."

Thank God she hadn't actually given Tonda's address to Hudson. If she'd lured him to his death, she'd never be able to forgive herself—never. Not that she'd be around long enough to forgive anyone. It was clear Knightly planned to kill her and Tonda.

Tonda whimpered. She was trembling with terror.

"Let me at least help Tonda. She's bleeding. You can take the cuffs off. I promise I won't go anywhere."

"You don't seriously think I'm stupid enough to take your word for it, do you? Anyway, helping her would be pointless."

"Why are you doing this?"

"That should be obvious. You and Vale were really close to finding out the truth. He talked to Detective Vilches's widow in the hospital. I'm sure she gave him my description. I couldn't wait around for her to identify me in a photo lineup."

"Detective Vilches? The one who investigated my mother's disappearance?"

"The very same. I must say, his notes on the case—which his wife very obligingly handed over—made for fascinating reading."

Hudson hadn't told her any of this. It probably would have made her mad that he was still stirring that pot. But damn it—he'd been right the whole time. Her father's murder was linked to her mother's disappearance.

"Don't worry, sweetheart. I'll still get away. Just not as clean as I'd hoped. A confession letter in Hudson's handwriting would be a nice touch. But one in yours should suffice."

"I'm not writing any confession letter." He could torture her, beat her, whatever. She refused to help him get away with his crimes.

"Oh, really?" He took a couple of steps toward her. No, toward Tonda. He grabbed Tonda by the hair and yanked, and she screamed in pain.

"Okay, I'll do it." He would have to uncuff her. That could work in her favor.

She had absolutely nothing to lose. She could just attack him, gun or no gun. If he shot her point-blank, he'd get blood on himself. That would make it much harder for him to slip out, maybe blend in with any law enforcement who showed up. She might not live, but Knightly would pay.

Maybe.

Did she have the nerve to launch an attack, knowing it would probably be the last thing she did?

Knightly let Tonda go then handed her a small key. "Unlock her cuffs."

Still sobbing, Tonda did as ordered. Her hands were shaking so badly it took her several tries to get the key in the lock and turn it.

When Elizabeth's hands were free, she rubbed her wrists to get the circulation back into her fingers. Knightly placed an old envelope and a ballpoint pen in front of her.

"Write down exactly what I say. If you deviate, if you even misspell a word, I'll shoot your friend in the knee. If you cooperate, you'll both die cleanly, no pain."

THE FIRST THING Hudson noticed about Cherry Blossom Lane, apart from the fact there were no cherry trees, was the lack of driveways—and parking. So much for his hope of spotting Liz's car in Tonda's driveway. If she'd come here, she might have had to park blocks away. But the street was blessedly short, only three blocks long. He cruised all the way down it. His heart jumped when he finally spotted a white Prius.

Was that it? He stopped in the middle of the street and got out so he could peer through the windows. The driver's window was open a crack. He couldn't see anything that definitely identified the car as hers, though it was neat and clean, the way he was sure she would keep her vehicle.

He stuck his nose near the crack and sniffed. There…a trace of that peculiar fruity mixture of scents that was hers and hers alone. She was here. He quickly parked behind her in a No Parking zone. Last thing he was worried about was a parking ticket.

Hudson had one phone and about two minutes left. How to spend it?

He had to decide fast; for every minute he delayed, Liz could get herself a minute deeper into trouble. With a sigh, he pulled the silver cell phone out. Plenty of minutes, but the moment he used it, Daniel could pinpoint his location.

Maybe that was the best solution. Daniel and his Project Justice people had every portable weapon, surveillance gadget and computer trick in the universe. They would figure out which apartment Tonda lived in among the six or eight buildings on this block.

He called Joe.

"Hudson?" Joe sounded amazed. "Dude, you're in some hot water."

"I know that. I think Liz might be in trouble—real trouble."

"Yeah, no kidding. She shook off her bodyguard. Daniel is livid. Usually people don't slip out of his custody, or whatever you want to call it. Big Brother knows—"

"Joe, I don't have much time. I think Liz might have walked into a trap. Todd Knightly is the dirty cop—I'm ninety-nine percent sure. I need you to collect anyone you can find and bring them to the 3300 block of Cherry Blossom—but without causing a stir. Any show of force might tip Knightly over the edge. I don't know which building Liz is in, but she went to help Tonda, and I need to find her. If I can just know she's safe, I'll turn myself in. Now. Please."

"I'm on it. Sit tight."

He loved that about Project Justice. They were all pissed off at him, but when the chips were down, if you needed help, no questions. They just jumped in with both feet.

He would owe them a lot when this was over.

Hudson expected it would take at least an hour before a team arrived. Joe would have to collect people, supplies, body armor, surveillance equipment. That was too long.

Liz had said an apartment, not a house. He would knock on the doors of some of the small houses sandwiched in between apartment buildings, see if any of them knew Tonda or…what was her pimp's name? Jackson, that was it.

A child of about five answered the first door he knocked on.

"Hi, is your mom or dad home?" Hudson asked.

The child continued to stare. Then he slammed the door in Hudson's face. He'd probably been left home alone while the parents worked. Sad fact of life among the poor—child care was too expensive.

No one answered at the next house, but a large dog sounded as if it was about to come through the door. Finally, at the third house, an elderly woman answered, took one look at Hudson and cursed him out in Spanish way too fast for him to follow, which was probably a good thing. She slammed the door, too.

One house left. A young woman answered, African-American, about Tonda's age, peering suspiciously at Hudson with three chain locks still fastened. "I'm looking for a woman named Tonda who lives on this block."

"You a cop?" she asked suspiciously.

"No." He hated the truth of his answer. But right now, he was not a cop. The cops were his enemies. "I'm a friend, and I think she might be in danger."

The woman studied him for a moment. "I know Tonda. We talk at the grocery store sometimes."

"Great—which building does she live in?"

The woman closed her door, but Hudson heard her sliding the chain locks open. She stepped out onto her porch and squinted into the afternoon sun as she looked down the street. "It's either the pink building or the gray one. I know it's down at that end, but I never been to her place."

"Thank you. Thank you." That narrowed things down considerably. Each of the apartments the woman had pointed out had maybe six or eight units.

Liz had told him not to come, that Tonda would run, that she would never trust Liz again. He would have to take that risk. If he was wrong, if this outing of hers was totally innocent, and she wasn't in any danger at all, she would be furious with him for causing all this trouble. That would be the nail in the coffin of their relationship. But when he weighed that risk against the possibility that she could be injured or, God forbid, killed, there was no contest. He had to go in. He had to trust his gut.

He started with the gray building, knocking on doors in sequence—Apartment 1, Apartment 2. With luck, he'd find someone who knew Tonda, rather than hitting Tonda's apartment itself. If he just knew which unit, he could listen. Peek in windows. Maybe get inside with no one the wiser.

But no one answered. He could hear TVs inside, dogs barking, saw curtains flicker aside, but no one was going to open their doors to a strange man. He was lucky that one woman had helped him.

Discouraged, he trudged upstairs to the second level. Rather than knocking, he simply pressed his ear to the door.

That was when he saw a Montgomery County cruiser turn down the street, inching along.

Carla.

She'd come. She believed in him regardless of the evidence. When this was over, he was going to kiss his partner for having faith in him. He could only hope Knightly didn't see the cruiser, so far out of its jurisdiction.

He trotted down the stairs and ran across the apartment building's weedy front yard. The cruiser's passenger window opened. Hudson took in the scene instantly; Ronnie Benson, in uniform, was driving, Carla in the passenger seat.

"Carla. You come with me. Ronnie needs to take the cruiser and his uniformed self out of sight. If Todd sees cops, he might do something crazy."

Carla turned to Ronnie. "Do what he says, Ronnie. We'll stay in touch with cell phones, not the radio. You can call for reinforcements if anything goes wrong."

Ronnie looked dubious. "If you say so, Sarge."

The cruiser glided out of sight. Knowing Ronnie, he'd find a shady spot and take a nap.

"Thank you for coming, Carla."

"This better be good. Knightly? Are you sure? I mean, he's such a stickler for rules, always has that stick up his—"

"It must be an act." Hudson pulled Carla to a more hidden spot, behind some overgrown honeysuckle that completely engulfed a trellis. "Two witnesses described him. More or less. But my baseball cap found in Mandalay's car—someone in our office took it from my desk and planted it. Clearly someone has been framing me from the beginning. At first I thought I was just an easy target because I had such an obvious motive. But now I see that it's personal. The murderer didn't just want to escape detection. He wanted me to go down. And you, too. He went to a lot of trouble to get hold of your backup weapon."

"Oh, God." Carla looked sick. "When I reported the theft, I had to fill out a bunch of paperwork. Todd said he would take it to Administrative Services for me."

"And he probably shredded it."

"Why? Why would he do something so…horrible?"

"Ambition? He always resented that I'd been promoted to Major Crimes when he had seniority."

"It doesn't seem like enough."

"People start wars over ambition. But I suspect he was also trying to divert attention away from his criminal operations. With both of us working to save our own skins, he must have figured we wouldn't have much energy to upset his applecart."

"But he was *defending* you."

"All part of the act. His reasoning isn't important right now. It's going to get a whole lot more horrible, Carla, unless we take action."

"We're just two people. We need a SWAT team or something."

Suddenly Hudson smiled, though it was with a sense of fatality. "We have something better than a SWAT team. We have Project Justice."

CHAPTER NINETEEN

ELIZABETH NODDED AND picked up the pen. Her hand was sweating, and the pen was slippery.

"'I'm sorry,'" Knightly said, using a high voice, pretending to be her. Obviously he enjoyed the dramatic. "'Hudson talked me into it.'"

She dutifully wrote the words, spelling everything correctly, though she deliberately altered her handwriting so the note would be questioned.

"'We did it for the money. We hired Munch.'"

She continued to write, as slowly as she dared. Not that there was any point in prolonging the inevitable. No one was coming for them. She'd given Daniel Tonda's address, but he had no reason to come looking for her unless she went missing.

"'Then Hudson didn't trust Munch and killed him. Tonda was a witness. He wants to kill her, too. I love Hudson, but this has gone too far.'"

She'd run out of envelope. She had to turn it over and use the front.

"'I'm going to kill him, then myself, so Tonda can live.'"

She looked up. "You'll let Tonda go?" she asked hopefully.

"Maybe." But she could tell he was lying. He couldn't let Tonda go—she knew way too much. "That's good enough. Sign it."

She signed it *Liz*. Knightly wouldn't know that Hudson was the only one to use that nickname. She put the pen down and looked up at him. For the first time in her life, she knew what true hatred felt like.

"You killed my father."

"You're only just now figuring that out?"

"Can I know why?"

"It was in self-defense. More or less. He had a meeting with Munch, but Munch wanted a witness. He was scared to death of your old man, and with good reason. I never met anybody as cold-blooded."

You're certainly giving him a run for his money.

She didn't say that out loud, though. Her expertise was in talking, in reasoning with people who were under extreme stress, in crisis, on the verge of making terrible decisions or regretting bad choices already made. That was the only weapon she had. She wouldn't resort to a physical attack just yet.

"Are you saying my father was a criminal?" She had to keep him talking. Obviously he had an ego. He was smart enough not to brag about his crime to anyone who could rat him out. But two dead women couldn't talk to anyone. This might be his only chance to tell his story, to gloat about how smart he was.

"Come on, Lizzy-baby, you knew that."

"I didn't know. I hardly ever talked to him once I went away to college."

"Oh, this started way before you went to college."

"I don't believe you. He wouldn't… Deep down, he was a good man."

"A good businessman, maybe. He was involved in prostitution, mostly. Yeah, the food on your table was paid for by young girls like Tonda, here. Opening their legs for a few dollars while people like Franklin Mandalay got rich."

Elizabeth's stomach turned again. Whether it was from the head injury, or the disgusting nature of Knightly's story, she didn't know.

"Supposing I believe you…how did you fit in?"

"I was in charge of the Montgomery County territory. It started out just as protection money. I looked the other way, made evidence disappear, that kind of thing. But your father's name kept coming up, and I started to wonder about him. Did a little research. Found out about the missing wife."

"Do you know something about my mother?" Though she'd told Hudson she didn't want to know, she realized she did.

"I know everything about your mother. Because I got hold of the investigating officer's notes. The cops were positive your father murdered his wife. But he was just too damn rich and powerful. He paid off someone high up. Maybe the chief of police. Your mother's case got buried."

Oh, God. She shouldn't have asked. Hudson's instincts were right on the money—this whole thing was connected to her mother's disappearance. But she hadn't wanted to hear these disturbing facts about her father. Any more than she wanted to hear them now.

But she'd already started down the slippery slope. Before she died, she had to know.

"I was going to blackmail him," Knightly continued, obviously enjoying his story. "I secured the information in a safe place where, if I were to die or disappear, it would all come to light. Otherwise, Franklin would have simply killed me. But I had him by the short hairs."

You think you're so damn smart. She'd never wanted to hit someone so badly. The anger surged through her veins, making her feel physically strong, as if she could pick up the coffee table and bash him with it.

"All I asked for was a bigger piece of the pie. I made him hand over all of Montgomery County. We became equals. I'm socking it all away. With Sanchez and Vale out of the picture, I'll make lieutenant within the year. Imagine what I can do then."

"If my father killed my mother, why did he do it?" she

asked, almost against her own will. "Did you discuss it with him? Did he tell you anything?"

Knightly flashed that evil smile. "Because of you. Your mother was threatening divorce. She'd gotten tired of his affairs, the prostitutes—he liked to sample the wares for free, you know—and she didn't like the way he wanted to raise you. She was going to take you away from him. And that was one thing he couldn't allow."

Now she was going to be sick. She leaned over and retched onto the carpet. It was her fault. Shouldn't she have seen what was going on? But looking back, she could see how Knightly's explanation made perfect sense. Her father always had been possessive with her. If her mother wanted to discipline her, her father stepped in and stopped it. But if her mother tried to give her ice cream or a cookie, her father would take it away, saying he didn't want her to get fat. Then, when her mother wasn't looking, he would give her an even better treat.

"It was painless," Knightly said, as if this made it okay. "Your father wasn't a sadist. He just liked to have his way. She's buried in the backyard, by the way. Under the tennis courts. Doubt anyone will find her now. You're the last person who would look for her, and—"

A knock on the door interrupted him. Knightly pointed his gun at Tonda's head and put a finger to his lips.

Elizabeth held her breath. She longed to cry for help, but she feared if she made a peep, Knightly would blow Tonda's head off.

HUDSON WATCHED IMPATIENTLY from the cover of the honeysuckle as Carla approached Tonda's apartment. Tonda had never met Carla and might be more likely to open the door to her. If she did, Carla would pretend to be selling something and assess the situation, see if Liz was there and if anyone seemed to be in imminent danger. If all appeared okay, Carla would withdraw, and Tonda would never know that law enforcement had intervened.

The sound of a car engine grabbed his attention. An ordinary-looking Chevy Impala made its way down the street, moving slowly, perhaps looking for a parking place. As it neared, Hudson could see that the passenger window was open, and Joe was scanning the area, searching for him, no doubt.

Hudson stepped out from his hiding place just far enough to wave to Joe. Joe nodded and the car continued down the street. Two minutes later, Joe appeared from the rear of the property, having approached from the alley. He wore a Kevlar vest and had another one in his hand for Hudson.

"What's going on?" Joe asked, stepping behind the bush.

Hudson quickly brought him up to speed as he donned the vest, while keeping an eye on Carla, who'd got one of Tonda's neighbors to answer her door.

"You're sure she's here?" Joe asked.

"I found her car parked on the next block. My partner is knocking on Tonda's door, but she's not getting an answer."

Hudson motioned for Carla to join them.

"Who'd you bring?" Hudson asked.

"Everybody we could pile into that car—Ford Hyatt, Jillian, Mitch, Griffin Benedict and, God help us, Celeste."

"Celeste?"

"Don't underestimate her. I've seen her take down a two-hundred-pound opponent with just her bare hands."

That sounded like someone he wanted on his team.

Carla joined them, looking troubled. "That lady I was just talking to? She heard what she described as 'an awful scuffle' about an hour ago in the apartment below hers. She said it sounded like someone was getting beaten."

Joe listened with interest. "So maybe Tonda's call was for real?"

"God, I hope so," Hudson said. Maybe Liz wasn't in danger at all. Maybe she was in there right now, simply trying to talk Tonda into going to the emergency room. Maybe Jackson was long gone, and Knightly was nowhere near here.

KNIGHTLY WANDERED OVER to the front window and peered out through a half-inch gap in the curtains. "Where, oh where, is Hudson?"

"He's coming. He was clear across town when I called him."

"Seems a little odd that it's taking him so long. Could it be that you're not really that important to him? He could be more interested in saving his own skin, fleeing the country. Maybe you should call him again."

If she did—if Knightly forced her to lie so that he would come here—she would be luring him to his death.

"Give him a few more minutes."

"But what if you're lying? What if you never told Vale anything about your visit with Tonda?"

Damn it. He was too perceptive, and she was a bad liar.

"Maybe he won't come," she said, trying to sound hopeful. "But if I call him again, he'll know something's up. He'll hear it in my voice."

"Let's just give it a try anyway."

Reluctantly, she stood up and pulled the silver cell phone out of her pocket. Probably Hudson wouldn't answer.

Knightly snatched the phone away from her and scrolled through her contacts. "You don't have many friends, do you." The silver phone only contained half a dozen numbers. But one of them was Hudson's.

Knightly located the number and dialed. He put the call on Speaker. If he answered, what would she say?

She couldn't risk double-crossing Knightly. He thought of Tonda as expendable and probably wouldn't think anything of shooting her to punish Elizabeth.

Please, Hudson, don't answer.

She got rolled to voice mail.

"Hudson, please hurry," she said. "Tonda's injured and she refuses to go to the hospital. *I'm really scared.*" Would he recognize that code phrase they'd arranged several days ago, when she'd met Tonda and Jazz at the restaurant?

She hung up and tried to find the app that would turn her phone into a wire, but Knightly grabbed it out of her hand before she could go that far. He powered it down. Now Daniel wouldn't be able to find her.

"That was perfect, Elizabeth," Knightly said. "But why didn't he take your call?"

"I don't know. Maybe he's driving."

"And I'm sure he would take every safety precaution when driving."

Knightly was so focused on Elizabeth, he'd stopped paying attention to Tonda, who was so cowed by his violence that he obviously deemed her a nonthreat. But Elizabeth hadn't stopped watching her. Tonda was moving, inch by inch, working her way to the very end of the sofa, waiting until he looked in the opposite direction before each move.

Elizabeth was in awe of the girl's courage. Beaten, bloody, probably in terrible pain, she was doing something to help herself—to help both of them. For her part, Elizabeth pretended to fidget, standing up, then sitting down again. Each time she moved, Knightly raised the gun in case she tried something, she supposed. But all she did was move toward the opposite end of the couch from Tonda, to draw his attention farther away from her.

"What are you going to do with Tonda?" Elizabeth asked, just to keep him talking. "It wouldn't make sense for me to have killed her. According to the note, by killing Hudson, then myself, I'm saving Tonda's life."

"Tonda will die from her beating. Jackson will go down for the murder, which suits my purposes. Jackson has always been a pain in the ass. He didn't play by the rules your

father set up. He was holding out, not paying the appropriate…franchise fee."

Tonda's one good eye widened at the mention of Jackson
getting into trouble for her murder. That, apparently, was
what it took to prod her into action. She grabbed a metal coat
hanger that was lying on the floor and, from behind Knightly,
slammed it over his head and around his neck. She jumped on
his back like a crazed monkey, wrapping her legs around him
and squeezing that coat hanger, finding the strength somehow despite her injuries.

"Get his gun!" Tonda screamed.

Elizabeth made a move to do just that, but Knightly pointed
the gun straight at her. Tonda had a grip on his upper arm
and was shaking it, still yanking on the hanger with her other
hand and screaming like a banshee. The gun waved wildly.
Elizabeth knew this was her only chance. She leaped across
the coffee table so she wouldn't be trapped between it and
the couch, then put her head down, intending to run straight
at him and head butt him, knock him down.

She never got the chance. He pulled the trigger.

The gunshot was deafening in the small apartment. Something that felt like a hot poker seared right through Elizabeth's arm, dropping her to her knees before she could even
make contact with Knightly. She forced her eyes open and
saw blood everywhere—her blood.

Jesus God almighty, she'd been shot. For a few moments,
she couldn't do anything but sprawl on the floor, clutching
her arm with the other hand. She heard screaming and realized it was hers.

Knightly spun wildly, trying to get Tonda off his back. He
reached behind him with the gun and attempted to whack her
in the head with it, but Tonda somehow managed to wiggle
around and avoid the worst of the blows.

Finally, he just backed up against a wall with enough force

to stun her. Then he swung her off and flung her literally across the room.

She collided with a lamp, slid across a small table and crashed into the front window. The window shattered, and Tonda hurtled all the way through to the outside with a horrendous scream. Elizabeth heard the smack of Tonda's body hitting the concrete outside.

Suddenly it was deathly quiet. Knightly was staring out the window, then back at Elizabeth, as if he wasn't sure what had just happened. But he was no longer smiling.

"SHE'S STILL NOT answering," Joe said. "Mitch is bringing an ultrasensitive microphone. We can use it to eavesdrop right through the wall."

The urge to just bash down Tonda's door was almost too strong to resist. But bumbling into a hostage situation could get someone killed.

"We need a plan."

"Daniel is attempting to get hold of the building manager now."

"Do these apartments have back doors?"

Joe nodded. "There's an alley. We've got people stationed back there."

That was when he heard the shot.

His heart in his throat, he looked at Joe and Carla. They each nodded; they were going in.

That was when the front window of Tonda's apartment shattered and a large mass came hurtling out. The mass was a female human being. Her head and shoulders landed hard on the concrete porch, and she somersaulted over the edge into some low bushes.

Hudson couldn't breathe until he realized it wasn't Liz.

"Tonda," he told Joe and Carla, feeling awful for his attitude toward her. She wasn't tough; she was a crumpled, bleeding little girl.

"He's got a gun," Tonda screamed. She lay partly in the shrubs, obviously injured or she'd have got up and run. "He's gonna kill us!"

Carla spoke softly into her radio. Sounded as if she was calling for Ronnie, then for emergency medical. Hudson wanted to do something for Tonda, but protocol dictated that they had to secure the area first before helping the injured. Otherwise, whoever was inside that apartment could shoot them all like fish in a barrel.

Liz was in there. It took every ounce of willpower Hudson had, and then some, not to throw protocol out the window and go to her.

Joe quickly reported to the rest of his team what was going on. Ford Hyatt and Jillian were covering the back door. Griffin Benedict and Celeste joined them in the front. Celeste, seeing the injured woman, tutted.

"We should at least get her out of the line of fire."

Seeing that Celeste was about to take matters into her own hands, Hudson put a hand on her arm to stop her. "I'll do it."

"I'll cover you." Celeste, her neon-orange chiffon shirt ruffles hanging out of her Kevlar vest, stepped into clear view of whoever was inside that apartment and pointed a gun the size of a small cannon. "I dare you to shoot me."

Not exactly standard police procedure, but Hudson darted out, grabbed Tonda by the shoulders and dragged her to the relative cover around the side of the building. It wouldn't be the most comfortable journey for her, but it was the safest way to move her if she had a spinal injury. Her eyes were closed, her face tense with pain. But at least she was alive.

It was quiet inside the apartment. Hudson returned to the front porch. The other three of his compatriots flanked the front window. Hudson joined them. By now, Todd Knightly knew he wasn't alone.

"Todd," Hudson called. "There's no way you're getting

out of this. You might as well cut your losses. Come out with your hands up."

Nothing.

Hudson broke off a long, slender branch from the bushes that lined the porch. He used it to reach through the shattered window, snag the curtains and slowly open them. The sight that greeted him chilled his blood. Todd Knightly stood in the center of the room with Liz in a headlock, his gun pointed at her temple.

"No one come any closer," Knightly said, his voice calm, even. "I *will* kill her. You saw what I did to Tonda."

"Don't hurt her," Hudson begged. He hated it that he'd been reduced to pleading with a bottom-feeding bastard like Knightly. "We won't move."

"Lower your weapons."

"That's not gonna happen," Hudson said. "Every person out here is a cop or former cop. You know what our directives are."

"Fine. Keep your weapons wherever you want. I'm leaving. With her." He nodded at Liz.

"Whose blood is that?" Hudson demanded.

Knightly didn't answer. "My car is out back. Tell whoever is back there to clear the area. I'm going out the back door. I'm taking Ms. Downey with me," he said again. "If I see anybody who looks like a cop or a Project Justice person or an undercover anything, if I see a suspicious-looking dog or a cat or a bird, I will shoot her clean through the head. Is that clear?"

"Crystal," Hudson ground out. No way was he letting this turd take Liz away.

He had a clean shot. He could nail Knightly in the head, drop him where he stood. Problem with that was, Knightly's index finger was tight against the trigger, the muzzle of the gun pressed against Liz's head. A reflex action could kill her.

"If you hurt her," Hudson said, "I'll end you."

Liz's eyes were huge. She was apparently too terrified to say anything, to do anything. She was paralyzed.

"I'm not going to hurt her. Soon as I get away clean, I'll let her out."

Would he? Hudson wasn't so sure. Knightly knew Hudson cared for Liz. Loved her. He'd already committed two murders, possibly a third if Tonda didn't make it. He would think nothing of killing Liz out of pure, venomous spite.

"Call your people off," Knightly said again. "Do it now."

Hudson exchanged a look with Joe, then nodded. He would at least pretend to be going along with Knightly's plan.

Joe spoke into his earpiece. "You guys need to stand down. He's coming out the back and he has a hostage. He says he'll kill her if he sees anybody."

Knightly began slowly backing up, never taking his eyes off Hudson.

Hudson had to do something. No way was he going along with this plan.

Liz spoke, but her voice was so faint, he couldn't quite make it out.

"What?"

"I'm really scared."

That was their code. Jesus, what did she mean by that?

She was trying to tell him something. She was going to *do* something. He tensed, ready for anything.

Suddenly she dropped. It looked as if every muscle in her body went limp. She fell like a stone, sliding down against Knightly's body.

Surprised, Knightly took about half a second to tighten his grip on her. During that half a second, his gun was no longer pointed at Liz.

Hudson didn't hesitate. He shot Knightly in the head. Death was instantaneous.

CHAPTER TWENTY

KNIGHTLY AND LIZ fell in a heap. Even in death, his arm continued to grip her. Hudson leaped through the window. Carla, Joe, Celeste and Griffin were right behind him.

Joe grabbed Knightly's gun and took it out of his grip, though there was no need. Knightly wasn't shooting anyone, ever again. Hudson pulled the dead cop's arm off Liz and she flew into his embrace.

"It's okay. It's all over. You're safe."

"Tonda," she said. "We have to help Tonda."

"Medical help is on the way. Baby, you're hurt, too." Clearly the blood he'd seen hadn't all come from Knightly and Tonda.

"I know. He shot me," she said matter-of-factly, and he realized she was going into shock. He scooped her off the ground and carried her toward the door. He had to get her out of this nightmarish scene where the smells of death and gunpowder mingled noxiously.

Carla stopped him. "Um, Hudson? Your gun?"

He still had the gun clutched in his hand. He loosened his grip. "Take it."

Carla took charge of his gun. He'd killed someone. A fellow cop, no less. There would have to be an investigation. *Another* investigation.

He didn't care. As long as Liz survived.

"Paramedics are on their way," Carla said. "Take her outside. Everybody!" she called to the Project Justice people.

"This is a crime scene now. I need everybody to clear out. I know this isn't our department's jurisdiction, but my directive is to secure the scene until Houston officers arrive."

She didn't have to tell them twice. They filed out the front door with Hudson. Celeste jumped out the window.

Outside, neighbors and strangers were already milling about, wanting to see what was going on. They wouldn't answer their doors and offer information that might have prevented this, but they sure were quick to want to watch the aftermath.

"You saved my life," Liz said, her voice full of wonder.

"I couldn't have done it if you hadn't taken action. You were so smart to use the code. You were amazing."

"I was a terrified blob of Jell-O. I think I might have wet my pants."

An ambulance pulled up, Ronnie and the cruiser right behind.

"Two injured," Hudson called out to the paramedics as he carried Liz toward the ambulance. "We have a gunshot wound here."

"Tonda first," Liz pleaded. "My injury is minor."

"You were shot. That is not minor."

"The night we met, you said getting shot was rare. Now look at me."

He was encouraged by the fact she could find any kind of humor in this situation. People didn't make jokes if they were about to die, did they?

One paramedic, a woman, headed for Tonda. The other, a male, came to Liz. Hudson was reluctant to let her go, but he set her on a patch of grass, and the paramedic started cutting her sweater away from her injured arm. Hudson wished the female one was attending Liz. He felt a totally inappropriate wave of jealousy as he watched this strange man touching his Liz, seeing her with only half a sweater.

She winced as he cleaned blood off her arm and examined the entry wound. "Bullet's still in there," the medic said. "There's a lot of blood. You probably nicked an artery. Best thing we can do is try to stop the bleeding and get you transported ASAP. Do you have any other injuries I should be looking at?" He pulled a roll of gauze from his bag and began wrapping her arm.

Liz pointed to her head. "Knightly hit me over the head when I entered Tonda's apartment."

Hudson held his breath as the medic took a look. That was when he saw Liz had blood in her hair, too.

"You better not die on me, Liz," Hudson said. "Not after I went to all this trouble to find you."

"I'm okay. I feel curiously free from pain. Earlier I hurt so bad I couldn't think, couldn't speak or move. But now there's this sort of euphoria. Relief, maybe..." She glanced over at Tonda, who was apparently conscious. More paramedics had arrived, and Tonda was moving a bit, but she cried out in pain when they put her on a gurney.

"Tonda..."

"She's conscious and moving and feeling pain. Those are all actually good signs." Hudson didn't say so, but it worried him that Liz didn't hurt. The situation had probably caused adrenaline to flood her system by the gallon; sometimes adrenaline could dull pain. But what if it meant something else?

Cop cars arrived in droves. If it was a slow day, every cruiser within five miles would show up, just in case they were needed.

Hudson realized he wouldn't be allowed the luxury of contact with Liz much longer. They would take him away and interrogate everybody ten ways to Sunday until they'd satisfied themselves that they knew exactly what had gone down here. Then Hudson would be taken into custody. No way around it. It would take many more hours to take everyone's statements and verify that Todd Knightly had been holding two women against their will, and longer still to prove he was a murderer. Even then, Hudson wasn't sure he was out of the woods, legally speaking. He had deliberately fled to avoid arrest.

It would all have to be sorted out later between the two departments, Houston and Montgomery County.

He didn't care. He'd sworn that if Liz's life was spared, any other breaks he caught would be gravy.

With limited time left, he realized he needed to say something.

"Liz, we don't have much time," he said. "But I want to tell you something. It's really important."

She blinked at him in surprise but said nothing.

"I know you don't think we have much in common, but we do. The deep-down, important stuff. I know I've made some mistakes, and I'm sorry. But I swear, I'll do better. What I'm saying is, I want us to have another chance. I'll trust your instincts. I'll learn to see the world how you see it—"

"This time, my instincts...were wrong." Her words were slow, a little breathy. "I should have...listened to you. You knew it was...a trap."

"None of that matters. What does matter is that I love you. More than my freedom, more than my life... Liz?"

Her eyes were closed.

"Liz? Are you okay?"

She didn't answer. She'd fallen unconscious.

ELIZABETH WAS FLOATING on a pleasant sea made of pink clouds. Her mother was right next to her, looking still young and beautiful, not much older than Elizabeth. They both relaxed in lounge chairs sipping some kind of fruity, frozen umbrella drinks.

"Did he really kill you, Mom?" It should have been a painful conversation, but oddly, it wasn't.

"Yes, he did. I wanted to take you away from him."

"And did he bury you in the backyard and put a tennis court over you?"

"I don't really know about that, sweetheart. I sort of stopped paying attention once I was dead. But it's really great to see you. You've grown into such a beautiful woman."

"Am I dead?"

"That's…undetermined. But if you are, don't worry. It's really nice here."

I love you, Liz.

Wait. That was Hudson's voice. Elizabeth looked around, but didn't see him.

"Someone's talking to you." Her mother sounded faintly amused. "Someone who is definitely not dead."

Don't you dare leave me.

"It's Hudson. He shot a man to save my life. At least, I think he did. It would be awful if I died anyway, after he went to all that trouble."

"Sounds like he cares for you."

"He does. He must. Mom, I think I'm in love with him."

"So, go back to him."

"Can I do that?"

She shrugged, as if they were talking about buying a dress. "It's up to you."

That was when her head started to hurt. In fact, everything hurt. Her mother went away. The pink clouds vanished. Elizabeth lay on a hard bed with a scratchy sheet.

She was still alive. Thank God.

She cracked one eye open, and the first thing she saw was Hudson's face, about six inches from hers.

"Liz?"

"Mmm." That was all she could manage.

"You're gonna be okay. Do you remember what happened? You were shot."

She tried to nod, but her body didn't want to cooperate. Yes, she remembered everything.

"Ya," she managed. "Shot."

"They took you into surgery and removed the bullet. Put some stitches in your head, too. Gave you about a gallon of blood. But the doctor said you'd be fine."

"Good." Suddenly she remembered…"Tonda?"

"She's okay. Pretty beat-up. Couple of broken ribs. But she's going to be fine, too."

"The baby?"

Hudson looked at the floor and slowly shook his head.

"Oh, no." Elizabeth could hardly imagine how Tonda must feel. Even though the pregnancy was unplanned, it had been obvious that Tonda already loved her unborn child. "How is she taking it?"

"She's upset. Jackson is with her, refuses to leave her side. He seems pretty shaken up, too."

That was interesting. Maybe Jackson wasn't all bad.

Suddenly Elizabeth remembered something. "I went to heaven."

Hudson raised one dubious eyebrow. "Really?"

"Well, I dreamed I went to heaven and saw my mother. Do you really think people sit around on pink clouds in heaven and drink daiquiris? That's how my mom used to describe it. Except she said they drank lemonade. I was too young to know what a daiquiri was."

"I…have no idea what people do in heaven. Maybe it's like a garden. With hummingbirds."

She managed to smile. "That would be nice, too. Oh, Hudson, you were right about everything. This whole business happened because my father killed my mother. Knightly found out about it and tried to blackmail him. But instead of paying him off in cash, Dad gave Knightly a chunk of his criminal business."

"We don't have to talk about this now, if you don't want to."

"No, I think we should. I need to talk about it while it's fresh in my mind."

She told him everything, recounting Knightly's words as closely as possible.

"So your dad sent Munch to kill me just because I arrested him?"

"My father's reputation and standing in the community meant everything to him. You threatened that. He knew you could identify Jazz, and you saw the exchange of cash. You could have caused his whole world to come crashing down."

"Then, when Munch bungled the job, your dad decided to eliminate him."

Elizabeth nodded. "But Munch suspected my dad's intention. He called Knightly for protection. Then Knightly, seeing an opportunity, killed my dad. At first he intended to blame it on Munch."

"Until he came up with better scapegoats—me and Carla. He must have given Munch her gun. Maybe he was planning our downfall for a long time, even stealing my DNA and Carla's gun, waiting for just the right opportunity."

"All so he could move up in the department?"

"Ambition can be a potent motivator. He probably saw himself as a captain—maybe even sheriff."

Elizabeth closed her eyes, suddenly exhausted just from talking. How unfortunate those two men had found each other. Each probably validated the other's ruthless ways.

"You okay?" Hudson asked, his voice laced with concern.

"I heard your voice. When I was in heaven…dreaming about heaven."

"Yeah? What did I say?"

"You said you loved me. That's what made me want to come back…from heaven. But I guess I can't hold you to something I dreamed."

"You didn't dream it. I mean, maybe you did, but I said it. I've been sitting here for two hours waiting for you to wake up, and I told you I loved you about a hundred times. I do. I want to try again. I'll do better, I swear. I just don't think we should throw out what we have because we hit a little bump in the road."

She hesitated. They were so different. But she didn't doubt that he loved her. She could *feel* it. They might not always agree, but what couple did? The important thing was how they dealt with conflict, and she felt they'd already learned a lot about how to respect each other's positions.

"Of course we can try again. I love you, too...." Elizabeth had opened her eyes again. That was when she noticed two uniformed officers standing against the wall, almost as if they were at attention. They stared straight ahead, but of course they'd just heard the entire conversation between her and Hudson.

"Who are those men?" she asked.

"Oh. I thought you saw them earlier. I'm sort of...in custody. There was still a warrant out for my arrest."

"How come you're not in jail, then?"

"Daniel. He pulled some strings so I could come talk to you."

"My God, he must have thought I was going to die. I'm not, am I?" She felt pretty horrible, like Riverdance and all their relatives were performing inside her skull, and someone had filleted her arm.

"You better not. Anyway, I think it's just a matter of some paperwork to get me released. Try not to worry about it."

She hoped he was right. But come to think of it, only she and Tonda had heard Knightly's confession. And who would take Elizabeth's word for it? She wasn't exactly unbiased.

Carla poked her head in the door of Elizabeth's room. "You're awake?"

"Sort of," Elizabeth answered.

"Good. Hudson, you have to go now."

Hudson squeezed Elizabeth's hand. "Get better. I'll be back soon as I can, okay?"

"Okay."

"We're good now, right?"

"We're golden, Hudson. I love you, and if you get me some morphine, I'll marry you."

"I'll hold you to that."

THE UPSTAIRS BALCONY off the master bedroom afforded an excellent view of the tennis courts.

It was almost December, six weeks since Elizabeth had been released from the hospital. She was done with physical therapy for her arm; the wound was healing nicely. She would always have a scar, but it wouldn't be that bad.

Elizabeth leaned against the balcony railing, watching as men with jackhammers tore up the tennis court concrete and hauled it away. A few days earlier, the police had come with ground-penetrating radar to search for her mother's grave site. They said Knightly could have learned the location from something he'd read in Detective Vilches's notes. Or he might have been making up the story about her mother out of sheer spite.

But the radar had found a suspicious area where the soil had obviously been disturbed to a depth of three to four feet. Cadaver dogs had been brought in; they'd confirmed that human remains were nearby. Amazing that they could sniff out a body covered with dirt and concrete. One of the handlers, Zeke, had said his dog could even sniff out a body that was submerged in a lake.

Now the police were going to find out exactly what was under that tennis court.

Hudson stood beside her, his arm around her waist, keeping the vigil with her.

"Are you sure you want to watch this?" he asked for the third time.

"Yes. I have to know. Once they find something...once they confirm it's human remains...I'll go inside. If there's a body, I'm sure it's hers."

She actually felt okay about all this. She'd done grieving for her mother years ago. When Holly had failed to contact her, when she hadn't come back to get her daughter, Elizabeth had known with a hundred percent certainty that she was dead.

Over the past few weeks, she'd come to terms with the fact that her father had killed her mother. For a long time, she'd clung to the belief that, despite his ruthless actions, her father had some good inside him, that he'd loved her, even if he'd chosen to show that love in an unacceptable manner.

But now she knew—the man had been bad through and through. When the police had finally released his remains, she'd had him cremated, and had asked the funeral home to dispose of the ashes. He didn't deserve the dignity of a proper funeral and burial. So, no more grieving for him.

As for her mother, she planned to give her the service she deserved—a celebration of her too-short life.

"The estate lawyer says my father's assets should be released soon." The authorities had tried to seize the whole thing, claiming it was all derived from criminal activity and should therefore go to the state. But her lawyer had successfully argued that Franklin Mandalay's legitimate business dealings had earned far more than his criminal enterprises. Elizabeth had offered to donate two million dollars to a victims' relief fund, and the government had dropped its claim.

"So, you're soon to be a very rich woman."

"Not for long."

"Are you really going to donate it all to charity?" Hudson didn't disapprove of her philanthropy. He seemed in awe of her generosity.

Elizabeth had originally planned to simply turn over the estate to one of the large, established charities. But then she'd got another idea.

"I'm not going to donate it. I'm going to take a page from Daniel's book and start my own nonprofit foundation. It's going to be a shelter for women like Tonda. Only it's not just going to be a safe haven. I'm going to help women who want to start a new life. Whether they're prostitutes who want to get out of the life or victims of abuse or addicts, I'll offer them a way out. The whole package. I'll help them get healthy, I'll help them figure out what they want to do with their lives, help them get education or job training, provide child care, nice clothes for job interviews. If they don't feel safe staying in Houston, I'll help them relocate."

"Wow." Hudson looked stunned. "Wow. That's a lot of helping."

"This house has plenty of bedrooms. And I already talked to Mrs. Ames. She wants to stay on and become a part of it. And Tonda—she wants to help, too."

Every time she thought of the recent choices Tonda had made, Elizabeth beamed with pride, as if she were responsible. And maybe she could take a little credit—she'd been counseling Tonda for more than a year.

As she'd been lying in the grass outside her apartment, waiting for medical help, Tonda had decided to quit selling her body to strangers. She was going to get herself and her unborn child out of her precarious situation—somehow.

Jackson had come to the hospital the moment he'd heard Tonda was hurt. She'd been prepared to tell him they were through. But Jackson had surprised her. Apparently, impending fatherhood, and almost losing Tonda, had been a wake-up call. He'd promised he was done with prostitutes and drugs. Although Tonda had lost the baby, Jackson wanted them to make a fresh start. He'd sworn he would straighten out his life, get a real job and treat her like the queen she was, if only she wouldn't leave him.

Elizabeth would have bet her whole fortune that he was feeding Tonda a line. But so far, he'd kept his word. He'd moved them to a better apartment in a safer neighborhood, started working at his uncle's mechanic shop and came home every night. He'd stopped drinking. Started running. From everything Tonda said, he was now a doting boyfriend, and they were even talking about getting married.

Such transformations were rare, but not unheard of, and Elizabeth was cautiously optimistic that Jackson was truly a changed man. She would welcome Tonda's help with her new foundation. Unlike Elizabeth, Tonda knew firsthand what these women were going through, and her insights would be invaluable.

"It sounds like a lot of work."

"I'm sure it will be."

"You gonna still have time for me?"

She turned away from the tennis court. Looking at Hudson was much more pleasant. "Of course. I seem to remember something you did that was really nice at the hospital."

"I did a lot of nice things at the hospital. There was that nice bouquet of roses I sent, the special meals I had delivered, the candy…"

"No, I'm talking about the morphine. Right after you left my room that first day a nurse came bustling in, and she was all about upping my morphine drip."

He grinned. "Oh, yeah, I did have something to do with that."

"And do you remember what I said I would do if you got me morphine?"

"I seem to recall something… Now, what exactly was it you said?"

Elizabeth felt suddenly self-conscious. "Let's go inside," she said. "I don't need to watch this." They exited the balcony through the French doors, but her father's old bedroom hardly seemed an appropriate place to have a serious conversation. She dragged Hudson all the way downstairs and into the kitchen, the room she still thought of as the happiest place in the house.

Mrs. Ames had obviously been baking again. The kitchen

smelled of yeast and vanilla. Elizabeth busied herself opening the refrigerator, getting out a carton of orange juice, pouring it into a couple of glasses.

"Is something wrong?" Hudson asked. "You seem a little nervous."

She took a fortifying gulp of the juice. "In all seriousness, with you living in Conroe, and me living and working in Houston, we do an awful lot of driving just to see each other. I was thinking... Maybe we could find a place halfway between—"

"I've already talked to a Realtor about putting my place on the market."

"But you love your lake house. And your boat. What if we want to go water-skiing sometime?"

"Well...I thought we should live closer."

"Oh, me too!"

"I can't afford two places."

"So, you'll move in with me. And we can keep your place as our weekend getaway." She said this casually, as if it was no big deal.

Hudson put his hand to his chin, seeming to think about her proposition. "Well, now, I don't know. It seems to me you promised something a little bit better than a roommate situation. And I did get the nurse to up your morphine dosage. I had to flirt with her, too, which, if you saw the nurse, was no easy feat."

Elizabeth's heart swelled. He did remember. "Even though I was drugged up at the time, I meant what I said. I would marry you, if you wanted."

Hudson dropped all pretense of teasing. He took the glass of orange juice out of her hand and set it on the counter, then took both of her hands in his. "Elizabeth Downey, I never in my whole life dreamed I could marry a woman like you. I would be honored and privileged to be your husband. We can live anywhere you want to live, keep the lake house or sell it, I don't care. As long as it's forever."

"I can't believe this." Her eyes filled with tears. "I was picturing something a whole lot more romantic. I mean, the tennis court..." She winced. "But yes. The answer is yes, anywhere, anytime."

* * * * *

Be sure to look for Kara Lennox's next
PROJECT JUSTICE *book,*
IN THIS TOGETHER,
available in October 2013!

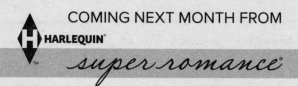
Available August 6, 2013

#1866 WHAT HAPPENS BETWEEN FRIENDS
In Shady Grove • by Beth Andrews

James Montesano has always been Sadie Nixon's soft place to land. Isn't that what friends are for? But something has changed. Instead of helping her pick up the pieces of her life, James is complicating things by confessing his feelings...for her! Suddenly she sees him in a whole *new* way.

#1867 FROM THIS DAY ON
by Janice Kay Johnson

The opening of a college time capsule is supposed to be fun. But for Amy Nilsson, the contents upend her world. In the midst of that chaos, Amy finds comfort in the most unexpected place—Jakob. Once the kid who tormented her, now he's the only one she can trust!

#1868 STAYING AT JOE'S
by Kathy Altman

Joe Gallahan ruined Allison Kincaid's career—and she broke his heart. Now reconnecting a year later, they're each looking for their own form of payback. But revenge would be so much easier if love didn't keep getting in the way!

#1869 A MAN LIKE HIM
by Rachel Brimble

Angela Taylor came to Templeton Cove to start over. But when the press photographs her in Chris Forrester's arms during a flood rescue, it's only a matter of time before her peaceful new life takes a frightening turn....

#1870 HER ROAD HOME
by Laura Drake

Samantha Crozier prefers the temporary. Her life is on the road, stopping long enough to renovate a house, then moving on. But her latest place in California is different. And that might have something to do with Nick Pinelli. As tempting as he is, though, she's not sure she can stay....

#1871 SECOND TIME'S THE CHARM
Shelter Valley Stories • by Tara Taylor Quinn

A single father, Jon Swartz does everything he can to make a good life for his son. That's why he's here in Shelter Valley attending college. When he meets Lillie Henderson, Jon begins to hope that this could be his second chance to have the family he's always wanted.

YOU CAN FIND MORE INFORMATION ON UPCOMING HARLEQUIN® TITLES, FREE EXCERPTS AND MORE AT WWW.HARLEQUIN.COM.

Staying at Joe's
By Kathy Altman

On sale August 6

Allison Kincaid must convince Joe Gallahan to return to the advertising agency he quit a year ago—and to do so, she must overlook their history. But when she tracks him down at the motel he's renovating, he has a few demands of his own.... Read on for an exciting excerpt of STAYING AT JOE'S by Kathy Altman.

Allison tapped her fingers against her upper arm as she turned over his conditions in her mind. No matter how she looked at it, she had zero negotiating room. "So. We're stuck with each other."

"Looks that way." Joe's expression was stony.

"I didn't come prepared to stay, let alone work," she said.

"I can see that." He looked askance at her outfit. "You'll need work boots. I suggest you make a run to the hardware store. Get something sturdy. No hot-pink rubber rain gear."

"I'm assuming you have a separate room for me. One with clean sheets and a working toilet."

"You'll get your own room." In four steps he was across the lobby and at the door. He pushed it open. "Hardware store's on State Street. You can't miss it."

When she made to walk past him, he stopped her with a hand on her arm. His nearness, his scent, the warmth of his fingers and their movement over the silk of her blouse made her shiver. *Damn it.*

Don't look at his mouth, don't look at his mouth, don't look—

Her gaze lowered. His lips formed a smug curve, and for one desperate, self-hating moment she considered running. But she'd be running from the only solution to her problems. "If I'm going back to the agency and delaying renovations for a month," he said, "then I get two full weeks of labor from you. No complaints, no backtracking, no games. Agreed?"

She shrugged free of his touch. "Don't worry, I'll do my part. Your part is to keep your hands to yourself."

"You might change your mind about that."

**Will they keep their hands to themselves?
Or will two weeks together resurrect the past?
Find out in STAYING AT JOE'S
by Kathy Altman, available August 2013 from
Harlequin® Superromance®.**

REQUEST YOUR FREE BOOKS!
2 FREE NOVELS PLUS 2 FREE GIFTS!

HARLEQUIN

super romance®

More Story...More Romance

Debut Author!

Samantha Crozier prefers the temporary.
Her life is on the road, stopping long enough to
renovate a house then moving on. But her latest
place in California is different. And that might
have something to do with Nick Pinelli.
As tempting as he is, though, she's not sure
she can stay....

Her Road Home
by Laura Drake

AVAILABLE IN AUGUST

The clock is ticking for Angela Taylor

Angela Taylor came to Templeton Cove to start over. But when the press photographs her in Chris Forrester's arms during a flood rescue, it's only a matter of time before her peaceful new life takes a frightening turn....

Suspense and romance collide in this sensational story!

A Man Like Him
by Rachel Brimble

AVAILABLE IN AUGUST

SADDLE UP AND READ 'EM!

This summer, get your fix of Western reads and pick up a cowboy from some of your favorite authors!

In August look for:

CANYON by Brenda Jackson
The Westmorelands
Harlequin Desire

THE HEART WON'T LIE by Vicki Lewis Thompson
Sons of Chance
Harlequin Blaze

TAKING AIM by Elle James
Covert Cowboys Inc.
Harlequin Intrigue

THE LONG, HOT TEXAS SUMMER by Cathy Gillen Thacker
McCabe Homecoming
Harlequin American Romance

Look for these great Western reads AND MORE available wherever books are sold or visit
www.Harlequin.com/Westerns